PASSPORT

To

Hiroshima

The Unthinkable, Inspiring Journey of a Japanese-American Family

Based on a True Story

TOSHIHARU and RITA KANO

First printing

The details of this book are drawn from the memoirs and memories of the Nekomoto family. Some names have been changed to protect the privacy of extended family members.

PICTURE CREDITS

All images courtesy Kano family archives except:
Shunichi Nekomoto drawing: Japanese American National Museum
(Gift of June Hoshida Honma, Sandra Hoshida and
Carole Hoshida Kanada, 97.106.2W)

Contents

Acknowledgements

Special thanks go to the members of the Edit Team for their support, contributions and encouragement: Yorie Kano, Annette Straub, Holly Smith, and Thomas Cantrell.

Preface

Providence snatched me from the jaws of death more than once in my life. I almost drowned as a child. A cousin pushed me into the current of a swiftly flowing river. As a young man scheduled on an ill-fated flight, the plane took off before I arrived at the airport. No, I wasn't dawdling. The itinerary given to me was incorrect. Later, I discovered that the seat I had been assigned was in a section of the plane where everyone died.

However, my first brush with death occurred much earlier in my life, even before I took my first breath.

I was the unborn son of Toshiyuki and Shizue Nekomoto the day the United States dropped the atomic bomb on Hiroshima.

The blinding flash of light reached 10,000 degrees Fahrenheit. A massive cloud of fire, smoke, radioactive dust, and a concussion force traveling 1,000 mph (greater than the speed of sound) slammed into our home. Statistics report the point of total vaporization from the blast's X-ray heated air reached 440 yards from the center of the blast.

Our home stood less than 800 yards from the hypocenter, within the area of total destruction. Statistically, my family should not have survived. Fifty percent of those exposed to the atomic bomb at greater distances died immediately or within hours of the explosion. Most of the other fifty percent died soon after from burns, wounds, or radiation related illnesses.

But, by some miracle, my family survived ... perhaps to carry a message of hope to the future.

Neither within these pages nor in our hearts, will the reader find criticism of governments or responsible officials. We hold no animosity towards anyone or any country involved for what happened. My family simply happened to be at the wrong place at the wrong time. Our concern, the reason for telling you our story, is that the desensitization of time will lead us to repeat the unthinkable.

The bomb dropped on Japan is a child's toy compared to the nuclear weapons the world possesses today. The horror of nuclear war must be forgiven, but never forgotten. If we do forget, or simply forget to care, the devastation, anguish, and pain of Hiroshima will be our planet's future.

As of this writing, there are more than seventeen *thousand* nuclear bombs scattered over our world. Each of these is a thousand times more powerful than the one dropped on Hiroshima. We have much to be concerned about, much to remember, and much to think about.

In my heart is a dream. I address the General Assembly of the United Nations on August 6, 2045 at precisely 8:15 a.m. It is the 100th anniversary of the bombing. At the age of 99, I will likely be the only living survivor of Hiroshima. Knowing first hand, the devastation of nuclear war, I plead with humankind, to lay down his sword, his weapons of mass destruction, and turn his passion to peace.

Let me be the last son of Hiroshima.

Toshiharu Kano

4

CHAPTER ONE

An Unforgettable Smile

He pops into my life with a short "hello" message and a casual photo. Toshiharu Kano and I have been connected.

We are a *FlexMatch* on a popular international dating site. *FlexMatch* means, "Okay, you aren't a perfect fit, but try each other on." It's like looking through the bargain bin of irregular sizes.

His smile glows with warmth and sincerity. However, these *possible* traits aren't what keep me going back to the dating site for another look at Mr. Kano. Rather, it is the feeling I know him already.

I turn the odd emotion over and around for a closer look. It isn't the ethereal weightlessness of love at first sight. No, this overwhelming familiarity is something even more intriguing.

As I look at Toshiharu Kano, memories stir; out of focus glimpses, it seems, of a life together. But that's impossible. I have never met him. Is it possible to "remember" the future? Yes, it is a curious notion. Maybe it should frighten me away from continuing to explore our FlexMatch connection, but it doesn't. Neither does another detail raising a red flag. In his photo, Mr. Kano appears years younger than his stated age. Is this only a singular, forgivable internet dating fib or does it portray a tendency toward deception?

There is another concern. Toshiharu is Japanese-American with his roots deep in Japan. I know little about Asian cultures, except what I have seen in *The Last Samurai* and *Shogun*. This is not solid footing for a southern girl who has never set foot on foreign soil.

I note my concerns and neatly fold them away in a mental drawer alongside two marriages and divorces. These keep me operationally cautious.

I consider my options. Shall I click *not interested* or proceed with caution? At this juncture in life, I am by no means desperate for a relationship. Couples with complicated histories often take on more problems than romantic love can ultimately bear. I have enough trouble carrying my own world-weary Samsonite. Should I even consider lugging someone else's baggage too?

I sigh. Sometimes caution thinks too far ahead. Fear of potholes doesn't keep me from taking my car out of the garage. "Relax," I tell myself. "Have some fun." Online communication combined with common sense should be safe enough. What have I got to lose, except my heart?

After a cordial icebreaker exchange followed by a four-step program of guided communication to determine if we are truly relationship compatible, Tosh sends an on-site email describing himself.

I am Shinto and Buddhist. Shinto believes in the Supreme Being who governs us and created us here on Earth. My family is the last of the Samurai who resisted the Emperor of Japan.

According to an astrologist (the friend of a friend of mine) who advised a presidential family, I am an ancient one who has lived here for many millennia. My astrological chart revealed to her that I am a teacher here to assist mankind with transition from the Piscean Age to the Age of Aquarius. I am a peacemaker. God asked me to come back to Earth for one last time for a very important mission. My grandfather gave this first name to me when I was born in March of 1946. My name means, "To Govern Peacefully."

I was born six months after the atomic bomb dropped on Hiroshima, Japan. Our family was in Hiroshima. Our home was only 800 yards from the center

6

of the blast. My father, my mother, older sister, and brother survived the bomb. My mother was the oldest survivor in the family and I am the youngest survivor of the bomb. I have survived two other brushes with death since then. I think I know my special mission. Thank you very much for expressing your interest.

Tosh's unique expression of who he is raises both eyebrows. Ancient One? Special mission? Last of the Samurai?

What? Who does he think he is, Tom Cruise?

Yes. Now is the ideal time to bow out gracefully. No real contact has been made. There are no heartstrings to break, leaving untidy frayed ends. Toshiharu Kano will simply disappear at my command.

I close my eyes. There is that haunting smile of his and a bucket full of curiosity.

Sprawled across a queen-size bed with my puppy, Indie, snuggled against my back, I ponder my cautious judgment. If I make Tosh disappear, will the hasty decision haunt me?

My brain isn't sure what to do. My heart doesn't know what to feel.

If doubts and judgments lead me to a quick-click escape, my life will return to familiarity. A humdrum job, shackled to a cubicle, hour after hour filled with productivity lacking the feeling of personal accomplishment. Although I enjoy many interests in the privacy of my head and home, there is no excitement beyond, in the sense of adventure and expanding horizons. Yes, familiarity is comforting. So are worn out sneakers and fuzzy bedroom slippers. Do I really want more of the same?

The intriguing Tosh with the Buddha smile lures me forward.

Who *is* this man? An ancient Shinto Buddhist Samurai who survived an atomic blast within the area of total destruction with a mission from God? This alone is more than enough to set off my Date-Alert alarm. But then, Tosh isn't the only one on a mission.

I'm working hard to remove the negativity of baseless judgment from my life. I don't want to *assume* dishonesty. So, I set out to *prove* it.

I Google his name. He shows up as the only Toshiharu Kano listed in the United States. No surprise there. His profession and place of employment are verified. Check and check.

What next? Well, let's see. I have no prejudice toward his religion, ancestry, or belief in reincarnation; but did he really survive an atomic bomb?

A thorough search of the internet validates Tosh's story. There were survivors within the half-mile radius of the blast. Newspaper articles and photographs of Tosh's family tell their unbelievable story.

Can *everything* he said be true? I reply to Tosh's email taking the risk to ask questions that may offend him. To move forward, I take the chance that Tosh may click *not interested* and make *me* disappear.

His reply reflects the gentle humor of his smile.

You have not offended me in any way. You probably think I am a weird person. I am a very fortunate person to be here today and talking with you. I hope I did not offend you in any way.

It is very difficult to explain what I mean when I say I am a teacher. I do not teach at any universities or colleges. I am a spiritual teacher and a guide. I have served the people of this State for over 40 years as Division Director of Public Works for Salt Lake County and as Assistant Transportation Engineer, and I will continue to serve mankind as God directs me. I will fulfill my ultimate mission on August 6, 2045 at 08:15 a.m. at the General Assembly of the United Nations. We were all given a mission to accomplish on this earth. I have served God very well over many millennia.

This will be my last and final mission.

I perfectly understand how you felt when you were growing up. I also was a misfit because of my health. I was exposed to radiation levels much stronger than what humans can sustain and yet I am here. It is very complicated to explain to you in such a little space and time. Thank you very much for listening to my story.

My wife understood perfectly why I am here. However, not too many people understand or comprehend what I am talking about. Ninety-nine percent of my co-workers and friends think I am a weird duck.

Everything happens for the purpose of fulfilling yours or their mission. No matter how small or large the incidents, they all move you forward toward fulfilling the appointed mission.

My wife helped me very well and I helped her very well for the last forty years. She passed away on September 7, 2008. She loved me and protected me for all those years. Now I am all alone.

And there they are; more red flags.

Tosh admits he comes across as odd. He says he is alone. *All alone.* Red Flag Translation: he is needy. I don't need needy.

I don't need that tug on my heartstrings. This is more than my second time around. I must remain objective, clear, and dispassionate. I am determined to keep my head below the clouds and both feet on the ground.

Once again, I consider clicking *bye-bye*; but then (sigh) there is that smile and a growing sense of affinity. I could be wrong about Tosh being needy. Perhaps, subconsciously, I'm looking for an escape route.

Curiosity still holds the reins.

The fact that Tosh may be different, even weird, isn't a deal breaker. I can easily relate to that. In grade school, my numerous "but" and "what if" challenges met with an authoritative frown.

Priests and nuns blocked my inquisitions with orthodox answers and expected me to accept them.

Tosh's frank revelations open a door I am growing more and more willing to step through.

I reply to his email with my own unorthodox story about my grandson, Damien.

As a child, Damien remembered a former lifetime in Japan, serving as a cook for the troops. Once, upon seeing Asian writing across the back of a truck, I asked him, "Do you know what language that is?"

"Chinese."

"How do you know?"

With a tone suggesting I should already know the answer to my question, he replies, "Because I can't read Chinese."

Adding to the mystery, Damien tended to put words together in an unusual way. He called his parents "Daddymama." Interestingly, there is one word for mother and father in the Japanese language, "Ryoshin." He used uncommon sentence structure, also. Asking if he could visit his Nanny (that's me), he was told, "Not today. We'll go another day." To which he responded, "Nanny, 'nother day no?" He also recalled a drink that looked like "white water".

When I tell Tosh about this, he replies:

Your Grandson remembers Doburoku, which is a rice wine. It is an old traditional drink that Japanese drink during the Cherry Blossom Festival that takes place around March 10 every year. Please give me a call any time. Thank you.

I don't call. Instead, I write asking more questions about the bombing of Hiroshima. Shuffled between is a question I type hesitantly. I ask if he felt anything unusual when he first saw my photo.

He replies:

I am sorry that I did not make myself clear. I would like to answer your questions in numerical order.

1. How did the radiation affect my health?

I was sick most of my childhood between 1 and 16. I had mumps three times and all of the childhood sicknesses except diphtheria and polio. I lost 20% of left lung capacity due to tuberculosis. I was off school one out of every three days with illnesses. However, I have only missed 10 days of work or school in the past 47 years.

2. How did I come to know that my mission ends on August 6, 2045 at 8:15 a.m.?

I will be the only survivor of the Hiroshima bomb on this earth. This is the date to commemorate the 100-year Anniversary of dropping the first Atomic Bomb. I will be addressing the General Assembly at the UN. I have a message from God to tell all of the world leaders that we cannot use the nuclear weapons to settle their differences ever again.

3. Do I have any defined sense of who I am and why you and I met on the dating site?

I do not know who you are, however if we are...

The message drops off.

Soon, another one continues.

I am sorry about this, my computer sent out my message before I was finished with it.

I was born in the year of the dog and I am also a fish, Pisces. I am sorry that I did not respond to your request sooner. I had too many things going on right now such as the Holladay Village Project and making arrangements for my wife's anniversary memorial service.

I do not know who you are, but we are meant to meet. We will meet. Thank you for your patience.

Again, I don't reply. There is much to think about. Tosh is confident that we will meet, yet I'm still not ready. Several weeks pass before I send another email. I am concerned that he is offended or discouraged by my delay, so my message says simply, "Are you still there?"

He replies in his usual relaxed, accepting tone:

Good Morning. Thank you very much for getting back with me. I thought that I was too weird for you to continue the conversation.

I grew up in Japan. My values are a little bit different from the normal All-American person. When I met my wife for the first time in 1968, she asked me, "Are you for real?" She thought that I just stepped out of a time capsule.

I did not date until I was 22 years old and my wife was the second girl that I dated.

When she kissed me on my lips for the first time, I fainted.

Did he say *"fainted"*?

The rusted, sagging door to my dreams creaks open. A thin stream of light illuminates nearly forgotten stories of knights in shining armor, castles, princesses, and dragon slayers.

I begin to wonder. "What if…" Could Tosh be "the one"?

Wait! What the heck am I doing? How foolish. Silly romantic notions. Unjustified hopes. Have I not learned anything from past relationships? What of all those dreams crushed under the heavy, grinding millstone of reality? Should I gamble now? Do I dare? No. I need more time and more answers.

I email Tosh asking what he does in his spare time. I also ask about his wife.

His response is simple. Honest. Open. Unguarded.

I met her at the University of Utah taking her PhD in psychology and I was finishing up my B.S. in Mechanical Engineering. This was in June 1968. She was born at Grand Forks, North Dakota. I miss her a lot but I know she is not in pain anymore. She was half German and half Swede.

I love to sit in my back yard taking in the beauty of nature. I love to watch the bees, doves, chipmunks, and magpies. I also enjoy looking at Mt. Olympus.

I do watch TV but I do not have a favorite show as such. I mostly watch the Discovery Channel. I love astronomy, anthropology, and archeology. I'd love to explore the ancient tombs like the Egyptian Pyramids and Chaco Canyons.

After surviving the most destructive bomb man ever created on this earth and also surviving drowning and the jet airline crash in August 1968, I have begun to ask a simple question, "Why me?"

My mother used to tell me that God saved our lives because we were placed here for a purpose.

I am the youngest survivor within 2400 feet from the center of the blast. I must attend a meeting; I will tell you my final mission later.

Doves? Chipmunks? I hear the chirping and fluttering of Walt Disney's pretty little bluebirds preparing Cinderella for the ball. This man cannot be for real. But … I am hoping he is.

CHAPTER TWO

One Golden Autumn Day

It is a bright, warm September day. I rock idly back and forth on my yard swing in the shade of a Maple tree, listening to song birds. Unbidden, my hands pick up my cell phone, my fingers push the buttons. The golden light of autumn inspires me to call Tosh.

"Tosh Kano speaking."

His voice is as unique and inviting as his smile.

"Hi, Tosh. This is Rita. Are you busy?"

Tosh doesn't recognize my name. I explain I am Rita from the dating site.

His voice is professional; his accent interesting. He doesn't comment on my North Carolina drawl.

We chat for a few minutes and then agree to meet the next day for lunch. I suggest Gardner Village; a group of charming cottages turned into shops. Stone walkways meander through patches of brightly colored flowers. Weather-worn wooden foot bridges crisscross winding streams accented by rush grasses.

This is it, the day I finally meet Tosh. It's my birthday and I've taken the day off from work.

Outside the restaurant, on the walkway near an old water wheel that once drove a grinding stone; I wait for Tosh to arrive. The village is crowded with shoppers. A breeze teases the hem of my ankle length gossamer skirt as I search for a man with a head full of white hair (I am still suspicious of the dark hair in Tosh's online photo).

Our scheduled time to meet passes.

14

Did Tosh misunderstand our meeting place? Is he waiting at another entrance? Or have I been stood up?

Fifteen minutes drag by. Five more make a tense twenty; still, no Toshiharu Kano. How much longer do I give him?

The old mill wheel squeaks round and round. Water drips and splashes. Footsteps tip tap on the walkway counting out the passing seconds.

I turn for one last look. There he is coming up the path wearing a short sleeve, beige Polo shirt neatly tucked into belted dark brown slacks. To my surprise, he has thick, straight, black hair just as his photograph suggested.

Tosh greets me with a smile and apologizes for his delay which was caused by a back-up of traffic at a road construction site.

The entrance to Archie's restaurant is only a few yards up the walkway. A cheerful hostess escorts us to a booth. From the start, there are no uncomfortable silent moments. Conversation flows naturally and advances without effort. In fact, we talk so much I don't have time to look over the menu.

The waitress arrives. Tosh orders the lunch special. Not wishing to interrupt the flow of conversation, I order the same, Archie's Wednesday Special: good old down-home meatloaf, mashed potatoes with gravy, and a vegetable.

The lunch is delightful. The company is even better. Our first meeting is going well. There seems to be no limit as to topic. So, for fun, I suggest, "Let's see who can be the first to make the other say 'you are weird'."

Tosh smiles that smile and leans into the contest. We each try our best to win, throwing out our most unorthodox ideas and unreal reality concepts. At the end of our lunch, neither has made the other say "you're weird".

The lunch ends too soon. What a great birthday present Tosh is. I'm pleased when he asks if we might have dinner together the following evening. He suggests a Japanese Restaurant, Suehiro. I agree to meet him there.

Tosh arrives at Suehiro with something wrapped in newspaper. It is my birthday present, a beautiful Japanese calendar. His gift is sweet and unassuming. He apologizes for the casual wrapping.

The more we talk the more we find in common; our interests and points of view, both conventional and unconventional. I am so caught up in Tosh's tales I am taken by surprise by one disclosure. "What?" I exclaim too loudly, forgetting that I'm in a public place.

Tosh smiles. I look around to see if my distraction attracted attention. No one is throwing sideways glances in our direction.

I lean over the table and lightly touch Tosh's forearm, "Did you say you have a rock containing fossilized *dinosaur poop*?"

Tosh nods matter-of-factly. "Yes. I also have a dinosaur egg; both verified by a friend of mine, a professor of geology."

Dinosaur egg? Dinosaur poop? Now we're talking.

I admit my most significant challenge in establishing social relationships with men has always been finding someone I could connect with in meaningful conversation. After two hours of pointless, superficial chitchat, I am desperate to escape. Not so with Tosh. There's nothing more meaningful than dinosaur poop!

It is *so* not so, that when he says goodnight outside the restaurant and doesn't ask to see me again, I am disappointed.

We walk to our cars and go our separate ways. Will he call and ask me out again?

Days pass. I look forward to hearing from Tosh. No call. A week passes. Then more days with no call. What's happening? Is Tosh taking it slow, or rolling to a dead stop.

Irma, a good friend and neighbor asks how things went on my date. My impressions spill out all warm and fuzzy. Tosh is open and emotionally accessible. My most significant impression is that he is honest, a man of honor, one who understands and values commitment and loyalty. Maybe even someone I can trust.

What I don't tell Irma is that I'm worried he may not be interested in me.

Two weeks pass. The phone rings. It's Tosh. He has been out of town. There were also pressing family matters to manage.

Tosh and I begin to date. It is an awkward process for both of us. We have been out of circulation for a long time; five years for me, forty years for Tosh. In the beginning, we simply meet at a restaurant for lunch or dinner and enjoy fun conversation.

On a sunny Saturday, we meet at a mom-and-pop café at the corner of a small shopping plaza. As I walk through the parking lot to the door, it is impossible not to notice a striking yellow and black hardtop Corvette convertible. Nice!

Tosh is waiting for me inside the restaurant.

The waitress seats us at a window offering a mountain view. With menu in hand, Tosh glances outside with studied casualty.

"Did you see the Corvette parked out front?"

"I did. That is a beautiful car!"

"It's mine."

"Yours?"

My quiet, conservative Tosh drives a hot, yellow Corvette? Imagine that!

"Would you like to go for a ride after lunch? We can drive up big Cottonwood Canyon over to Park City."

Until now, Tosh and I have met only at designated locations. I have not yet told him where I live. At this invitation, I decide to move my trust up a notch. I share my home address, which happens to be only a couple of blocks away.

He follows me home. I park my well-used ten-year-old white Toyota and join him in his sleek, yellow Corvette.

Driving a gorgeous, flawless, expensive car on narrow mountain roads with extreme drop-offs ending in rocky creek beds, mirrors my inner turmoil of starting over; moving forward on a cliff's edge.

Will I fall or will I be lucky and fly? The risk is there. No matter how many fail-safes anyone thinks they have in place, betting on love is a gamble. The nature of the game, with its individual rules and perspectives, is always one of illusion and shadows.

In spite of my apprehensions, I manage to enjoy the drive with Tosh, just as much as I've relished every one of our simple adventures to date. Our topics of conversation are limitless with the sweet spontaneity of naïve teenagers.

The past five years alone have brought with them plenty of opportunity to ponder past decisions and consequences. What have I learned? Have I learned enough? Have I learned anything? Can I trust my instincts yet? Better take things slow and careful, if not cautiously.

Well, Tosh may drive fast cars, but when it comes to dating, he stays in first gear. After our drive up the canyon, it takes him three months to work up the nerve to hold my hand. That's okay. Maybe this way he won't faint when we kiss for the first time!

One crisp October evening I discover that something more than the weather is in the flux of change. With the bite of early winter accentuating the evening breeze, we pull into the parking lot of Goodwood Restaurant. I'm anticipating one of my favorite meals; good, down-home North Carolina style pulled pork barbeque.

We sit in the car and chat before going inside. I have a gift for Tosh, a deck of Marilyn Monroe playing cards. We are both big fans of Marilyn. He thanks me for the present and then casually asks if I am okay if we are *friends*.

"Friends…" I catch my breath. I force a smile. "Sure. Of course, we can be friends."

Inside I am *not* smiling! "Friends?"

Am I being dumped? I can't believe it! My degree of disappointment surprises me. I have been so careful being cautious I never realize I'm not the only cautious one. Apparently Tosh doesn't have stars in *his* eyes either.

Wounded, I consider skipping dinner. Maybe I will ask him to take me home. I can sulk all the way from Draper to Sandy.

But, I'd miss dinner. No way am I forsaking North Carolina style barbeque. Food first; strategy later.

To my surprise, our meal and time together is as enjoyable and comfortable as always. With my craving for barbeque satisfied, things start to look better. Did I overreact to Tosh's suggestion of friendship?

The waitress brings our check to the table. Tosh puts on his eyeglasses to read the bill and calculate a generous tip. Although there is nothing unusual in what Tosh does, *it* happens again. Time slips into slow motion. There is that casual comfortability I have felt with him since the beginning. The feeling of familiarity I experienced when Tosh was just a face on a photograph passes through me again.

Sitting across the table from him feels so natural, so right. I could get used to being with this man.

Tosh suggests we sit on a bench outside and enjoy the brisk air. Now, I'm certain his comment earlier meant something other than how it sounded. Then, as if reading and correcting my thoughts, Tosh tells me he is dating other women.

Well, of course. We met on a dating site. It makes sense that I'm not the only one he's met. I don't know why I am so surprised. But I am! *I'm* not dating anyone else.

In one clear, unguarded moment I realize I have decided, albeit subconsciously, that Toshiharu Kano is the man I want in my life. He treats me with great respect. He patiently developed a friendship before demonstrating any romantic notions. I have been courted as every southern girl dreams of being courted.

Tosh has made "friends first" beautiful.

Now it's "friends only"?

He's not just seeing other women; he wants me to *know* he's seeing other women. Is this his way of softening a decision he has already made. Is there no future for us? Friends for a while, then he finds someone else and our relationship ends?

Oh, crap.

I don't expect to hear from Tosh again.

Who would have guessed? Tosh keeps calling. We continue to date. Could it be he hasn't made up his mind about me? Maybe we do have a future.

And then, Tosh tells me about one of the women he is dating. She is a widow, who has been left exceptionally wealthy.

It turns out, Tosh doesn't just talk to me about other women; he keeps them apprised of his dating status also. He has told the wealthy widow about me and the job that minimally supports me. I can't help but wonder if he told her the driver's side door on my ten-year-old Toyota only opens from the outside!

Well, he told her something, because this woman felt compelled to tell Tosh that I am a "nothing" and a "nobody." Not only that, she had the audacity to tell Tosh that he should stop seeing me.

Now, processed and labeled based on superficial circumstances, will I be discarded?

Where Tosh and I are going, remains up in the air. I know only one thing for certain. If a relationship with him doesn't happen, I am through looking for a companion. This will be it for me.

Okay, I know, not the most productive thinking. After all, Tosh never even held my hand for three months! Who knows *what* he is thinking!

Not only does Tosh continue to call, our dates become more frequent, more comfortable and more fun.

One of our dates is a drive to Wendover, a casino town straddling the State line. Part of the desert town is in Utah and the other in Nevada. Tosh enjoys gambling; slot machines and the tables. I played a little back in the days when real quarters were inserted and, if you were lucky you'd get a waterfall of tinkling silver to reward you for your efforts. It's not so much fun getting paper tickets like a report from the accounting department. Unfamiliar with the new system, I follow Tosh around watching him play and win at the machines.

After a buffet lunch at Montego Bay, we drive to the Rainbow casino, where Tosh plays more. I watch and observe the patrons of the casinos. It all feels alien to me; especially the patrons of the High Limit section. So far from frugal; the driving force in my life.

On the way home, Tosh and I talk amiably about this and that. Somewhere along the 122 miles of desert and salt flats, our conversation turns to our feelings toward each other.

When we reach Salt Lake, it finally happens. After months of courting, we kiss for the first time.

Tosh doesn't faint.

I don't know if that is a good sign or not!

It is.

Tosh proposes as we share a meal together. A year later, we marry. It is a simple church ceremony with family members.

I am so grateful I hung in there while we took time to create a solid relationship, filled with friendship and conversation before the commitment of marriage. I'm also grateful I walked through my fears during moments of doubt.

There are, of course, more bumps and turns on the road of matrimonial bliss after the chapel ceremony in April of 2011. Our misunderstandings are most often due to cultural differences. We always talk things through and invariably land in a stronger place.

I am now far removed from my childhood vision of life and fairy tale coloring books when I always colored within the lines and thickened those lines with a darker color of the same hue. In books of white paper I created a safe, flawless, predictable, beautiful world with 16 magic wax crayons.

That world no longer exists. Now, I experience unclear lines and am challenged to color wherever I may with whatever color presents itself to me.

Getting to know Tosh is one discovery after another, with more unclear lines. The subject of reincarnation surfaces often. Tosh reveals to me what he meant in those early emails on the dating site when he said he was an Ancient One. He tells me he has lived many lives and remembers being present at major historical events.

My grandson remembers a life in Japan. I have memories of past lives. Tosh has memories of many lives. What could it mean? Perhaps there are no lines.

This story is about the world's foundation. It is about the pursuit of happiness and the unhappiness the pursuit often inflicts. It is about the many opposing, senseless ways life's players go about getting their needs met and where it takes us ... all of us ... no matter the literal distance between "you and me".

If reincarnation is the wheel of life, each one of us will eventually walk in everyone's shoes, "their" shoes. Names, race, sex, status, beginnings and endings are all interchangeable.

Tosh opened up to me about the role he believes he will play in the destiny of mankind. That role brought me to these white pages to write his family's story.

It is difficult to pinpoint where anything originates. As far as Tosh's life is concerned I'd say his destiny began with a simple wish. Grandmother Nekomoto of Furuichi, Japan wanted her granddaughter, Shizue, to marry her grandson, Toshiyuki.

CHAPTER THREE

Grandmother's Matter of Importance

In the early Twentieth Century it was common in Japan for cousins to marry in order to maintain the family name and fortune and, in some cases, to preserve their bloodline. The Nekomoto bloodline is very important to them. They are descendants of Samurai, the military nobility of medieval and early modern Japan.

Toshiyuki and Shizue Nekomoto are paternal first cousins, born in Hawaii on the island of Oahu in 1914. They now live in the village of Furuichi, Japan.

Toshiyuki's parents are Shunichi and Tonoyo Nekomoto. Shizue's parents are Waichi and Misao Nekomoto.

Toshiyuki, a self-acknowledged "rascal" did not move to Japan by choice. His father, Shunichi, sent him here for rehabilitation after his expulsion from a very prestigious school in Honolulu. From the age of 10, the rebellious boy was immersed in the Japanese way of disciplined living and respectful interaction. His father believed Japan's traditions of decorum and veneration would teach his only male heir self-control and respect.

Shizue first arrived in Japan at the age of eight. Her mother, Misao, was bedridden after the birth of Shizue's brother, Katsumi, due to complications. Doctors in Honolulu told Waichi she was terminally ill and they could do nothing to improve her health. Waichi decided to send his wife to the family estate in Furuichi, Japan to give her a peaceful, countryside life for the remainder of her days. He knew Grandmother Nekomoto would take good care of her.

Six months after Shizue's mother left Hawaii for Japan, Shizue, her older brother, Kiyoto and several cousins went to a beach near their home to collect shells. They were so busy searching for shells they forgot the time and did not realize how far they had roamed. The sun was almost setting on the horizon. It would soon be dark. They started heading for home.

On the way, they saw a ball of fire moving on top of the sea, coming from the direction of Japan. The ball of fire grew brighter and brighter; heading towards them. Just before reaching the spot where they stood watching, it shot straight up into the air and vaporized. Terribly frightened, the children ran home as fast as they could. Not one of them spoke to anyone else about what they had seen. They were sure it was something out of this world.

Shizue would soon learn that the fireball she, Kiyoto and her cousins saw appeared around the same time Misao passed away at the mansion in Furuichi, Japan. Waichi had received a telegram informing him that his wife died the same day.

Shizue believes the fireball she saw was her mother's spirit. Her mother had come to say good-bye. Shizue did not discuss her feelings with anyone, not even her brother, Kiyoto.

Waichi remarried a couple of years later. His second wife, 12 years older than Shizue, treated her and her brothers poorly. The stepmother did not want to be bothered with another woman's offspring. Waichi did nothing to stop his young wife from harassing his children. To appease her, Waichi sent the two younger children, Shizue, age eight, and her three-year-old brother, Katsumi, away. They sailed alone to their ancestral home in Japan, a strange, faraway place, where they would live with their grandparents.

Grandfather and Grandmother Nekomoto accepted the children, loved them and raised them as their own until Katsumi, at

13 years of age, decided to return to Hawaii. Shizue would not let him go back alone to face their stepmother

Shizue and Katsumi sailed back to Hawaii.

Their stepmother had not changed her ways. Life with her was difficult. Katsumi, however, fared better than Shizue. He had grown into a very resilient boy. He would not take his stepmother's abusive behavior. One day when she yelled at him, he yelled back, "What did you say? Say that again!" The stepmother would say nothing to him after the incident. However, she continued to harass both Shizue and Kiyoto, as they would not talk back to her.

Uncle Shunichi was very kind to Shizue knowing how her stepmother treated her. When he learned that she wanted to take a tailoring class, but could not ask her father for the tuition, he paid the fee.

Every morning before she left home to attend class, Shizue had to complete a list of chores: clean the bathrooms, fill the Japanese Goemon-buro (bathtub) with water, and more. Running late one day, she forgot to fill the tub. Her stepmother called her back as she was stepping out the front door. Shizue had to remove her silk stockings and finish the chore before she could leave home.

Kiyoto protected Shizue as much as he could, but finally reached his limit for abuse, had a terrible fight with his stepmother and left home. He moved into his uncle Shunichi's house until he married and moved into a small rental home.

Shizue wanted to leave also, but she did not have the funds. The small allowance received from her father every month wasn't even enough to pay her bus fares. She was able to manage with a little help from Kiyoto.

To earn extra money, Shizue decided to take in orders making and tailoring shirts, pants, suits, etc. from neighbors and relatives. After returning home from her class, she completed the chores piled on her by her stepmother and then, bent over her sewing machine, worked on orders until late at night.

Her stepmother complained to Waichi saying Shizue should not work at home. "I can't stand the noise. She is using our electricity. We should make her pay for it. We should confiscate her earnings. We deserve it!"

For the first time, Waichi did not agree with his wife. "No! She is working so hard. Don't you see that? I don't have the heart to take her hard-earned money."

Stepmother was upset, but did not pursue the matter further.

Shizue graduated from the school as a certified seamstress, with a State certificate in the "Men's Suits and Shirts" category. She passed the State of Hawaii examination and found a job at a shop downtown. The owner, who was old and ready to retire, wanted someone trustworthy to take over the business. She asked Shizue to carry on the name and reputation of the business.

Shizue regretfully declined her offer, as she wanted to go back to Japan before her grandmother passed away. She had no intention of living, indefinitely, with her father and stepmother. Along with saved earnings, she had been collecting fabric remnants and other items she could take with her back to Furuichi.

Shizue and Katsumi did not have to deal with their stepmother's ill treatment for long. Waichi learned that his wife was pregnant. It was not his child. An illness had left him sterile. They soon divorced.

Shizue returned to Japan with over 20 precious items (sugar, fabrics, sewing machines, shoes, clothing, etc.) in trunks and boxes. Some of the goods were given to her by friends and neighbors to be given to their families. These items were treasures in Japan due to years of war.

Shizue's relatives in Japan picked her up at Yokohama Harbor. Workers were waiting to unload her belongings from the ship. Shizue spotted her luggage and boxes in one area and started checking them against her list. She could not believe all her possessions were miraculously there, all together, even the small boxes her friends gave her at the time of boarding.

A cousin took out a knife and started to cut the rope bundling some packages together so that the custom's officer could examine them. Shizue stopped him from cutting the rope as it was very precious in Japan. Her father, Waichi, had instructed her to keep the ropes intact. He wanted to make sure that the family in Japan could reuse them.

As they waited for the custom's officer to show up, a man in uniform approached them. He was tall and quite handsome. He asked Shizue if she had found all her belongings.

"Yes. They are all here," Shizue had replied.

The customs officer proceeded to check Shizue's luggage without asking her to open any of the trunks and boxes. He marked "Checked, Passed Inspection" on everything. Then, he stepped back, stood for a moment and said, "Will you marry me?"

Shocked, Shizue replied, "No. I came back to Japan to take care of my grandmother".

The impressive man smiled, "Of course, I understand." He walked away with no look back.

Shizue's aunt urged her to get his name and contact him later. She would have ample opportunity as they would be staying in Tokyo for several days. Shizue did not intend to do any of that.

Shizue, now 27, is back in Japan caring for her aged, ailing grandmother. Her grandfather passed away a few years earlier.

The very day Shizue returned to Furuichi, she saw a fireball a second time. It was late afternoon. The sun was setting as she talked to a friend in the vegetable garden. Her friend yelled, "What was that?" The fireball came and went in the same manner Shizue had seen from the beach in Honolulu. Shizue is certain her mother followed her back to Japan to let her know, "I am here with you."

Shizue now believes her mother's spirit follows her and protects her. Misao had not wanted to leave her children in Hawaii to live out her dying days in Japan. She missed her children so much, especially Shizue, she had found a way to be with her.

Now, Shizue is determined to take care of the grandmother who loved and cared for her for ten years. She has no interest in returning to Hawaii, even though several men there were very interested in her and talking about marriage. She was not interested in them. Also, she vowed she would not get married before the age of 28 as her mother passed away at 28.

Today, in the countryside of the village of Furuichi in the ancestral Nekomoto mansion, Shizue is happy to fulfill her duty and honor her grandmother.

Shizue's cousin, Toshiyuki, also lives in the home. He, too, had returned to Hawaii, but chose not to stay. Everything there had changed for the worse. The Great Depression of 1929 left his father's construction business in Honolulu in crisis. Toshiyuki had come back to Japan for a college education and opportunities for a good career.

Seventeen years after being expelled from Punahou School, Toshiyuki is still a rascal. Shizue disapproves of her cousin's insubordinate ways. She is distant to him, although modestly polite. He will be out of her life soon enough. He has a girlfriend and is talking of marriage.

On this gray September day, Shizue looks like a schoolgirl moving about the large kitchen of the Nekomoto mansion. She is a tiny five feet tall, dressed in black monpei slacks and a kimono top. During wartime, with a shortage of manpower, women help out farmers, clear roads, clean buildings, even fight the enemy when necessary. Monpei slacks and blouses are very versatile, made of lightweight cotton fabric. This is Shizue's daily attire, except when she goes into town on an errand. On those occasions, she wears a western style skirt and blouse.

The sizeable kitchen of the mansion echoes with the sounds of Shizue chopping vegetables. This environment is so far from the small, intimate, white frame house in Honolulu where Shizue lived from the age of 18 to 27.

The kitchen/dining room, designed to entertain a large family and many guests, has three levels: the highest, where men are served, a secondary level for women, and the lowest for children and servants. Pillows for sitting and bento trays are stored in a nearby closet leaving the dining area clear, except when meals are served.

Shizue stops chopping to adjust the comb in her hair and tame a strand of smooth, black hair that insists on dangling in front of her eyes. Her delicate features are serenely beautiful.

Rain begins to fall as she prepares a breakfast of Miso soup, green onions, seaweed, and fish. A black cast iron kettle hangs in the opening of a large wood and coal burning stove. She opens the window above the stove just enough to let out some of the smoke.

Every day, Shizue sweeps, dusts, irons, picks up after her cousin, and carries meals plus loving attention to her grandmother's bedroom.

Today, the sky remains overcast with a steady drizzle.

The persistent, pattering rain falls on 20 acres of centuries old gardens. Water drips from roof tiles, fogs window panes, and soaks the twelve-foot high, two-foot thick wall that fortifies the property.

Shizue has a fondness for the sound of rain. Especially, raindrops falling on smooth stepping stones that meander through the three-inch, luxuriant lichen in the ornamental garden. She may go out today and watch the rain fall on gray stone lanterns, Japanese Koke, maple, and pine trees lining the path to the Koi pond. She will stop at the edge of acres of bamboo forest and listen to the gentle rush of wind.

Beyond the gardens and the protecting wall of the mansion, Japan is at war with the Republic of China fighting for control of Korea. The ongoing hostilities are beginning to wear on the fabric and stamina of the people of Japan.

Inside the walls of the Nekomoto mansion, survival is the task at hand. Years of government conflict are destroying the longstanding roots of prosperity and prestige. Security and peace of mind surreptitiously lose ground in the procession of ever-darkening days.

Today, the lumbering clouds dull the edge between day and twilight.

After a long day, her chores finally completed, Shizue goes to her room and slips into an evening kimono. The rain has settled into a downward windless fall. She slides the paper panel wall of her room and the outer heavy oak panel across the hallway open to the mansion grounds.

Sitting on a pillow, Shizue listens to the pit-pat symphony of rain drops, brushes her long silky hair, and daydreams about the special young man who has been visiting her ever more frequently. A particularly pleasing thought brings a smile to her face. She whispers "Sugu ni" (soon).

"Shizue! Shizue!" The insistent call from Grandmother interrupts her pleasant distraction.

Shizue plops down the hairbrush and rushes along the hallway on tiny feet. The floorboards do not even creak under her slight weight of 80 pounds.

"Obaasan, (Grandmother) are you okay? I thought you were…"

Shizue screams and points to a corner of the room. "Snake! Snake!"

She shrinks back toward the hallway, as a large white snake slithers across the floor and out of sight beneath the chest of drawers.

"My goodness, child, calm yourself." Obaasan runs her fingers through long, loose hair. Despite advancing age Obaasan's hair is still dark, except for an almost perfectly centered streak of white.

"But there … there's a…" Shizue continues to point to the spot where she saw the snake.

"Yes, I know. It is only Hogo-sha."

"Guardian?" says Shizue.

"Yes," answers Grandmother. "Hogo-sha snakes have lived here, watching over our family since I was a child."

"But, it…" she doesn't take her eyes off the chest of drawers, "but, it's hiding under the…"

"She is hiding because you frightened her. She will not bother you. Hogo-sha always comes inside when it is raining."

Shizue backs away.

"Come back. She will not bite. Come back," encourages Obaasan.

Shizue stands at a fair distance from the bureau.

"You will get used to Hogo-sha. She is an Iwakuni. She eats rats and brings good fortune. For you to see her is a good omen. Now,

32

sit here beside me." Grandmother pats the embroidered pillow beside her futon.

Shizue takes two steps forward and gasps. The ivory white snake with ruby colored eyes peers out from under the chest.

"It ... she ... it's looking at me."

"She's only curious. Sit down. Sit down," insists Obaasan.

Grandmother's room is simply decorated as are all the sleeping rooms. Tatamis, thick woven straw mats, cover the wooden plank floor. A paper panel slides open to the hallway. Two other sliding panels open to the inside of the house. A chest of drawers and a closet hold all of Grandmother's personal items and treasures. A vase of fresh flowers sits on a low, mother-of-pearl inlaid table. Grandmother lies on the traditional Japanese futon, a mattress of cotton about four inches thick.

After commenting on the tenacious rain, Grandmother picks up the conversation where the snake interrupted, "As to your question 'am I okay?' No, I am not. There is a matter of great importance we must discuss." Obaasan then reveals a deep desire; a wish she can no longer conceal. With firm, but quivering words, she tells Shizue she must marry her cousin, Toshiyuki, for the sake of the family.

Grandmother seldom jokes, but this request Shizue cannot take seriously. She laughs.

Grandmother does not laugh.

Shizue searches her grandmother's face. "This is the desire of your heart? This ... *this* is the matter of importance? You wish me to marry Toshiyuki?"

"Yes. It is my wish," says Grandmother. The downward pitch of her voice implies this may be her last wish.

"But ... no Obaasan. I cannot marry Toshiyuki. I don't love him. I will marry for love." Shizue speaks with a rare, bold defiance. Her smile and wistful eyes soften her firm refusal.

33

Grandmother touches Shizue's hand. "Yes, of course. Love is the fancy of all young hearts. It is not, however, wise. Your own dear mother, Misao, married for love. Waichi did not take good care of her. Love, my child, is the broken dream that put your mother into an early grave."

Shizue closes her eyes. She does not want to remember.

"Much unhappiness has befallen our family at the hands of its men," Grandmother shakes her head. "Yes. My sons are too much like their father. Oh, how I loved your grandfather, but... Do you know why Toshiyuki's mother is paralyzed?"

"Uncle Shunichi said she suffered a stroke. It is terribly sad."

"Yes. It is terribly sad. Perhaps more than anyone knows. My son refuses to speak of Tonoyo," she shakes her head again. "There is a dark secret hidden in Shunichi's silence. I..."

Grandmother does not complete her thought.

"Shizue, listen to old Obaasan. You must marry for honor and for love of your family. Marry Toshiyuki and you will preserve what is most important."

Shizue stares at her grandmother's frail, withered hands; blue veins bulge underneath delicate, transparent skin. Shizue does not look into Obaasan's discerning eyes.

"Look at me, Shizue. Look at me. You were a child when Waichi sent you away and far too young to understand why he chose his new wife over his children; his blood. What does this tell you about a man's love ... even when that man is your father?"

"I have not forgotten. Katsumi cried all the way here. People on the ship threatened to throw him overboard. I..."

Shizue draws a quivering breath, "Obaasan, maybe what you say about love is true, but there's something you don't know."

"Tell me. What is it?" Grandmother urges, "You may speak to your obaasan without fear."

34

Encouraged, Shizue blurts out her feelings, "I don't like Toshiyuki! He is spoiled. Selfish. A disgrace to the family. He still jokes about getting kicked out of Punahou School."

"Yes. Yes. Toshiyuki was a rebellious child," Grandmother agrees, although dismissively. "But he has grown into a fine young man."

"He is a man, but he is not grown! What manner of husband will Toshiyuki be? He is a rascal. He does not deny it. Deny it? No! He is proud of it!"

"Shizue, you…"

"No, Obaasan. Toshiyuki broke Uncle Shunichi's heart. Japan has not reformed him. Japan has not made an honorable man out of Toshiyuki."

"My dear, dear child, Toshiyuki is still young. He is having fun. One day he will know and do what must be done. He has the blood of nobility. He has the blood of Samurai."

"As do I," replies Shizue. "It is a deep honor to me, but to Toshiyuki, it means nothing."

"Toshiyuki will grow into his blood. He will grow into the spirit living in his blood. This old Obaasan knows."

"When? Some day? I will not wait for some day. The man I marry will be a man of honor now. I will marry for honor and love."

Grandmother nods. "Yes. Yes Shizue. You can have love. It is good to love. Love kittens. Love puppies. Love children." Grandmother squints, "If you could see your future, you would not want to love a man."

"But, I do want to love a man. I will not abandon my dreams. I will marry the man I love."

Grandmother sighs. "Oh, my child, I understand. I understand more than you know. When you see me in this wrinkled and failing body, you think I don't know your dreams. But, I do. Ah, yes. I have not forgotten the desires of youth. I remember. I remember well."

Obaasan closes her eyes. Through labored breaths, she whispers, "My dear, beautiful Shizue, you are far too hard on Toshiyuki. Yes, Shunichi spoiled him. Those days are gone. Your cousin has a good heart. I see this in him. He will be a fine man. Sharing Samurai blood, the blood of nobility, spirit, and honor gives you much in common. You will see. Marry Toshiyuki and I will be happy. Marry Toshiyuki and you will be happy."

"Obaasan, with all my heart, I want you to be happy. But, even if I agree to marry Toshiyuki, he will not agree to marry me. He doesn't like me any more than I like him. He calls me Nekoyanagi! (Pussy Willow) Besides, you know he has a girlfriend and talks of marrying her."

"The young woman he has chosen is unsuitable ... not of our class. She will not become my grandson's wife. The family will not allow it."

"Toshiyuki does not care what the family wants."

"Toshiyuki is in love today and out of love tomorrow. He will honor his family's wishes."

"But I ... Obaasan, I also have someone ... someone I..."

Grandmother interrupts. "Yes. I have seen you and the young man walking together. Forget him. Duty is your concern ... your only concern. Duty to family, preserving family honor and your noble heritage, this only will bring you happiness."

Shizue turns away from her grandmother. Silence engulfs her as if she is about to grant her grandmother's wish. Her silence, however, is not a sign of defeat. Grandmother is right. Seeing the Hogo-sha was a good omen. Her downcast eyes disguise a clever thought playing in the corners of her mind.

"So, Toshiyuki calls you Nekoyanagi?" Grandmother laughs.

"It is not amusing."

"No. No, Shizue. You misunderstand. I am not laughing about the name he calls you, I am happy about what it means."

"What it means?"

"It means your cousin likes to tease you. This is good."

"Good for what?"

"Agree to marry Toshiyuki and you will see. Tonight as you sleep, listen to the whispers of your heart. Tomorrow you will know what to do."

"No, Obaasan." Shizue closes her eyes for a moment before she continues. "Sleep will not dull my senses. Whispers of the night will not blind my heart. I will not give you my decision tomorrow. I ... I will give it now." Shizue pauses for a hasty second appraisal of her plan and then releases the words that could change her life forever. The shadows of lamplight disguise her intentions. "Yes, Obaasan, for your happiness ... to strengthen and safeguard our family... I will marry Toshiyuki."

"Oh, Shizue, you are my joy," Grandmother Nekomoto touches her granddaughter's cheek with the tip of a trembling finger. "My dear, dear child." Her failing eyesight does not see tears welling in Shizue's eyes.

Amber lamplight flickers over Obaasan's aging face and sparkles in her eyes, "Where is my grandson? I will speak to Toshiyuki now."

"He isn't home. He is out. Remember? It's Friday. He is always very late on Fridays."

"Friday ...yes ... I had forgotten. Then, I will reveal my wish to him tomorrow."

"And tomorrow you will tell him this marriage is not the desire of my heart?"

Grandmother's vacant nod does little to ease Shizue's concerns.

"Please, Obaasan. Promise you will do this. I have agreed to marry Toshiyuki only to honor you. My love is for you, not him. It is right that he knows my true feelings. Tell him. Please."

"I am too old and forgetful for promises. Tomorrow I will speak the words the morning brings."

"But you must tell Toshiyuki the truth. The truth is my only request."

"The day has been long, Shizue. Go now. I am very tired."

Shizue glides toward the hallway.

"Granddaughter?"

"Yes?"

"Sunday, when your young man returns, you must dispose of him discreetly."

"Yes, Obaasan." Shizue bows to the matriarch of the Nekomoto family and slides the wall panel closed.

In the hallway outside her grandmother's room Shizue draws a heavy, fulfilling breath. She agreed to Obaasan's wish; yet she remains faithful to her belief that only love brings true happiness. Shizue is certain the rebellious Toshiyuki will not agree to the marriage. He does not want to marry her. He too wants to marry for love. *He* will say "no" to Grandmother.

Shizue will let her rascal cousin, Toshiyuki, be the one to break their grandmother's heart. She smiles at her cleverness.

All will be well.

CHAPTER FOUR

A War of Hearts

Late that night, Toshiyuki guides his wobbling bicycle down a waterlogged street toward home. He holds a black cloth umbrella in his left hand to prevent inadvertently pressing the handle brake connected to the front wheel, which would send him tumbling off the road into the mud. The cloth umbrella is more than a shield against the rain; it indicates he is a member of a prestigious family. The poor can only afford oil paper umbrellas.

He arrives home dripping wet. In the shelter of the exterior hallway, he shakes water from his uniform and cap and tries to wipe the moisture from his round frame spectacles. Yes, Toshiyuki has grown into a man since leaving Hawaii. But, no matter how much he jokes around and laughs with apparent abandon, discerning individuals sense his smile hides a little lost boy. Young women find the endearing quality irresistible. For Toshiyuki, there has never been a shortage of women.

Another week of military training has gone well, followed by another Friday evening with college buddies at a sushi bar eating and drinking sake or beer. Toshiyuki has a reputation for holding his liquor better than most. The truth is he drinks very little as it makes him sick to his stomach. Only a small amount actually goes into him. At social gathering, when friends or employers aren't looking, he pours the alcohol into a bottle he keeps hidden in his jacket. It's very important to Toshiyuki to fit in and not be the object of ridicule.

Friends have questioned him about his high tolerance level to liquor without response. They chalk up the phenomenon to pure stubbornness.

Toshiyuki never reveals the truth that keeps him sober.

Tonight, he falls into bed exhausted. As he sleeps he dreams of his island paradise. He walks barefoot on the white sands of Honolulu beaches. He fishes, swims, and flirts with girls wearing daring, revealing two piece bathing suits. In dreams he returns to the home he knew before the Great Depression; the life of a privileged son of wealth and prestige. He dreams of the life he has lost.

Toshiyuki's university days in Japan revolved around serious issues, but they weren't all work and no play. He wasn't shy or inexperienced with the opposite sex and managed to find some off time for socializing with girls and dating.

Now, Toshiyuki has met a special young woman and plans to marry her one day. Realistically, there is much to do in advancing his career before taking on the responsibilities of marriage.

Another stage of Toshiyuki's life has begun. It appears straightforward and simple. Build a career, marry, have children, and live happily ever after.

Destiny has other plans, however. Like the borders of a great puzzle growing inward, tighter and tighter, pieces of the past and decisions of the present will lead him to a place and a force of destruction no one can possibly fathom.

As an American born Japanese, a "Niseis", the son of immigrant parents, Toshiyuki has dual citizenship. He is a citizen of the United States and a citizen of Japan. The Imperial Japanese Army drafted Toshiyuki when he reached recruitment age. Because he was a university student at the time, the army postponed his enlistment.

After graduation, he entered the 5th Engineering Supplementary Regiment in Hiroshima.

Behind him now are three rough months of basic training. He will never forget this time in his life. The grueling training brought some recruits to tears. Worse, there were those who could not handle it and committed suicide.

The military required Toshiyuki, a spoiled privileged kid from Americanized Hawaii, to strictly obey his superiors, even same-ranked privates who completed basic training ahead of him.

There was no free time, absolutely not a single minute. When not in training, Toshiyuki had to perform common chores: wash clothes, clean the recruits' room, the sergeant's quarters and the most offensive chore of all, wash the sergeant's loin cloths. It was impossible for recruits to catch up with the duties. The rookie soldiers had to do what they were told without question and without complaint.

One aspect of basic training infuriated Toshiyuki.

The government supplied each recruit a limited number of each item of clothing and shoes. If items were damaged or lost, they were not replaced by the military. To maintain their clothing supply, recruits had to wash, hang, and then watch their clothing put out on the line to dry. This was the only way to prevent their items from being stolen. Punishment for lost or stolen clothing was a blow to the face with the sergeant's leather slipper. To avoid this punishment, recruits stole from others what had been stolen from them. This was Sashikuri, "take if taken from", a practice without fairness or justice.

The sergeant always had something for new recruits to do. For Private Nekomoto it was worse than for the others. He could never meet the sergeant's expectations when it came to folding his uniform shirt. Shirts had to be folded perfectly square at the shoulders. This sergeant did not determine the accuracy of the folded shirts by sight. He used an L-square to determine perfection.

The spoiled, rich kid from Hawaii encountered a problem.

"Nekomoto, do you think that's square, Nekomoto? I WANT IT PERFECT! DO IT OVER!" the puffy-eyed sergeant, who had found the perfect niche for his undeveloped manhood, slammed the uniform down to the floor.

The new recruit refolded his shirt and submitted it for another inspection.

"DO IT OVER!" he heard again.

With each attempt at folding the shirt properly, the sergeant expressed extreme dissatisfaction and threw it to the floor.

No one had ever treated Toshiyuki this way. The other recruits had to stand at attention during the entire ordeal. Toshiyuki was not only embarrassed, he was humiliated.

No matter how hard recruit Toshiyuki tried; he could not fold the uniform shirt to the satisfaction of his sergeant.

Finally, the sergeant gave up on Private Nekomoto. "You are STUPID, Nekomoto! USELESS!"

That night, Toshiyuki, too infuriated to sleep, stared up at the ceiling. The spoiled, rich kid being treated like a commoner came up with a plan to restore his pride. For the next uniform inspection, he would stuff the shirt with stiff, smooth newspaper and fold the shirt around it.

The following morning, Tosh leapt out of his bunk anticipating the success of his plan; the chance to get the sergeant off his back and end the increasing derision from other recruits.

Inspection hour came. New recruit Nekomoto stood at attention beside his perfectly folded uniform shirt, precisely square at the shoulders. He stood confident, fully expecting to get away with the artful illusion. The poker face he wore as the sergeant approached his bunk would have inspired any professional gambler, even his Uncle Waichi.

The sergeant walked over slowly, hands behind his back. He examined the shirt with a stare that turned suspicious.

Recruit Nekomoto didn't blink as he waited for the sergeant to move past his folded masterpiece.

The sergeant did not move along. He scowled at the new recruit.

Toshiyuki didn't breathe.

"NEKOMOTO!"

"Sir!"

"Do you think I'M STUPID, Nekomoto?" The sergeant snatched the shirt into the air and the newspaper fell out. "Fold that shirt properly. NOW! What are you ... some pathetic kind of clown? I'm watching you!"

Nekomoto retrieved the shirt, folded it and waited.

The sergeant continued inspection of the other recruits. Upon completion, instead of returning to Toshiyuki's bunk, the sergeant strolled out the door.

Sighs of recruit relief filled the room.

Toshiyuki tried not to think about the next inspection.

Yelling was the least of the sergeant's insults.

Military training, versus the privileged life, pushed recruit Nekomoto to experience unfamiliar emotions. Sometimes, he felt like crying. He questioned his life and why he had to suffer like this. To hold back the tears, he vowed silently, to get revenge on the devil in the sergeant uniform. One day, Toshiyuki Nekomoto would be an officer of higher rank and order the sergeant to perform the humiliating and degrading tasks he had been forced to do.

"Just wait, Sergeant, I'll get even with you." This was Toshiyuki's pledge.

Private Nekomoto survived basic training on plans for vengeance.

The months of basic insanity, finally, approached conclusion. Toward the end of the ordeal, Toshiyuki began to appreciate the many things he had learned from his sergeant. In three short months, he received manual and technical training on the proper use of simple tools such as wire cutters, saw, hammer, and sledge. He learned the art of gun positioning, tunneling, trenching, building wooden bridges, and transporting infantry across rivers.

The boy Toshiyuki had become a man equipped to deal with whatever might come, with patience and endurance. He abandoned plans of retaliation against his sergeant, but not his plan to become an officer, which was the best way to survive and succeed in the military. He set his first military goal. Private Nekomoto will become an officer.

After passing the required exam for officer candidate school, Toshiyuki was sent to the South China front for advanced training in battle practices. He ranked eighth in a class of fifty; one of fifteen selected to return to Japan to the Engineering Academy in Matsudo. In Matsudo, he advanced from Private to Sergeant. He returned to Hiroshima, completed Officer's School in September of 1941 and advanced to the rank of First Lieutenant.

Instead of being sent to the front like the other cadets, Toshiyuki remained in Hiroshima for further instruction as a Civil Engineer.

This morning at the mansion in Furuichi, in the dim light before the first rooster's crow, the family matriarch enters Toshiyuki's room, sits down at his bedside and shakes her sleeping grandson's shoulder.

"Grandmother!" exclaims a startled Toshiyuki. "What wrong? You sick?"

Toshiyuki grew up speaking Pidgin English, a form of communication that originated on sugar plantations between immigrants and natives of Hawaii. It affects how he speaks Japanese, his second language.

"No, Grandson, I am not sick."

Toshiyuki pushes up on his elbows. "Is it burglar? Are we robbed?"

"No." Grandmother places one hand against his chest to restrain him. "There is an urgent matter we must discuss."

"Urgent matter?" mumbles Toshiyuki, trying to focus his vision in the faint light. "Now?"

"I am worried," says Grandmother.

"Yeah, I know. Soon, I go off to battle."

"Yes ... and while you are away ... until you return I need someone I can trust to be at my side. I know who is best for this."

"Shizue," he rubs his eyes. "She takes good care of you. Shizue will be by your side."

"Yes, Shizue is trustworthy. I rely on her. She will take good care of the house and me when you are gone."

"Then why you worry?"

"There is a special reason to worry."

"What you worry about?" Toshiyuki yawns, as the fog in his head slowly begins to clear.

"Shizue is a beautiful young woman. She is also kind and generous. Do you agree?"

"Yes," he clears his throat and nods. "She is beautiful and wonderful girl. Why that make worry? You want Shizue to be ugly, mean, and selfish?"

"Stop that! You joke too much. This matter is serious. A young man has noticed Shizue. He stops by every Sunday afternoon at exactly 2:45. They walk together. When they return, she cannot stop smiling. Sometimes I hear her singing."

"Shizue sings? I tell her joke and she hardly smile."

"The young man's punctuality concerns me." Grandmother's brow wrinkles deepen.

"Why? You like better him to be late?"

Grandmother does not understand the humor of Americans. A tilt of her head cautions Toshiyuki that she has had enough of his amused attitude. "He is dependable and responsible, also handsome. This young man has admirable qualities. If Shizue marries him she will leave the mansion. I will be alone with no one I trust to care for me or our beautiful home. Do you understand my worry? You must keep Shizue with us!"

"Keep her with us? Me? If Shizue wants to be with him, how can I keep her here?"

"Toshiyuki, if you care for me..." Grandmother Nekomoto covers her face with trembling hands. A tear rolls to her chin.

"Grandmother, don't cry. I care for you. You know I do. Please don't cry. I listen."

Grandmother puts her hand on top of her grandson's. "You must see to it that Shizue does not leave."

"How? Shizue does not listen to me. I don't think she likes me. Nothing I can do if she wants to marry and leave."

"Grant my wish and Shizue will not leave."

"Your wish? What you wish?"

"Toshiyuki," Grandmother's jaw sets firmly. "You must marry Shizue."

"Marry Shizue!" Toshiyuki laughs, but seeing the despondence in his grandmother's eyes stops abruptly. "I? Marry Shizue? No. Shizue is wonderful girl, but after war with China over, I marry my girlfriend."

46

Grandmother holds out one hand. "Help me up."

"Wait, Grandmother. Understand why I say no? Why I cannot do this?"

"Help me up," Grandmother repeats.

"No. Wait," Toshiyuki shifts to a different tactic. "It not be fair for me to marry now, leaving wife behind with hard days would not be honorable. If I am killed in war, Shizue be young widow and will not feel free to marry again."

"Your worries are honorable. However, there is no need to worry about leaving Shizue behind. I have spoken with her. She is willing to take on the responsibility and hardship if you do not return." Grandmother closes her eyes to the vision of war and death that is all too real. "Shizue wants to marry you."

"Say what? Shizue want to marry me? Shizue tell you this?"

"Yes. She has agreed."

"But, what about ... what is the man's name?"

"His name does not matter. Shizue has agreed to marry you," the words wheeze from Grandmother's chest.

"No. No. I can't marry Shizue."

Another tear rolls down Grandmother's cheek. A rooster's crow sends a chill through Toshiyuki. He is going off to war. He may not return.

Toshiyuki reaches for Grandmother's hand and holds it firmly between his. "Grandmother, don't cry. I ... okay, yeah. I will talk to Shizue. I hear her words. Then I decide what I do."

"Do not waste time." Grandmother coughs. "Tomorrow is Sunday. Her suitor will come again. One hour with Shizue could change everything. I know he is planning to ask our beautiful Shizue to marry him."

Toshiyuki helps Grandmother back to her room.

"Have Shizue wash everything in your room." She pulls up her bed covers. "It smells of cigarettes."

"I am sorry, Grandmother. My buddies smoked last night."

"And you did not?"

Toshiyuki shakes his head.

"You are a good boy. Go! Go now! Hurry! Do not delay speaking with Shizue."

Toshiyuki does not obey. He saunters to his room indignant over his grandmother's request. He picks up the Samurai warrior sword of an ancestor, pulls it from the sheath and applies dots of oil to the cold blade. Up and down. Down and up. He polishes it with a slow, entrancing motion. The feeling of his hands on smooth, razor sharp steel calms his nerves. Toshiyuki is unaware that morning light casts his shadow and the shadow of the sword on the paper paneled wall.

"Toshiyuki, what are you doing?"

It is Shizue. She can see the silhouette of the sword in his hand.

Toshiyuki doesn't answer. He slides the sword into its sheath and listens for Shizue's footsteps to fade down the hallway.

He lies back on his futon. He stares at the ceiling for an hour. When he is certain Shizue has finished her chores in the kitchen, he creeps past his grandmother's room and down the stairs.

Miso soup warms on the stove. Toshiyuki eats alone, as he usually does after a late night out on the town. With a full stomach, he walks for hours in the back acres of bamboo forest. He smokes a pack of cigarettes while pondering what to do about his grandmother's request.

After grinding his last cigarette into the boggy ground, he returns to the mansion and finds Shizue sweeping puddled rain off a sagging portion of the east side walkway.

The broom swishes through rain water as he walks up behind her.

"Shizue?"

Her sudden turn tosses the comb from her hair. It falls into a puddle. Her silken locks swirl down around her shoulders.

Toshiyuki picks up the wet comb and dries it on his trousers.

"Your hair is beautiful." He hands Shizue the comb. "You look pretty this way."

"Grandmother has spoken with you?" Shizue braces the broom against a porch beam, piles her hair back into place and secures it with the comb.

Toshiyuki nods, yes.

"Good! Of course, you refused her request." Shizue brims with confidence.

"No," answers Toshiyuki.

"No? Why *no*?"

Toshiyuki leans in close to Shizue, "Grandmother is stubborn ... hard to fool. We must make look like we take her wish seriously."

"Yes," Shizue's eyes dart about avoiding her cousin's gaze. "Yes, Grandmother is terribly stubborn. We must do as you say."

The cousins agree on a time and place to meet and discuss how they might skillfully deny their grandmother's request.

They meet in the garden by the edge of the Koi pond.

Toshiyuki speaks first.

"Grandmother's wish cannot be granted." He opens a fresh pack of cigarettes. "It is not wise for anyone to marry in uncertain times."

"It is out of the question," agrees Shizue.

"You do not wish to marry me?"

"No. I do not."

"But Grandmother ... Grandmother tell me you agree."

49

"Yes," replies Shizue.

"What? How you say 'no you not want to marry me' and 'yes, you agree to Grandmother's wish'?"

"I agreed to marry you, because I knew you would not agree."

"Ah," says her cousin. "I see."

In a spout of words connected by threadbare breaths, Shizue lists all the traits she does not like about Toshiyuki. His rebellious nature. His selfish ways. His crude jokes. She fans away his invasive cigarette smoke as her words grow louder and more emphasized.

She will not marry Toshiyuki only to make their grandmother happy.

"But Grandmother said…"

Shizue interrupts, stiffening her spine, "Yes. Yes. Yes. I told Obaasan I would not marry you unless you want me as your wife. And you do not want me as wife. Is this not so?"

"I see," Toshiyuki repeats. "You want your rascal cousin say 'no' to Grandmother."

"That's right. It is easy for you to say no."

"Yeah." Toshiyuki crushes his half smoked cigarette on a stepping stone.

"Good. Tell Grandmother you do not want to marry me and this nonsense will be finished. Even Grandmother cannot resist both of us together."

"But, you put burden of breaking Grandmother's heart on my heart. You think that fair?"

"Is marrying you fair? You are a big, strong man. You always do only what you want. Obaasan will cry two days and then forgive you. She always forgives you."

"Two days?"

"She will cry many more days if I am the one who breaks her heart."

"That makes no sense."

"What do you know of sense!" huffs Shizue.

Shizue does not want to marry Toshiyuki. Toshiyuki does not want to marry Shizue. The one and only desire the two uncommon cousins have in common is the deeply heartfelt desire to please their beloved grandmother.

They sit for a while looking at everything in the garden except each other.

Toshiyuki counts stepping stones, buried deep in the ground for stability and permanence. Marrying Shizue, marrying within the family, would give him that kind of security.

"Grandmother love and trust you," he says to Shizue. "She not like my girlfriend."

"Your girlfriend is a commoner with a disgraceful family history. You will not be allowed to marry her..." Shizue pauses, "and retain your standing and inheritance in the family."

Shizue, honest to a fault, has spoken the truth and inadvertently pushed Toshiyuki in the direction she does *not* want him to go.

"Family say that?" questions Toshiyuki.

"Yes."

"I did not think of that."

"You do not see, hear, or think what family wants because you bury your head in love."

"Why you say that?"

Shizue doesn't answer. Her words have traveled full circle. Has she, too, buried her head in dreams?

Toshiyuki and Shizue, amid bird calls and a breeze rustling through the branches of bamboo trees, feel the turmoil within.

Shizue snaps the stem of a tiny cluster of blue wild flowers growing at her feet. She has pulled every petal off when she breaks the silence. "Obaasan says if I knew what she knows, I would not

51

want to love a man. She says I would marry for family honor and for stability."

Toshiyuki scoops up a fallen pine needle and twirls it absentmindedly between his fingers. "She say I will not be allowed to marry the woman I love."

Shizue tosses the wild flower stem into the pond. Koi rush in with open mouths.

Toshiyuki crushes the pine needle and throws it aside.

"Shizue..." Toshiyuki ruffles his hair.

"Yes?"

"Shizue, you are Grandmother's happiness. How can I not want such wonderful and beautiful girl?"

Did Toshiyuki call her wonderful and beautiful? Shizue blushes. "You ... what are you saying? You can't mean ... do you want me as your wife?"

"Yeah." Toshiyuki flashes a smile that has finally figured everything out.

"But, you don't..." Shizue folds her arms over her chest, "We can't. You don't like me. I don't like you. We cannot marry."

"You are beautiful. You are sweet. You are smart. I am smart. It is good you be my wife."

Shizue's eyes widen. She stares into the clear water of the pond watching the Koi move in slow motion. Her heart pounds.

"Well," says Toshiyuki.

"Well, what?" says Shizue.

Toshiyuki pulls the pack of cigarettes from his pocket. "I tell you, you beautiful, sweet, and smart. What you like about me?"

"Grandmother doesn't want you to smoke."

"I know." He strikes a match and lights the cigarette. "So, what you like about me?"

Shizue picks another flower and brushes it across her cheek. A tear Toshiyuki cannot see slides beneath the petals.

"I ... I don't know ... maybe I like your smile."

"What else you like about me?"

"Nothing."

Toshiyuki chuckles.

"Why are you laughing? I do not understand you."

"I understand you." Toshiyuki's eyes twinkle.

Shizue flushes wild rose pink.

Toshiyuki draws on his cigarette. Withholding the draw, he taps his cheek with one finger, releasing the smoke in rings. "So, we marry?" He drags in another draw, lifts his head and blows the smoke upward, through shapely, full lips.

The blush on Shizue's skin brightens as the word she prepares to speak tightens around her heart. "Yes," she answers.

"Okay, then. We marry on my birthday," decides Toshiyuki.

"On your birthday," says Shizue.

Toshiyuki stands and holds out his hand to Shizue.

Shizue puts her hand in Toshiyuki's for the first time.

As they walk through the garden, back to the mansion, Toshiyuki envisions his grandmother's joy upon hearing the news of their engagement. He also envisions how heartbroken his girlfriend is going to be when she hears the announcement.

Shizue pulls back. "I will tell my gentleman friend he should not come here again. You must tell your girlfriend too."

Toshiyuki pats his clothing to remove smoke residue. "She won't hear it from me. Rumor reach her soon enough. Will be easier that way."

Easier for whom? Shizue wonders.

Stone benches, hungry Koi, and stepping stones immersed in a sea of green lichen recede from view as the cousins walk back to their home.

Toshiyuki opens the kitchen door for Shizue, for his bride-to-be.

Together they step into a future that neither one of them could ever envision.

CHAPTER FIVE

Forces that Bind

Toshiyuki's birthday and marriage is a mere four months away.

Nothing else changes for the couple in the weeks following their consent to wed. Toshiyuki is away at military school or at sushi bars with his buddies. Shizue goes about her duties. There is no courtship.

Grandmother, however, is ecstatic over their plans to marry. She talks incessantly at every opportunity to fill a willing ear about the bright days and years awaiting her grandchildren.

About two months later, destiny takes another step.

On a cold morning in November, a bold headline splashes across newspapers and radio waves.

U.S. Shows Strong Attitude
Talks Reach Serious Stage

Japan is in a corner as a result of the ABCD line, a series of embargos imposed on the Pacific island nation, by America, Britain, China, and the Dutch. These Western powers stopped selling iron ore, steel, and oil to Japan. Attempts to avert war between the United States and the Japanese have brought about extreme tension. When new leaders with differing views are put in charge, hope for peace begins to fade.

The Japanese government and nationalists consider embargos acts of aggression. Japan's economy and the military are grinding to a halt. Japanese Ambassador John Grew warns the United States Government that an armed conflict can and almost certainly will come with dangerous and dramatic suddenness if this strategy to control Japan continues.

On the 20th of November, Japan offers to withdraw forces from southern Indochina and cease attacks in Southeast Asia provided the four Western countries cease aid to China and lift their sanctions against Japan. The Western power's counterproposal of November 26th requires Japan to evacuate China without conditions and enter into non-aggression pacts with Pacific powers.

It is an ongoing tug of war that someone is going to lose.

Shizue has not seen the morning headline. Going about her usual daily chores, she is unaware of the electrified chatter in the neighborhood streets puffing out into the frozen air like the steam of a runaway locomotive. It isn't until the mailman knocks at the door to deliver a package that she hears her already uncertain future has now become ever more uncertain.

She doesn't tell Grandmother the serious news until after lunch. Through a bowl of miso noodle soup, she listens one more time as the old matriarch chirps high-pitched sounds of happiness. Her words, like brightly colored songbirds, perch on branches of sheer imagination.

Grandmother shrugs off the headline. "That's how they sell papers. They're always exaggerating something or other." She retains her happy attitude.

Shizue gathers up the lunch bowls and then continues down the hallway back to the kitchen. An ominous quiet settles through the house, dimming the sunlight shining through paper doors.

Toshiyuki hears the morning news when a commotion interrupts a training class. His teacher shouts out to the disruptive offenders for silence. One soldier leans into the room and blasts out his interpretation of the headline. "War is coming! War is coming!"

Many at the military school feel Japan is being bullied by the large continent nations. They are revved up. Schooled for war, they want war, and are certain Japan's spirit can prevail against any foe.

Toshiyuki stares out a window. Through the tangled branches of a tree, he remembers his university days. He had been an initiating force behind the organization of international conferences to build up American-Japanese student relations. He is disappointed that the nations have not been able to work out their differences.

With clamor surrounding him, he remembers the greetings given by Joseph C. Grew, the Ambassador of The United States to Japan and Iesato Tokugawa, President of the America-Japan Society at the first America-Japan Student Conference. He particularly recalls President Tokugawa's ending message:

"It is my earnest hope that when the conference is over you will be able to return to your respective colleges and universities in America and Japan, greatly enriched with lasting friendships and understanding heart and that your experience during these few weeks will equip you in no small measure for the leadership in shaping the future relations of our two countries on the basis of peace and harmonious cooperation."

These hopes were optimistically spoken on August 1, 1936.

Toshiyuki's lips move to the words of the conference theme song.

Shake hands, firm hands
Far across the sea
I say, "Kon-nichiwa" to you
You say "Hello" to me
Bow low, so low; let's show them how it's done

Let Stars and Stripes
Fly side by side
With the flag of the Rising Sun

Questions without answers pile one on top of another. Is his dream of peaceful relations between Japan and the United States only a dream? Is an already difficult situation going to grow worse?

The answers come too soon.

On December 8, as Toshiyuki walks to class along a street crowded with shops, a radio announcer's voice blasts out.

"Special announcement from the headquarters of the army and navy; The Imperial Army and Navy forces entered in to war before day break this morning with American and British forces in the western Pacific area."

Toshiyuki turns toward the voice on the radio, straining to catch every word.

The announcer repeats the bulletin then says, "Don't switch off your radio today. We will have much more important news."

Toshiyuki knew it would take time to realize his dream of stable, peaceful relations between Japan and the United States, but he had felt certain it would happen.

Now, unable to escape a new reality, he sighs. The dark cloud threatening his family and his future has burst. War has broken out with America and the British.

"What will happen to my parents and sister in Hawaii?"

"What about Japanese people living in the United States?"

Toshiyuki lights a cigarette to calm down. He is late for school and has missed his normal training. He doesn't care. He has always seen himself as a survivor. Today, however, as an American citizen living on the other side of the fence, he doesn't feel so lucky.

He stands in front of the shop waiting for the next wave of news. Others gather around straining to hear. No one is talking. They all wear serious, worried faces, waiting for the next words from the radio. It is easy for Toshiyuki to understand their thoughts. They are also his thoughts.

What will happen to us? Can Japan, a poor and small country withstand a war with bigger and richer countries?

The repeated radio report stops. Instead of more news, the radio plays marching music of the Navy. The initial announcement comes back repeatedly followed by the same marching anthem.

Toshiyuki pulls out his cigarette case and lights another one. Others do the same, smoke and wait. The music stops and the same news repeats.

Growing impatient, Toshiyuki decides to go on to the academy, where he may hear more details. He hurries to the station and catches the train.

On the train are more serious faces.

"At last the war has started!" someone says.

Another, "Yes, it has begun."

That is all they could say because that was all they knew. Some people are happy, some concerned, some relieved because the tension of waiting was finally broken.

An elderly man says, "Even a rat, when cornered by a cat, will turn and fight. The situation for Japan is like this rat. The pressure has been too much. The ABCD line forced Japan into war. If the other countries had not set this line around Japan and blockaded all the trade and economies, Japan would not have started the war."

"Can we win? Can we last this war?" someone asks.

A young man replies, "We fought Russia and won, didn't we?"

The man sitting next to Toshiyuki turns to him, "Heitai-san (soldier), what do you think about this?"

"I don't know."

Toshiyuki turns away from the stranger and stares through the window. He doesn't give his opinion to the passenger, but he gives it to himself. The man is right about the economic blockade. This had been the straw that broke Japan's back. He is saddened and discouraged that it has come, finally, to war.

At the academy, a message is on the chalkboard: No Class Today. Assemble at the Officer's Club. General Tojo has gone to the Emperor's palace and an announcement will be soon forthcoming.

At the Officer's Club, 11:45 a.m., the radio plays the Marching Navy anthem. After the music, the announcer turns on the recorded Imperial Rescript. All stand respectfully and listen with bowed heads as their Emperor declares war on America and Britain.

Toshiyuki's eyes fix on the floor. His body tightens. When the declaration ends, he feels as if he has been awakened from a long, restless dream. He has lost all strength. It isn't that he is afraid of war or afraid of death. He can't name or even describe the feeling coursing through him.

Toshiyuki's initial questions and concerns about his family in Hawaii are well founded.

America's first response to the surprise Japanese attack on Pearl Harbor is shock and disbelief, then anger. Immediately, American government officials on the islands round up all Japanese citizens they consider potentially dangerous aliens. Of the 150,000 plus Japanese Americans in Hawaii, approximately 1,500, are interned.

Japanese Americans living on the west coast sent to interior camps total 110,000. The internees are housed in make-shift camps; race tracks, fair grounds, and livestock stables. After review of each individual's potential power to harm the US, some, those advanced in age or otherwise considered harmless, are released.

Toshiyuki is certain that his father, Shunichi, a prestigious and powerful man in the Japanese community in Honolulu, will be singled out, and along with him, Toshiyuki's mother and sister.

The following day, the 9th of December, Toshiyuki receives orders to form a new Special Engineering Company in Hiroshima and wait there until further notice from his superiors.

The waiting is torture. Conversations between family and friends are superficial, tense. Neighbors and strangers on the streets of Hiroshima and Furuichi peck at isolated facts like hungry chickens. War is on the horizon. The heavy stillness shadows their every move.

Shizue suggests postponing their marriage. Toshiyuki does not object. He will do whatever Grandmother wants.

Grandmother will not hear of postponing the marriage.

"Nonsense," she exclaims, pulling on her small reservoir of strength. "Life does not wait to be lived!"

Grandmother's mind is set. Shizue makes no other attempt at reason.

For days following, at breakfast, lunch, and dinner, Grandmother repeatedly mutters "Nansensu!" (Nonsense) under her breath.

Toshiyuki, soon to be sent off to battle and possibly never return, visits his oldest sister, Nishiyo, in Tokyo to say goodbye. She attends high school there under the care of his mother's sister.

He no sooner walks inside the house, when his aunt says, "I am very sorry to say this to you. I can no longer look after your sister. I have a son to send through the University. I am not rich enough to have him and your sister continue schooling. Your father sent money for her expenses, but as you know that has stopped. I am very sorry. You must take Nishiyo back with you to Hiroshima."

Toshiyuki knows his father sent enough money for Nishiyo's support and the support his aunt's entire family. In this time of crisis, with Toshiyuki going off to war, can't his aunt manage for one more year? But he says nothing to her.

He speaks with his sister about returning with him to the country home in Furuichi. She cries and begs him to let her stay in Tokyo for her final year of high school.

"Okay. I will try."

Toshiyuki attempts to persuade his aunt it will be best for his sister to live with her for one more year. His aunt replies with a simple, firm "No."

"If I send you money will you keep her here?" asks Toshiyuki.

"Send me 25 yen a month. Then, I can look after your sister."

Toshiyuki receives 75 yen a month from the Army and 25 from Ishihara Industries, a copper and iron mining company he landed a job with during his college years. Ishihara Industries agreed to pay him 1/3 of his monthly salary while he is in the military, until he returns to work again. The total amount is barely enough to support the house in Furuichi. If he cuts down on his expenses, however, perhaps he can manage.

He agrees. His aunt is happy. His sister is happy.

He bids them farewell and returns to his country home.

On December 10, 1941, the radio announces the landing of the Japanese Army in the Philippine and Guam islands. A Japanese aircraft attack sinks the British man-of-war, Prince of Wales; shocking news to the British. They believed the battleship was unsinkable. This success revolutionizes the Japanese Navy's air attack tactic.

December 23, 1941, Wake Island falls.

December 25, 1941, Hong Kong is captured.

January 2, 1942, Manila also falls to the Imperial Japanese Army.

January 11, 1942, Japanese forces occupy Kuala Lumpur, Malay.

On January 15, 1942, under the pounding, crushing steps of World War II, Toshiyuki and Shizue are married in a simple ceremony at the Furuichi mansion.

Two weeks after the wedding, Toshiyuki receives orders to join the 5th Army in Malay.

On February 17, he leaves for the Singapore front.

The marriage of Toshiyuki and Shizue has been consummated.

Toshiyuki goes off to war feeling certain he planted a fertile seed. He is quite correct.

In October 1942, a precious daughter, Yorie, will come into a world torn by war.

CHAPTER SIX

The Lucky Years

Time passes in the fog of daily survival. Few dare to look beyond the day at hand. *Now* is all they have the strength to handle.

Days of war turn into months of war.

Toshiyuki's luck holds out. Following the Japanese attack on Pearl Harbor, he survives every frontline encountered without firing a shot, without taking a life and without injury.

With the Singapore project completed and POW camps relocated to Burma, Toshiyuki's company prepares to return to Japan. A week after turning in their equipment and arms, they are called to retrieve their items. Toshiyuki's company will not be returning to Japan after all.

The army allows Toshiyuki to send a letter to Shizue informing her of his relocation from Singapore to an unknown destination in the south.

When his company boards a warship, rather than a freighter, Toshiyuki suspects it is not good sign. Their destination must be a dangerous one.

Warships are not built for passengers. The soldiers' quarters are stretched tents on the deck. On sunny, humid days of travel close to the equator, the tents turn out to be more comfortable than cabins or holds, as they welcome fresh, ocean breezes. Tents, however, are not so great on days of rain and strong winds.

The first day in the dining room, Toshiyuki sees a familiar face among the naval officers. It is Mas Yamane, a former high school classmate. Toshiyuki and Mas spend the evening catching up on the six years that have passed since they last saw each other.

Mas asks about Toshiyuki's family in Hawaii.

While in Singapore, Toshiyuki learned from Red-Cross workers that after the attack on Pearl Harbor his father had been taken to a concentration camp in Texas. With no one to care for his paralyzed mother, she had been sent to Queen's Hospital. Tonoyo died three days later. The government sent his younger sister, Shigemi, to the Texas internment camp, to join her father.

Something in Mas's manner concerns Toshiyuki. He feels an emanation of pity from his high school friend as though Mas knows that he and his company's destination is a land of no return.

Mas informs Toshiyuki that after unloading the soldiers at the destination, the ship will sail to a Kure City port. Kure City is only 50 miles from Hiroshima. Mas offers to stop by Toshiyuki's home in Furuichi and give Shizue news of their meeting.

Toshiyuki couldn't have wished for better. He is certain Shizue is worried and would like her to know more than he was able to tell her in his latest letter.

After sailing amid the hot sea for seven days, up and down the equator twice, the ship's captain stands at the end of a dinner table and taps his glass.

"I am now allowed to give you the true news of Japan's standing in the south sea. The situation is very bad. Our convoys were sunk almost completely before reaching their destinations. Japan is losing battles in the air and at sea. The enemy grows more powerful every day. I am sorry to bring you bad news. You are going to Rabul. I wish you all good luck."

The news of Japans standing in the war is a shock. Until this moment, the soldiers thought Japan was winning the war. Only a few weeks ago they celebrated the unveiling of a monument and temple in Singapore. They thought they were certain victors. Now, the powerful Rising Sun is about to fall.

Mas bows his head and will not look Toshiyuki in the eyes. Now he knows why his classmate feels sorry for him. He already knew about the Japanese situation and the ship's destination. Mas knows his friend and his company are headed for their graveyard.

The ship arrives in Rabul the morning of December 20, 1942. The wharf at Rabul is under constant attack by United States planes. The regiment makes camp outside the town, deep in the jungle. There, they wait for boats to take them to the island next to Guadalcanal.

While Toshiyuki is in camp outside Rabul, he contracts dysentery and malaria. He is put in a crowded field hospital. Even with professional treatment his condition grows worse. He can't keep any food down. Even a glass of water upsets his stomach.

When his company moves out, Toshiyuki goes on board a hospital ship, which pulls out of the harbor bound for Takao, Formosa. He is aboard the ship on New Year's Day; unable to eat or join in the festivities.

On January 2, 1943 the ship arrives in Formosa. He is carried off the ship and bused to a military hospital.

In the Takao hospital, Toshiyuki begins showing signs of recovery. He is moved from Takao to the northern city of Taipei. After a month, his health improves, but he is not yet back to normal.

On February 15, the military transfers him from Taipei to Ujina, Japan. He sends a message to a cousin living in Hiroshima informing her that he is at the 1st Army Hospital. The cousin contacts Shizue. When Shizue hears Toshiyuki is back in Japan and in the hospital, she assumes he has been seriously injured. Maybe he has lost an arm or a leg. She wastes no time getting to the hospital.

Seeing Toshiyuki's body normal and looking healthy, her anxiety gives way to joy that he is alive.

Toshiyuki sees his baby girl for the first time. Yorie is four months old.

There is sad news from Shizue. Grandmother passed away. She didn't live to see the birth of her great granddaughter. But, something wonderful happened before she drew her last breath.

"It was almost exactly like with Grandfather's death," she tells Toshiyuki. "Obaasan looked out onto the garden and said, 'Look at the beautiful birds. I have never seen such exquisite birds.' I looked out and there were no birds. I knew in that moment, that Grandfather had come for her. Grandmother smiled and was gone." Shizue's eyes well with tears, "Their spirits are together now."

"I don't believe in spirits," remarks Toshiyuki. "You know that. You must not either."

Shizue does not reply. There is other news she wishes to discuss, but Toshiyuki only wants to get to know his daughter. He tries to hold Yorie in his arms. She screams and struggles to get back to her mother.

"Darling, this is your daddy. You understand your mama? This is Daddy."

Toshiyuki's little girl doesn't care one bit about that. She only wants her mama. Since her birth there has been no man in her life. Yorie screams and wails as if her father is the devil.

Soon, however, she gets used to him and feels secure enough to let him hold her.

After three months of healing, Toshiyuki is released from the hospital on March 20th and assigned to the 5th Engineering Regiment under the command of Colonel Yasuji Tamura, in Hiroshima. Tamura Butai, the colonel's regiment is called.

To aid in his recovery, Toshiyuki is put in a temporary position in charge of supplies. Three months later, after regaining his strength fully, he is transferred to the Engineering Headquarters in Tokyo where he receives three months of fortification training.

After the training period, he spends time in the Shimizu, Shizuoka area. From there he goes to Matsue on the coast of Japan and then to Kagoshima, Kyushu to work on defense lines. Eventually he returns to Hiroshima to help the city plan protection against fire bombs. Upon completing his duties he is transferred back to his own regiment, where he is promoted to Captain and made a company commander to the 2nd Company of the 5th Army Engineering Regiment. Toshiyuki fulfills his military duties Monday through Friday, returning to Furuichi each evening and weekends to spend time with Shizue, Yorie, and a new addition to the family, their new baby boy, Toshio.

In his absence, Toshiyuki's two younger sisters and his father, Shunichi, have joined the household in Furuichi. Nishiyo, who had been living with her aunt in Tokyo while attending high school, is the older of the two. She has graduated and is eager to find a husband.

The U.S. government repatriated Toshiyuki's father, Shunichi, to Japan. He is penniless after being incarcerated in the Lordsburg Justice Department Camp in New Mexico and three years in the Heart Mountain internment camp in Wyoming. Shigemi has come to Japan with her father as she has no other place to go since the United States government took all Shunichi's possessions, including the family home in Honolulu.

On an extraordinarily warm Monday morning in May, Toshiyuki's friend and commanding officer, Colonel Kubota, calls the now Major Toshiyuki Nekomoto to his office.

"Colonel?" Toshiyuki stands at the entrance way.

"Nekomoto, come in … and … ah … close the door."

Colonel Kubota wipes his forehead with an already damp handkerchief and opens the window behind his desk a few inches wider. His khaki colored uniform melts into the earthy hues of a distressed, wooden desk. The room smells musty. Stacked books lean against walls. Unsteady piles of papers spill over the top of his desk and onto the floor. The Colonel looks as disheveled as his office.

"There's not a bit of breeze today. And it's not even June." He shakes his head. "Looks like we're in for an uncommonly hot summer. Put that on top of everything else."

Major Nekomoto nods.

"Nekomoto, as you know, air raid alarms are becoming more frequent. Cities are being bombed all around us. Our luck, if it is luck, isn't going to hold indefinitely. Your family estate in Furuichi is about 10 miles north. Is that right?"

"Yes sir."

"I thought so." He draws a decisive breath. "Yes, as I thought. That is too far, Nekomoto. I need you in the city to fulfill your duties quickly, any time of the day or night."

"Yes sir. I understand."

"I've been told certain officers of other companies are growing lax in their duties. What is the old American saying? 'The boy cried wolf too many times.' False alarms have made them careless."

"Yes sir, I hear the same."

"Don't bet on our luck continuing, Major. I will not allow such an attitude in my command. I suggest you move here … ah … to Hiroshima, near the barracks. You can visit your family on weekends."

Before the Major can speak, Colonel Kubota's suggestion becomes an order. "I arranged a room for you in a boarding house ... about, ah ... about a half mile away. The rate is cheap, of course. No one comes to Hiroshima for pleasure any more. The landlady is holding it for you. Move your personal belongings." The Colonel wipes perspiration from his forehead, "The sooner the better."

"Boarding house...?" starts the Major, "I ... yes, thank you, Colonel, I will."

"Ah ... Nekomoto, you should be warned. The landlady is ... well, I've heard the woman has a reputation for disliking military men. Rumor is she prefers rich businessmen. No matter, I say. You won't be spending much time there."

"No, Sir. The landlady will be no problem."

The Colonel, nicknamed "Smiley" by Toshiyuki for his naturally amused expression, appears lost in thought and sits gazing, apparently scrutinizing Toshiyuki.

"Okay, then..." picks up Toshiyuki, "I will return to Furuichi and prepare for move."

Kubota stares at him.

"Colonel ... is there another matter?"

"What? Ah ... no..." The Colonel's chair squeaks as he pushes it away from his desk and over to the window, "that's it Nekomoto."

Toshiyuki turns to leave.

"Wait." The Colonel spins around. "Yes ... ah... there is ... there is one other concern. Stay focused, Nekomoto. Be vigilant. Stay on track with your career and your marriage. Shizue is a wonderful woman. Like a daughter to me. You and I are more than officers. We are friends and ... ah I have not forgotten a certain weakness of character you confided to me. Do you remember that confidence?"

"Yes, sir, I do." Toshiyuki's brow furrows.

"Good. If you should find yourself facing any situation requiring guidance, any situation of a sensitive nature, I am here to help ... as a friend, without judgment. What is it you Americans also say ... I have no stones to throw?"

"Thank you for your candor, Colonel."

"There is much more to my words than candor."

"Sir?"

"Yes. How should I say..." the Colonel wavers, "...life is different here in the city than in the field. Certain things ... doings ... are allowed by the Japanese Army and happen out there on the front that should not happen at home."

"Things, Sir? What do you mean?"

"Have you been away so long you play games with me, Major? The things of which I speak are professional prostitutes who follow soldiers to the front. The doings ... well..."

Toshiyuki looks down at the floor, embarrassed. He remembers the Chinese town of Nannei, where he was stationed for a month of training in advanced battle practices. Nannei is a typical old Chinese town. A muddy, yellow river flows through it. Even the shallows of the river bottom could not be seen clearly. Toshiyuki bathed close to the bank, never venturing out for fear he might encounter a poisonous devilfish hiding under a rocky ledge.

It was in Nannei Toshiyuki learned a hard lesson.

His regiment received instructions to assemble at the town opening to witness the execution of a soldier who had broken a Division regulation. The soldier to be executed had raped a local woman.

The Army made every effort to prevent soldiers from being tempted to rape local women and thereby contract sexual diseases. The government provided women for the men. These women received medical examinations by Japanese military doctors to determine virginity and health. They followed soldiers to the front in order to *reduce* the incidence of venereal disease among the troops. Some were volunteer prostitutes. Most "comfort woman" and "Western Princesses", as they came to be called, were lured into service with promises of employment, purchased from family, or abducted from their homes and forced into sexual slavery by the Imperial Japanese Army. Some were Japanese; the majority was from occupied countries.

As soon as an infantry division stopped and settled down, the "prostitutes" opened their business. They set up three camps of tents, segregated for commissioned officers, non-commissioned officers, and soldiers. Long lines of military men waited in front of the tents for their turns at "comfort".

The man whose execution Toshiyuki witnessed had gotten drunk before going to a "comfort station" and had been refused services. On his way back to camp he passed a Chinese hut, peeked inside and saw a beautiful young woman. He raped her. In his drunken state, she *looked* young and beautiful. He had, in reality, raped a 60 year old woman. The soldier would have gotten away with it had he not gone back to the hut again later. On his second visit, the Military Police caught him in the act.

This soldier had been a very honorable policeman in his home town and a good soldier when sober. Before his last breath he regretted what he had done and cried out for mercy; if not for him, for his wife and children. Mercy was not granted.

The Colonel continues, "If the women here at home saw these sights, they would think that men are animals with no self-control even on the battle front." Kubota snatches up a sheet of paper, crumples it, and tosses it into a waste basket. "We are an honorable people..." His voice trails off.

"I see." It is clear to Toshiyuki that his friend and commander is not having a good day.

"Do you, Nekomoto?" Kubota punctuates his question with a frown.

"Yes Sir. I do."

"Make sure you do. Words are easy. Far too easy I have seen for American born Japanese. I make no allowances, even for an officer and friend."

"You have my word, Colonel. I will not dishonor my uniform, my family, or you."

Colonel Kubota squints under bushy eyebrows.

"See that you do not," his voice softens, "You may go. Instruct your men and leave for Furuichi immediately."

Toshiyuki has never seen his friend so overwrought.

At home in Furuichi, Toshiyuki reveals the nature of his unexpected arrival.

"I must move to Hiroshima closer to barracks. Colonel Kubota's orders," he informs everyone gathered around him. "It takes too much time to travel back and forth by bicycle. I will come home on weekends."

No one is happy with Colonel Kubota's decision. But, they understand its necessity. Duty to country outweighs duty to family.

Toshiyuki moves into the boarding house chosen by his commander the following day. His new residence is less than a mile from the barracks.

He finds the rented room suitable, though accustomed to better accommodations, he doesn't require it. This is a temporary solution and he expects to be there only to sleep.

The owner of the house is younger than Major Nekomoto imagined her to be. To him "landlady" conveys the image of a plump, gray-haired woman on the dim-witted side, who talks too much, maybe drinks too much, and adds fulfillment to her mundane life by spreading gossip.

Fully aware of his thin defense against beautiful women, Toshiyuki is relieved to find the landlady only average looking. Her thin lips sit crooked on a square jaw, centered by a thin nose. There is no physical attraction. Duty to wife, family, honor, and his commander and friend, Colonel Kubota, will certainly not be jeopardized by temptation.

Colonel Kubota's decision to move him closer to the base for the sake of his military career appears to be a sound one.

After the initial settling in, the landlady, who identifies herself only as Mieko, gives her new tenant little more than adequately clean accommodations. Conversation hovers at the minimal level necessary between tenant and landlord.

Other than curiosity about why Mieko reveals no last name, Toshiyuki feels comfortable. He is, however, surprised when he glimpses Mieko smoking a cigarette outside in the shade of a tree. In Japan, smoking is a habit seen only in women of bad reputation. He is not aware that his new landlady moonlights as a prostitute.

Late nights, before retiring, Toshiyuki spends time conversing with the only other boarder, Mr. Shimizu. Mr. Shimizu, who soon asks to be addressed by his first name, Daichi, is in Hiroshima on a matter of business and anxious to return home to Nagasaki. Both men are troubled about leaving their wives and children alone at such a perilous time.

Daichi thoroughly enjoys Toshiyuki's stories of Honolulu. He wishes to visit one day. Every night he asks to hear more of the American island boy's exploits.

Toshiyuki delights in sharing stories about the freedom he enjoyed in Hawaii, until being imprisoned in Punahou School behind stuffy walls with snooty teachers as wardens.

Punahou School, founded by missionaries for the purpose of educating Royal Hawaiian families, provided elementary through high school instruction. Shunichi believed it would be in his son's best interest to be educated in the American tradition, while faithfully preserving his Japanese heritage. However, Shunichi's good intentions, combined with extremely indulgent parenting, would ultimately fail.

Toshiyuki extremely disliked attending Punahou School. Its strict policies extended far beyond the classroom. School administrators didn't want the boy selling Sunday newspapers on the street or going around barefooted when not in class. They insisted he discontinue these activities for the pride of Punahou.

The fifth grade student had no use for the pride of Punahou. He wanted to live like the other kids in his neighborhood. They attended public school without ties and with nothing on their feet, while he attended a sissy school confined by neckties and shoes.

Boys want to be free, to have fun. Outside the school windows, frothy blue waves crashed onto warm white sand. Sweet and salty ocean breezes whispered through palm fronds. Fish waited to be caught or speared, cooked and savored. His favorites were Mahi-Mahi and Tilapia.

Adventure, excitement, and discovery called from beyond Punahou walls and stern faced teachers.

"Time is a great teacher, but unfortunately it kills all its pupils." Perhaps it would have been better for Toshiyuki had he not heard this quote.

Time and many dedicated teachers failed to reform Toshiyuki. In fact, he grew more rebellious. His youth wouldn't come again. Paradise would not wait. There were plenty of years ahead to grow up and become serious about his future.

Toshiyuki's youthful enthusiasm transforms his face as he speaks about his life in Honolulu. The war is forgotten as he recalls his exciting daily discoveries and adventures on the beaches. Wonderful quests constantly lured him from the antiseptic white halls of the sterile school and strict teachers who smelled like wet muskrats and mothballs.

Toshiyuki laughs. He calls himself "The Rascal of Punahou".

On one occasion, "The Rascal of Punahou" sneaked up behind a teacher as she wrote on the chalkboard and lifted her skirt, exposing her white panties to the entire class. By the time the teacher collected her wits and turned around, Toshiyuki sat innocently at his desk.

Both men laugh as the Major lights up a cigarette.

Passing in the hallway, Mieko overhears the story of Punahou and covers her mouth to hide escaping giggles. Her giggles are not heard over Mr. Shimizu's laughter.

Now, Mieko often tiptoes to a spot near their rooms where she can hear the two men talking. She listens, entranced, as Toshiyuki chuckles about the pranks he pulled in Punahou, and the one that got him expelled.

A buddy, who sat in front of him, passed a note and whispered "Read this." The sexually funny note caused Toshiyuki to snicker. The teacher overhead and caught Toshiyuki smirking.

The old maid teacher snarled, "What's so interesting, Nekomoto? Let me see what you are reading!"

Toshiyuki refused with a tremor of his head.

Again she demanded, "Tell me what caused you to disrupt the class with a snicker and a smirk!"

Toshiyuki kept silent as the teacher pried for a response.

"Stubborn boy … you will obey." The teacher's patience had run out. She stared at Toshiyuki; her arms folded; her chin tucked into the folds of her neck.

The troublesome Toshiyuki kept silent as did the entire class. No snickering. No giggling.

"I'm waiting," the teacher snapped.

The more the teacher forced the issue the more Toshiyuki withdrew. The tension in the room thickened.

Faced with daring rebelliousness and insubordination, the teacher became angry. Embarrassed by her student's lack of respect and furious because of the bad example Toshiyuki set for the other children, she tried to force him to hand over the note which he held tightly behind his back.

She held out an open hand. "Give … me … that … note!"

Toshiyuki remained stubborn.

"You are an obstinate boy, Nekomoto, but you are also smart. Be smart and consider the consequences. My patience has it limits. Give the note to me now!"

Toshiyuki glanced at his buddy. His friend is wide-eyed and terrified.

This incident was a larger matter than a childhood prank; more than a common contest of wills between a stern teacher and a willful, playful student. Toshiyuki's friend was son of the Head Postmaster. Such a crude note as this one could ruin the boy's father's reputation and bring disgrace to his family.

Toshiyuki heard the silent plea in his buddy's eyes, *"Hold fast! Don't tell!"*

The teacher cracked a ruler on Toshiyuki's desk and ordered the students sitting near the disruptive boy to move their desks away from his. She then circled Toshiyuki. Her hard-heel shoes click-clacked on the tile floor. "How long do you think you can sit there?"

Toshiyuki held the crumpled note within a fist as the teacher took a stance in front of him and fired harsh, authoritative words.

"Repulsive behavior! Offensive character! What will your future be, Nekomoto?"

Toshiyuki withdrew his hand from behind his back as though to give the teacher the incriminating note.

The teacher held out her hand and aimed a smile full of self-satisfaction.

The boy, Toshiyuki, having thoroughly considered the consequences, crushed the paper, tossed it into his mouth, and gobbled the note down with a burp of defiance.

The teacher's face flushed a violent red as she withdrew her hand. The old maid teacher with a reputation for always winning classroom battles experienced her first defeat ever.

Having failed to obtain evidence or confession, the indignant teacher clomped toward the classroom door, snapped to a stop and turned back to face the students. "I am going to report this matter to the Principal's office. This door will remain open. I expect each of you to think carefully about unacceptable, disruptive behavior. There will be severe consequences!"

She glared from one student to another before focusing on her adversary, "Nekomoto! Come with me!"

Down the hall Toshiyuki stood, unchastened, before the ample breasted body of the principal. She leaned back in the chair, folded her arms, nodded, and bared the smile of a hungry crocodile about to feed. She had waited for this precious moment, longed for it, vividly dreamed of the satisfaction soon to be attained.

This installment of insubordination, the swallowing of the note, was her opportunity to be rid of a rebellious student who continued to embarrass the school by disrespecting their high standards of dress code and activities in their private lives. Selling newspapers in bare feet, like a common street urchin. Oh no. Oh yes. Justice is sweet. There remains no chance for redemption.

Without a word spoken to Toshiyuki, the principal lifts the receiver of her desk phone and dials a number scribbled on note paper.

Toshiyuki's father answers the call. The principal informs him there is an urgent matter she must discuss with him in her office. He must come to her office immediately.

Shunichi arrived within the hour.

"Mr. Nekomoto, I am very sorry to say this." The principal's demeanor is at great odds with her carefully chosen words. "Your son has failed time and time again to conform to the honor, principles, and strict discipline of Punahou School. Attending this school is an honor. Toshiyuki's teachers have worked tirelessly to redeem him and to prevent the decision I must of necessity now make."

She placed her plump hands together in prayer fashion, tapped her fingers together as one sorrowfully considering a decision and announced her verdict.

"Your son must attend another school next year. He may stay at Punahou to the end of this year … no more."

A professionally polite dismissal, on the surface; even a sad one, but Toshiyuki saw a smile of satisfaction trembling to escape behind her closing office door.

Shunichi said nothing. He sat for a moment, then arose from the chair, politely bowed, took one long look at his incorrigible son and walked stiffly from the room.

Although his father never punished or even scolded him, Toshiyuki knew the discouragement, disappointment, and shame brought about by this incident was almost too much for his father to bear.

Toshiyuki tells Daichi that the only regret about his childhood antics is the injury to his father's pride for his son having been expelled from a renowned school.

This is how Toshiyuki came to be in Japan. Shunichi believed his son, surrounded by the culture of his ancestors, would be redirected and outgrow his rebellious nature.

"Let your beloved child travel to the unknown country." Toshiyuki draws on his cigarette. "A smile. A snicker. My defense of a friend's honor at the expense of my father's changed the course of my life. I didn't want to leave Hawaii. I refused my father's wish until he said to me, 'I am sad in my heart for you to leave and go to an unfamiliar country. My strength comes from my deep love for you and for your future. My love for you until now has been a blind love. Keeping you by my side will only spoil you more'."

Toshiyuki grinds the stub of his cigarette, "These ... my father's words, made me understand his feelings. I did not want to hurt my father any more. I agreed to go to Japan."

Toshiyuki continues his narrative in a low voice, pitched with notes of remorse.

"What was it like..." Mr. Shimizu, who walks with a limp, squeezes his arthritic knee, "coming here as an American born child?"

"Not bad."

Toshiyuki recounts his arrival in Japan. The 5th grader had stayed with his Uncle Akira Sekishiro, in Yagi-Mura, twelve miles north of Hiroshima City, four miles outside the castle town of Himeji. Uncle Akira was a kind man, who devoted himself to the education of his nephew. Toshiyuki, however, believed his uncle's efforts were not for the sake of devotion, but out of obligation to Shunichi, who, a few years prior, had bought Akira a sake brewery business. Toshiyuki assumed his uncle's dedicated attention in his behalf was only an attempt to pay a debt.

This perception gave the boy who had been expelled from Hawaii against his will a sense of power. If he was not happy in Japan under his uncle's guidance, his father would not be pleased; his uncle would lose honor and Toshiyuki would return home to his beloved island.

The boy played the "keep me happy" card often, as often as his uncle's attempts to discipline him. He thereby resumed his mischievous and rebellious ways.

In Hawaii, Toshiyuki was King of the Mountain due to his father's prestige in the Japanese community. The same attitude now carried over to Japan. Toshiyuki resisted, even rebelled against, rigid tradition. He built a motorized go-cart and drove it wildly through the streets of the old village of Yagi-Mura, causing dogs to yap incessantly, disrupting the peace and quiet in the conservative farming community.

Villagers complained to the constable. Police officials did nothing to stop Toshiyuki's antics even though his behavior violated town rules. The boy from a prestigious, wealthy family in Hawaii, far away from his influential father, continued to demand and get what he wanted.

"I..." Toshiyuki pulls another smoke from his pack, "I was wrong about uncle. He was good and patient man. He stayed for long hours teaching me to speak and read Japanese. He began with animal picture books and then advanced to children's magazines. I never thanked him for sacrifice he made. I behaved like brat. He is dead now. Even when he called me to his deathbed, I did not go."

Toshiyuki nods absently as his heart looks back on a decision he cannot correct.

"I went back home to Honolulu after graduating middle school. Hawaii was in big depression. Nothing was same as I remembered. My father struggled to regain business profit. Employees were no longer friendly and faithful because boss was behind in their pay. I was only another burden. My mother was paralyzed. My sisters were too young to help. I learned as old saying goes, people are friends when you are in prime, but enemies when in distress. Big depression teach me big lesson. My future can no longer rely on money or family power ... only on me."

Toshiyuki stands, stretches, and walks to a window. The window glass casts back his reflection. The invisible quiet outside is a moment standing on edge in this time of war. At any second the peace could be split open by air raid sirens or bombs exploding.

"I stay up nights thinking about my future. Japan has slogan, 'Go Manchuria. Build your future'. I think I be able to find opportunity here. Have chance to make new future. I come back to Japan at own will."

Daichi has a few tales of his own. Growing up, he dreamed of serving Japan as a military pilot. Poor eyesight prevented any performance of duty for his country.

Toshiyuki trudges back to his pillow seat, anxious to share his experience as an officer in charge of a group of British prisoners of war.

Being American born with a comprehensive view of both sides of the war, he treated Prisoners of War (POW's) with exceptional respect. He relied on their sense of honor to keep order in the camp. His unusual method yielded great results. Japanese and British soldiers became friends. When the British were eventually transferred to another camp, they knew they would not be treated as well and were sad to leave their Japanese friends and the command of Major Nekomoto.

As much as Mr. Shimizu enjoys the Major's military experiences, Mieko, eavesdropping from around a corner, is more entranced by the tales of Toshiyuki's Samurai ancestors.

The Nekomoto family line traces back to the Asano clan, a Samurai family who for much of the Edo period, controlled the fief centered at Hiroshima Castle. Descended from Emperor Seiwa and a branch of the Toki family, these Samurai served Daimiyo Asano, Lord Asano Takumi no Kami, who committed seppuku (hara-kiri) for an alleged breach in protocol. After the ritual suicide, the shogunate confiscated Asano lands and dismissed the Samurai who served him, making them Ronin, that is, Samurai with no lord or master.

Forty-seven of these Ronin avenged Lord Asano's death. Revenge brought a heavy consequence for all the clan. With a price on their heads the clan had no choice but to flee their homes in search of a safe place to live. Because few people would associate with Ronins for fear of being punished by the Shogun, these Nekomoto ancestors traveled to Hiroshima Prefecture, a district located in the Chugoku region on Honshu Island, and settled down in a small village where no one knew their history. Having been trained only in the skills of warriors, the Nekomoto Ronin worked at anything they could find, no matter how humble, to survive. In order to protect their identity, they called themselves "Neko-ya gumi" Neko-ya Clan.

Many were unhappy with their new circumstances. At the turn of the Meiji-era, the majority of the Neko-ya Clan sailed to Hawaii seeking opportunity to build a better life by working as common laborers in pineapple and sugarcane fields. It was a hard existence, but in Hawaii, life had possibilities.

Mieko's heart skips a beat when she hears that her handsome boarder is a direct descendent of noble Samurai. Her heart skips

83

several more beats when she hears Toshiyuki's father regained the estate the family lived in for hundreds of years; a magnificent three story house on twenty acres of countryside land with a teahouse, two barns, and five storage buildings.

Three days later, Daichi completes his business in Hiroshima and returns home to Nagasaki.

Toshiyuki is now Mieko's only tenant. After Shimizu's departure, he spends more time at his office, arriving back at the boarding house later and later before retiring. No matter how late the hour, however, Mieko remains, oddly, still engaged in household chores.

She nods to her boarder when their paths cross upon his entering and leaving, but she doesn't reply to his greetings. Mieko gives Toshiyuki no reason to suspect her attraction to him and his wealth. Nor does he know this clever, calculating woman, skilled in the arts of temptation, is known for having her way.

The first time Mieko bumps into the Major as he turns a corner is barely noticed; military duties and family responsibilities are on Toshiyuki's mind. Nor does he show concern the second time their bodies touch … accidently.

Unknown to the Major, like a cat playing with a mouse, Mieko is tenderizing the wealthy, tempting Toshiyuki.

In the deep of the night, barely a week later, the panel to his room glides open and closed. Startled awake, Toshiyuki bolts upright. The intruder is confronted by the sound of his sword hissing from its sheath.

"Shush…" a soft voice whispers. "Listen. Someone is outside. They are here to rob me. Help me, please."

Recognizing Mieko's voice, Toshiyuki advances toward the entrance to investigate sounds he has yet to hear. He senses Mieko's closeness in the darkness.

"Stay where you are." He cautions Mieko. "Do not move."

But move she does … with clear intent.

As Toshiyuki reaches out to open the wall panel, her hand grasps his and guides it to her bare breasts.

Major Toshiyuki Nekomoto, husband of Shizue, surrenders to temptation, without resistance.

His weekend trips to Furuichi to spend time with his wife and children grow less frequent. Duty to family soon gives way to nefarious pleasure.

CHAPTER SEVEN

Colonel Kubota's Solution

Colonel Kubota stands stoically at the door of the Nekomoto mansion. A personal visit from Toshiyuki's commanding officer can mean only one thing. Shizue gasps and covers her mouth when he requests a few minutes in private.

In a mansion filled with family, paper walls are thin. She escorts the Colonel to a far room, upstairs.

Shizue offers a cup of tea, which the Colonel declines with exaggerated politeness that appears to be stalling for time. He clears his throat and nervously taps the hilt of his sword.

Shizue's fear screams over the dull throb in her head. *Toshiyuki! My husband has been killed.*

"Mrs. Nekomoto, I … ah … I am very sorry to inform you…" Kubota pauses; unable to speak out loud that which has brought him to the Nekomoto estate.

Instead of completing his thought, he unbuttons a shirt pocket, pulls out a folded paper and hands it to Shizue.

Shizue opens it.

The Colonel walks over to a window, staring out, with hands clasped behind his back. It is another overcast spring day. Raindrops trickle down the window panes. Mercifully befitting; once Shizue reads the message there will be no room in her heart for sunshine.

The letter informs Toshiyuki's wife of the affair with Mieko, the landlady of the boarding house. Shizue looks up, puzzled. "He… My husband is not dead?"

"Dead? Oh, ah … you thought … no, he is not dead. Forgive me. My wife scolds me daily for my insensitivity."

"Forgive…" Shizue's single utterance dangles helplessly in the suffocating air.

Colonel Kubota pulls a clean white handkerchief from his pocket for her, but Shizue does not cry, even after the commander reveals the decision he has made; a solution for Toshiyuki's disgraceful behavior and embarrassment to Shizue and the 5th Engineering Regiment.

Standing soundly, Shizue listens without emotion and thanks the Colonel for his discretion.

He thanks Shizue for her hospitability and strength. "I would rather face gunfire than tears. You understand why I have come to this decision … what must be done."

"I do." Shizue bows.

Shizue escorts Colonel Kubota to the door. She watches his departure. When he exits the gate, she drops to her knees. The pain of betrayal has doubled her over, cutting into her as surely as the cold steel of a sword. She knows now, why Toshiyuki's weekend visits steadily became less frequent. His absence has nothing to do with the war, increased air raids, or his duties as an officer in the Japanese Army as he so skillfully explained. His excuses are all lies. Her husband is unfaithful, deceitful, and a liar. He has betrayed her.

Shizue's eyes are dry and only a little reddened when Shunichi asks why the Colonel stopped by. She tells him it was a quick hello, in passing nearby, only the courtesy of a kind man.

The night following the collapse of Shizue's world couldn't be more perfect. The sunset radiates rose gold across the sky. Birds sing. The sweet fragrance of new spring blossoms promise to fulfill every heart's desire; every heart except Shizue's.

Shizue Nekomoto stands on the bank of the Ota River. On the ground at her feet is 5th Engineering Regiment letterhead, ripped to shreds. Bits and pieces flutter about on a breeze as if gasping for breath until a compassionate gust sweeps them into the water. Some sink. Others float away on the current. Shizue watches and listens, as if possessed, to the sound of whispering water.

To the couple sitting under a tree, the gentle lapping waves promise tomorrows of romance and happiness.

Children, catching slippery tadpoles at the water's edge hear the promise of another playful day.

Shizue hears long, deep sighs; echoing the desire that brought her here to end her life.

She holds baby Toshio in her arms. He has fallen asleep. Yorie clings to her mother's skirt. Tears roll down Shizue's face, glistening warm against pale skin. The young mother cries without the slightest sound. Practice makes her sorrow perfect and keeps her intentions secret. Her broken heart has gone unnoticed by family, friends, and neighbors.

By morning everyone's eyes will be opened. She gave up love for her grandmother. Duty and honor replaced her dreams. She will now break her husband's heart as he has broken hers. She will take his family. He will suffer the loss of those he loves most; his beautiful, precious children. Toshiyuki will live out the remainder of his years in disgrace with the ghosts of those he cherished.

Shizue, focused on her intent, looks around. The teenagers sitting under a tree are gone. The fisherman, with fresh catfish hanging from a cord and flapping for breath, is almost out of sight. No one is on the bridge.

Long shadows cast by the late sun seep into the porous night. In minutes it will be dark enough to walk into the water with her children, unnoticed.

Perhaps if grandmother had not passed, but she had, and there is no one to guide her. Prayers for relief and guidance have gone unanswered. There is no salvation. There is no hope for happiness.

Shizue will wade into the water with her children; drown her heart and theirs as well. Yorie and Toshio will never know the pain of love or the heartache of betrayal.

Shizue prepares for death.

Yorie tugs on her mother's hand, "Okasan, Okasan, eko."

Shizue holds the tiny hand tighter as darkness encroaches.

Yorie looks up at her mother. Short black hair and bangs frame her bewildered expression. She begs to leave. "Home, Okasan. Eko. Eko."

Little Yorie's pleas are not answered. The night swallows her helpless cries. Her tears ache with the very pain her mother wants to spare her. When Shizue pulls her into the water to drown, Yorie will also feel betrayal, however brief.

Yorie's cries become sobs. Her tears begin to loosen the grip of death on Shizue and the lure of a painless future. Shizue shivers, blinking spasmodically as muscles twitch out of their oxygen deprived stupor. Irresponsible. Selfish. Unforgivable. No. She will not end the precious lives of her children because of her husband's infidelity.

She squeezes Yorie's hand. "Baby, it's okay. Mother … mother is back. Don't cry."

Yorie, too lost in fear, is inconsolable.

"Yorie, listen to mother. I am here. Don't cry. Look." Shizue moves away from the water. "See? We are leaving. We are going home to grandfather, Shigemi, and Nishiyo. Okay?"

Yorie wipes her nose with her free hand and nods.

As they walk toward home leaving the river behind, Shizue vows there will be no more thoughts of suicide. From this day forward she will live for her children not for Toshiyuki … not even for herself. She offers this sacrifice to her children and to the memory of her beloved Obaasan. She will reveal the pain of her husband's betrayal to no one.

Saturday arrives and Toshiyuki does not show up in Furuichi to visit his family. Shizue packs a few items and prepares the children for a special, unannounced trip to Hiroshima City to see their father.

"We are going to the city," she informs Shunichi over the hollow chatter of the radio, "to Toshiyuki's boarding house for a surprise visit."

Shunichi hovers over the radio every day listening for news about Hawaii. He holds up one hand to keep Shizue quiet until he hears all he wants to hear out of the box. He turns, "The boarding house? Do you even know where it is?"

"I will find it," replies Shizue.

Shunichi returns his attention to the radio program. "I will expect dinner at the usual time."

"You will have it."

At the door of the boarding house, Shizue raises her hand to knock and hesitates. Inside are a man and a woman engaged in spirited conversation.

Yorie recognizes the male voice, "Daddy!"

"Shush," Shizue signals with a finger placed over her lips.

"Mama?"

"No baby. Shush."

Toshiyuki and Mieko are sharing stories of their rebellious pasts when they hear the casual knock at the door.

"Come in," Mieko calls out. Close to Toshiyuki's ear she whispers, "I hope it isn't someone looking for a room."

90

"Tell them you are full. Very full," Toshiyuki laughs as he reaches for the last red bean cake.

Mieko laughs too. "Door is open. Come in, please."

The door creeps open.

Toshiyuki gasps and almost chokes on the swallow of bean cake.

He scrambles to his feet, "Oh, it's you," he manages to say before rushing to his room and closing the door panel behind him.

"Daddy!" Yorie calls after her father.

"Daddy will be back." Shizue holds her daughter's hand and introduces herself to Mieko.

Mieko, more puzzled by Toshiyuki's relaxed demeanor than embarrassed by the surprise visit of her lover's wife, invites Shizue inside.

Adhering to proper Japanese custom, Shizue offers a gift, a pair of Japanese dolls, man and woman, to the woman sleeping with her husband. Was her intention to remind her Toshiyuki is a married man and Shizue is his wife? Did Mieko get the message?

Mieko politely says, "Thank you for the beautiful dolls".

Mieko offers a cup of green tea. Shizue nods acceptance and sits between her children, who look around the room absorbed in the unfamiliar surroundings.

The two women, with tea cups in hand, engage in polite conversation. Their voices are low. Each word, carefully chosen, exquisitely balanced and disconnected from the assessments behind their eyes.

At the door of his room, Toshiyuki strains to hear. To his surprise, the two women, his wife and his mistress, are not talking about him, but casually discuss what is going on in Japan and in Furuichi with the Nekomoto family. Toshiyuki is perplexed. He hears no angry words. No sounds of agitation. His eyes dart about.

91

Any moment, the chit-chat will elevate to accusations and then ... he can only imagine.

The children grow restless. The conversation between Shizue and her husband's lover ends the same way it began, cordially. Shizue informs Mieko that dinnertime is approaching. She must leave to prepare a meal for her family.

Shizue rises to leave. Her demeanor is pleasant, as though nothing out of the ordinary has happened.

"Bye-bye." Mieko waves to the children.

Shizue walks out the door, her back straight and strong. Pain etches the face Mieko cannot see.

Toshiyuki, an officer in the Japanese army, a leader of soldiers, is left hiding in his room thoroughly baffled. How did Shizue know? He has no doubt she knows. She didn't say one angry word to Mieko, but she knows. She would not have come to the boarding house if she didn't. Who told her?

Shamed by the incident and Shizue's graciousness in light of his conspicuous infidelity, he makes the only decision a man can make to recover his pride and shattered honor, outside of seppuku, that is. He will move out of the boarding house to another, away from the scheming temptress who took advantage of his weakness and seduced him.

Toshiyuki opens the wall panel a couple of inches and peeks out.

"She's gone." An edge of scorn sharpens Mieko's words.

Toshiyuki steps out and examines the room with quick turns of his head, like a wild man expecting to be ambushed.

Assured Shizue is gone; he walks over to Mieko and plops down. He covers his face, breathing heavily into his hands.

"What was that?" Outrage punctuates Mieko's voice. "Why did you leave me alone to face your wife and children?"

"I must move out," Toshiyuki mumbles.

"Move out? A descendant of great Samurai warriors runs away?"

Toshiyuki heaves himself to his feet and heads toward his room.

"Where are you going?"

"I tell you already. I leave."

Shrieking a stream of obscenities, Mieko grabs his arm. "You will not leave me! No!"

"Let go! I get my things. I leave now." Toshiyuki jerks his arm from her grip.

"No. No! *No!* You will not get things! You *leave*. Leave *now!* Get out! Get out! Get out!"

Toshiyuki throws up his arms and backs up toward his room.

Mieko screams with distorted ferocity and hurls a vase at Toshiyuki ... a near miss.

Toshiyuki, fearing curious neighbors will overhear and come rushing to Mieko's aid, ducks out the front door to avoid further embarrassment and injury, as another object, a tea cup, soars past his head.

Major Nekomoto wanders through the neighborhood in his uniform pants and a tee-shirt, without purpose or direction, giving Mieko a chance to cool down.

Two hours later, surely enough time for a rational resolution, he returns to the boarding house and politely asks Mieko for his possessions.

Mieko has not cooled down. She refuses to allow Toshiyuki access to his possessions; hurls insults and cries intermittently.

Toshiyuki begins to feel the full weight of what he has done. His weakness, evidenced in succumbing so easily to temptation has not only broken his wife's heart, it has hurt Mieko. For Mieko, he had not been business as usual. Though a life of prostitution has hardened her heart, she still has one. Tough, calculating Mieko glimpsed a shadow of a dream; a magnificent dream, embroidered

93

with love, respect, and nobility. It is a dream she is not ready to give up.

Mieko sees the spark of understanding in Toshiyuki's eyes. Her demeanor relaxes. "Stay with me." She throws her arms around him. "I forgive your betrayal. Your proper wife will not. Toshiyuki … I love you. Stay with me."

"Get off!" Toshiyuki shoves her away.

Mieko stumbles backward, "I see." Anger ignites her eyes. "Go home. Go home to your boring wife. Beg for forgiveness with your noble tail between your legs."

"Yeah. I get things then I leave."

"You will not!" Mieko liberates another gut ripping scream.

Toshiyuki backs out the door. Mieko slams and locks the door behind him.

Humiliated, Toshiyuki goes directly to the Army barracks and Colonel Kubota's office.

"Colonel?"

"Nekomoto?" the Colonel drops his pen and leans back in his chair. "You look … ah … disturbed. Is there a problem?"

"Yes Sir. I…" Toshiyuki reaches up to adjust his cap, as he often does when he's nervous. His hand grabs air. Mieko has his cap.

"Let me decide." The Colonel leans back and crosses his arms.

"It is about…" he hesitates, "situation at boarding house. I decide to move … to another…"

"The accommodations were unsatisfactory?"

"Yes … and…"

"The matter cannot be corrected?"

"No. It cannot. I tell landlady I leave. I go to get personal items. She screams. She throws me out. She is crazy woman. I am embarrassed. I leave."

"Is that all?"

"Yes Sir."

"I see," Kubota slumps forward. He decides, on the moment, not to tell his friend he is aware of the indiscretion with Mieko. "I'll send soldiers to the boarding house to retrieve your belongings and take them to your office. Is there anything more, Nekomoto?"

"No Sir. Thank you, Sir."

Colonel Kubota waves one hand through the air, a dismissal reserved for officers who are considered regiment pests. Toshiyuki can only wonder what lay behind the uncharacteristic brushoff.

Within the hour, soldiers return to the regiment barracks with the Major's possessions. As they exit the building, they burst into laughter. Too soon. Toshiyuki has excellent hearing. In their merriment is a tone he recognizes. The same amusement he feels when retelling the story of lifting a teacher's skirt at Punahou School.

Did Mieko spill the intimate details of this embarrassing departure to inferior soldiers?

From the window of his office, he watches the men walk across the grounds, still laughing and poking jest.

The Major flushes with embarrassment and anger. Has he had *his* skirt lifted?

Toshiyuki goes home to Furuichi and tells Shizue they must speak in private, upstairs. She follows him and stands at a distance, within a shadow.

He tells Shizue that Mieko tricked him into the affair. He explains that she is a witch; a truly evil woman. A wicked siren to whom he fell victim at a time of immeasurable stress.

Shizue listens without comment or perceptible emotion.

Toshiyuki assumes Shizue's demeanor indicates she believes him and will forgive his weakness; a man's weakness.

95

"Tomorrow I will find other room in Hiroshima. I will make this right, Shizue. I will…"

"No…" Shizue steps out of the shadow, "that is not what Colonel Kubota wants."

"What you mean? Not what Colonel wants."

"You are not as clever as you think. Your betrayal… Your dishonor did not go unnoticed."

"Colonel Kubota knows? He knows about… What he tell you? What does he want?"

"He wants…"

Toshiyuki throws up his hands and grabs the back of his head. "Colonel knows?" Toshiyuki loosens his shirt collar. "What about my men… Do they know?"

"I don't know."

"Does anyone besides Colonel know?"

"I know!" blurts Shizue. "Toshiyuki! How could you do this to me … to our children?"

Toshiyuki turns his back. "Tell me what Colonel Kubota want."

"He wants me and the children to move to Hiroshima, so you will not succumb to another temptation and be of further embarrassment to your company."

Toshiyuki whirls around. "No! You cannot. It is too dangerous in city."

"You will not change the Colonel's mind. He believes this is the only way to… He is your commander. It is your duty to obey."

Shizue reveals the details of Colonel Kubota's visit to inform her of Toshiyuki's improprieties. How the news crushed her heart. How close she came to ending her life and the lives of Yorie and Toshio in the Ota River.

Toshiyuki slumps. "Did family ask why the Colonel's visit? Did you tell them?"

"Your father asked why, but I did not tell him. I could not bear the shame of your betrayal. I could not bear to see his shame. Neither have I told him of my moment of weakness."

"Better family does not know."

"Yes, it is best."

Toshiyuki walks over to the window and stares out. The branch of a pine tree screeches against a pane.

Shizue comes up behind him. "Toshiyuki…"

"Yeah?" He does not turn around.

"Have you nothing more to say … nothing to say to me?"

"I am betrayed."

Shizue steps back. "You are betrayed? *You* betrayed me. You broke my heart. I went to the river to die … to drown in the water with your children." Shizue's face flushes, tears fill her eyes. "I thought we … Grandmother said…" standing with the man who brought her this pain; a man who thinks only of *his* inconvenience, she can no longer contain her tears. Shizue drops to the floor and sobs.

Toshiyuki does not attempt to comfort her. Neither will he speak about what might have been. Saying "I'm sorry," would be foolish. It would change nothing. He cannot bear the weight of Shizue's pain on top of his dishonor and the humiliation of getting caught.

"Father must not know why you and children move to Hiroshima." He starts to walk away.

"Wait." Shizue wipes tears from her face. "I am sorry."

Toshiyuki looks over his shoulder. "You are sorry? Shizue … you believe me? You understand that wicked woman tricked me?"

Shizue does not answer his questions. She stands and moves slowly to the window. She stares at the pine branches, heavily laden with raindrops. "I dreamed of having a family … and love…"

Toshiyuki hears her footsteps behind him. He feels her hand on his shoulder. He whirls around. "Shizue? You forgive me? You forgive my weakness?"

Shizue wipes another tear from her cheek.

"No dear. I only want to look into your eyes and tell you I am sorry Obaasan was right. I do not want to love a man. I do not want to love you."

CHAPTER EIGHT

Tomorrow's Shadow

"Father ... I'm moving Shizue and children to Hiroshima," Toshiyuki announces.

Shizue stands nearby holding baby Toshio. She doesn't look at her husband as he speaks to Shunichi.

"Yorie, come to mother." Yorie plays at her grandfather's feet as he listens to his radio. She picks up her doll and obeys her mother.

Shunichi clicks off the radio. Disbelief deepens the wrinkles of his face.

Toshiyuki's father is only a shadow of the man he used to be. His once sturdy jaw line droops, as do the corners of his mouth. He chuckles. "My hearing isn't as good as it used to be, son. Surely you didn't say you are moving Shizue and my grandchildren to Hiroshima City."

"Yeah, I move family."

"Move ... to Hiroshima..."

"Yeah."

"Don't joke with me, son. No one is moving to the city. Everyone expects an attack from the United States. Rumor says they have a special, larger firebomb they are going to drop on Hiroshima."

"Yeah, I know."

"You know everyone who can flees to the country and you move your family to Hiroshima City?" Shunichi leans over, plops his hands on his knees, and stares at his son. "Are you stupid?"

Toshiyuki's placid expression distorts into shock. He has always done as he wished with little challenge from his indulgent father.

Never has his father raised his voice to him in anger or called him stupid.

"Why? Why would you do this? Answer me!"

Toshiyuki remains speechless in the face of his father's rising fury.

"Answer me! Or tell me you will not do this."

"I tell you what I must do," says Toshiyuki.

"Must do? That is not a good enough answer! Why? Tell me why!"

Shunichi waits for an explanation. He needs something … anything to help him understand his son's preposterous, irrational, insane decision.

Toshio whines and struggles to break free of his mother's tense embrace. Yorie clings to her mother's slacks.

Toshiyuki walks casually to the kitchen and pours himself a glass of water.

Shunichi interprets his son's tight-lipped stand as defiance; a step above Toshiyuki's classic rebelliousness. *This* he will not allow. He looks at Toshio, and then from Toshio to Yorie and Yorie to Shizue before leaping to his feet so aggressively the stool beneath him tips over. He tromps over to Toshiyuki waving his arms in the air. Inches from his son's face, Shunichi repeats the question. "I said … are you stupid?"

"Yeah!" A deflated Toshiyuki slams down the glass. It shatters on the counter. "Yeah! I am stupid." Blood trickles from his hand.

Shizue stares; shocked by Shunichi's uncharacteristic anger and Toshiyuki's uncharacteristic response.

Shunichi exhales an exasperated breath; turns away from his errant son and returns to the stool in the corner. He clicks the radio dial on.

"Go to Hiroshima," he says. Years spent in internment camps have weathered the once powerful and prestigious man beyond repair. "You will all die." His voice trails off in frustration and despair.

The next morning, Shunichi joins Toshiyuki, Shizue, and his grandchildren in the kitchen for breakfast, as usual. Nishiyo and Shigemi are not present. They often sleep late as they enjoy being catered to and putting Shizue to extra work.

Rested and revived, Shunichi approaches his son's decision to move Shizue and the children to Hiroshima from a more rational perspective.

"Who will run the household?" Shizue places a bowl of steaming miso soup before him. "We have no one to depend on other than Shizue. How will we live without her? Your family will suffer."

"It is war. Everyone makes out. You will make out." Toshiyuki holds his bowl out for a refill. Toshio reaches for the bowl.

"No. No. No, Toshio," says Yorie. She plays "mommy" whenever she can. This morning she has ample opportunity. Shizue is distracted.

"When they have to! When there is no other way. I know you have other way." Shunichi shoves his bowl away. "This isn't hot enough. Heat it up." Shizue takes his bowl. "You are keeping something from me, Son. What have you not told me? Tell me why you do this."

Toshiyuki shakes his head as he picks a slice of carrot out of his soup.

Getting no response, Shunichi issues a proclamation. "I am your father! Before war … before America betrayed me, I gave you everything."

"Shizue," Toshiyuki glances at his wife. She gathers the children and leaves the room.

Toshiyuki and Shunichi are alone in the kitchen.

"Father, I am soldier with duty to Japan. You must accept my decision."

"No! This is not about duty. This is about disrespect. Listen to me. I had everything in Honolulu!" Shunichi grits his teeth. "Successful business, prestige, power... I gave it all to you and now you give me this? Defiance!"

"That is not what I give you. What I do is necessary."

"It is not *necessary*. It is *disrespect*. How can you disregard my suffering? You saw how hard I worked to build a good life. Now, everything is gone. Why?" Shunichi pounds a fist on the table. "Because I am Japanese. "Yes!" He pounds the tabletop again. "Being Japanese is my crime for being hauled off to prison like a common, penniless derelict. My body, my mind, and my heart wasted away for three long years in a cold, drafty, dusty, ramshackle..." He pounds again. "...prison camp. You cannot know what that was like."

Shunichi has kept the details of his experience in internment camps at Lordsburg Justice Department Camp in New Mexico and the Heart Mountain Camp in Wyoming secret until now. He had been taken to Heart Mountain in the summer of 1942 after eight months detainment in New Mexico. Finally, Shunichi liberates his pain.

"In dark miles lit only by a shrinking moon, soldiers marched us along a narrow road. Coyotes howled. Desert rattlers sounded warnings. One prisoner left the road to relieve himself and ran back screaming for help. He had been bitten by a viper. A guard thought the prisoner attempted an escape and shot him. We were not allowed to help. They forced us to march on. The young man was left to die.

At the end of the long march, in the light of dawn, we saw our new home. Huh!" Shunichi scowls. "Our new home they called it. Home? No! It was a prison; seven hundred and forty acres of dry buffalo grass and sagebrush, surrounded by barbed wire fence and nine guard towers. The tarpapered buildings had cracks in the walls so big we had to stuff them with rags and newspaper to keep out the dust and cold.

Soldiers forced back-breaking work on us. They treated us like slaves, especially the strong men. When the weak and sick became too much trouble they disappeared. The guards shot them in the back so they could claim they were shot trying to escape. Sharpshooters in watchtowers watched every move we made. No one knew if we would leave there alive."

Toshiyuki pushes his bowl aside, still half full of breakfast miso, "I have heard about internment camps. It should never have happened. But Father, past is gone."

"Past is not gone until mind is gone. I still have my mind and you add more hurt on top of pain. Son, you cannot move family to Hiroshima. I need them here. In city they will die. Our family will be lost!"

"Father..." Toshiyuki shakes his head.

"Do not shake your head! Listen to me! Understand why family must not go to Hiroshima."

Everything Shunichi has not revealed in the five months since returning to Japan pours out.

FBI and Secret Service agents went to the family home the very morning of the Japanese attack on Pearl Harbor, broke down the door and took him away to a military jail, handcuffed and blindfolded.

103

Shunichi had not, however, been taken by total surprise. He knew government officials saw him as a threat to United States security. He held a position of leadership in the Japanese community, occasionally entertaining high ranking Japanese officials in his home. But, his interests were never political. They were personal. Success in business and family security were his only concerns.

Always, prepared for an unfavorable turn of fortune, Shunichi kept a significant amount of cash hidden in his home. Immediately following the bombing of the harbor, he put his security stash, tens of thousands of dollars in large denominations, in a money belt and fastened it around the waist of his paralyzed wife, underneath her clothing. If he was taken away, his family would be safe.

As with the best laid plans, this plan too went awry. Federal agents took Shunichi, his wife, Tonoyo, and Shigemi, his 14 year old daughter from their home. Agents detained Shigemi for questioning and then sent her to live with her uncle, Waichi. They took ailing Tonoyo to a Navy hospital. The fortune in cash hidden around Tonoyo's waist disappeared.

"Shigemi has not been the same child since," mumbles Shunichi. "I do not know what they did to her." Pent up pain, frustration, and fury shatter Shunichi's typically passive façade.

Toshiyuki has never seen his father like this. The details of his family's abduction from their home are shocking and disturbing, but what can he do? He has his own situation, and humiliation to deal with right now.

"It is done." Toshiyuki's voice is monotone. "There is nothing I can do. There is nothing you can do." He doesn't mean to sound cold and insensitive, but he cannot become absorbed in his father's frustration. Out of respect, he also can't turn on his heels and leave.

"Do you hear me? They took everything! Not only from me, from you and from your children. Where is your anger?"

"Father, I remember how it was in Honolulu before war. Every day employees give you respect. 'Yes, Boss. No, Boss. Anything you say, Boss.' Now, world no longer lay at Mr. Nekomoto's feet. World changed. We must change. I remember something else. You teach me to make the best of anything. You say, better to be head of chicken than tail of cow."

"Yes," says Shunichi. "That was a long time ago. Look at me, Son. I am old ... too old to begin again. All my life I provided for you. Now, I need my family. Don't take Shizue and my grandchildren away."

"I tell you already. There is nothing I can do."

"You can change your mind. You are this family's future. Not me. There is nothing *I* can do, but sit in the corner and listen to the radio for news that my land and property will be returned. Don't do this to me."

"What I do I must. War took my dreams, too. You say I am future of family. What future do I have with empty pockets? United States not care I born American. Japan not care I born American. Before war, military was good career. Now, I am swept into corner. I follow orders. I do my duty."

"Yes! Yes! Do what you must do. *You!* Not Shizue and the children. A big firebomb will fall on Hiroshima. Do not put our family in such danger."

"Shizue wants to be with me."

"What?"

"Shizue tell me if I must stay in city ... she will stay in city. We will share danger together. If we die ... we die together."

"You are both crazy!"

"Yeah! We move to Hiroshima as soon as I find house."

"I am still the head of this household. I will not allow this. Shizue and the children will stay in Furuichi. You are eldest son. It is your duty to honor my decisions. Only when I am dead are family decisions yours to make."

"I will not tell you again. I do what I must do, Father. You do what you must do."

"How dare you speak to me in such a manner! Am I now the tail of cow? No! I am head of this household."

Toshiyuki sighs, shakes his head again and walks away. He stops in the doorway.

"Son...?" Shunichi assumes Toshiyuki has a last second change of heart.

"Goodbye, Father."

"No... Son... Don't do this to me!"

CHAPTER NINE

Paper Walls and Open Sky

Major Nekomoto has no difficulty finding a house in Hiroshima City. Many are vacant. The wealthy have left the danger zones and are glad to have someone live on their property, even for free. He rents the house of a rich stockbroker on Nishi Hakushima Street. It is a comfortable two-story wood frame house; 10 minutes walking distance from his regiment barracks; half a mile from beautiful Hiroshima Castle, the ancient home of a feudal lord.

Shizue is happy to learn that a young couple lives next door, Kenji and Ami Suzuki. They are expecting their first child. Perhaps new friendships and good neighbors will ease the burdens weighing on her heart.

One week later Toshiyuki, Shizue, daughter Yorie, age three, and Toshio age one, move to Hiroshima City to Nishi Hakushima Street.

B-29 bombers pass over their new home almost every day. They fly high in the sky, appearing as a glint of silver with a long white cloud tail, accompanied by a distinctive deep droning, a sound the residents describe as boom-boom.

People on the ground feel safe when they hear the boom-boom. The B-29 bomber is flying high and fast and will not attack. They grow familiar with the sound and don't get excited or worry that a bomb will be dropped. They only pause for a moment, search the skies for the plane, and then continue what they are doing.

More than three years into the war, the Japanese people are now in deep distress. The ABCD line, the economic blockade formed by the allied forces of America, Britain, China, and the Dutch, succeeds in choking the life out of Japan. Her people are heart-weary and close to starvation. A wayward breeze could blow their frail bodies over. Military pressure pushes them forward. They move mechanically, obeying their superiors who ferociously seek victory.

To zealots of war, death is preferred to defeat. Deep rooted instincts of honor and obedience flow in the blood of Japanese warriors. Undaunted bravery, fierce family pride, selfless, at times senseless, devotion to master and man, are valued virtues. War is purifying, death an honor. The people persevere believing the outcome of the war depends on the firm and united soul of the nation. The deaths of their beloved sons are a sacred sacrifice to the spirit of Japan.

On a Sunday morning, the droning of a B-29 is in the sky over Hiroshima. The plane is *flying low*. Fear strikes at the hearts of the people. They look up and gasp. Something is falling. Millions of propaganda leaflets drift down from the sky and settle over the city.

Toshiyuki picks one up and reads:

"Springtime in March and April,
The Cherry blossoms season,
But July and August will be
The season of ashes"

July and August are the hot summer months, the dry season and the best time for the effectiveness of firebombing. After reading the leaflets, firebombs are what everyone in Hiroshima expects.

The United States of America Air Force has adopted a policy of saturation bombing in its attacks on Japan, using incendiaries. This tactic is burning and devastating Japan's cities.

Monday night brings another air raid siren alarm. The mournful, wailing sound rises and falls signifying mortal danger. But no bombs are dropped. The B-29 passes over Hiroshima. The sound of its engines fade as it heads south toward Kure City.

The distant boom of explosions and the staccato rhythm of anti-aircraft guns shatter the peaceful silence of the Hiroshima City evening, triggering waves of barking and howling. Fire ignites the southeastern sky. A sister city burns. The dead and dying, strangers by name, are family in Hiroshima's heart.

Tears streak the faces of Hiroshima as Kure City burns. There are fewer tears today, however, than in the beginning of the war. Some people no longer cry. They whisper prophetically, *"This is the season of ashes. Tomorrow we will be the distant glow."*

The young and inexperienced do not worry about a bomb falling on their homes. They think bad things only happen to others. And it certainly appears true. Hiroshima, although the largest city in the Honshu region, is one of the very few Japanese cities untouched by American bombs.

Kure City, the location of Japan's largest Naval Base, Iwakuni City, the largest military refinery plant with vast storage facilities, and almost all the other large cities in Honshu, the largest and most populous island of Japan, are damaged heavily by the bombs. Many people in Hiroshima believe that because most Japanese living in the United States are immigrants from Hiroshima City, and many of their friends and family live in Japan, the United States will spare their city.

Others disagree. They fear the United States plans to use a special bomb, larger than the ones they use on other cities.

Hiroshima City authorities expect that firebombs will eventually be dropped. Hiroshima is a tinderbox, crowded with wood and paper structures.

Young and old are drilled in the techniques of firefighting. All residents keep a drum full of water in front of their houses with buckets, ladders, and a long handled straw-rope duster to strike fires.

They build large, concrete storage tanks on every block, and keep it filled with water.

City authorities use the five branches of the Ota-gawa, a 65-mile river running through the city, to create natural fire lines. They carve a   100-meter wide roadway for a horizontal fire prevention line stretching from east to west through the center of the city. They tear down houses in the location needed for the road and haul the debris away.

The work on firebomb protection goes on from dawn to dusk every day.

Thousands upon thousands of volunteers from adjoining rural districts help the city build roads to create protection against firebombing. Along the banks of the roadways, they plant potatoes to help feed the starving people.

All civilians, young and old train to fight, military style, against potential occupation forces. The training takes place after the work day ends, every day. Saturday and Sunday do not exist. There is only Monday, Monday, Tuesday, Wednesday, Thursday, Friday and Friday. Men and women learn to fight with bamboo spears against guns and swords. They prepare to die honorably, exemplifying the spirit of war in the traditions and history of Japan.

They also pray for a miracle. The Japanese believe in "Kamikaze". This is the sacred wind that protected Japan in olden days when the great China fleet attacked. The divine wind blew and destroyed the entire enemy navy. The people believe and expect this wind will blow again and save Japan.

Whether going to work, school, or to market, the civilian warriors are on constant alert. By order of the military, each wears a helmet, carries a gas mask, a bag of food, and a canteen of water. Men wear quasi-military uniforms with woolen leggings. Women dress in loose monpei slacks for better mobility. This is Hiroshima's armor. Enthusiasm. Cooperation. Fighting spirit.

Every day B-29 Superfortress bombers fly over Hiroshima City. Still, not a single bomb drops.

Will Hiroshima be spared? Or is the eye of the war storm upon them?

The days wear on.

CHAPTER TEN

The Beast in Shining Armor

Sunday night, August 5, 1945

Mothers tuck their children into bed with a kiss to their foreheads. Fathers promise to scare away pasty green goblins. Grandmothers read fairytales as grandchildren drift off to sleep.

Monday morning, August 6, 1945

The aroma of scant breakfasts; miso soup, fish, and seaweed, spice the muggy air. Roosters crow. Streets come alive with muffled activity. Determined minds and undernourished bodies begin their day. Mothers give young children last minute warnings not to play or linger in the open, and then hurry them out the door with stern instructions to come straight home after school. They watch them out of sight wondering what the day will bring.

The crystal water of the nearby Ota River reflects stark sunlight. An old man walks to the shore with a bamboo fishing pole against his shoulder. Chickens scratch at parched ground. Dogs bark at the tension in the air.

Next door to the Nekomoto home, Kenji and Ami Suzuki's newborn son cries.

They have all awakened to a day that will become the nightmare of *Once Upon a Time* and, for 240,000 thousand people, the end of *Happily Ever After.*

Inside the Nekomoto house on Nishi Hakushima Street, Shizue is changing Toshio's diaper when her body stiffens and her eyes reveal alarm. She tilts her head, listening intently to a sound growing in the distance.

The guttural hum of an engine pushes its way through the barking of dogs and the neighbor's crying baby. The droning sound grows louder. Shizue whispers a hurried prayer, rushes to the window, and scans the sky searching for a low flying bomber. There is no plane. The engine sound is that of a road construction truck, not a B-29.

Shizue draws a staggering breath, returns to Toshio and kisses her curious and agile toddler. Impatient with his mother's slow, careful manner, he struggles to get up and resume his play.

"Toshio," she touches his nose, "there's plenty of time to play, my little warrior." Her eyes, soft as her voice, fill with love for her son. She finishes the task of diaper changing and releases her precious child to the tatami covered floor.

Dropping his soiled diaper into a bucket, she calls out to her daughter.

"Yorie? Where are you?" Adventurous Yorie is much too quiet for Shizue's comfort.

Yorie plays in an adjoining room with a doll strapped to her back. Fully immersed in her make-believe mommy world, she doesn't answer her mother's call.

"Yorie," Shizue calls again. "Come to…"

Footsteps on the porch jerk Shizue's attention away from her daughter's possible mischief to someone approaching the entrance.

A shadow falls across the floor planks. Burglars often invade in broad daylight.

Shizue snatches Toshio up from the floor and prepares to run as the footsteps reach the open door panel. She glances over her shoulder. It is Toshiyuki!

Curiosity quickly replaces fear. Toshiyuki left for the barracks at his usual scheduled time. Something has caused him to return. But what? Shizue doesn't ask. Since her husband's affair with Mieko, they avoid each other as much as parenting allows.

Toshiyuki paces the porch several times and then halts near the entrance. With hands clasped behind his back, he stares off, over the wall and the irregular rooftops of the city, into the horizon.

Shizue observes her husband. She isn't immune to the attraction of a man in uniform; cap, high brown boots, sword hanging by his side. He is close enough for Shizue to smell the leather of his boots, belt, and scabbard.

Why has he returned so soon from his office? Did he come home to speak with her? If he did, why is he hesitating? What secrets hide in her husband's thoughts? Does he care that he broke her trust and violated his honor? Did something more than lust pass between Toshiyuki and Mieko?

Shizue resists the thoughts. She does not want to entertain such ineffectual wonderings. Her husband may be secretly tormented by his infidelity.

Shizue sighs as her slender flame of hope flutters and poofs into smoke, snuffed out by the brutal reality of common sense. Toshiyuki often disappears inside himself. His secretive behavior will not let her forget what he has done and may do again.

Shizue scolds her heart for entertaining the thoughts of a naive school girl. She remembers Obaasan's warning, "You do not want to love a man." The words seemed cold and heartless at the time, but Grandmother was right. Brutal experience has proven the naivety of Shizue's youth. Toshiyuki is a man. He is not to be trusted with her heart.

Toshiyuki, her husband, the stranger, stands erect and motionless, his head held high, like a man of honor, like...

Shizue's thoughts mercifully disconnect. She repositions a tortoise shell comb holding her upswept hair into place. The comb belonged to her mother. Whenever she touches it, she feels her spirit.

Today the spirits of her mother and grandmother feel unusually close.

"Oh!" Shizue places a hand on her stomach. New life flutters inside her womb. Her pregnant condition does not yet show through her favorite blue house kimono top. Toshiyuki is not the only one with secrets. He is unaware Shizue carries his third child. There is little reason for him to suspect.

Since learning of her husband's infidelity with Mieko there was only one intimate night together. She had awakened and seen him sitting in the dark. His face was in shadow, but sensing a deep unhappiness, she tip-toed over and sat down beside him. One warm touch led to another and then more.

It was a moment of weakness that changed nothing. She has not forgiven him. The man on the porch, the father of her children, remains a stranger to her heart. For all appearances, he does not consider her feelings. He has not given her even a simple "I am sorry."

Shizue is in Hiroshima City because of his dishonor. Miles away from the relative safety of Furuichi, she goes through the motions of living, waiting for bombs to drop and burn their lives away. Even a fine house within concrete walls provides scant security.

Any day in Hiroshima City could be her family's last day on earth.

An old Japanese proverb says, "Bad causes bring bad results." Shizue no longer hopes that being a patient, loyal, forgiving wife will lead to happy endings. Shizue no longer hopes. Shizue simply exists.

Her attention turns to Toshio, playing noisily on the floor. She smiles modestly. In family there is life. With her children there is meaning. Meaning is better than happiness.

Curiosity finally gets the better of her. She walks to the door. "Toshiyuki...?"

He is gone.

A rush of morning sickness twists the young mother's stomach. She reaches for a tea cup and herb tea to relieve her nausea. "Yorie. Come to Mother. Yorie!"

The water pot steams as she plans her day. She will take the children outside to play in the yard while she goes about the morning chore of washing diapers.

Toshiyuki has not left home. He stands outside the gate, searching the road in the direction of the army barracks. He greets passing neighbors as he anxiously waits for his horse to be delivered by Private First Class Ito. The designated time, 0730, has passed. This isn't at all like Private Ito. He is always reliable, and yet it is now 0800 and he has not arrived with the Major's horse.

Toshiyuki begins to rationalize an excuse for his subordinate. The troops were on high alert the previous night because the neighboring cities of Kobe and Nagoya had been firebombed. He instructed his soldiers to take an extra hour of rest. Other battalions on their regular schedule are, by this time, finished eating and outside receiving orders from their commanding officers.

Private Ito and the other soldiers of the Major's battalion are one hour behind their normal routine and ... Toshiyuki glances at his watch ... are right about now, most likely finishing breakfast in the company mess hall. Yes. He will give his soldier a few minutes more.

Toshiyuki's thoughts drift as he waits idly, searching the morning sky for enemy bombers. The fingers of one hand wrap around the

116

hilt of his sword as he reflects on the consequences of his most recent indiscretion. He knows and respects the Bushido Code of eight virtues: Justice, Courage, Mercy, Politeness, Honesty, Honor, Loyalty, and Self-control. However, Toshiyuki finds them easier to apply in his professional life than in his private one.

Shunichi taught Toshiyuki to devote himself honorably to career and family in all ways but one, self-control of physical desires.

Enough of this waiting! He whirls around. His sword flaps against his leg. He tromps back through the gate, retrieves his bicycle from the porch, and heads out for the barracks.

He approaches the first intersection and is about to make a left turn, when the bike's front tire flattens. Already frustrated, now perturbed, he hurls his bike to the ground, snatches the cap from his head and wipes away perspiration. Up the road in the direction of the barracks there is still no visible Private Ito or horse. Toshiyuki picks up the bicycle and whirls around, headed back to his house.

No Ito. No horse and pushing a bicycle with a flattened front tire. Toshiyuki senses more is going on this morning than bad luck. Something isn't right. The sky is too clear. There are no clouds. No breeze. To Major Nekomoto it feels as though Hiroshima's sky is holding its breath.

Arriving home, wet with perspiration and fully defeated, he tosses the bike onto the porch. It thuds, bounces, and clanks against the wall by the front entrance.

Shizue hears the commotion and rushes to the door with Toshio in her arms.

"Toshiyuki, what...?"

"I am late!"

"What happened?"

117

"Papa," Shizue restrains Toshio as he stretches his arms out for his daddy.

"No time to explain."

Halfway across the yard, he turns around and hurries back to Shizue.

"Yorie must not play outside today. Keep her inside the house. You and Toshio must stay inside also."

"But, I…"

"Shizue! Do as I say."

"But, Toshio's diapers … I must go outside to wash his diapers."

"Okay, wash diapers, but only that."

As they speak, Yorie slips outside.

"Yorie, no. Come back. Yorie. Come back to mother. Your father does not want you playing outside today."

"Oka-san nande? (Why mother)" Yorie is always full of questions.

"Don't ask why. It is not polite. Obey Mother."

Yorie ambles back to the porch with a pouty face. The Obi, a long sash that wraps around a Japanese kimono, is still on her shoulder.

"Where did you get that? Have you been plundering through mother's chest of drawers again? Give that to me."

"Watashi Obi! (*My* Obi)" Yorie darts past Shizue.

"Your daughter is out of hand." Toshiyuki touches Toshio's outreached hand. His son wants his daddy. "Discipline her."

"This is not like her. Maybe she is also sensing what we feel this morning."

"You too? You feel something is not right?"

Shizue nods.

"Yeah. Okay. But keep her inside today." Toshiyuki cautions Shizue one last time.

Every morning, Yorie follows her father on his way to the barracks and visits a neighbor, "Heitai-basan" (Soldier Mom). She is very fond of this woman's daughter and plays with her most of the day. For some reason, Yorie did not follow her father today.

He heads for the barracks, this time, on foot.

On the straight concrete road near the overpass, he sees a group of high school girls walking toward him. They are laughing and giggling.

"Say you girls!"

The girls stop.

"Don't you know alarm is still in Condition II? Stop laughs and giggles. Be serious."

"We are very sorry," the girls reply. "Gomen-nasai (Forgive us)."

Before the Major can accept the girls' request of forgiveness for their carelessness, the humming of a B-29 turns his attention upwards. High in the sky is the glistening silver body of the bomber.

"See you girls. There is the bomber." Toshiyuki points up to emphasize the validity of his concerns and spots another object in the sky. This one is falling, attached to a parachute.

Bomb!

His body braces. He squints through his glasses lenses. No. It doesn't look like a bomb. It is, most likely, the usual propaganda papers.

Anxious to be on their way, the schoolgirls ask to be excused.

"Sumimasen (excuse us)," they say in harmonious unison.

Assured the B-29 isn't a serious matter; Toshiyuki excuses the schoolgirls and resumes his walk toward the barracks.

"Be careful, girls," he warns as they pass.

At home and also running late, Colonel Kubota hears the unmistakable drone of the B-29 in the sky over Hiroshima. Having just finished breakfast and in the process of dressing, he reaches for his uniform shirt, but his hand doesn't carry through. There is no comforting boom-boom accompanying the bomber's droning. He grabs his binoculars instead and rushes to an upstairs window to confirm what his gut really already knows. Naked to the waist, his hands trembling, he watches the bomber approaching.

It's the Enola Gay, a U.S. military Boeing B-29 Superfortress bomber, piloted by Colonel Paul Tibbets. Only seconds before, the crew released an atomic bomb, code named "Little Boy". The Enola Gay is accompanied by two other planes. One of them, Necessary Evil, carries photographic equipment to record the explosion and the effects of the bomb. The other, The Great Artiste, drops instrumentation by parachute that will measure the power of the blast. This instrumentation will radio-transmit an energy yield of 15 kilotons, the equivalent of 15,000 tons of TNT.

Hiroshima City has a civilian population of almost 300,000. Military personnel and soldiers are 43,000. The city had been spared from conventional bombing to serve as a pristine target for the purpose of observing the effects of a nuclear bomb on an undamaged city. As a result of the blast, resultant firestorm and radiation, approximately 237,000 people will die.

"Little Boy" is the first nuclear bomb used in warfare. It is attached to a parachute to slow its descent so the B-29 bomber has time to escape.

Little Boy, 10 feet in length and weighing 9,700 pounds, speeds toward Hiroshima sparkling in the morning sunlight for 44.4 seconds before detonation at 1,890 feet; the height predetermined to inflict the most damage.

With less than a minute to spare before detonation, the Enola Gay speeds away.

In seconds, not only will Hiroshima be forever changed so will the world.

The Japanese reply "Mokusatsu" to America's request for the surrender of Japan, was mistranslated to the sender, as we, Japan, are "not considering" rather than the intended message: the cabinet has not yet made a decision, but is considering. This mistranslation caused the Atomic Bomb to be dropped on Hiroshima.

Colonel Kubota sees the bomb dropped from the plane and watches its descent. He has no idea that this bomb is an armored beast with the power to wipe God's world from the face of existence. He waits, ready to assess the damage and take control of the situation. The weapon of mass destruction grows larger, brighter, and closer to its target. He stops breathing. His heart pounds out the seconds.

seven... six... five...

Major Toshiyuki Nekomoto is one step outside the railroad overpass on his way to the Army barracks.

The high school girls are a few yards beyond the shelter of the overpass, walking in the opposite direction.

Inside the Nekomoto home on Nishi Hakushima Street, Yorie plays mommy with a doll strapped onto her back with an Obi.

Shizue holds Toshio, breastfeeding her hungry boy. His crying has delayed her going outside to wash the laundry.

Inside Shizue's womb beats the new heart of her three month fetus.

Born and unborn, the children's chances ... the family's chances of living through this almost ordinary August day are zero.

Shizue hears the dreaded sound of the bomber growing stronger. She waits for the reassuring boom-boom!

It doesn't come.

The baby in her womb flutters like a fish thrown into a dry bucket. Her heart skips a beat. Neighborhood dogs explode into a barking frenzy, silencing the chirping of birds and the incessant chirr of cicadas.

Shizue stops breathing. Each pounding beat of her heart ticks off the last seconds of promises tomorrow will never keep.

four... three...

CHAPTER ELEVEN

The World the Day Ended

two... one...

Pika-Don! (Flash-Boom)

The Enola Gay is eleven and a half miles from ground zero when Little Boy explodes. A 1,000 mile per hour fireball shock wave rocks the bomber. The mushroom fire cloud climbs to 40,000 ft.

The bomb destroys everything within eight miles of the hypocenter. Sixty-nine percent of Hiroshima's buildings are destroyed. More are damaged.

Nine out of ten people half a mile or less from ground zero are dead. Eighty thousand people are killed instantly. Twenty doctors and one hundred and fifty nurses survive to care for the sick and dying.

Major Nekomoto is one step out of the shadow of the railroad overpass, facing away from the blast. A flash blinds him. A force from behind, like a strong wind rushing out of a narrow passage, catapults him into a roadside drain ditch. His cap, eyeglasses, and briefcase are blown away. His sword, detached from its hook, dangles against his leg.

Toshiyuki lies low in the ditch, covering his face with his hands. What happened? Was he hit by a direct blast nearby? He raises his head to look around. A choking cloud of dust and debris whirls about him with the force of a tornado. Dirt and roof tiles pelt his body. His mind races, desperately trying to understand. Fear overcomes caution. He lifts his head again. Through reddened, squinted eyes, he sees a ball of fire crawling beneath the overpass, hissing and creeping toward him like the gaping mouth of an ancient fire dragon.

Too disoriented to run, he can do nothing but stay flat on the bottom of the ditch and wait to be devoured.

He squeezes his eyes shut, certain death has found him. The hissing grows louder. Heat burns his back. The sizzling fireball is on top of him.

Trapped in a nightmare with no awakening, face covered, eyes tightly closed; languishing in boundless space void of familiar sounds, Toshiyuki loses all sense of time and sanity. This is his end.

As Toshiyuki braces for the final touch of death, the sizzling and crackling diminishes. And then it's gone. The fire cloud passed above the ditch. It passed over him! In its place is an odd, gassy, choking odor. Gases from explosions are extremely poisonous. He tries not to breathe.

He remains still, keeping his face covered. Finally, he gasps for breath and his eyes open. A pinkish cloud surrounds him now; thick, nauseating. He can see nothing through the pink haze; not the railroad overpass, the high embankment, or houses. Where are the houses? He knows they are there. Has he lost his eyesight? But, there are no sounds. Where are the sounds of the city? Is he deaf, too? He feels the ground around him. Only naked warm earth returns his touch. What happened? What is happening? He wants to get up, but is too afraid. He stays still, listening for a sound; watching for a distant movement. A cough. A cry. Something … anything. He hears nothing. Is he alone within the noxious cloud?

But, he can't be. Toshiyuki remembers the school girls whispering and giggling on the road before the explosion. They should be out there. They have to be.

Panicked thoughts crash into each other and tumble through his mind trying to find safety in reason. He shouts his name, "Major Nekomoto!" He isn't deaf, but... Perhaps he didn't escape the fiery, hissing monster. Could he be dead? Has he been ripped from one world and blasted into another?

"*Shizue!*" he whispers her name. Toshiyuki never listened to Shizue's warnings about an afterlife. He laughed at her prayers. He ridiculed her beliefs in the spirits of their ancestors. Was she right? Was Shizue right about everything? Is there a heaven and a hell? Is he in hell?

No-o-o-o! He refuses to listen to the voices in his head. Shut up! *Shut up!* If Shizue was right, it's too late! Too late to change; too late for forgiveness! Toshiyuki's every thought is torment.

He struggles to shut out the jangle of confusing, overlapping voices vying for a place in the line of reason. An audible groan escapes as he wrestles with invasive doubts and regrets. The menacing thoughts and pure, unbridled fear scream out through his collapsing reason.

Stop! *Stop!* He must get up. He has to stand. He must put sense back into the head of the soldier. If he is in hell, he is still Major Toshiyuki Nekomoto, Officer in the 5th Army Engineering Regiment of Japan, son of Samurai. He must command his broken mind! His body must obey!

"That's an order, Major!" he shouts out loud. But, muscle and bone do not obey. Fear beyond reason, beyond sanity pins his flesh to the ground. The more he strains to force his body up, the more his stomach fights back waves of nausea. He can't get up. Toshiyuki cannot even move. He can only listen and wait, but for what? And worse, what is out there waiting for him?

Little by little, the pinkish cloud turns dark and murky; smelling of dust and earth.

"*Help*," a faint call. Did he really hear it? Or was it a voice in his head.

He waits.

"Help," the voice comes from his distant right.

"Help me." Another comes from his left.

Faceless, ragged, shriveled cries begin to rise and fall from everywhere and nowhere. Some are hollow like echoes. Others, torn and gnawed with pain, scream out names. Tomomi! Aiko! Kazumi! Chiyoko! Their loved ones do not answer.

"Shizue. Yorie. Toshio." Toshiyuki whispers his loved ones names. Tears gather dust and ashes as they roll to his chin.

In weary anguish, the Major buries his head in the crooks of his arms and attempts his first prayer.

"Grandmother, if you are here. Help us. Help Shizue. Help our children."

He waits. Seconds? Minutes? Hours? He has no sense of time. Time is now an eternity; an eternity taking pleasure in inflicting pain. Yes. This could be hell. Pain. Suffering. Hope. Dashed hope. More suffering.

Slowly, the air begins to clear. He looks around to see if it's safe enough to stand. He sees something. A shadowy form moves through the gray haze. Someone or something is out there.

A surge of hope moves his legs. He belly crawls out of the ditch. Feeling his way forward, his outstretched hand touches something hot and crisp. Uh! Without his glasses, he cannot make it out. He crawls closer. Inches from the object, he strains to see. Oh! Oh, no! It's a face! Toshiyuki gasps and recoils. The hot, crisp thing is a face, burned beyond recognition. One of the school girls? Toshiyuki backs away. If it is one of the school girls, that fate could have been his. Maybe, it still could be. He stays still.

The leaden gloom begins to rise. Bit by bit, Toshiyuki sees a specter worse than any imagined Hell. Houses lay flat on the ground. No tiles on roofs. No roofs. Not a leaf on any tree. Not anything green. Ash and dirt bury the colors of life. The potato patches planted along the railroad embankment are gone. The high embankment itself is gone. Flat, bare ground smolders, strewn with charred, smoking debris.

Men, women, and children crawl out of collapsed homes. Bleeding, charred, half naked, crying, screaming, and dazed, some crawl back in for family members who are trapped and calling out from inside. Others run in circles, stunned and bewildered.

Muffled cries seep out of the ruins onto an endless landscape of rubble.

"I'm here."

"Help me."

"Help."

Most cries go unanswered, fading into the silence of hopelessness and death.

The injured who manage to struggle out of the wreckage of their homes don't know what to do. Seriously hurt, shocked, confused, and helpless, no one can help them.

Toshiyuki pulls himself shakily to his feet. He brushes the dirt off his uniform and tries to locate his eyeglasses and cap. He can't find them, but he locates his briefcase a couple meters away.

Now more aware of how vast the devastation, Toshiyuki ceases to wonder what happened to him. His question becomes, "What has happened to the world?"

The blast struck Toshiyuki at the halfway point between the barracks and the home where he left his wife, daughter, and infant son. Should he go to the barracks to aid his men or return to the place he left his family? Duty first or family first? Military training

127

insists he put duty first. He trained Shizue to take care of herself and the babies in case of emergency. If she is alive, she will know what to do.

All this happened, not in hours, but in minutes. At 0815 the bomb exploded near the center of the city. Its focal target, the famous 'T' shaped steel bridge, Aio-bashi, three-quarters of a mile from the place Toshiyuki was hit. He had been protected from the direct force of the blast by the high railroad embankment. The sizzling cloud that passed over him was the result of the fireball produced by the explosion; 1,200 feet in diameter with a surface temperature of 10,830 degrees Fahrenheit.

The reinforced concrete of the overpass protected him from the 1,000 mile per hour concussion wave of the atomic bomb. The only place on his body burned by the explosion is the back of his neck, between his collar and cap. The clothing he wore and the direction he faced when the atomic bomb exploded were major factors in his surviving with relatively minor visible injury.

The officer, Major Nekomoto, goes into action. He leaves his heart to fate and turns his feet toward the barracks.

"Heitan-san!" Two of the school girls he met earlier on the road and cautioned about the B-29 stagger toward him.

"Heitan-san! (Soldier) Heitan-san, what shall we do? We are burned. Please, help us."

The girls' cries are screeches, terrified and unrecognizable as the same giddy voices the Major heard only moments earlier. Their blouses are burned so badly, the fabric barely hangs onto their bodies. The heat of the explosion burned through their black monpei slacks, leaving only their white underwear. The girls' faces are burned nearly beyond recognition. Skin hangs from bones like melted plastic. How they are alive is beyond understanding.

Toshiyuki is certain they will not be alive for long. He conceals his shock. "Okay. I am going to the barracks. You girls follow me."

The girls stumble behind the Major as he pushes through debris-choked roads toward the barracks. He could move faster alone, but the girls haven't the strength to keep up. He can't leave them behind, however bleak their ultimate fate.

"Please sir, will you help my mother. Mother can't get out! Please get her out!" A young girl runs up to the Major with tears streaming down her dirt-smeared face. She points toward a pile of wood that had been her home. "Over there. Help her. Help my mother, please!"

"All right, lead me to her. I will help. It's going to be okay." Relief turns the child's pleas to uncontrollable crying. Toshiyuki takes her by the shoulders. "Look at me. What is your name?"

"Chi … Chi … Chiyo," she manages to whimper.

"Chiyo. Okay, Chiyo. Stop crying. Where is your mother? Show me."

The child stops crying. However, it is not Toshiyuki's order that interrupts her tears. It is the appearance of the school girls who have caught up with him. The child gapes at them, trembling, but she doesn't scream. Perhaps she believes this is only a nightmare from which she will soon awaken. Toshiyuki is thankful for that.

"Look at me," he turns her face to him and holds it gently in his hands. "Show me where your mother is. Chiyo."

"Stay here and rest," Toshiyuki tells the school girls. "I will come back for you."

"No! Don't! Don't leave us! Please, don't leave us."

"Okay. I won't. Come then."

Major Nekomoto follows the child to her house and finds the mother buried except for one arm reaching out from under a pile of timbers.

"Get back. I help you. Get your arm back."

He shoves and kicks away the light debris. The school girls, in spite of their horrifying condition, try to help. Underneath the light debris, the mother is held down by a larger timber. Together, Toshiyuki and the school girls pull on her arm. Even with their combined strength, the beam does not budge.

"Too heavy! We can't move it. I am going to my barracks. I will send soldiers to help as soon as I get there," Toshiyuki turns to leave.

"Soldier!" The child grabs his jacket. "Soldier! Don't go!"

"Don't leave us!" pleads the mother's muffled voice.

"But, I must," the Major says. "I go to barracks. I send help from there."

Toshiyuki and the high school girls are only a few yards along when they hear a whimpering cry. The child is following them.

"No. Do not follow us. You must stay. Look after mother. Watch for soldiers. They get your mother out. Watch for soldiers. Can you do that?"

The child only stares at him.

"Can you do that, Chiyo?"

Still, she does not answer.

Toshiyuki holds his hand out, palm forward. "Stay here. Stay here with your mother."

He leaves the child, not knowing if she understands. Not knowing what will happen to her and her mother.

The school girls follow. He can't help them along. They can't help each other. The slightest touch will tear skin from bone.

As the Major pushes on, over and through piles of scattered debris, buttons fall from his uniform coat. A pocket falls off. A shoulder separates at the seam and the right side sleeve slides off.

130

By the time he reaches the barracks, his jacket barely hangs on his body.

At 0830 he passes through the main gate. His soldiers rush toward him.

"Major! You saved our lives! You saved our lives!" They repeat the words as if they can't believe them. "We were inside. We stayed inside like you told us. We were not outside."

Major Nekomoto looks around the desolate grounds, "Where are the others? Where are the other companies?"

"Dead and dying, Sir," a soldier replies.

"The recruits?"

The soldiers shake their heads. "All dead, Sir."

This morning, the Major's company had new recruits, almost to the limit of the drafting age. They were called to duty by 1½ sen stamped Special Delivery red post cards. On this, the first day of duty, these young men, were in the midst of roll call on open ground in front of the Headquarters building when the bomb exploded. Parted from their families only a few hours before, they are gone.

The soldiers barely manage to repress their shock and horror when they see the school girls' injuries. It's one thing to see burned corpses. It is another to see walking corpses.

"Find a safe place for these girls. Give them water. See if you can find a medic," orders the Major. "You girls go with soldiers."

Toshiyuki takes another look around the 5th Engineering Regiment grounds. His company barracks, a two-story log structure nearly fifty years old, the oldest building in the regiment, is the only one left standing. The south side facing the blast center is damaged. Window spaces are empty, imploded by the force of the blast. Walls are shifted and tilted. Roof tiles stripped away.

Major Nekomoto's company, composed of 5 officers and 250 men, has no casualties. His men were having breakfast in the barracks at the time of the blast and their building, the old sturdy log building, didn't collapse.

Other companies' men were going about regular morning duties on open ground. Most were killed instantly or critically injured.

Toshiyuki goes inside the barracks building and forces open the door to his office. The ceiling lay piled up on his desk. Rubble and broken glass litter the floor.

If the Major's horse had arrived that morning on schedule or his bicycle tire had not flattened, he would have been in his office at his desk when the bomb exploded. Most surely, he would have been crushed.

The Major walks across the room, kicking debris aside, broken glass cracking under his boot heels. He looks out through the space in the wall where a window had been. The big camphor tree growing between the barracks and the main gate stands completely stripped of leaves. All buildings far into the distance are flattened. Soldiers trapped under collapsed structures call out for help, filling the void where their lives had been. Other victims of the blast lie on the ground motionless or writhing in pain. Some injured wander around calling for medics, who are now dead or in need of assistance themselves. Only the major and his men are left able to help.

From what he can see now, the Major knows his first assumption about the cause of the blast was wrong. No incendiary bomb could create such devastation.

Major Nekomoto orders his men to assemble in front of the barracks for roll call. They move quickly into formation. Twenty-two of his soldiers are injured from flying window glass and debris. Miraculously none are seriously injured (except by radiation, the

132

unknown adversary, which will later take its toll). Two sergeants are away on mission to the 5th Army Headquarters.

The Major finishes roll call at 0840. He must relocate his men to a safer place, tend to the injured, and rescue those still trapped under debris. Necessary supplies must be retrieved from the barracks building, which could collapse at any time. Temporary shelters must be built. Food and water scavenged, as they expect no supplies will come from outside the devastated area for some time.

As survival plans go into action, a B-29 returns to the sky over Hiroshima. The few soldiers and civilians who survived the blast run for cover, but the aircraft doesn't fire guns or drop bombs. It circles the devastated city like a buzzard, observing, taking photos, recording evidence of their victorious assault on the people of Hiroshima.

Toshiyuki stops worrying about the aircraft. He feels certain the enemy will not attack again. He contains any resistant doubts in a calm authoritative demeanor, assuring surviving soldiers they are safe to work and move around freely.

To accomplish the urgent tasks, the Major divides his men into groups.

One group is assigned to search, rescue and attend to survivors as best they can.

Another group will obtain clothing, blankets, medical supplies, and ammunition.

A group is ordered to build shelters, making use of the tunnels in the back hills of their training grounds, for what is left of the company. They will also build storage units for food, water, and other supplies.

One group goes out to gather whatever supplies of food they can muster, starting with the pumpkins scattered across the regiment grounds from a farmer's field. They will search ditch banks for potatoes planted along the roadsides. All these items will be assembled at the new campsite.

A small group of soldiers will locate and provide aid to other companies.

Another is sent out to rescue civilians trapped under collapsed structures and otherwise provide aid to those living near the barracks.

With rescue, aid, and survival efforts in effect, Major Nekomoto attempts radio communication with the 5th Army headquarters. There is no response. He will learn later that the regiment commander is alive, although injured. Out in the open, on horseback when the bomb detonated, he was thrown from the horse, which resulted in a broken right arm.

Overwhelmed with military responsibilities, Toshiyuki forgets about Shizue, Yorie, and Toshio.

The officer in charge of helping civilians dispatches two soldiers to Major Nekomoto's house.

CHAPTER TWELVE

The Warlord's Sword

Less than one-half mile from the Nekomoto home on Nishi Hakushima Street, the nuclear bomb explodes. Temperatures at the hypocenter reach 10,000 degrees Fahrenheit. The city does not burn; not immediately. The force of the concussion wave creates a vacuum, snuffing out fires as quickly as they start.

The mighty shock wave and concussion force wind slams into the home blasting Toshio out of his mother's arms. Pressure rises from beneath the house and blows up the floor, lifting Shizue and the children with it. The three of them, along with tatamis, furniture, and household items, everything … is flipped over. Shizue, Yorie, and Toshio fall and drop under the floor to the ground as a secondary force, this one from above, disassembles and smashes the house flat upon them like the clapping of giant hands. Floor timbers protect Shizue and the children from most of the large falling debris, but one supporting beam strikes Shizue on the forehead, inflicting a three-inch-long gash to the bone. The blow knocks her unconscious. As if in a dream, far away, somewhere in the darkness she hears children crying for help. With their cries, she hears her grandmother's voice echoing as though from the other side.

"Shizue, wake up. Shizue, wake up. Shizue, wake up."

Shizue awakens to the terrified screams of Yorie and Toshio. The gash on her forehead is bleeding profusely. Through the red of blood covered eyes, she looks around and thinks the house is on fire. The smell of smoke fills her gasps for air. Heat from the blast stings her skin.

"Toshio! Yorie! My babies! My babies!"

With one stroke of a giant warlord's nuclear sword, the world Shizue knew ended. In its place are massive clouds of smoke and dust, darkness, silence, and the metallic, salty taste of blood and choking befouled air.

Lead by screams of terror and pain, Shizue crawls through the rubble, searching for her children. She finds Yorie buried face down under debris. She pulls her out and tries to comfort her three year old daughter by repeating soft, familiar words. "Mother is here. Mother is here." Yorie opens her eyes. Her terrified cries become shrieks.

"Yorie. Yorie, it is mother." Yorie thrashes her arms and intensifies her terrified screams. In the dim, dusty light, Shizue's blood drenched face looks like a monster.

Shizue wipes blood from her eyes and speaks calmly, "Yorie, baby, I am your mother. See. This is your mother's voice. You know Mother's voice. Don't be afraid. Mother is here."

Convinced the bloody apparition is her mother, Yorie stops screaming, but continues to cry.

"That's a good, Yorie. You are a good girl."

Blood gushes from a gash on Shizue's right arm at her elbow. A main artery is cut. She gathers Yorie into the injured arm thinking the pressure of her daughter's body against the vein will ease the blood flow. Supporting herself with her other elbow, she pushes forward toward Toshio's screams.

Toshio's cries going unanswered, he screams louder. Wrenched from his mother's arms by the force of the explosion, he is more than 10 feet away.

Shizue crawls through the wreckage to the sound of her baby's cries and finds him buried under loose debris with only his legs visible. She digs Toshio out of the rubble. His head is bleeding severely. With each pump of his heart blood spurts from his many wounds. She carefully feels his skull, fearing it is crushed.

"*Get out!*" Shizue hears the voice again.

Yes. She must get out. But how? She can't crawl through the debris carrying two children.

The Obi! The Obi sash is still strapped on Yorie. The sash is the only clothing not ripped from their bodies by the explosion. They are all naked. Shizue removes the Obi and ties Yorie to her back. Now, she can hold Toshio in her arms and use her elbows to move. But, move where? Where is safety? Which way is out?

Shizue picks up Toshio with her injured arm, keeping pressure on the deep gash. Toshio screams and struggles to get away from her. He, too, doesn't recognize his mother. Neither Yorie nor Toshio will stop crying.

"Mother is here. Don't cry. Mother is here." Her repeated reassuring words, intended to dispel her children's fears, do little to ease Shizue's own simmering panic. She smells smoke. They must get out before the house bursts into flames.

She looks around. This way? That way? There is scarcely enough room to move beneath the floor beams. How can she escape the suffocating dust and smoke? How can she get her children to safety?

Yorie and Toshio continue to cry. Toshio continues to struggle, trying to break free of the monstrous being that has snatched him from his mother.

On the verge of panic, Shizue sees a sliver of light reflecting on the dusty darkness. Is it a kindling fire or a ray of sunlight from outside; a way out? She struggles through the rubble toward the glint of hope.

"Get out. Out. Out now!" She pushes herself beyond human limits guided and commanded by the hollow voice of her grandmother.

The ray of light widens as she squeezes through the rubble carrying Yorie on her back and Toshio with one arm, still struggling to get away from the monster.

The light guides her to the front of the house. There, standing open, intact, is the frame and door, free of debris, without a single glass pane broken.

Shizue crawls through the doorway, stumbles over the debris of the concrete wall that surrounded the home and out onto a dim, dusty, eerie, landscape. No one is outside. What has happened? Where are the people? She hears someone crying for help and finds a neighbor buried from the waist down in the rubble of her home. Shizue tries to pull her out, but can't. She tells the unfortunate woman she will find help.

Shizue looks around for assistance. There is none. Every house, every structure within view, all the way to the far side of the city, lies flat on the ground.

Reason tells Shizue there must be something left standing; somewhere to find help. She peers into the gloom searching for Hiroshima Castle. The magnificent, old structure, only half a mile away and will provide shelter and assistance. She looks to her left; to her right and turns around, but does not see it. She turns again. There is no castle. It too, is gone.

Now Shizue's world is truly gone. A beast without face, eyes, teeth, or claws; unleashed by an unknown power has transformed their once beautiful city into a smoldering wasteland.

There is only one thing Shizue can think to do; head for the barracks for help and pray Toshiyuki is there and alive. She tells the neighbor trapped under the debris of her home that she will send soldiers from the barracks to help her.

With little left to recognize around her, she heads out in the direction she believes she will find the barracks and comes face to face with a woman covered in blood and dirt.

"Ami?" Shizue stops.

The young mother holds her disemboweled baby boy. The newborn's innocent blood stains his mother's arms and clothing.

Ami stares vacantly at Shizue, rocking her baby.

"Ami..." Shizue says again.

"Yes," Ami smiles and begins to sing the Hawaiian lullaby Shizue taught her just days before.

"I can smile when it's raining, touch the warmth of the sun
I hear children laughing in this place that I love."

"Look," she whispers to Shizue. "He is asleep now. He loves your song." Ami giggles. "Yes. Just like you said he would."

"Ami..." Shizue can't find the words she wants to say. "Ami, I am going to the barracks for help. Come with me."

"Shhh! My baby is asleep." The young mother hums the gentle lullaby.

"Ami ... Ami ... Takeshi is dead. Put him down. There is nothing we can do for him. Come with me."

"Dead? My baby is not dead!" Ami flashes an angry glare at Shizue and rushes away.

There is nothing she can do to help Ami or her baby boy. Only then does Shizue remember the third child she carries. She holds her own babies tighter. The Army barracks ... she must get to the Army barracks.

Farther from the remains of her home are bodies of the dead and dying. One survivor reaches for her. The skin of his arms has slipped over his hands and dangles; held on only by fingernails.

139

Another victim scrambles over a flattened home. She digs through the rubble, frantically calling out the names of missing loved ones. Shizue can't see mothers, fathers, children; entire families trapped inside the wreckage.

Shizue's shock intensifies as she hears the names of children who played with Yorie only yesterday. She knows them. She knows their faces, their laughter ... their smiles. She knows they are gone.

Shizue runs as fast as she can, carrying her children. She runs barefoot, over hot melted glass and splintered debris.

One by one, smoldering ruins begin to burn. Without help, those trapped in the rubble will burn **alive**.

"Leave me!" someone screams. "Run. Get away, before you die too!"

Shizue runs. Her children are alive. She must live. She must run.

"Toshiyuki," she whispers. The sound of her husband's name propels her forward.

Suddenly, at the railroad overpass, Shizue stops running. On the ground is a military cap. It looks like Toshiyuki's. Is it... her heart pounds. Is it Toshiyuki's cap? She moves closer. Beyond the cap, in the ditch, she sees a body.

Shizue stumbles toward the sprawled remains. Skin and clothes are charred black. There is little left to recognize.

"It is not Toshiyuki. This is not your husband," a voice whispers in her head. She turns to escape the horror and a glint catches her eye. There is a ring on the right hand of the charred remains. Toshiyuki left home this morning wearing a ruby ring given to him by his grandmother.

"Toshiyuki! No, Toshiyuki!"

Shizue drops to her knees and slumps beside the body she believes is her dead husband. She cannot hold back the tears. She weeps for her loss of hope. She weeps for the future of her children.

"Mommy…" Toshio, who has finally recognized his mother and stopped crying, pulls her hair.

Shizue's despair blocks her son's voice.

Toshio pulls harder. "Chichi iya" (Papa, no)."

"What?" Shizue lifts her head. "Toshio? What did you say?"

"Papa no."

"No? This isn't daddy?"

Toshio shakes his head.

How could her baby know?

Shizue scrapes her knees, scrambling to get up onto her feet. Hope rises in her breast. She can make it. She will make it. The barracks isn't so far away now.

A half mile away, Toshiyuki does what he can to save his men and others who live nearby. Sitting upon his horse, he directs the soldiers in their rescue and survival efforts. His uniform has now completely disintegrated and fallen off. Nothing is left on the Major's body except white underwear, his sword and revolver.

In the mix of civilian and military survivors, he sees a woman being helped along by the two soldiers sent to find his family. The woman's clothing is ripped and stained with dark blood. She is barefooted. Her face is covered with blood and dirt. An Obi sash holds a child onto her back. The child on her back has little clothing left on. She is bloody; as is the baby the woman carries in her arms. Toshiyuki looks closer. The woman is bleeding from cuts on her forehead. Fresh and black, dried blood mixed with dirt make her face unidentifiable, but Toshiyuki recognizes the Nekomoto family crest on the sash. The soldiers sent out to help his family had found Shizue and the children on the road along the way.

"Shizue?" Toshiyuki shouts. "Is that you?"

141

"Yes! Yes!"

Toshiyuki leaps down from his horse.

"Papa. Papa," Toshio reaches for his daddy.

Toshiyuki scoops his wounded child into his arms.

Shizue has a gash on her forehead and a serious laceration on her arm inflicted by a nail. Toshio's head is bleeding. Yorie, strapped to her mother's back, cries softly. She has a gash on the back of one thigh and many cuts and abrasions on her back.

"Our children are hurt! Help them, Toshiyuki! Help our babies!"

Toshiyuki calls the only active company medic and orders him to attend to his family. Immediately! He orders another soldier to look for clothing for Shizue.

"Sir, there are only uniforms," informs the soldier.

"Then put her in uniform."

"Wait," says Shizue. She tells Toshiyuki about the neighbor buried in the rubble of her home. The two soldiers who brought Shizue to the barracks go back into the city. They will find the home too late. The woman's burned body lies among ashes and smoldering timbers.

The medic wraps his jacket around Shizue, and leads her, with the children, to Major Nekomoto's temporary shack, where they receive medical treatment, food, water, and clothing.

Toshiyuki remains to give additional orders to his men before going to his shack. He takes Shizue into his arms. "I thought you and the children were dead." His words mix with tears streaming down his face. "You make me proud. You got babies out. You saved our family."

"No. It was not me. Toshio saved us. We wouldn't be here if not for Toshio."

"Toshio?"

Shizue sniffs back tears. "On the road are many dead. At the overpass, I saw a body ... burned ... dead. Near him I saw a cap like yours. I thought this man was you. My spirit abandoned me. I felt so tired I wanted to die and be with you and mother and Obaasan. I collapsed and as I cried, Toshio said, 'Chichi iya' (Papa no)! I looked into his eyes and I believed him. Strength returned to me. We are alive because of our son. He knew the body by the ditch was not his daddy."

"My son," Toshiyuki's voice brims over with pride and amazement. "My son saved my family." He holds Toshio tenderly and whispers, "One day you will be a great man. You will be the man that I am not."

Twenty minutes after the bomb exploded, the smoldering debris of Hiroshima City had burst into flames.

Shizue realizes if she had not awakened when she did; if her grandmother's voice had not given her strength; if the light, where there was no light, had not guided her out of the debris, she and her babies would have burned alive. She calls their escape ... a miracle.

143

CHAPTER THIRTEEN

The Day After Never

The rubble of Hiroshima burns. Many people remain trapped and burn, dead or alive. If the fires had not started more than half of the trapped could have been saved.

Spontaneous fires spread rapidly toward the Army barracks. If they are not stopped, flames will destroy the little that is left over from the bomb.

Despite the valiant efforts of surviving soldiers and civilians, people at greater distances from the bomb's hypocenter remain trapped under collapsed buildings. The fire danger increasing, Major Nekomoto orders the group of men gathering food and supplies, together with the group helping civilians, to stop what they are doing and fight the approaching flames.

The soldiers create firebreaks between the burning city and the barracks. There is no heavy equipment available. Soldiers and other survivors push collapsed structures toward the burning debris with make-shift tools to form a sweeping open area. This strategy stops the fire from reaching the old log structure. A great shout arises from the soldiers when the building is saved from destruction.

At approximately 1030, the two sergeants who were on errand to the 5th Army Headquarters return to the regiment safely. One reports that at the time of the blast, he was in the toilet shack behind the Headquarters main building. The sudden blast collapsed the shack on top of him. He pushed the lightweight remains of the outhouse away and saw the main building had been destroyed. It began to burn almost immediately. There was no one else in sight. Alone and frightened, he returned to his barracks.

The other sergeant, on his way to 5th Army Headquarters at the time of the explosion, survived relatively uninjured, also. The Japan Railroad Hospital, a concrete building, protected him from the deadly force of the blast.

From these two sergeants, Major Nekomoto learns more details about the devastation inflicted on the 5th Army and on Hiroshima City.

At 0815 when the bomb exploded, the General of the 5th Army was conducting a staff meeting inside a one-meter thick concrete encased shelter. On this uncommonly humid morning, the door had been left open. The door faced the hypocenter of the blast. Pressure from the explosion smashed the soldiers against the far wall, killing them instantly. The concrete shelter then collapsed on top of them.

Toshiyuki had not been able to make contact with the 5th Army Headquarters because headquarters no longer existed.

Throughout the expanse of the city, transportation and communications are cut off. From the scattered bits of word-of-mouth intelligence, the Major realizes the devastation brought by this one extraordinary bomb is beyond comprehension. No one in Japan knows it was an atomic bomb.

Over three-fourths of the city of Hiroshima sustained severe damage. The devastation extends from the south of Hijiyama, a small hill at the western end of the city, to the eastern end. The flat terrain of the area offered no protection from the explosion, except in the shadow of Hijiyama. The narrow rivers offered only limited protection from the ensuing firestorm.

There were no fire-fighting plans in place sufficient to deal with destruction of this scale. Hiroshima City had been preparing for incendiary bombs or an invasive attack, not a weapon as devastatingly powerful as "Little Boy." The nuclear blast destroyed all fire-fighting facilities. There is no electricity, no water pressure, and no water pumping stations.

With no way to fight the widespread, instantaneous fires, those who survived the explosion had rushed away from the flames to the river, for safety and to quench their agonizing thirst.

The two sergeants, on their way back to the barracks, witnessed an appalling sight. Thousands of dead and injured men, women, and children lay on the riverbanks, many writhing in agony. All were severely burned. Those few who were able to stand wandered about with hands stretched out in front of them to avoid contact with their bodies. They moved stiffly, like zombies, hands drooping at the end of outstretched arms, vacant unfocused eyes, faces frozen in agony.

Unknown to Hiroshima's survivors, the bomb dropped on their city is far from finished; its power continues to wield agony and death.

Four hours after the blast, there is another booming sound in the sky; thunder booms, followed by lightning strikes. Black rain and hail begins to fall; filled with dirt, dust, and radioactive particles sucked up by the explosion. It falls oily and sticky. The ice and rain are so heavy they sting the bodies of those out in the open. Survivors dehydrated and overwhelmed with thirst, look up and open their mouths to catch the rain drops. Thousands outside the city, who were not directly affected by the explosion, are caught in the deadly precipitation. As soon as the hail hits human flesh, skin

146

turns to purple and then to black blisters, spreading over the entire body. Many sicken and die from radiation poisoning.

The black rain and hail descends over the city and beyond. Toshiyuki, Shizue, Yorie, and Toshio are safe inside Toshiyuki's temporary shelter in the hills behind the barracks building.

Survival is the only task at hand.

With the firebreak protecting the old barracks building, soldiers return to constructing temporary shelters. The campsite, situated on a hill a short distance from the destroyed headquarters building, is completed by nightfall. All available food and supplies are hauled to the makeshift storage units. In front of the Major's temporary dwelling sits a great pile of pumpkins.

He moves his company to their temporary Headquarters.

After dining on a meager fare of pumpkin and potatoes, those in the company well enough to move go outside. They sit on the hilltop and watch helplessly as the once beautiful city of Hiroshima burns like Nero's Rome. The light is bright enough to read by. Mercifully, they are far enough away to not see or hear the human agony as flames consume the light of life.

Toshiyuki, being overcome with a deep weariness, moves away from the others to a spot near his shack, where Shizue and the children are sleeping.

He pulls his knees tight against his body and wraps his arms around them. As exhausted as he is, he cannot relax. Every nerve is on duty, ready to issue a new command to ensure survival.

His senses jump to full attention upon hearing footsteps behind him.

"Shizue! It's you. I thought you were asleep."

"Toshio and Yorie are asleep." Shizue, wearing the oversized uniform of a recruit, slides down beside her husband and leans her bandaged head against his shoulder.

"Are children okay?"

"They are afraid in this strange place. I told them a happy story, like at home, and they fell asleep." The fire of Hiroshima reflects in her brimming tears.

Night doesn't fall. The massive fire lights up the sky as it consumes the rubble of Hiroshima, burning as if it will never extinguish.

"We are lucky to be alive." Toshiyuki fumbles through his pockets for a pack of cigarettes. There is none. "In that fire our beloved people lie dead and dying. But, my family is saved. I cannot stop thanking God."

Surprise enhances the beauty of Shizue's face. Yes, the man beside her is Toshiyuki, her husband; yet he is not the same man who left their home this morning.

Shizue bows her head, "Yes. Our friends and neighbors ... Yorie's playmates ... are all gone. We should thank God. It is the honorable thing. But, I ... Toshiyuki ... you have never before spoken of thanking God. You tell me engineer's wife should think like 'two plus two is four, not five and God is 'five'. God makes no sense. Now you say we should thank God."

Toshiyuki turns away from her inquisitive gaze. "Do you think I am weak now?"

Shizue begins to realize what is happening in her husband's heart. She places her hand on top of his. "You do not grow weak. You grow strong. I am happy for this."

"Then I ... Shizue ... there is something I have not told you."
Toshiyuki picks a small rock up from the ground. He rolls it
between his palms. "Remember that odd feeling I tell you about this
morning?"

"Yes. Of course I remember."

"It was not a feeling only. I heard a voice as I walked to barracks.
The voice said my name. The voice say, *Toshiyuki be careful.*"

"Obaasan!" exclaims Shizue. "The voice was Grandmother's!"

"Yeah. I think so."

If it were not for the glow of Hiroshima burning, Toshiyuki
would have seen his wife glowing with hope for her husband and
their marriage; a new strong hope forged in the flames of disaster.

"Shizue, there was another time…"

Toshiyuki breathes in so deeply Shizue can feel the breath
shuddering within his chest. "Toshiyuki? Are you all right?"

"No. I am not all right, Shizue. This day has … I … I have kept
much from you … things and feelings I think make me weak."
Toshiyuki draws another strengthening breath. "When I was in field
hospital in Rabul, sick with malaria, I heard a voice. Voice tell me I
will live and see my family again." Toshiyuki sighs. The liberation of
his long kept secrets deflates him. He slumps forward.

"So, the smart engineer, son of Samurai, no longer thinks I am a
silly superstitious girl?"

Toshiyuki squeezes her hand and leans into Shizue. "You are not
a silly superstitious girl."

Shizue sighs. "I cannot tell you how much this means to me.
Now I can tell you something that happened before the bomb."

"What is it?" Toshiyuki asks.

"I saw a spirit light. Like the one I saw on the beach in Honolulu after my mother died. This morning the light came floating from the direction of our country home. It lit up our yard, circled the trees, and then faded away. I think this light was my mother's spirit. She and grandmother came to guide and protect us." Shizue cries softly.

Toshiyuki strokes her cheek and Shizue continues.

"And then, after the bomb, when the house collapsed, Obaasan's voice called my name and told me to get out. She gave me strength to save our children. I carried them toward a light I thought was shining in from outside, but there was no light outside. This light was Grandmother's spirit. She guided us from the house before it burned. She saved us. She saved you. We must always remember this wonderful thing."

"Yeah. We will remember," promises Toshiyuki.

Shizue nods. The yellow-orange light of fire devouring Hiroshima ripples over her tears, "Toshiyuki. Something moved. There..." she points, "over there in the shadows."

Toshiyuki moves cautiously to investigate the spot where Shizue pointed. There are shadowy shapes crawling toward the pile of pumpkins outside his shack. He draws his revolver.

"Don't shoot! Don't shoot!" Hungry soldiers, isolated from their companies, stand shakily to their feet.

"Soldiers! What you think, sneaking around? You stupid? You get bullet that way!"

The three soldiers back away. "Hai Sensei (Yes Sir). Sori (sorry), we are hungry."

Toshiyuki snaps his revolver back into its holster. "Take a pumpkin. Take two pumpkins. Ask, don't steal! Every head is crazy with fear. Don't you know? Shoot before think."

"Hai. Sori, Sensei! Arigatou (thank you)! Arigatou!"

Toshiyuki flops back down at his wife's side. "Shizue, there is much suffering and death in this place. It is not safe. You and children must go home to Furuichi tomorrow. Go early, before sun gets too hot. I send soldier to take you. Go sleep now. I stay here. I have much to think about."

"I cannot sleep. We are surrounded by the dead. Ghosts will be in my dreams. Spirits of the dead will follow us forever."

"You are always good and strong woman, Shizue. You must be strong now. Yorie and Toshio are sleeping. You must sleep. They will need you tomorrow. Come. I go with you."

"Yes. You are right. I will try to sleep."

Toshiyuki lifts Shizue to her feet. They walk, hand in hand, to a temporary shelter with the rubble of Hiroshima blazing in the distance.

"Shizue, remember how Grandmother tricked us to marry? I think she play another trick."

"What do you mean?"

Toshiyuki stops. He places both hands on Shizue's shoulders. "Do you believe when a person almost dies they ... change? I think I have changed, Shizue. Not so much ... not enough, maybe, but less stubborn ... less pride..." He pauses, sorting out his thoughts. "In the hospital at Rabul, when I had malaria, Obaasan's voice tell me something else. Voice say I will live and..." Toshiyuki shakes his head.

"What is it, dear? Please tell me?"

151

"Shizue ... voice tell me I will bring another child into world. I did not believe voice before, but now..."

Shizue shivers.

"Shizue? What's wrong? You okay?"

"Toshiyuki ... I am pregnant."

"You are ... a baby?"

"Yes. I am three months along. This morning our baby moved. I did not tell you I am carrying your child because..." Shizue closes her eyes, "because I could not forgive your betrayal with Mieko. I am sorry."

"No. It is my fault. I am stupid man. I hurt you. I am sorry. Maybe tomorrow ... maybe someday you will forgive me."

"No!" Shizue stiffens her spine and wipes away a tear. "I will not forgive you tomorrow. No."

"Yeah, I see." Toshiyuki releases her hand.

Shizue slips her hand back into his, "No, Toshiyuki. I forgive you now."

CHAPTER FOURTEEN

Morning Meets the Nightmare

Nuclear War, Day 2

The land of Hiroshima is dead. No dogs to bark. No cicada sings. No trees give shade from the intense August sun. Stark, unrestrained light shines on dreary dust and ashes. No mercy. No respite. Within the heat of summer, the blood of survivors flows like ice water. Victims give up to sorrow and injury. More die.

By mid-morning, the heat is already unbearable. Shizue changes her plan to leave for the country. She will leave after sundown, in the cooler hours. The children will fare better then. They will also be spared the searing visions of carnage.

Toshiyuki agrees to the change of plan and leaves camp with two officers and a couple of soldiers to survey the damage inflicted on Hiroshima. They will offer what help they can to survivors.

The oppressive smell of burned and decaying flesh fills the air. Hundreds of corpses lay twisted and scattered about. Some bodies have swollen beyond recognition. Others are so dehydrated they appear mummified.

The five soldiers, unaware of the type of bomb dropped on Hiroshima, are shocked by the victims' extensive burns.

They trudge through the debris choked streets. Less than 24 hours ago, these streets connected a thriving city. Thousands of dwellings and shops that yesterday crowded together filled with friends and neighbors are destroyed. Some still burn. Others are only smoking ashes. They come across a burned out streetcar packed with human skeletal remains.

Distorted, scorched frames of concrete buildings stand as mute sentinels; witnesses to the worst devastation by the hand of man in the history of the world.

"Wait!" The Major comes to an abrupt stop, as if a cold hand slapped his face. Only now does he recall the woman trapped under her collapsed home and the little girl, Chiyo, he promised to send help.

"This way," he shouts to the others with him. "Follow me!"

He runs to the place where he thinks the house stood. The charred body of a woman lies in smoldering ashes. There is no sign of the little girl.

The mother's face and the face of her daughter flash and sear into Toshiyuki's mind. He had forgotten them. He will never know if the child lived.

The group of soldiers continues their assessment of the destruction.

Reaching the railroad overpass where Major Nekomoto caught the force of the blast, they look around for potatoes that had been planted on the embankment. There are no potato patches, only scorched earth.

Nearby, a gutted, derailed train burns. Railroad ties on the bridge are destroyed, leaving twisted rails dangling.

The men set out to find Toshiyuki's house on Nishi Hakushima Street.

The high concrete walls once surrounding the home are rubble. The house is burned to lumpy ashes. Trees in the yard, even the bomb shelter are consumed. The Major stomps out a small fire.

The skeleton of Toshiyuki's bike lay burned and contorted by the tremendous heat.

Toshiyuki is about to abandon his search for a few possessions, when he notices a small bucket sitting upon remains of the bathroom floor. Toshio's soiled diapers are still in it, waiting to be washed.

The bucket is the only possession retrieved from the house.

From Nishi Hakushima Street, the men walk toward the center of the city. Major Nekomoto leads the way with a secret personal agenda. He will make sure he and his soldiers pass Mieko's boarding house.

The sun bears down mercilessly with no shade to give relief. The soldiers' uniforms are soaked with perspiration. The scorched earth reflects and magnifies the oppressive heat. A few lost souls wander about searching the remains of their homes for possessions or the bodies of their loved ones.

Major Nekomoto falls behind the group.

"Major!" One of the soldiers calls to him. "What is it you see? Have you found someone alive?"

"Say what?" Toshiyuki first replies, distracted. "No. No. Nothing," he shouts back. "Go on that way." He points. "I'll catch up."

Toshiyuki kicks a pile of charred wood. "No," he mutters to himself, "there is nothing here."

The boarding house is rubble. There is no Mieko screaming for help, or sobbing. There is no Mieko hunched over, rummaging through ashes for a small bit of memory; a tea cup, the cigarette lighter Toshiyuki left behind. Nothing.

The five soldiers soon abandon hope. The widespread, devastating results of the bomb have left nothing to inspect, little to salvage, and few survivors.

Major Nekomoto turns the expedition toward the central river to Aio-bashi Bridge, at the center of the attack.

The heavy steel bridge has been shoved by the force of the blast a meter upstream. The streetcar rails, although still connected, curve in the shape of the bridge's movement. The sides of the bridge are blown away leaving only a barren platform.

At the riverbank, the Major and his small team of soldiers observe the same horrible sights they have witnessed elsewhere, now multiplied many times. The number of burned bodies is so overwhelming, so unfathomable; the vision before their eyes distorts the soldiers' sense of reality. The bodies of their countrymen no longer resemble anything human. Their corpses look like baked brown potatoes scattered across a dusty field.

The people who survived the initial firestorm, burned and consumed by thirst, headed for the river, where they believed they would find relief and safety. Some never made it to the water. They stare with vacant, dull eyes; their arms stretched out toward the river, reaching for life. All are nearly naked; their skin blackened, showing raw pink where dark clothing burned away taking seared flesh with it. Other burn victims made it to the water and jumped in, only to be boiled alive.

Dead fish by the thousands float belly up in the water. A few, barely alive, move sluggishly amongst the corpses. Their flesh is ghastly white in contrast to the black, bloated human bodies.

The soldiers wade into the water, push aside the dead and retrieve what fish they can catch with their hands and caps. The dying fish are half cooked. Their spines are as white as their underbellies.

In trance-like, staggered formation, the soldiers return to their camp. They clean the fish and add them to their meager supplies.

Sometime around noon, Dr. Yoshida, head of the Hiroshima Railroad Hospital, arrives at the camp to ask for assistance. His hospital, far enough away to survive the blast and the ensuing fire, now overflows with wounded and dying patients. Every room is filled to the limit, but with more bedding, he can make use of the halls and basement.

Major Nekomoto sends men to the hospital with all the supplies they can spare.

An hour later, Toshiyuki rides out on horseback to inspect the perimeters of the temporary camp.

"Stop! Wait! Wait! Stop!"

Toshiyuki reins his horse toward the frantic voice.

"Son!" It is Shunichi, Toshiyuki's father, drenched with perspiration and out of breath. "You are alive! We heard..." he gulps in air. "We heard the explosion. We saw the explosion cloud. Son! I'm sorry. I'm sorry I said you would all die! Forgive me! It is a miracle! It..." Shunichi's forehead furrows as he realizes his joy is perhaps premature. "Shizue? Yorie? Toshio? Are my grandchildren ... are they..."

"Father! You should not have come."

"What are you saying? Shizue? The children? Are they...?" Shunichi braces for devastating news.

"Alive. They are wounded, but alive at shelter. I take you there."

Shunichi jogs alongside Toshiyuki's horse. He looks over his shoulder at the smoldering ruins. "I can't believe what my eyes are

157

seeing, Son. I can't believe how lucky you are to be alive. What did this?"

"Yeah. We are lucky to be alive. Nobody knows what kind of bomb did this. It was a special one, just like rumors said."

Shunichi tells his son that before making his way to the barracks, he had first gone to their house.

"Look," says Shunichi. He holds up a tea kettle. "I found this in the kitchen area and brought it with me. It was the only thing I could recover".

Fortunately, Shunichi did not dig up the rubble searching for other valuables. Many people who came to the city looking for their loved ones possessions inhaled radiation gas, became sick and died.

Toshiyuki pulls his horse to a stop. "Father, it is not safe here. You..." He points at his father's shirt. "There is blood on you. Are you injured?"

"No ... I mean, yes ... it is blood ... but, not mine. Along the way were thousands of people escaping the city. It is their blood. They begged me for water. I let them drink from my canteen. 'Thank you,' they said. And son ... they drank and collapsed as if dead. I don't know what happened to them. I stopped no longer when they called to me. Water did not help them. I only wanted to find my family."

"How is family at home?"

"Okay. No one is injured. The bomb shook everything. The windows facing the city were blown out. But, house is not seriously damaged."

"Is Furuichi damaged?"

"Not much. Many wounded go there for help. They tell us how bad the bomb was. They tell us everybody in city is dead. No one is left alive, they say. They tell us everyone who survived has left. I had to come look for you. The family begged me not to, but I had to know if you were alive."

"Father, after you see family, you must go back to Furuichi. Take Shizue and the children with you. I will send soldiers along to protect you."

"Yes son. I will do as you say."

That evening Shunichi, Shizue, and the children leave for Furuichi. Their journey is sad, but quiet and uneventful. They arrive at home safely.

Safe, however, is not how they feel.

Nuclear War, Day 3

Major Nekomoto receives a message from the newly established 5th Army Headquarters. Officers and staff are being rushed in from Tokyo to reestablish the destroyed command post in Hiroshima. All personnel receive orders to assemble at the former 5th Army site by noon.

At the meeting, the Major and his officers are finally given the details about the unbelievably devastating single bomb dropped on Hiroshima. It is called an Atomic bomb and only the United States has it.

Because the effects of nuclear radiation are still unknown, no one understands the increased ill effects of staying in the radioactive area. They immediately began working to restore the city's infrastructure.

The Major's orders are to see to the repair of the city's roads and bridges. Help from outside is nearing and access to the city is needed.

The first priority is to clear all the main roads of debris and bodies. It is an overwhelming and gruesome task. Every able-bodied man is required, including officers.

The soldiers use shovels and pitchforks, whatever makeshift tools they can find, to load corpses into the back of trucks. When the prongs of pitchforks penetrate swollen bodies, fluids spatter out and ooze onto the ground. The soldiers struggle to load the rotting torsos into truck beds as arms, legs, and heads separate and fall off. The dead occasionally groan or sigh eerily as gasses pass through vocal cords. The stench is unbearable and unforgettable.

The dead are hauled to the river bank, piled into mounds, doused with fuel and cremated.

After the first exhausting day, an important communique arrives from the Chief of the Military Police in Hiroshima City. At the time of the blast a number of American prisoners of war were being held in the city. They have utterly vanished. No bodies were left behind. They are simply gone.

Toshiyuki gets more information from a school classmate. Hiroshi Yanagida, a warrant officer in the Japanese Military Police had been in charge of the American POWs, twenty-two men and one woman. These pilots, navigators, and gunners, captured when their planes were shot down, died instantly, vaporized by the explosion. Only one young man buried in the wreckage, somehow survived. Not for long. He was assaulted, beaten, and killed by angry Japanese survivors.

Warrant Officer Yanagida was in the basement of his office building when the bomb hit and thereby escaped injury.

Nuclear War, Day 4

Shortly after 11a.m., on August 9, 1945, the terror that struck Hiroshima City strikes again. Two hundred and sixty-one miles away, Hiroshima's sister city, Nagasaki is destroyed by a second atomic bomb.

The nature of war and future of the planet are forever changed.

CHAPTER FIFTEEN

The Field Hospital at Hesaka

Nuclear War, Day 5

Having heard nothing of Colonel Kubota's fate, Major Nekomoto leaves his soldiers in Hiroshima to search for his friend and commanding officer.

Although Toshiyuki is fully aware the Colonel told Shizue of his indiscretion with Mieko, he knows his friend did this with the best of intentions. He and the Colonel have not spoken of the incident, nor will they.

Toshiyuki journeys on foot to a temporary field hospital established in the nearby village of Hesaka, two miles north of Hiroshima. Hesaka, protected from the direct blast by a mountain and therefore relatively undamaged, is now the site of the field hospital.

Hundreds of victims of the nuclear attack on Hiroshima City arrive daily; walking, limping, crawling, and carried on improvised stretchers. The small farming community of Hesaka is soon overwhelmed and spilling over with the injured and the dying. They are housed in homes, barns, chicken coops, any roofed structure. When all the buildings are full, they lie on cool grass, under bridges and trees; anywhere they can find shelter from the sun's radiant heat. Groans of the wounded and dying, punctuated by the cries of children, charge the air.

The nauseating stench of burned human flesh replaces the once delightful countryside fragrances of flower blossoms and hay. The smells of decay and cremation will remain in the memory of the survivors forever.

Trees line the winding road to the village. Beneath their canopy of branches, the emaciated, dehydrated victims of the flames of Hiroshima wait for help. Wounded and dying victims appear to wear hardened masks bearing no expression. Occasional groans of pain, sorrow, and despair rise from deep within and escape through blistered, thirsty lips.

They call out to Toshiyuki.

"Help me."

"I burn. Please ... help me."

"Water ... do you have water?"

They reach for him as though he is an ancient healer.

Struggling to clear his expression of the horror and distress he feels, Toshiyuki gives a sip of water, here and there. For many, the swallow will be their last.

He asks those who are strong enough to speak, "Where are the people in charge? Where are the doctors and medics?"

"I don't know, Sir," answers an old man holding a dirty rag over an eye injury. "No one knows."

"We have waited for days. My leg is broken, but no doctors are here."

"There are no doctors. We walked many miles for help, but we have come only to die."

Toshiyuki's canteen is empty. He can no longer supply even a sip of relief.

Finally, he locates the main tent of the field hospital. There is no one in military uniform. Villagers are doing what they can to help the refugees.

"Where are officers in charge? Where are the doctors and medics?"

"We don't know, sir. Soldiers brought victims to our homes, and then they left. We try to ease the suffering of the wounded, but most die. The dead must be cremated immediately because of the awful smell. We don't know who the dead are, so we put handfuls of ashes in small boxes, stacked on the table there. Families who come looking for someone and can't find them, take a box home … any box … for the shrine of their loved one … to honor them. A box of ashes is all they have."

"I look for my friend, Colonel Kubota. Do you…"

"Sir … if you want to find your friend, all you can do is search among the people. If you do not find him, you may take a box of ashes."

Toshiyuki searches the village, home to home, barn to barn, shack to shack. An hour into his quest, he wonders if perhaps he will return to Hiroshima with a box of ashes.

With few buildings left to search, he approaches another home. From the doorway, he hears a familiar, high pitched voice reciting a Buddhist prayer for mercy. It is Mrs. Kubota. She is surrounded by bodies, injured and dying, suffering, emitting sounds of agony that should not be heard in any world.

Lying on a straw mat next to her is the Colonel. His arms stretch stiff alongside his body. His eyes are open, but unresponsive. Water and puss ooze from burned flesh. The skin of his face, lips, chest, and abdomen have melted away. From the waist up his body is red, raw meat.

Toshiyuki would have passed by without recognizing his friend had Mrs. Kubota not been by his side, fanning the heat and flies away from his horrific wounds.

"Mrs. Kubota … Colonel, at last I find you." Toshiyuki's friend does not respond. There is no sign of recognition or awareness even to pain.

"Ah! Major Nekomoto!" Mrs. Kubota bows to Toshiyuki. "It is wonderful to see you. Are you injured?"

"No. I am okay. I come here looking for Colonel."

"Thank you! Thank you so much."

"How are you?" Toshiyuki sees no visible wounds on the Colonel's wife. Mrs. Kubota, never the epitome of health, is skinny thin, with a permanent harsh expression.

"Well enough. I am well enough to care for my Colonel."

"How is he?" the Major asks, although he can plainly see his friend's condition.

"Worse. Each day he grows weaker. He does not speak or move. He only stares up at the ceiling."

"How did you and the Colonel escape the blast?"

Mrs. Kubota recounts their terrifying experience.

Standing at the window in an upstairs room of their home, Colonel Kubota caught the radiating blast of the bomb on his naked upper body. He and his wife were buried under collapsing walls, but managed to crawl out of the rubble minutes before the house caught fire. They fled to the northern part of the city toward the river where they thought they would be safe.

Along the way, Colonel Kubota felt a stinging sensation on his face and upper body. He applied boot grease, which he found on the street. Anything oily, he thought, would be good for his injury. They stayed the night in the cover of a bridge, waiting for help. The Colonel's burns became more painful. His face and body began to swell.

The next morning, they heard the military had opened a temporary field hospital. So, they came to the village to this farmer's house with other refugees.

They had been in Hesaka for four days when Toshiyuki found them.

"He moaned in pain for two days. Now, he makes no sound. He will soon be gone." Mrs. Kubota speaks matter-of-factly as though her sorrow is simply exhausted.

"Did the Colonel receive treatment?"

A young man, one of the mobile patients slides over, making a small space for the Major to sit.

"Thank you," says Toshiyuki.

"Arigatou." Mrs. Kubota bows to the young man. "No. We have seen no doctor or nurse. At first there were people with Red Cross bands. But they left. No one knows why or where. This is no hospital. It is a graveyard."

"This makes no sense." Beads of perspiration roll down Toshiyuki's face. He removes his cap. "Red Cross and the military put medical emergency preparations all around Hiroshima. Where are they? Where is medicine?"

"Maybe they are injured and suffering too."

"Yeah." Toshiyuki contemplates what will happen to his friend and all the other injured.

166

Mrs. Kubota sighs. "Everyone will die without treatment. And now there is more bad news. The owner of this house wants us to leave. He cannot stand the awful smells any longer. He is afraid the scent of death will stain the house and the spirits of the dead will haunt him forever. It is the same at all the other houses. They say we must go."

"They make you leave? But where? Where will you go?"

"I don't know. Our house burned to ashes. Our land is there, but I am not able to build even a shack. Friends and neighbors houses are also gone." Mrs. Kubota turns the fan on herself, for a moment. "My husband will not live long. I want him to die under a roof, not in an open field."

Toshiyuki wipes away perspiration and replaces his cap.

"Major, you say you are fine, but you don't look well to me," observes Mrs. Kubota.

"I am tired, but I am okay. Kubota-san..." Toshiyuki lifts and adjusts his cap again. "I know a place you and the Colonel can go."

"You know a place we can go? Yes, please."

"My house in Furuichi is only three miles away. There is teahouse in the garden with two rooms."

"A teahouse? Yes. Oh, yes. Thank you. Thank you. Yes, we will go. You are a true friend to my husband."

"Okay, then. We do that. I will come back with help to move you and the Colonel."

"Thank you. Thank you." Mrs. Kubota bows repeatedly.

Toshiyuki steps carefully around the suffering and dying as he leaves to make arrangements.

"Thank you," Mrs. Kubota stands and calls out to him, again. "Thank you!" Her shrill voice cuts through the groans of misery and the silence of dying spirits.

The Nekomoto Family 1916
Front row from left: Shunichi with son, Toshiyuki, and Tonoyo
Grandfather Nekomoto
Shizue with mother, Misao, and Waichi with Kiyoto

Toshiyuki and Mother, Tonoyo Nekomoto 1917

Toshiyuki Nekomoto in Sanyo Middle School uniform
1930

Toshiyuki, in Sanyo Middle School uniform
with Uncle Akira Sekishiro
Miyajima Shrine, Hiroshima, Japan
1930's

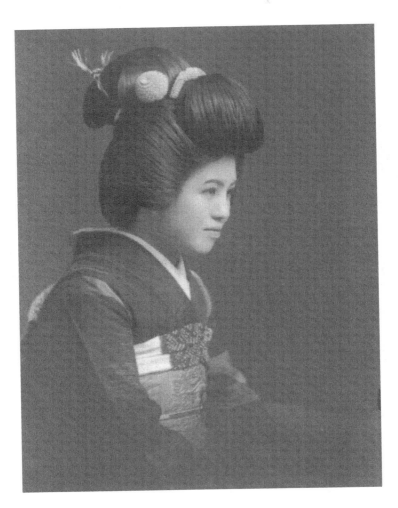

Shizue Nekomoto
Age 20
1934

American-Japanese Student Conference
Stanford University, Palo Alto, California
1937

Toshiyuki reporting on his trip to the
American-Japanese Student Conference
Stanford University, Palo Alto, California
1937

Toshiyuki Nekomoto
Standing near barracks building
1940

Wedding photo of Toshiyuki and Shizue
January 15, 1942

2nd Lt. Toshiyuki Nekomoto
Singapore, 1942

Drawing of Shunichi Nekomoto (left) during internment
Lordsburg Justice Camp, New Mexico
1942

Shizue and Yorie
Furuichi, Japan
1943

Shizue with daughter Yorie, and son Toshio
At home in Furuichi, Japan
Spring of 1945
(This is the only existing photograph of Toshio.)

Engineering Company Barracks, Hiroshima, Japan

Yorie, Toshiharu, and Shizue
Furuichi, Japan 1948
Family portrait with bear to make four

The Nekomoto/Kano Family 1950
Back row: Shunichi, Shizue, Kome, Waichi, and Toshiyuki
Front row: Yorie and Toshiharu
Miyajima Shrine, Hiroshima, Japan

Toshiharu Kano, age 6, in school uniform
April 5, 1952

Shizue, Toshiharu and Yorie
1952

Colonel Kubota after healing from radiation wounds

Monument built for British Soldiers
POW camp, Singapore

Friends Reuniting 1976
Middle: Geoffrey Adams, British Officer and Japanese POW
Toshiyuki on right

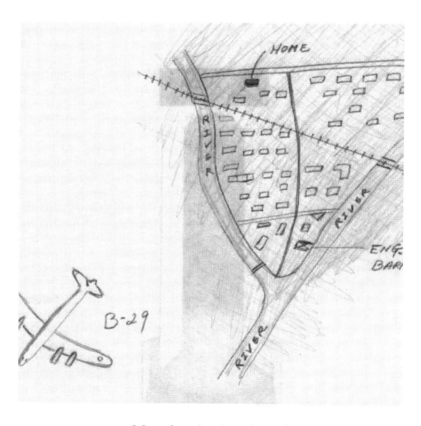

Map showing location of
Engineering barracks and Nekomoto home

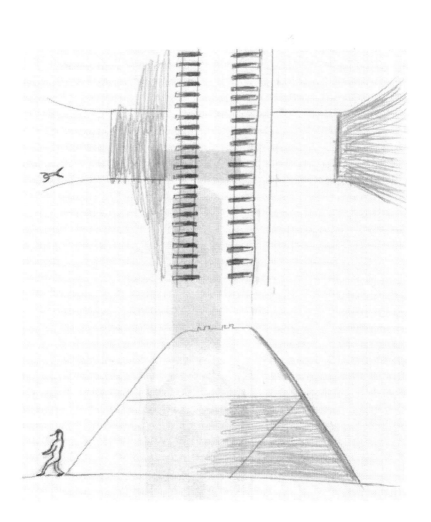

Two views of railroad overpass showing
Toshiyuki one step beyond embankment

東京都　　番号 27077

特　　別
被爆者健康手帳

氏名 加納 俊治

Front cover of
Atomic Victim Health Benefit Book
Issued to Toshiharu Kano

法 第2条に よる区分	㉑第1号・ 第2号 ・ 第3号 ・ 第4号
令 第6条に よる区分	㉑第1号・ 第2号 ・ 第3号
被爆の場所	広島（市）町 西旭町小学校裏 郡　　村 爆心地から　0.8　キロメートル
被爆直後の行動（おおむね2週間以内）	
被爆当時の外傷、熱傷の状況	
被爆当時の急性症状（おおむね6箇月以内）	
過去の健康状態とかかつた主な傷病名及び時期	

Page in Atomic Victim Health Benefit Book
recording Nekomoto address and distance
from hypocenter of bomb dropped on Hiroshima

CHAPTER SIXTEEN

Surrender of Dreams

Nuclear war, Day 6

The Colonel and Mrs. Kubota move into the teahouse of the Nekomoto mansion in Furuichi.

Toshiyuki spends a few precious hours with his forgiving wife, his children, and family, and then returns to devastated Hiroshima.

Nuclear war, Day 7, Day 8, Day 9

Living conditions in the aftermath of the bomb are dreadful and grow worse each day. The destruction and suffering is a nightmare from which no one can awaken. The huge death toll has left thousands of charred, mutilated corpses still unburied or cremated. More than one hundred thousand people injured are in unsanitary shelters.

Water supplies have been destroyed. Failing sewage systems promote a plague of flies and other pests. The filthy conditions cause an epidemic of infectious diseases and high fevers. Radiation burns and radiation sickness bring a steady increase in agony and death. Doctors, having no knowledge of radiation poisoning, attribute the victims' cause of death to a puzzling phenomenon they label "mysterious illness".

The enemy Hiroshima now faces is a silent killer, wielding a ruthless invisible power.

The morning of August 15th, transportation and communications are still not back to anywhere near normal. Major Nekomoto neither hears nor reads about what is going on in the outer world. Radio stations and broadcasts remain under control of the government. Only news considered beneficial to Japan is aired.

People coming into Hiroshima from Tokyo spread news learned from USO air-dropped leaflets. According to the leaflets, the Emperor and Liberal Japanese believe the Potsdam Declaration, a proclamation defining terms for Japanese surrender, is a very acceptable basis for defeat. The Emperor, the leaflets say, is considering the proclamation. Accepting it unconditionally will provide the continuance of the Imperial Household and rights of Sovereignty.

Toshiyuki does not trust the source. He is certain the USO leaflets contain only United States propaganda.

At noon on August 15, Major Nekomoto receives a message from the 5th Army Headquarters, instructing him to set up the camp radio with loud speakers. Then, gather his men and civilians for a special announcement from the Emperor, scheduled to air at 5:00 P.M.

The news is shocking. There will be an announcement from the Emperor to the public ... in person? Never in the history of Japan has such an event occurred. The Emperor is revered as divine. It is considered disloyal to look directly at him. His words and his decisions are unbreakable and sacred to all. The Emperor's voice is the voice of God.

Now, the people will hear the Divine voice?

Soldiers and civilians are upset. Many are suspicious. This announcement is sure to be something very important, if not devastating.

"Commander, do you think this special announcement will be that of surrender as the rumors say?" the Major's men ask.

Major Nekomoto shakes his head and shrugs. He knows nothing more than they know.

Toshiyuki's heart cannot imagine surrender. Once war is declared, the military demands continuance to the last. Japan has never surrendered. Surrender is disgraceful. Capture is equally disgraceful. Japanese people, military and civilian alike, die with the castle and their superiors. Death is the most loyal of acts.

He thinks perhaps the Emperor's announcement will be the last encouraging address in the people's struggle toward their honorable end ... death.

Questions grow as the day passes and the hour of the Emperor's announcement ... the hour of decision ... the hour of answers ... approaches.

"Is the rumor of surrender true?"

"What will happen to us?"

"Will we be slaves?"

"Will we be starved to death?"

"What will become of Japan?"

Toshiyuki is certain Japan will not accept defeat. Still, if by chance the Emperor announces a decision of surrender, the Major has a plan. He will escape to remote mountains where he will never again be disturbed.

Toshiyuki thinks, too, about dying. If the Emperor's message is one of encouragement to the people of Japan as they fight to their death, he doesn't want to be reborn as a cow, to be eaten, or a dog, to be kicked around, or as a human being in a world with endless conflict. His wish is to be a shell in the deepest part of the sea. There, in the depths of the ocean no turmoil in the upper world will affect him. He will rest in peace, forever.

As the appointed time for the Emperor's broadcast draws closer, military personnel and civilians gathers in front of the radio with static excitement and wrenching concern.

At 5:00 P.M., the Emperor's special announcement begins.

The Emperor's rescript as translated by Toshiyuki:

"After making a comprehensive study of the international situation with regard to the present condition of our Empire, I wish to stem the crisis with urgent action. Therefore, I wish to announce to you, my faithful subjects that I have ordered the Imperial Government to announce to the four countries, the United States of America, Great Britain, China, and the Soviet Russia, the acceptance of the Potsdam Declaration.

Originally, it was the will of my ancestors to promote the peoples' interests and share the happiness of the mutual prosperities of the world, which I solemnly obeyed. The reason for the declaration of war on the United States of America and Great Britain emerged from the will to maintain the independence of the Empire and the security of Eastern Asia. Originally, rejecting the sovereignty of other countries and invading their domain was not my desire. We have seen four years of hostilities. Despite the utmost efforts of each, the courageous fighting of my braves of Army and Navy, the endless endeavors of

197

my officials, and the sincere services of my people, the development of war situations were not favorable.

Also the international situations were of no advantage to us. Besides that, the enemy, by the usage of the new brutal bombs, continually killed and wounded many people. Destruction was beyond estimate. Furthermore, if we still continue to fight, finally it would not only lead to the downfall of our nation, but the demolition of the civilization of mankind.

Thus, with what could I retain the million lives of my beloved people and with what could I apologize to the spirit of my ancestors? This is the reason why I came to the conclusion to making the government accept the Potsdam Declaration.

I can only express my deepest regret to the allied countries that cooperated with our Empire to gain the liberation of Eastern Asia. My heart burst when considering the grief of the bereaved families of my faithful subjects who died in the battlefields, in their occupational posts, or in the air raids. I fell into deep sadness when it came to the promotion of welfare of those who were injured in the war and to those who lost their property and businesses in the disasters.

I can imagine, hereafter, my faithful subjects, the many difficulties of our Empire, which we will face and suffer, will no doubt be uncommon. I can surely feel your sadness, but I wish you would all, as time proceeds, bear the unendurable, stand the insufferable, and with it reclaim the undisturbed peace for the coming generations.

Now we are able to preserve our National Character, and by the trust in your sincerity, my faithful subjects, I will always be together with you. But if you are enraged with your passions and recklessly cause troubles; or dispute with each other and together disturb the situation; it would result in a mistake to the road of success and loss of the Faith of the world. Such I exceedingly warn you.

Instead of these, properly consolidate in a united effort with your descendants; believe in the imperishability of our sacred country; realize that our responsibilities are serious and the road is far; devote yourselves totally to future constructions; have a high moral sense; firm your purposes; swear to raise the essence of our country; and determine not to fall behind the advancement of the world. You, my faithful subjects, do well in the obedience to my will."

The Emperor's recorded voice, the voice of God, delivers his message to the people of Japan. The people listen intently, out of honor ... and confusion. The Emperor spoke in formal classical Japanese and made no direct reference to the surrender of Japan.

Few listeners present understand the message. The classical Japanese combined with the poor audio quality of the radio broadcast, create a buzz of whispers. Heads turn this way and that. Hands gesture their bewilderment. The future of Japan is still uncertain.

Finally, the radio announcer clarifies the Emperor's message.

Japan is surrendering!

The decision is made. The war will end with Japan's unconditional surrender.

Unconditional surrender! Two words the people of Japan have never heard before.

The eyes of everyone in attendance dart about with disbelief.

Men stand mute, with heads bowed. New worries etch their faces. They must begin a new life ... an unknown life ... with little or no resources.

Civilian women drop to their knees one by one, like balloons losing their air. They bend over and cover their faces. Their strength gone, tears mingle with mixed emotions. Their husband and sons fought and died for their country. They died for honor. They died for victory. Now, Japan has lost the war, but still … still they have their soil, their mountains, and rivers!

"The Lord is our shepherd. May he lead us to good green pastures." This is their prayer.

It is done.

Japan is in the hands of a strange foreign power. What will happen now?

Toshiyuki anticipates trouble. Fanatic officers will attempt to persuade their men to fight on and die with honor.

This is not Toshiyuki's choice. He and his men face another fate as demobilization and disarmament of the Japanese armed forces, at home and abroad begin immediately.

Each Japanese commander is ordered to report to the senior United States Army commander in his area. Military staff is required to produce locations of regiments, strength figures, status of demobilization, etc. They are directed to disarm all personnel found with weapons. Only Japanese police are permitted weapons; only such weapons considered necessary to maintain law and order.

Toshiyuki's military duties continue.

Nuclear war, Day 11

Toshiyuki's strength wanes. His joints ache. He feels tired; more tired each day. He thinks little of it until he loses his appetite and lethargy takes over. Military duties push him through the long hours. Within days from the onset of his mysterious but apparent illness, he is exhausted beyond recovery and unable to oversee his men.

He calls Dr. Yoshida requesting treatment.

Dr. Yoshida, a plump, elfish man with a nervous twitch in his left eye, listens to Toshiyuki's list of symptoms and nods after each is named.

"Yes." The doctor's tone of voice is solemn. "You are having the same troubles as most of my patients. This, we have learned is Genshibyo, the disease caused by what is called "radiation sickness". It comes from the atomic bomb."

Toshiyuki has radiation sickness in its first stage. He is devastated. After surviving his war duties and the atomic blast, he may still die miserably.

Treatment for the illness is only guesswork. Various methods are being tested and their effectiveness, or lack of it, recorded for posterity. So far nothing tried has been successful.

Dr. Yoshida has his own ideas. He believes the cause of this sickness is the decrease of white blood cells. The best chance at turning the destruction of these cells around is to build the blood back up to normal.

For a slim chance at survival, Toshiyuki must follow Dr. Yoshida's instructions precisely.

"Watch the hair on your head and eyebrows. If the sickness grows worse, the hair on your head will fall out. If the sickness continues to progress, the hair of your eyebrows will fall out. When this happens, there is less chance of surviving. Follow my instructions with no deviation ... *NO* deviation! Do you understand?"

Toshiyuki stares vacantly as the doctor chatters on.

"The treatment will be painful. You may want to die. Stop the treatment and you will die. If you want to live there can be no..." Dr. Yoshida folds his arms over his belly, "Major..."

"Yeah. Yeah. I hear you. No deviation."

"Not the slightest," the doctor stresses with a wag of his forefinger. "If you succumb to the weakness of will..."

"Yeah. I hear."

The doctor's severe words sink into Toshiyuki slowly, but fully. There are no options. He must obey to the letter or die.

Dr. Yoshida instructs his patient to stay in his shack. He must lie in bed very still to conserve all his remaining strength. Take lots of vitamins and at every meal ... this, he emphasizes, is critically important ... eat half a regular size raw onion, plus five cloves of raw garlic. Instead of water he must drink tea. There will be an injection administered daily. Dr. Yoshida will take care of the injection personally.

The first instruction on the doctor's list is easy to accomplish. Toshiyuki does not have the strength to move.

Two days later, Toshiyuki's lips begin to swell from diligently eating the raw onions and garlic. His eyes bulge. His nerves strain. With death as his only option, he holds fast to Dr. Yoshida's treatment.

Toshiyuki doesn't want Shizue to learn of his condition. Toshio has not recovered from his injuries. Her responsibilities are greater than ever before. He decides Shizue must be spared this worry.

Nuclear war, Day 12

Toshiyuki dispatches a soldier to Furuichi. The soldier informs Shizue that due to the bomb's vast area of devastation, the Major's responsibilities in Hiroshima continue to grow, requiring his constant attention day and night.

"It will be weeks … maybe months before Major Nekomoto can take time out for a visit." The lanky, young Private relays the message standing outside the main entrance to the mansion.

Shizue doesn't reply immediately. Exhaustion and worry for her children slows her reactions. As the soldier waits for her reply she wonders how the young man survived Hiroshima's destruction. She knows why his eyes appear to be swept bare of emotion.

The Private clasps his hands behind his back. When the Major's wife does not acknowledge the message delivered, he begins to fidget.

"Major Nekomoto says you should not worry…" the soldier swallows hard, as if a word has stuck in his throat.

"Thank you," replies Shizue. "Tell my husband hard times require hard decisions. He must do what duty requires of him."

"Yes Ma'am. Thank you, Ma'am." The messenger pivots on his heel and strides on extra-long legs toward his horse.

The young man, little more than a child, has not yet learned to lie with persuasion. Shizue watches, attentively, as he attempts an escape.

"Wait!" she calls out, "Come back. My husband has forgotten."

With disciplined reluctance, the boy soldier returns to the entrance.

"Forgotten, Ma'am?"

"Yes, my husband has forgotten the anniversary of our grandmother's death. He must return to Furuichi in three days for the memorial service."

"But, Ma'am I … I don't think…" The young man blinks repeatedly, clutching his cap in his hands.

"The arrangements are in order. A quick trip here and back is all it will require. Major Nekomoto will be angry if I fail to remind him. He will not dishonor Obaasan's memory to build bridges."

"Yes Ma'am."

The messenger prepares to mount his horse again when Shizue calls out for him a second time.

"Come back!"

The soldier returns. He stands rigid, holding his cap, now with trembling hands.

Shizue notices. "Are you ill?" she asks.

"No, Ma'am.

"But, you're hands are trembling."

He replaces his hat and clasps them behind his back again.

"Private, is there something Major Nekomoto does not want me to know?"

"No Ma'am," he bows, concealing his lie under downcast eyes. "Is that all, Ma'am? Is … is there anything more, Ma'am?"

"Yes…" Shizue steps closer to her husband's messenger. "Tell my husband this. Tell him I will speak to Obaasan in my prayers. She will understand his absence at the memorial service … duty before family. Tell him, also, I will journey to Hiroshima tomorrow for a short visit."

"But you…" the young man blinks frantically, before completely unraveling. "No, Ma'am … you can't, Ma'am!"

"What did you say?"

"Ma'am, what I mean is ... I mean, yes, I will tell him."

"Very well, you may go, now. I will keep you no longer."

The messenger does not go. He remains in place, staring at the ground.

"You may leave now," repeats Shizue, "and see to more pressing responsibilities."

"No! Ma'am! I mean ... you cannot go to Hiroshima to see the Major! He has the radiation sickness. He does not want you to know. He does not wish to burden you. Forgive me!"

"Radiation sickness..." Shizue repeats the monstrous words invading everyone's reality.

She falls silent. Her dark eyes stare into a secret void.

"Ma'am? Ma'am, what do you wish I do? Major Nekomoto trusted me to spare you worry. I cannot tell him that I have told you."

"Do not tell him," Shizue's eyelashes flutter. "I will not tell him. But I ... wait ... please ... wait here. I have something to give you ... something for my husband."

Shizue returns with a small package.

"Take this. An Obi sash is inside. Place it under my husband's bed."

"Under his bed ... but, what should I tell him?"

"Say nothing. You must do this in secret with the greatest of caution. When my husband recovers return the Obi to me."

"In secret? But, how? How can I..."

"You are a brave soldier. You will find a way. You must. Our grandmother's spirit is in this Obi. She saved my life. She saved the life of our children. With this Obi beneath Toshiyuki's bed, she will protect her beloved grandson and he will live."

"Yes, Ma'am, I will find a way to … yes … and I will return the Obi when Major Nekomoto recovers."

"I can put my trust in you? You will not fail me and your commander?"

"No, Ma'am. Yes, Ma'am, I will find a way."

"Soldier," Shizue places one hand over her heart, "my husband's life depends on you.

CHAPTER SEVENTEEN

The Miracle in Ashes

Nuclear War, Day 13 and Day 14

The full extent of suffering following the bombing of Hiroshima will never be adequately described. Initial shock turns to panic, then to loss of the ability to react to external stimuli. Survivors simply follow others until they find a safe place where they rest, sleep, receive care until their mental functions return, or die. They live in constant fear. They may die, that would be terrible. They may survive, that could be worse.

The survivors are numb, going through days and nights like living corpses. Nightmares increase in number and severity. Depression ensues, then anger and in some cases, denial of the event itself. The only way to live with the unthinkable is believe it never happened.

Every day victims struggle with indelible images of grotesque forms of death. Most wrestle with guilt for having lived through the tragedy. It is difficult to trust others and impossible to find meaning in what has happened to them. Nothing makes the suffering go away. The effects of the bomb are endless and mounting ... if that is even conceivable.

Toshiyuki's treatment continues. He checks his hair and eyebrows often. None falls out. Little by little, he feels strength returning.

Toshiyuki receives word from Furuichi that his son, Toshio, shows signs of radiation sickness. He immediately consults Dr. Yoshida.

"Your son is too young for the treatment of onions and garlic," Dr. Yoshida informs him in his half-whisper, mumbling fashion. "The injection too, would not be good for such a young child. Instruct your wife to keep him quiet, feed him small amounts throughout the day and let me know if his hair begins to fall out."

Shizue receives word from another soldier. She sends a message back to her husband that she will carefully follow the doctor's instructions. She also informs Toshiyuki that relatives in Hawaii are helping out as much as possible since becoming aware of the shocking situation in Japan. Shizue's family has shipped large boxes filled with sweaters, candies, blankets, sugar, powdered milk, fabrics, and other essential items to aid their survival.

Even with help from the outside world, the dismal aftermath of the bomb worsens day by day. Refugees from the fire-bombed cities of Tokyo and Osaka roam the countryside looking for a place to live.

"Please," they beg on their knees, "we have nowhere to go. No shelter. No food. Will you help us?"

Some of the more fortunate families help the homeless victims. Most, however, cannot bear the additional strain.

The few who can help the destitute victims are not enough. The Japanese government takes control. They order citizens who live in the countryside to take refugees into their homes. The number of refugees allocated to be placed in a home is determined by the number of tatamis each household contains; the larger the house, the more tatamis and the more refugees the families are ordered to take in.

The Nekomoto mansion is huge. It contains hundreds of tatamis. The family cannot bear the strain of the many refugees the government will order them to take in based on the number of mats.

Even without refugees, life is difficult and demanding. Toshiyuki is fighting for his life. Shizue is pregnant and caring for an already large family, plus two injured children. Now with orders from the government, her burdens and stress will increase.

There are currently 13 people in the home (not including Toshiyuki): Shunichi, Shizue, Yorie, Toshio, Toshiyuki's two younger sisters, Nishiyo and Shigemi, Colonel and Mrs. Kubota, the Kubota's adopted daughter, Yoko, and four girls from farming villages, who Shizue is training to cook and clean in preparation for marriage.

Colonel Kubota's brother and his wife were killed when the United States bombed Tokyo. Their daughter, Yoko, survived. He and Mrs. Kubota have taken her in.

The four young farm maids are most often more responsibility for Shizue than helpful. They require constant supervision. The situation is made worse by Toshiyuki's two spoiled sisters, Nishiyo and Shigemi, who are constantly calling the maids away from necessary chores to perform trivial tasks and errands.

"Tie this for me!"

"Stir my tea!"

"I am bored. Read to me."

"Take this note to the river and toss it into the water, so my wish will come true."

The sisters have an endless well of nonsensical ideas for the maids to entertain them.

Spoiled family, the lack of money, and never-ending chores are not Shizue's only concerns. Family members hear rumors that pregnant women exposed to the A-bomb near the hypocenter, are giving birth to deformed babies. Some are born with small bodies, small heads, and underdeveloped mental faculties; emotionally and intellectually disabled for life. That is, if the fetus survives at all.

As Shizue's pregnancy enters another trimester, she becomes increasingly drained, physically and mentally.

During this time of struggle, the government gives Japanese people the opportunity to change their surname. Family registers were completely destroyed by American attacks and will now be reconstructed on individual declarations.

Shunichi has been unhappy with the Nekomoto name for years. Neko means cat. Traditionally, Neko is associated with an evil. However, it is also linked to Lucky and Blessed. Japanese businessmen display Maneki-Neko, meaning welcoming cat, lucky cat, money cat or fortune cat, in their place of business expecting their business to prosper.

Shunichi, however, dislikes the association to cat, has found it embarrassing, and wishes to change the name to a more respectable one. He sends word by messenger asking Toshiyuki how he feels about choosing another name.

During his university days, Toshiyuki was the butt of jokes because of his last name, being called pussycat. Although the

Nekomoto name is no longer a source of embarrassment, he agrees to the change because it is his father's wish.

Nekomoto isn't the ancestral family name, anyway. It is a name adopted by their ancestors to escape the dangers of being Ronin; Samurai without a master.

The Nekomoto's Samurai ancestors, once Japan's highest social caste, the warrior nobility, after losing their master, were forced to flee their homes in search of a safe place to live. They found it necessary to protect themselves further by changing their names. Each displaced family took the first letter of Neko to be included in their name. Toshiyuki's and Shizue's ancestors became Nekomoto, as they were the leaders of the clan. Moto means the head of the household. Others came up with Nekonishi, Nekoda, Nekooki, and so on.

Shunichi reads an article in the newspaper about a wealthy and successful entrepreneur by the name of Kano. Kano means "to double your investment." Being the eternal businessman, he likes the positive meaning and the surname Nekomoto is changed to Kano.

Relatives in Hawaii are more than surprised by the name change. They are shocked. Nekomoto is a very distinguished name in Hawaii. They immediately assume Toshiyuki, known by all to be rebellious, is the one who wanted the change. Later, they learn Shunichi came up with the idea. They are told his reasons, but are still puzzled why he would do this.

Shizue has little interest in the name change or what relatives in Hawaii think about it. Every day she cooks and cleans, with limited assistance from the farm maids. No family member offers to help. It is not because they are physically unable, rather because they are simply unwilling. Shizue is baffled by their behavior. The family's survival depends on selflessness and cooperation.

Shizue shares her concerns with Toshiyuki's two sisters, Nishiyo and Shigemi. Her effort to open their eyes to the family's desperate situation, fails. They refuse to help with household chores. Shizue suggests another way for them to help the family and put their time to good use ... find a job.

The sisters are highly offended by the suggestion they work for a living. They march straight to their father, Shunichi. How dare a family member in Shizue's position tell them to consider the benefits of duty and honor to family over their own youthful needs.

"Shizue hates us, Father!" Nishiyo's stern expression is accented by an extended chin. "We do not like her tone of voice. She wishes to ruin our lives. If she has her way we will become old maids with calloused hands and weary faces. Our friends will laugh at us. Father, tell Shizue to leave us alone! She is a devil! Her nagging voice hurts our ears. She wants us to be unhappy so she can have leisure time!"

Shigemi stands nearby, but does not speak.

"Is this how you feel too, Shigemi?" Shunichi asks.

The timid younger sister, a true beauty in any country, looks back and forth from Nishiyo to her father. Shigemi is fond of Shizue, but her overbearing older sister, Nishiyo, has bullied her for as long as she can remember. She is conditioned to obey her elder sister and will not disrespect her now, even if she does not agree with all that Nishiyo says.

"Yes. It is true, Father. Shizue will not leave us alone."

"I see. I will speak with Shizue about her disrespect."

212

"Thank you, Father," Nishiyo's left eyebrow arches with a crooked, satisfied smile. When Shigemi does not follow Nishiyo's lead, she nudges her.

"Yes, Father. Thank you," says the obedient sister.

Shunichi finds Shizue upstairs in the midst of cleaning Toshio's head wounds. With no preface as to the condition of his grandson, he commands her to stop trying to force work on his daughters.

"Is this what Nishiyo and Shigemi have told you?"

"Are you suggesting my daughters are not truthful?"

"I would not, Ojisama (Uncle)," says Shizue using a respectful term for the head of household. "Perhaps Nishiyo and Shigemi misunderstood my intentions and my concerns. They are young women who will one day marry and have responsibilities. I only suggest now is a good time to learn, while they can learn at their leisure."

"My daughters' futures will not be like yours," Shunichi huffs. "Their life will not consist of performing menial chores. You will stop speaking to them of such trivial things. I do not want to hear of this again!"

"As you wish," Shizue nods.

"Do not think I am so deaf I do not hear defiance in your voice, Shizue. I will see to it that Toshiyuki hears about this ... the inappropriate things you say to his sisters and how you disrespect me behind his back."

Toshio wails in apparent pain.

"What are you doing to my grandson?"

"I am cleaning his wounds. He will be fine as soon as I am done."

"Fine? I can see he is not fine! My son should see this ... and your disgraceful behavior."

"I too wish Toshiyuki were here to see me."

"So ... you disrespect me and mock me. My son will hear of this. Discipline is not for children only!"

The head of the household has spoken. Shunichi stomps away.

Shizue is not sorry for anything she said, only for how it was received. She must learn not to beat her head against Shunichi's wall. Toshiyuki has warned her repeatedly to keep her mouth shut when it comes to his father. Nod. Agree. Then she is to tell him and he will settle whatever matter is at hand.

Yes, when Toshiyuki hears of this matter, he will not be happy.

And then, Shizue remembers the battle her husband is fighting; a battle far worse than her own. She will be happy to see him again, whether he is happy or unhappy.

"There. There, baby. Mother is finished."

Toshio's crying brings on labored breathing and exhaustion.

Shunichi is right about one thing. Toshio is not fine. While Shizue has been encouraged by Toshio's head injuries continuing to heal, he is eating less, sleeping more, and his stools are loose. Shizue does not want her father-in-law to know because she does not want Toshiyuki to hear of his son's decline. Not yet. She is doing everything as Dr. Yoshida instructed, but baby Toshio's overall health is not improving. She will wait, but not much longer before she tells her husband. For now, though, her husband needs time to recover from the radiation sickness without more worry on his mind.

Baby Toshio is not the same child as before the explosion. He wants Shizue to pick him up and carry him around, when before he struggled to escape her protection. In Shizue's best thoughts, her son only needs time to forget what happened and feel safe again. Behind her most shining assessment, however, is a deepening shadow of fear and foreboding loss.

She has little time to spare for Toshio's care. Soon, she will have less time. Refugees will be moving in. Although the government provides rations and each refugee family will be responsible for doing their own cooking, their presence in the home will certainly add more demands and responsibilities.

To control the number of refugees sent to their home, Shunichi lessens the number of mats by converting several tatami rooms to wooden floor rooms. One room, a meeting hall that holds over 200 people, is stripped of tatamis. The number of refugees assigned to the home would be desperately unmanageable without removing these tatamis and more.

As a result the government assigns five families to the Furuichi household. In addition to these, Colonel and Mrs. Kubota and their niece still live in the teahouse.

Without assistance from Toshiyuki's sisters, Shizue is desperate for help. She tries to teach the four maids the rules of housekeeping, but they do not follow her instructions. Shizue must re-do everything they attempt.

Between sports event broadcasts, Shunichi takes notice of the haphazard manner in accomplishing household responsibilities. That night when dinner is not ready on time, he scolds Shizue. "Why do you clean up after the maids? Who is the boss here? Why can't you control these young girls?"

"If I don't help the maids the housework will never be finished," Shizue is on hands and knees scrubbing the hall floor.

"The maids are lazy. I see them out chitchatting with Mrs. Kubota and the neighbors."

"Yes. Yes. I know. They are more trouble than children. It is easier this way."

"Look at me, Shizue. You will not treat me as if I am a bother. Disrespect! I will not tolerate it! Stop what you are doing. Now! I am hungry."

"I must finish this chore or the refugees will spread rumors about our lack of cleanliness. I will ask one of the maids to cook your meal."

"A maid? Cook? Hog slop tastes better than their meals!"

"Then dinner will be late."

"I will not put up with this! Send those girls away ... all of them. Send them home to their parents. Today. Find a good maid! One good maid."

In two weeks' time, Shizue goes through several other maids. One proves to be trustworthy. Her name is Narumi. Like the others, she comes from a farming community and her family does not want money for her services. She is one of many whose parents send their daughters to strangers' homes to learn housekeeping basics as part of marriage prerequisites.

Narumi's efforts are satisfactory. No one is as meticulous as Shizue, but the young maid lightens Shizue's load, giving her more time to look after Toshio and Yorie. As they work together, Shizue quietly and privately gives her new maid specific instructions regarding the demands of the two sisters, Nishiyo and Shigemi.

"When the sisters ask you to perform silly tasks for them, be polite. Tell them *yes*. Say you will get to it right away, as soon as you finish what you are doing. Then forget what they have demanded.

216

Act innocently obedient if they remind you. Their demands are always insignificant, 'stir my tea' 'listen to the birds for me' ... silly things so they can feel important and bossy. Both are scatter-brained. They forget quickly. Can you do this ... keep our secret?"

Narumi giggles. "Yes. I will do as you say."

With the loyal help of Narumi, Shizue can now squeeze in time to tend to the garden grounds nearest the house. In her pregnant condition and weakened health there is not much extra she can do. Her small efforts, such as picking pine straw out of the beautiful lichen, accomplish little to restore the grounds former beauty, but it is a labor of love and it gets her out of the house. She carries Toshio outside with her. Sunshine, bird songs, and wind rustling through the tops of bamboo trees are good for both mother and son.

Soon after this occurrence, the five refugee families move into the home by government order. There are now 22 people living in the home; family and refugees.

The daughter of one of the refugee couples, Hoshi, is bed ridden with a soft vertebrae disease that causes her body to twist and wobble like an octopus. She has a beautiful face. Although she is much older than Yorie, they become good friends and play all day with dolls her mother made. Shizue overhears Yorie call Hoshi "tako onna", Octopus Girl, as she tries to imitate her movements. The three year old didn't think about the name hurting her friend's feelings. After a gentle reprimand from Shizue, Yorie promises she will never say it again.

Along with the increased workload, an old problem gets worse. There are six bathrooms in the Furuichi mansion, but only one bathtub. The tub is the huge, round Go-emon style like those of the

Edo-era, about the 17th century. A wooden plank lid floats on top of the water. Bathers stand on the lid and their weight sinks it to the bottom of the tub, which comfortably holds six or seven adults.

With 12 families living under the same roof, a very complicated bathing time ordeal develops. They must take turns. No one, family or refugees, helps Shizue fill the huge tub with water.

From a well in the courtyard, she pumps the water by foot pedal. It takes over 200 pumps to fill the family size tub. Shizue's legs cramp from the strenuous effort it takes for a small, pregnant woman. She then carries wood to place beneath the Go-emon to heat the water. It takes hours to prepare hot water baths for everyone in the household.

The kitchen becomes a problem also. Too small now for the number of residents it serves, it is expanded to accommodate the demand. Still, even with the expansion, not everyone can fit in the kitchen to prepare meals. It becomes necessary to schedule feeding times.

The meals are scant. Family and refugees go to bed with gnawing, empty stomachs. Yoko is hungry all the time. Another refugee witnesses her eating grains from a broom made of milled wheat sticks.

Colonel Kubota's condition does not improve. Family and friends believe he will die at any hour.

Mrs. Kubota devotes herself tirelessly to the seemingly hopeless task of saving her husband. Somehow, she finds her second, third, and fourth wind. She refuses to accept the outcome that appears to all to be inevitable. She applies every method of treatment she thinks of herself or hears from others might be good for burns.

Neighbors try to dissuade her exhausting efforts. "You are injured yourself," one says to her. "You need rest. Do not waste your energy on a dying man."

"Maybe I cannot save him," replies Mrs. Kubota, "but, I must try to alleviate his suffering."

Colonel Kubota hangs on to life. His loyal wife continues her efforts. One by one, all methods turn out to be useless; nevertheless, she does not lose faith, diminish her efforts, or stop her ear piercing chanted prayers. Perhaps the Colonel will survive if only to silence his wife's shrill voice.

Mrs. Kubota, hearing a rumor that human ashes are good for burns, goes to the riverbank where the dead are cremated, picks through the ashes and gathers bones.

Neighbors see her rummaging through the ashes, "Mrs. Kubota, what are you doing?"

"I am going to put human bone ashes on my husband. I hear it is good for burns. I will grind the bones to powder and apply it. I don't know if it will work, but at least I will try."

"That is good," they say, with a pretend smile to give her hope. They don't think anything is going to help the Colonel.

When her basket is full, Mrs. Kubota carries the bones to the tea house, grinds them and carefully applies the powder to her husband's infected burns. Overnight the powdered bone ash dries and hardens. She then peels the crusted ash off the wounds and applies fresh powder to absorb more puss and poison from the burns. Colonel Kubota shows only slight movement of his eyes during the process of applying and removing the hardened ashes.

After two days of treatment, Mrs. Kubota is convinced the ashes are curing her husband. Her demeanor lightens. She tells everyone at the mansion and in the village that human bone ashes are curing her husband.

From then on, when she is not with her husband, she is at the riverbank gathering left over bones into a basket. Upon returning to the teahouse, she crushes the bones and repeats the process of pounding and grinding. Extra bone powder is stored in a large earthenware pot.

One morning, she finds her husband covered in hundreds of flies. They are all over him, on his face, arms, and chest. She swats and swishes them away, but they only keep returning.

The following morning Colonel Kubota is covered in thousands of squirming maggots busily consuming his dead tissue. His wife, not realizing the maggots are aiding her husband's recovery, removes the maggots one by one with tweezers. Her husband screams in pain and slaps at his wife, as he tries to fight her off. Mrs. Kubota does not relent.

On a Wednesday afternoon, as Shizue removes pine straw from the lichen beds, she hears Mrs. Kubota scolding her husband. "Oh, be quiet. Let me peel it off."

Colonel Kubota has recovered enough to complain about the pain when his wife peels off the crusted ashes. It is the first sign of recovery.

Her husband's steady, miraculous recovery gives Mrs. Kubota time to socialize with the refugees. It is then that unexpected changes come to the Nekomoto household. Mrs. Kubota, the devoted wife who works tirelessly to save her husband's life, is a troublemaker when her attention has less focus. She begins to bad-mouth Shizue and the family who took her family in.

One of the rumors she ignites labels Shizue a gold digger. In addition, she tells everyone that the family is not wealthy, as their fortune was lost due to business failure in Hawaii.

It is sadly true their fortune has been lost. Having everything taken by the United States government after the attack on Pearl Harbor is much worse and more heartbreaking than business failure.

Relatives living across the street fuel the malicious gossip. They have shown jealousy over Shunichi's success as a businessman for years. Now they spread their happiness over his misfortune, which they describe as failure.

The gossip started when Mrs. Kubota heard the story of Shizue being raised by her grandparents after abandonment by her father, Waichi. Mrs. Kubota then assumed Shizue manipulated the marriage to Toshiyuki so she could be the grand, fancy lady of the mansion. She is wrong of course, but the rumor spreads and others who hear it begin to look unfavorably toward Shizue. They become suspicious of her outwardly kind manner. They whisper behind her back, calculating selfish motives for the woman who works from dawn to dusk to provide shelter and care for her family and the refugees.

CHAPTER EIGHTEEN

Good News – Bad News

After weeks of fighting radiation sickness, Toshiyuki begins to regain some strength. His hair, eyebrows, and eyelashes have not fallen out. The healing continues and soon he is well on his way to recovery.

Nuclear War, Day 25

Toshiyuki receives word from Furuichi that Toshio's wounds have healed but his precious son is thin, weak, and his hair is falling out.

Having great faith in Dr. Yoshida's abilities, Toshiyuki immediately sends men to bring Toshio and Shizue to the temporary barracks in Hiroshima.

When Shizue arrives with Toshio, Toshiyuki stares at his emaciated baby boy. "He is skin and bones! What happened?"

"I don't know. His weight changed so quickly. I sent the message to you as soon as I grew concerned."

Toshiyuki and Shizue waste no time taking their baby boy to Dr. Yoshida. The doctor examines the child. He finds a severe case of diarrhea and blood in his stool. In addition to suffering from radiation sickness, Toshio's digestive system suffered damage when the explosive force of the bomb hurled him out of his mother's arms and across the room.

"How long has he been without nourishment?" Dr. Yoshida looks over his spectacles at Shizue.

"Without nourishment? No." replies Shizue. "Toshio has not been without nourishment," Shizue's tone reveals she takes offense to the physician's assumption. "He eats a little several times a day, every day."

"It has not been enough. Nurse! Bring food for the boy ... something soft and warm ...lukewarm."

Everyone takes turns trying to coax gruel into little Toshio. Each fails. Toshio lacks the strength to eat.

"What is happening? What happened to my baby?" Shizue bursts into tears. "He was not like this before we came."

"Mother ... stop crying or I must ask you to leave. You are distracting me and upsetting your baby. How far did you travel to get here?"

"I'm sorry," Shizue sniffs and catches her breath. "Twenty miles."

"A very long way for sick child."

Shizue covers her face.

"You must be strong. No one is to blame." Yoshida, who has aged years in a matter of weeks, speaks in his distinctive mumbling manner. "Radiation sickness changes nearly every rule of medicine we know."

Dr. Yoshida shares his own frustration. He dreads waking up in the morning, wondering how many patients died during the night. He treats Hiroshima's radiation victims by trial and error. He is literally working in darkness.

Dr. Yoshida admits Toshio to the hospital. He and Shizue stay in a makeshift room with no walls. Patients sleep on floors with

223

mosquito nets hanging around them to keep off the flies. The medical facility is so overcrowded there is no space to lie down. Shizue must sleep in a sitting position.

The conditions are so unfavorable to Toshio's recovery that Toshiyuki orders his men to build a shack beside the hospital for his wife and baby.

After a week of treatment from Dr. Yoshida, Toshio begins to show promising results. His diarrhea and internal bleeding stops. The physician is cautiously certain Toshiyuki and Shizue's baby boy will continue to improve. However, the road to complete recovery will be exhausting and very slow. It may take months.

Shizue stays by Toshio's side every moment possible. Toshiyuki has less time to spare. Together, they comfort Toshio ... afraid to hope too much.

Shizue gives Toshiyuki the good news that Colonel Kubota has recovered enough to complain when his wife removes the hardened bone powder.

Toshiyuki is strengthened by the news of his friend's grumpiness.

Nuclear War, Day 27

Sept. 2, 1945, Japan formally surrenders in a ceremony aboard the U.S.S. Missouri.

The war is over ... finally, really over.

Relief overwhelms Shizue. As soon as Toshio recovers, she and Toshiyuki will return home to Furuichi. There they will begin their lives again. They will have another chance at happiness.

Holding Toshio's hand, Shizue remembers sitting on the hill with Toshiyuki the night following the bombing of Hiroshima. Toshiyuki had told her he was sorry for his infidelity and the pain he caused her. He had spoken of spirit voices and their grandmother's role in their survival. He now believes in the protection of their ancestors and their love from beyond the grave.

Out of pain and suffering, life has given Toshiyuki and Shizue another chance at love.

Within hours of Shizue's exhilaration, bad news arrives by way of messenger. Toshiyuki will be among those put on trial for crimes against Prisoners of War.

World War II is over for some. For others it is not. Toshiyuki served in Singapore as commander of a prisoner of war camp. The actions of Toshiyuki and all others who had connections with POWs will now be confronted. A war criminal court is scheduled to be held in Singapore.

Immediately, the 5th Regiment Commander, Colonel Tamura is put in the cell of a ship and delivered to Singapore. Officers of his regiment are told to remain in Hiroshima and stand by. Every movement they make is reported to the local police. They can do nothing but wait for the result of their commander's trial and wonder what is going to happen to them.

Toshiyuki and the other ex-officers arrange a meeting to discuss and second guess their actions in Malay. At the time, it seemed they had done everything they could to honor the Bushido Code, the honorable way of treating prisoners of war. Had it been enough? Most thought, yes. But from the British soldiers' perspectives, would there be another less positive account?

Their concerns are understandable with the frightening prospect of being executed by hanging as war criminals.

Toshiyuki has more faith in their actions as officers than the others present. He reminds them how candidly he had spoken with the British POW Commander.

"If any of your men think they can escape by swimming the channel, they are welcome to try," he had told the British officer, Colonel Geoffrey Adams.

This casual attitude, plus the amount of freedom allowed the British soldiers, had surprised the commander.

Although this had been Toshiyuki's first and only experience with prisoners, his tactic worked and relieved tensions between soldiers at war.

Even in the circumstances of being a prisoner of war, the British soldiers did not lose their pride or abandon their gentlemen ship. They were obedient to commands, kept strict military regulations in their camps, and were very orderly. All the Japanese officers of the 5th Regiment respected the British war prisoners.

Toshiyuki visited each camp once a day. Although of lower rank than the camp commander Colonel Adams, the then Lieutenant Nekomoto received respect as a superior officer.

On one occasion, Colonel Adams invited Lieutenant Nekomoto to his room. He proudly shared pictures of his family and discussed each one as if the young Japanese soldier was a friend.

Toshiyuki reminds the officers awaiting judgement that in the crisis of war, although there had been many problems in the POW camps, most were successfully solved through cooperation and conciliation. He believes they all went above and beyond the requirements of their code of honor. He believes they exemplified humanity.

One officer disagrees, citing the incident of using the British soldiers as laborers.

There had been a lot of work required in the camps. Japanese Companies didn't commonly use prisoners as laborers because they couldn't spare men to control them. There was also the language barrier that made it difficult to communicate detailed jobs and work orders. Yet, despite these challenges, British officers wanted to send their men out on work details, partly to mitigate boredom and despair.

A meeting between Japanese and British Camp officers came up with a mutually beneficial solution.

The Japanese Companies could use more POWs as laborers if they were under the control of the British officers. The Japanese project officer would give the job order to the British officer and the British officer would instruct his men and have them work accordingly.

Toshiyuki does not think that using British prisoners for labor will become a problem as the British officers had cooperated fully.

"The enemy often turns," reminds another less optimistic officer.

"Yeah," says Toshiyuki, rolling a cigarette between his fingers, "but I think the British will not turn against us. Remember how they disliked eating so much rice. Even this complaint we not ignore."

The British were not used to eating rice as their main food as were the Japanese. They wanted wheat flour bread. Lt. Nekomoto requested wheat flour from the Headquarters Supply Office. The supply office denied the requisition. The British prisoners would just have to learn to eat rice.

With the requisition denied, Toshiyuki called the camp mess staff to discuss the matter. Together, they decided to grind rice into flour for bread. The trial proved successful. Rice flour bread turned out to be rather good. Better than boiled rice, at least to the British.

The most difficult problem encountered with POW's involved clothing and boots. No replacements for worn out apparel were available from the Headquarters Supply Office. Each prisoner had two shirts, two pairs of shorts, two pairs of stockings, and one pair of boots. The only way for them to continue having adequate clothing and boots was to avoid wearing them out. To this end, Nekomoto suggested the POW Camps send their men out to work without shirts.

The camps agreed and the prisoners went out to work bare chested. This not only saved wear on clothing, but also gave the soldiers tanned bodies and made them look healthier.

One problem solved. Next, Nekomoto asked the Quartermaster for worn out tires that had been discarded and piled up in the yard. With the rubber the prisoners could make boot soles. The Quartermaster approved the request. It was a great way to get rid of useless tires.

The clothing and boot problem soon improved through efforts of the Australian Red Cross. Toshiyuki's company received a shipment for their prisoners of war. The boxes contained assorted canned foods, clothing, boots, and wide brimmed Australian hats. Thanks to the Red Cross, the regiment had a warehouse full of goods for their prisoners.

As for medical problems, skin diseases increased due to the shortage of bath water. To attack this problem, one stone killed two birds. By letting the POWs work without shirts, sunshine healed many of the skin disorders.

This worked for outer skin diseases, but not the areas under clothing. Chaffing was difficult to cure. The POWs discarded their traditional style underwear and used the Japanese soldier's loincloth type undergarment, a piece of cloth two feet long, about seven inches wide with straps sewn to both ends, like an apron only it is put on the back and tied in front. The hanging cloth end is brought to the front between the legs and pushed under the straps. The British POW's found this underclothing much more comfortable and easier to wash.

To treat subcutaneous skin diseases, patients lined up in front of medics sitting on chairs. With iodine and paintbrushes in hand, Japanese medics held the patient's male genital organ up with chopsticks and busily painted iodine on the rash. After having this sensitive area painted with alcohol based iodine, patients jumped up and fanned themselves frantically ... to the great amusement of the Japanese medics.

To relieve leisure time boredom, the British prisoners requested pianos for their recreation rooms. Lieutenant Nekomoto located and gathered damaged pianos from nearby villages. The innovative British soldiers took whatever parts were needed to assemble usable instruments.

It turned out there was always some expert for whatever the British prisoners of war needed or simply wanted.

Another British request became the biggest problem to solve. The POWs wanted to organize a search party to gather their dead left unburied in the nearby jungle.

Lt. Nekomoto sympathized and reported the request to his commander. The Commander also respected their sentiment and felt the petition should be granted.

"When in battle," said the Commander, "we are enemies, but after it is over, we are fellow human beings ... even friends."

Commander Tamura promised he would do his best to get permission from General Tomoyuki Yamashita, Commander-in-Chief of the Japanese Armed Forces. He went one step more, saying he would try to get permission to construct a monument for the British dead like the one under construction for the Japanese dead. He believed it would be fair and humane to do so.

The Commander spoke to General Yamashita about organizing a search party and also building a monument for the British dead. The General approved the permit for the search party without question. However, he denied the building of a British monument.

Commander Tamura, in support of the monument for the British dead, got into a hot discussion with General Yamashita.

After listening to Tamura's passionate arguments in favor of the monument, General Yamashita eventually conceded. The turning point in the argument came when the General realized the Japanese military could use this matter for propaganda purposes. He would make a film of the monument and give a grand write up to the news media, so the people, both locally in Singapore and in Japan, would appreciate and respect the hospitality of the Japanese military. Yamashita never missed a chance to promote his military agenda through "positive" propaganda.

For Toshiyuki's commander, the General's reasons for giving permission to build the British monument didn't matter. He was pleased with the outcome. The British POWs truly appreciated the commander's effort.

Toshiyuki, too, appreciated the 5th Regiment Commander Tamura. Tamura was a full colonel with the manner of a civilian rather than a professional soldier. His demeanor was that of a good old grandfather. Once a week he invited the POW officers to dinner at the Headquarters building. Toshiyuki attended the dinners as an interpreter.

Tamura enjoyed talking with the British officers about their civilian lives, their country, and their hobbies. Tamura's hobby was playing the bamboo flute, which he liked to show off after dinner. After the flute concert, the group enjoyed a Japanese movie.

After the Singapore project reached completion, the 5th Army Headquarters received orders to return to Japan. This was great news. The 5th Army was always in the front fighting the hardest battles. The soldiers turned in their equipment and arms. Everyone in the camp was happy, except the British Prisoners of War.

The Japanese troops, who treated the British with the greatest of respect and had become their friends, were returning to Japan. What would happen to the British prisoners without their care? Who was going to be in charge? Would they get the same good and fair treatment?

The British POWs asked Lt. Nekomoto to find out where they were going; back to Ft. Changi or to another place. Lt. Nekomoto learned the POWs were to be relocated to the Thai-Burma Railroad building site as soon as transportation could be arranged.

When the British learned their destination, all were worried, not only because of monsoons, hot, humid summers, and mosquitoes, but the hardships they were sure to endure.

The POWs were scheduled to be put on a train to Burma a week later. Farewell parties were held at the camps.

On the day the British left, the "enemy" soldiers who had become their friends saw them off at the station. The Japanese soldiers said farewell in broken English. In turn, they received words of appreciation in broken Japanese from the British soldiers.

The train pulled away with the unknown approaching steadily from every direction for both the British and the Japanese.

Now, with the surrender of Japan, for Toshiyuki and his fellow officers, it had come to this … waiting for news of their fate.

One officer, who has listened in silence to Toshiyuki's positive outlook on their situation, speaks out. "You have forgotten the temple we built, Shonan Jinjya, temple of the shining south. A good name, then, when our forces were successful in the war. We had the south in our hands. We had rubber and oil. Everything we needed. The war was going in our favor and soon Japan would be on top of the world. We did not expect to be here waiting for judgement … waiting to hear if we live or die!"

"Yes," agrees another. "Our victories made us drunk. There is a saying, don't crow too much over your enemy'. Japan did not obey this saying. We must prepare for the worst. A great thinker once said there are no facts, only interpretations."

The Japanese officers fall silent as another unknown, "perspective", may cost them their lives.

The officers can do nothing but wait. There will be weeks of fitful sleep and many days of worry.

Shunichi returns to Hiroshima to the hospital where Dr. Yoshida cares for the gravely ill Toshio. There are problems at home in Furuichi.

Nishiyo and Shigemi are annoyed and terribly unhappy. Shizue left them with all the household responsibilities; the care of family, the care of refugees, plus care of Yorie. Yorie wakes up screaming every night. She is more rambunctious and mischievous than ever. No one at home in Furuichi is getting adequate sleep.

The sisters believe their subordinate sister-in-law, Shizue, lounges in the big city of Hiroshima, receiving luxurious treatment. They refuse to continue the arrangement and insist on sending Yorie to Hiroshima. They will not care for the troublesome little girl any longer.

Toshiyuki and Shizue cannot believe the sisters are behaving so selfishly at such a time of crisis.

"Father ... you came here for this ... for sisters' petty grievance? You know how hard things are here. Sisters know this too. You told them, yeah?"

"I did not." Shunichi squares his shoulders. "Young ladies are full of dreams. They do not ask for much, only to be happy. They want to meet young men and get married. It will help no one to tell them about the suffering here in Hiroshima."

"Help no one?" Toshiyuki sweeps one hand toward Toshio. "Is your grandson no one?"

"Your sisters nag me constantly. I cannot hear the radio above their badgering. Do not question me. I have not come to ask your

233

permission. I am telling you what must be done. I will return with Yorie in one week. You must make arrangements!"

Toshiyuki and Shizue, stunned by the outrageous demand, discuss the matter privately.

"It is not safe here." Shizue's eyes cast back fear. She knows too well Shunichi intends to get his way. "Yorie must stay in Furuichi village. We cannot care for her and Toshio too."

Toshiyuki agrees, but sees no way out of granting his father's "request". If his sisters do not get their way, there will be no rest for anyone. Toshiyuki does not want to deny his father's wish and stir up more family trouble.

"No..." Shizue hesitates and then powers forward. "No. No, Toshiyuki, this is not a good place for our child. She is safe in Furuichi, in the family home. Talk to your father again. You must stand up to him. You must tell him we cannot do this. Shunichi is not a bad man ... only a broken man. When he understands fully, he will change his mind and not insist we do this. You must find a way to reach your father's heart."

"Father will not change his mind. We must agree. We have no choice."

"No!" Shizue exclaims. "We do have a choice. Our world has changed. Your father must change. He spoils your sisters not for their sake, but for his own. You must stand against him, Toshiyuki. You must do this for Toshio and Yorie. You must do this for us."

Toshiyuki knows that everything Shizue says is true. He cannot deny it. He walks away from Shizue shaking his head and turns back around with a groaning sigh.

"Yeah. Okay. I tell Father we cannot do this."

Toshiyuki relays his decision to Shunichi. It is impossible to care for both Yorie and Toshio in Hiroshima. Toshio's life is in jeopardy. Nishiyo and Shigemi are adults and must behave as adults for the sake of their family.

"I see," Shunichi purses his lips; his head bobs, "Yes …"

"Thank you. Thank you." Shizue almost falls over as her knees weaken with relief. Too soon.

"You thank me? No. You misunderstand," says Shunichi. "If you cannot care for Yorie here, you and my grandson must return to Furuichi."

Shunichi wields his unmitigated power as head of the household. He will not put his foot down and demand his daughters grow up. He will not deny the demands of his daughters and become the target of constant nagging.

Toshiyuki closes his eyes for a moment and then watches Shizue for a sign of approval.

Shizue shakes her head. "No! You cannot do this! We cannot do this. Toshio is not well enough to travel."

Shunichi addresses his son. "Will you hide behind your wife's weakness and deny my request?"

"I go speak to Dr. Yoshida," says Toshiyuki. "If he agrees the trip to Furuichi will not harm Toshio … that is what we do."

"Toshiyuki, no. Our baby cannot make the long trip. It will harm him. I won't do it!" Shizue rushes out the door.

Toshiyuki follows and calms her down. Together they speak with Dr. Yoshida, explaining Shunichi's demands.

Dr. Yoshida examines Toshio and gives an emphatic, absolute "No" to the request. "Your son must not be moved! If you wish, I will speak with your father."

"Yes. Yes, Please." Shizue's voice is hoarse from crying and begging Toshiyuki to stand against his father. "Please, speak with Shunichi. Make him understand."

"Toshiyuki?" Dr. Yoshida settles a hand on Toshiyuki's shoulder.

"Yeah. Do that. Maybe you can make him see how bad is situation."

Shunichi hears Dr. Yoshida out, but is not swayed. "I am the head of this household," he repeats again and again, like a gorilla pounding his chest. "I know what is best for my family."

Dr. Yoshida speaks to Toshiyuki outside. "I did my best. I'm sorry. You are in a tough spot. But if you want your son to live, he must not be moved from his bed."

Toshiyuki nods.

Dr. Yoshida walks away with slumped shoulders.

"Well?" says Shunichi when Toshiyuki and Shizue return.

Father and Mother stand before Shunichi like stone sentinels … and just as helpless.

"You have a choice," Shunichi grumps. "Either I bring Yorie here or you return to Furuichi. I will not suffer my daughters' complaints one more day. If they are not happy they will not let me be happy."

"Father," Toshiyuki's tone wavers between respect and anger. "You are not hearing us. Toshio is very ill. He needs more time here in Hiroshima under doctor's care for rest and treatment. Shizue cannot do this treatment at home. You cannot risk your grandson's life for your convenience. Father, you must understand."

Shizue's swollen eyes plead with her father-in-law. She cannot say aloud the panic filling her head.

Shunichi folds his arms and paces a few steps away, "I understand."

Shizue's face brightens.

"Now *you* understand *me*. I am the head of household. I give you three days. Come back to Furuichi with Toshio … or Yorie comes here."

"Father…" Toshiyuki begins.

"Yes. I am father." Shunichi waves his arms about. "A woman's skirt and tears will not change my decision. Three days. You have three days."

"Do not bring Yorie here. We will return," says Toshiyuki.

"When?" asks Shunichi.

"In three days, as you say."

Preparations to leave the Hiroshima hospital begin as soon as Shunichi leaves. They will first return to Toshiyuki's shack, 10 miles away, spend the night there to gather items necessary for the trip, then continue on to Furuichi. This will break up the miles and make it easier on Toshio.

Shizue says little to her husband the remainder of the day.

That night, however, when they arrive at Toshiyuki's shack in the make-shift barracks, her demeanor shifts. She remembers how she and the children miraculously survived the bomb and how Toshiyuki survived radiation sickness. And she remembers why.

"Toshiyuki, I am sorry I say too much. I do not wish to put bad feelings between you and your father."

Shizue does not wait for a reaction from Toshiyuki. She has a surprising question for him.

"When you learned you had radiation sickness, you sent a young soldier to Furuichi to inform me you could not return on weekends. Where is he?"

"Kenshin? He died. Why do you ask about Kenshin?"

Shizue's face washes pale.

"Shizue, what's wrong?"

"The Obi sash ... where is it?"

"Obi sash? Why do you ask about Obi?"

Shizue looks under her husband's bed for the sash. It is not there. "You don't have it? But ... you must. Toshiyuki, where is the sash?"

"Shizue, you are not making sense. Why would I have your Obi sash?"

Shizue tells her husband what happened during the young soldier's visit. How she learned of Toshiyuki's radiation illness and the sash she sent back with the soldier to ensure his recovery.

Toshiyuki is touched by her love for him. But no words comfort Shizue.

"The Obi must be here. That young man put it here somewhere. He promised! He promised me!"

"Why are you so upset? You can make another Obi with the family crest."

"No! Grandmother's spirit is in that Obi. You are alive. No other can replace it!"

Toshiyuki cannot console Shizue. With the Obi lost she believes the spirit of their grandmother is lost. Obaasan will no longer be able to guide them and save them from misfortune.

Shizue holds Toshio in her arms and cries herself to sleep.

As promised, Toshiyuki, Shizue, and Toshio leave Hiroshima for Furuichi. Toshiyuki rides a bicycle which pulls a wooden cart holding all their belongings. Toshio is nestled in a blanket between their possessions and supplies as snugly and safely as possible.

Shizue walks beside the bike and cart. Toshiyuki stops and waits when she falls behind.

The road from Hiroshima to Furuichi is 10 miles of cart wobbling bumps.

Toshio vomits twice. Toshiyuki and Shizue assume it is from motion sickness.

Upon arriving at home in Furuichi, they summon a doctor … only to ease their mind about Toshio.

The diagnosis, however, is devastating; the prognosis, worse. Toshio's sensitive intestines have been damaged further by the rough cart ride. The doctor attending him gives no good news. He does not expect the baby to recover. The injuries are too severe. There is nothing he can do.

He advises the family to prepare for Toshio's death.

Toshiyuki stares at the floor.

Shizue does not accept the doctor's diagnosis.

"You are mistaken," she defiantly tells the doctor. "Dr. Yoshida has great confidence Toshio will recover in a few months." Her words fall oddly one upon another as if all the good doctor need do is correct the prognosis and Toshio will live.

"I am sorry." The physician gathers his instruments into a leather satchel.

After he leaves, Shizue has harsh words for her husband.

"This cannot be true! Did we barter our son's life to make your father and your spoiled sisters happy?"

"Toshio is alive," says Toshiyuki. "Dr. Yoshida saved my life. Toshio will not die. Our love and the love of our ancestors will save him."

"Our love?" Toshiyuki's sentiment takes Shizue by surprise.

"Yeah," replies Toshiyuki with a hopeful tilt of his head.

"Yes," Shizue says, wanting to believe. "Yes, you are right. We must trust Dr. Yoshida. We must trust the doctor who saved your life. We must trust love."

CHAPTER NINETEEN

The Sound at Heaven's Door

Toshiyuki returns to Hiroshima and resumes his duties.

Shizue is left in Furuichi with the responsibilities of household, family, and injured children. Yorie has nightmares. She follows her mother everywhere. Toshio keeps some food down, but begins having bloody stools again. Shizue cannot give him the time and devoted care he needs. Her position in the household requires she attend to her demanding family. Toshio is left alone in an upstairs room most of the day.

Although, Toshiyuki's sisters have nothing to do all day, they do not help with housework or assist in the care of their sick nephew.

Shunichi spends his days and nights listening to the radio. Men are exempt from the responsibilities of household chores and the care of children. It is the traditional Japanese way.

Between chores, Shizue rushes upstairs to feed Toshio and change his diapers. Shizue wants to keep her son nearby as she cooks and cleans. But, she cannot. If Toshio is moved repeatedly, his internal injuries will not heal. It is often after dark when household responsibilities are completed and she returns to his room for the night.

Shizue feels certain Toshio understands her difficult position. He does not cry. He sleeps most of the time. When he is awake he makes baby noises and stares at the ceiling. Every time his mother enters the room, he smiles.

"That's a good boy," she whispers. "Every day you will get better. You will grow stronger ... a little stronger every day. I promise. Soon, you will laugh when Mommy tickles your tummy."

"Shizue!" Shunichi calls from the foot of the stairs.

"Your grandfather is calling, Toshio. Mother must go prepare lunch. I'll be back soon. Do you understand your mother?"

Shizue kisses her baby. A tear falls onto Toshio's cheek.

After lunch, Shizue returns to check on her son, she repeats the words aching in her heart. "I am sorry. Please forgive me." His shallow breathing cannot be discerned by sight. She kneels beside him, placing her hand on his chest. Toshio smiles when she touches him.

"Shizue!" Shunichi calls again.

"Oh! What does he want now?" Shizue whispers. "Well, he will just have to wait."

When Shizue doesn't answer Shunichi's call, he climbs the stairs to Toshio's room. He hears Shizue whispering; pleading for her son's forgiveness.

"The boy is dying!" Shunichi steps into the room. "There is no hope for him. Why do you waste time crying and begging for a baby's forgiveness? Prepare for his death. Let our ancestor's receive him. Those living need your attention."

Shizue hears the first words out of Shunichi's mouth and then hears no more. She is lost in the same deafening silence as when Colonel Kubota brought her news of Toshiyuki's infidelity with Mieko.

Shunichi's downward turned mouth prattles on as she searches the face of the man who has spoken the heartless words. *The boy is dying!* Where is compassion for his grandson? Why is there such great distance between Shunichi's needs and his heart? Perhaps, if Obaasan were alive, she would help Shizue understand.

"I can't find my baseball stat notebook. What have you done with it?"

"I saw it on the floor under the radio table," says Shizue.

"Oh. That's right. I remember now."

Shizue's head throbs with every heavy footstep descending the stairs.

As the thudding fades away, Shizue's thoughts drift to a time that feels now like a lifetime away…

"Haha!" (Mama)" Her heart remembers Toshio's voice calling, "Haha!"

"No. No. Baby," she called back over her shoulder. "Stay upstairs with Yorie. Yorie, play with your brother. Stay with him like a good big sister. Mother must attend to chores."

Yorie always obeyed her mother's instruction to stay upstairs, with no resistance. She had tumbled down the stairs, attempting to crawl down head first.

But Toshio, determined to be with his mommy, had learned to work his way down backwards, one step at a time, giggling and cooing victoriously as he went bumping down. Again and again, he did this, never fearing. When Shizue scolded him for being so adventurous, he only grinned and jabbered his victory back at her.

Tonight, her son lies still and weak. If he lives … if ever he defies her and descends the stairs … she will not scold him. She will praise her tiny, brave warrior.

When he is well again and asks to go to the river to chase butterflies, pull petals from flowers, and screech at the buzzing of

243

bees, she will not say, "Mother has too much to do today, Toshio. Tomorrow, we will go. Okay?"

Toshio will never again need to protest, "Haha, matadaide e ko." (Mommy, no wait … go now).

Never again will he be denied the joy of living. Instead Mommy will smile and say, "Yes, let us go now while the sun shines."

Shizue caresses Toshio's pale cheek and leaves, again, to attend the family's needs.

The day stretches long; her thoughts with her child upstairs. After preparing and serving the evening meal she will be free to be with her son.

"Ah… Yes. That was delicious," proclaims Shunichi. "We are happy to have you back, Shizue."

Prodded by their father's compliment, the sisters mumble a compulsory "Thank you."

The family's words of appreciation echo hollow in Shizue's heart. Their actions and their lack of action, reveals more than Shizue ever wanted to know; how little those of whom she cares and loves, reciprocate love or care for her and her children. This family, of the same blood, the same ancestors, is more uncaring than strangers.

She hurries through her duties with one thought. She must return to her baby boy.

Her responsibilities finally completed Shizue rushes to the upstairs room with Yorie. Dusk crowds the room with shadows. She lights an oil lamp and sets it down bedside the futons. "Mother is here," she says to Toshio as she tucks Yorie into bed. Yorie is asleep almost instantly, exhausted from her nightmares.

"I'm here, Toshio. Mother is here." Golden light washes over the ashen face of her suffering child. He smiles up at his mother, his dark eyes move over her face as if he is tracing every loving feature.

Shizue sighs with relief. "Mommy is sorry she was gone so long. I am here now. I will not leave again tonight. I am here, baby. Mommy is here."

She lies down beside Toshio. She will rest through the night, holding her son's hand, loving his face in the glow of the bedside lamp. She will not fall sleep. She will watch over him. She will listen to his breathing and feel the warmth of her son's frail body next to hers.

Mother, daughter, and son share the peaceful darkness and the freedom of the night.

Morning radiance illuminates the room. Birds flutter and twitter outside the window. Shizue opens her eyes. Oh, no! How long did she sleep? No sound, no movement, had awakened her. Yorie usually wakes her up whimpering, having had another terrifying nightmare.

"Yorie?"

Yorie is not there. She must have awakened early and slipped downstairs.

"Toshio?"

Shizue touches his pale body. "Toshio!" Her hand recoils. Her baby is cold.

No! No! No! No! No!

The inaudible voice screams out of Shizue's every pore, whirls about, plummets into her gaping mouth and strangles out her cries. Only a whisper escapes her heart, "No ... Toshio ... No."

There is no life in her beautiful baby boy.

CHAPTER TWENTY

Out of Ashes

Nuclear war, Day 66

Shizue descends the stairs. Pressed to her breast is the lifeless body of eighteen-month old Toshio. She staggers toward the kitchen where the family is gathered, waiting for breakfast.

"Where have you been?" Someone calls upon hearing her footsteps.

"Where is breakfast?" Shunichi's words sound muffled. "Toshiyuki has returned. Did you forget…?" His words trail off. Everyone turns to see what has stopped his heart.

Shizue stands in the doorway. "My baby … the bomb … why? I should have held him tighter. I should have protected him. I will never forgive myself."

Toshiyuki pushes himself up and forces his legs to move toward Shizue. "Toshio? No! Not Toshio! Not my son!"

Tears well in the eyes of Shunichi, Nishiyo, Shigemi … tears empty of meaning for Shizue and her baby.

Family members look from one to the other. They are speechless. It matters little. Shizue would not have heard their compulsory words.

Yorie scampers over to Toshio, reaches up and shakes his little body. "Wake up, Toshio. Wake up."

Toshiyuki grabs Yorie up into his arms and leaves by the kitchen door.

Three days later, Toshio is cremated at the temple in Furuichi.

Toshiyuki and Shizue's precious baby boy had died, too weak to resist death's call, on a mid-November night, three months after the bombing of Hiroshima, two weeks after Toshiyuki's recovery from radiation sickness. Massive internal hemorrhaging claimed baby Toshio's life.

After the funeral service, family members have little to say to each other, only what is necessary. Shizue finds nothing necessary to say. She answers questions with a nod or a shake of her head and resumes household responsibilities without thought or emotion and wonders how her heart keeps beating. The mansion reflects Shizue's emptiness with creaks and moans and long, narrow hallways.

Two weeks later, as Shizue puts Yorie to bed, Toshiyuki sits down beside her.

"Shizue, I am troubled. I rebel to customs in Hawaii and Japan except..."

Shizue interrupts, "Yes, Toshiyuki, you rebel to all customs except honoring your father's wishes. That you do ... no matter."

Toshiyuki stares down at the floor heavy with Shizue's unfinished accusation. "Shizue ... do you blame me for Toshio's death?"

"Yes..."

Toshiyuki exhales and rises to leave.

"...at first," Shizue continues, "at first I blamed you. I also blamed your father and your sisters. If I do not blame them ... if I blame war, do I blame Japan? America? Who do I blame? Tell me who to blame. What could I have done to save our son? If I had not sent the Obi sash to you, would you be dead ... not Toshio?

The Obi is lost. Obaasan's spirit has left us. That is why Toshio died. I am to blame."

"Shizue, you must not say that."

"Our son is dead. My heart is empty."

"We have Yorie."

"Today ... yes ... today we have Yorie." Shizue's words drag across her fears. "Many children are still dying of radiation sickness."

"Yorie is healthy. Another baby is on way. We will have another son ... a son like Toshio."

"I pray only for a healthy child." Shizue presses her hands against her expanding abdomen. "It is not wise to ask for more."

"Yeah. That is best. Shizue ... when Yorie is fast asleep, come to my bed."

"Yorie needs me with her." Shizue pulls a cover over Yorie's shoulders. "She has nightmares. Every day she searches for Toshio. She thinks he is playing hide and seek. She asks me to help her find him. I must be here when she wakes up crying."

"Okay." Toshiyuki's acceptance clashes with his disappointment.

Days, weeks, months pass. Everything changes and nothing changes. The past will not leave. The future will not come. Many exposed to war's wrath and the A-bomb's radiation refuse to leave the homes where they have found relative safety. They will not go to work. They numbly move through the motions of living. They are not alive and they are not dead. Nightmares haunt them. Depression, fear, anger, and denial all increase. Some continue to deny the event even happened. Their eyes are open, but there is no awakening.

Each day victims struggle with haunting images of grotesquely twisted death. The effects of the bomb are endless. Meaning in what happened to them is impossible to find. Suffering lingers, physical, psychological, and spiritual ... burdened by guilt for having lived while others died. Perhaps guilt would have held less power over them had they known the destruction inside their bodies is irreversible. Radiation remains in cells, tissue, and organs. They are highly susceptible to blood disorders: leukemia, multiple myeloma, malignant lymphoma, and many more. For the rest of their lives victims of the bomb will be *hibakushas*, explosion-affected people. They and their descendants will face discrimination. They will be refused employment. They will experience social exclusion and romantic rejection. Those hoping to marry may never find a partner willing to risk passing radiation defects on to their children.

At the Nekomoto home, however, some pressures have diminished. All the refugees have left the mansion and re-joined what is left of their families. Only the Kubota family remains, as the Colonel is still recovering from his extensive burns.

Mrs. Kubota now runs a part-time business out of the teahouse, making Japanese kimonos to help pay their way. Her effort is appreciated, but the use of an iron all day increases the cost of electric power and leaves no surplus for the family.

One day there is a knock at the front door. Former refugee guests are gathered outside. They have come to thank Shizue for taking such good care of them. The relatives who took them in are not treating them kindly. It seems those who did not experience the bombing of Hiroshima do not grasp the horror the victims lived through or understand their struggles. These refugees do not want

249

pity, but are burdened now with insensitivity. The refugees apologize for their bad behavior while in Shizue's home. They regret believing Mrs. Kubota's foul gossip, which caused them to disrespect Shizue. They beg for her forgiveness.

Shizue serves tea, accepts their apology, and wishes them well.

There are now 12 people living in the Furuichi home. Food is still scarce. Everyone is malnourished and weak. The government ration of rice is one bowl (about two cups) per month for the household, calculated by ages and occupation of family members. Rice is so scarce it becomes known as "silver rice".

In Japan, it is the woman's job to obtain food. Shizue travels to farms where she trades goods and some of her belongings, for whatever crop is available. Obtaining food consumes most of her day. She mixes the vegetables with rice to make the ration stretch as far as possible. The most abundant crop is daikon, a radish. Shizue chops the radishes into rice size particles, adds a small amount of rice and cooks it into porridge. The family is not fed properly, but they are much better off for her efforts.

Nearing her sixth month of pregnancy, in the early morning hours, Shizue straps Yorie to her back and pulls a small wooden, two-wheeled hand cart to neighboring farms. The ground is saturated with yesterday's rain. She pushes and pulls the unwieldy cart through the mud.

She trades her goods for potatoes, onions, squash, and daikon, then drags the loaded cart home, arriving spattered with mud and exhausted.

Shizue continues to sleep with Yorie, even though Toshiyuki is tiring of her excuses not to join him in his bed.

250

Not long after the refugees visit, another blessing comes. Nishiyo marries a local boy and moves out of the mansion. Shizue almost cries when she meets the young man. Nishiyo bosses him unmercifully, doing all the talking. He says only, "Yes, Nishiyo. Yes."

A week later there is yet another blessing. Shigemi, who has not found a satisfactory suitor in Furuichi, returns to Honolulu.

Shizue's workload is lightened. The bickering ceases. A quiet peace descends on the household.

Shunichi listens to baseball on his radio, jotting down players' names and statistics in a notebook. Ever the eternal business man in Honolulu, he developed a liking for baseball during his three year internment at Heart Mountain. Playing baseball was pastime allowed the prisoners. Shunichi shouts and cheers as the roar of the crowd filters through the tiny speaker, like the chirp of crickets.

Sumo wrestling is his other passion. He contorts his body as if that will help his favorite contender. Shunichi is once again lord of his castle. He will never admit it, but he too is happy his spoiled and demanding daughters have moved out.

The two blessings bring Shizue peace, but no true happiness. She still struggles with Toshio's death, blame, and regret. A steady line of "what if's" march through her conscious hours. Her dreams are happy and sad, the loss of her son, the approaching birth of another child.

She focuses on a third blessing. Toshiyuki has embraced the change in him. He truly is the new man he became the day the world they knew ended. He is kinder, more patient, and understanding. He comes home every night to be with his family unless duty requires his presence in Hiroshima.

In her seventh month of pregnancy, Shizue returns to Toshiyuki's bed.

Soon after, Toshiyuki's day of reckoning arrives. January 21, 1946, the British war crime trials begin in Singapore.

Colonel Geoffrey Adams, a British officer who survived the Burma campaign and the POW camp at Singapore, speaks up for Colonel Yasuji Tamura, the 5th Regiment commander on trial. In his testimony, Colonel Adams vehemently insists that the British Prisoners of War had been treated well. His captors had passionately obeyed the Geneva Convention laws relative to the treatment of POW's.

He relates specific incidents of fair treatment and many kindnesses. He tells how the Japanese Colonel gave permission for a search party to find and bury British soldiers who died in the fields and forests of a foreign land. He lists additional unrequired kindnesses that fell outside of international regulations. The foremost was being allowed to construct and erect a Christian symbol, a 10 foot tall wooden cross as a monument to their fallen comrades.

The British officer offers a compelling argument, that this Japanese Colonel and his regiment did no wrong, no harm, and should not be punished.

Based on Colonel Geoffrey Adams testimony, Colonel Yasuji Tamura and his regiment are acquitted of all charges. The 5th Regiment commander is set free and returns home to Japan on a British plane.

Major Nekomoto meets Colonel Tamura at the airport and transports him to his temporary home in Hiroshima.

The Major then phones or sends telegrams to all the officers nearby asking them to assemble in Hiroshima for a celebration of their Commander's freedom, restoration of his honor, and their own.

It is a happy meeting. All who attend are thankful to be alive. They never expected that a simple wooden cross, constructed out of respect for the beliefs of their enemies in honor of their dead, would redeem their own lives.

The military hearing is finally over. The officers and men are now free of the trials of war.

The people of Hiroshima and Nagasaki, however, are still imprisoned in the hell of radiation sickness. For the prisoners of atomic war, there will be no courts, no judges, no release, no reprieve, and no freedom.

CHAPTER TWENTY-ONE

The Perils of Survival

Toshiyuki is back in Furuichi as a civilian with no income. He is unable to return to Ishihara Industries, the company he worked for during his college years. The up and coming company failed during the war.

He and his father put their heads together to discuss how the family is going to survive. Shunichi suggests his son form a company to construct bridges in Hiroshima City. In the aftermath of the bomb, there is much to rebuild.

Shizue does not favor Toshiyuki returning to Hiroshima. Her due date is nearing and she wants her husband close by. However, no other financial prospects appear and the decision is made. Toshiyuki will form a construction company in Hiroshima City.

As Shizue prepares the evening meal her water breaks. Toshiyuki helps her to the bedroom, where a problem becomes evident. His wife is losing an alarming amount of blood. Shizue is hemorrhaging.

Shunichi sends for the young midwife hired to deliver the baby, but she is unavailable. Her backup, an old retired midwife, rushes to the mansion.

Toshiyuki answers the knock at the door. The old, stooped midwife stands a foot shorter than Toshiyuki. Salt and pepper, short cropped hair seems to float over her protruding jaw and oversized teeth. She holds an oil cloth umbrella in one hand.

"Mrs. Akiyama," she says squeezing past Toshiyuki.

She catches his glance at the umbrella. It isn't raining out. There's not a cloud in the sky. "You would not believe how many babies are born in the middle of the night during a downpour. I was certain I wouldn't make it here without opening this up." She moves the umbrella up and down like a piston. "Finally, I'll bring a baby into the world without a thunder cloud over his head. Where is the mother?"

Mrs. Akiyama examines Shizue and informs the family that the delivery will be a long and extremely risky one.

Two hours into labor that will ultimately last over twelve hours, Shizue and the midwife overhear Toshiyuki telling Shunichi the baby had better be a boy. If the baby is a girl, he vows to give the child away.

"You would not do that," says Shunichi.

"Yeah, I will. I lost a son. I have a daughter. I want another son like Toshio."

Shizue continues to hemorrhage. Her body grows cold. Her skin looks pasty. Pain depletes more of her strength. Fear that her baby, exposed to a deadly dose of radiation, will be born with abnormalities overwhelms her. Shizue's pulse drops. A transfusion to offset the blood loss is not possible. No blood is available. Shizue is dangerously close to slipping into unconsciousness.

The old midwife by her side has never lost a mother or baby and will not start now. She shouts at Shizue, "Stay awake! Do you hear me?" She slaps Shizue's face. "Mrs. Kano! Do you hear me?" The midwife repeats her commands until she sees a slight nod of Shizue's head.

"Good!" Mrs. Akiyama rubs Shizue's arms and legs vigorously to get her blood circulating. "Our baby is almost here. Hold on. Yes! That's a good girl. Our baby is almost here. Not long now. Almost here." The midwife holds Shizue's attention by shouting loud enough to be heard by neighbors.

Shortly after 8 a.m. on a magnificent spring morning, a special child joins the world. "It's here!" says the midwife. "Your baby is here. See your beautiful baby."

Shizue does not open her eyes. "So tired. I am so…" she mumbles, "I…"

"Mrs. Kano! Open your eyes! *Look!* You have a beautiful baby girl!"

Shizue's eyes open in panic. She catches a waning breath. "No… no… not a girl… I cannot have…"

"Yes! It is! You have a baby girl." The midwife carries the baby to a porcelain bowl to wash. "Yes. Look at that … a beautiful baby girl… sweet baby girl…"

Shizue strains to see the baby. She blinks several times. The midwife is washing a baby boy.

"A boy…? Do I … have twins … a girl *and* a boy?"

The midwife having overheard Toshiyuki's statement about what he would do with a female child and feeling she was losing Shizue, jolted her into consciousness with a calculated deception.

Adrenaline born of fear for her child shocked Shizue into full awareness. She did not give birth to twins. She did not give birth to a baby girl. Her baby is a boy. The canny old midwife's clever pretense saved Shizue's life.

The baby's lusty cries bring Toshiyuki and Shunichi rushing into the room.

"Is it a boy?"

"Yes, it is a boy," the midwife answers, "a beautiful healthy boy! Look, 10 fingers … 10 toes … all perfect. Your son is beautiful."

This baby boy, perhaps the youngest survivor of "Little Boy," the bomb that destroyed Hiroshima City, is named Toshiharu, which means "to govern peacefully."

Outside the mansion gate, Toshiyuki and Shunichi raise the traditional blue paper Koi to signify the birth of a male child. They raise the symbol high into the air for all the villagers to see. Father and grandfather are extremely happy and proud they have a male child to continue the family name. Neighbors, friends, and family are amazed to see a healthy child with no deformities. Their fears of atomic radiation defects are relieved.

Shizue, however, has difficulty recovering from the trauma and complications of the long and arduous delivery. She loses weight and becomes anemic.

As with the birth of Yorie, Shizue does not produce enough milk. During war time only a cupful of powdered milk was rationed for an entire month. The milk ration is more now, but not enough. Shizue is fortunate to have goats milk available from a neighbor. Also, her Aunt Kome moves into the mansion and becomes the newborn's wet nurse.

Aunt Kome is crippled, having lost her leg above the knee due to gangrene when she was in her twenties. After Kome lost her only son to war, Shizue looked after her.

"Who would do that for old Aunt Kome? Shizue. Only Shizue." Tears fill Kome's eyes.

Even with Aunt Kome wet nursing and some goat's milk for the newborn Toshiharu, it soon becomes clear his appearance of healthy normalcy at birth was deceiving.

Toshiharu weakens with every passing day. His immune system is not strong enough to fight off common infections and illnesses.

Shizue and Toshiyuki search for a physician who can help their baby. Many doctors are called. One after another examines the baby boy. All give the same prognosis. Little Tosh will not survive.

As she did with Toshio, Shizue refuses to accept the prognosis. The wartime doctors have seen too much death. There are too many patients and too little time. They are tired, discouraged, and frustrated. They have grown used to losing battles. It is easy for them to give up, but Shizue will not. Toshiharu is a miracle baby, a gift, spared from nuclear destruction by the grace of God. Shizue believes her baby boy will be spared for a special mission. She believes in his name, Toshiharu, *to govern peacefully*.

The baby's health continues to decline. Heavy congestion causes great difficulty in breathing, allowing only brief periods of sleeping time for mother and child. Shizue places hot towels on his chest and directs vaporizer mist onto his nose and mouth to keep the nasal passages open.

She stays up nights, lying with the baby on her chest so she will know when his breathing becomes labored. Not the smallest detail necessary for her son's welfare is overlooked. This time, Shizue will not put demands, duties, family status, not even honor above her baby. This child will live.

The new arrangement of Shizue's priorities deprives Toshiyuki of her company. The baby's constant crying irritates him. Toshiyuki relocates his sleeping quarters to a far corner of the house where he will not be kept up at night.

Travel time and business responsibilities in Hiroshima put Toshiyuki under a tremendous amount of stress. There are no comforts of home, or wife, to give him relief. Unknown to Shizue, he is looking for a room for rent in Hiroshima.

In a few weeks, baby Toshiharu shows slight improvement. He begins to sleep longer, although he does not move. Shizue, while grateful for the increased rest, is concerned about his lack of motion. She continues her vigil, moving him in the night and shifting his little head often, to prevent deformity.

However, Toshiharu's overall condition does not improve. Another doctor is called to the home.

He examines the boy. "Um-huh," he nods. "Your baby has lived longer than expected. I thought this was a good sign. As it turns out, it is not. I am sorry. You and your family must prepare for the worst. In my opinion, your baby has no chance of surviving ... two weeks ... not much more ... maybe less. You should prepare."

When the doctor leaves, Toshiyuki leaves. He is angry. Toshio is dead. Now another son is dying.

Hours later he returns and tells Shizue their baby's death will be a blessing. The world is rough for the strong. The weak die. It is best that way. They must accept little Tosh's death.

Her husband's calloused words break Shizue's heart.

Within days, Toshiyuki drops another blow on Shizue. The stress at home, combined with the stress of his construction company is too much. He has rented a room in Hiroshima City and is moving out. He will return to Furuichi when he can find the time.

The next day, Toshiyuki moves out of the mansion.

Shizue does not try to stop him. Seeing to Yorie's recovery and keeping Toshiharu alive is all that matters to her now.

Shizue does not leave little Toshiharu alone. She carries him from room to room as she performs the daily household chores.

Three weeks pass. In spite of the negative prognoses regarding fetuses exposed to the effects of a nuclear bomb, little Tosh holds on to life. Though weak and sickly, struggling every hour of every day and night ... little Toshiharu survives.

CHAPTER TWENTY-TWO

Trust – Hope – Deception

Two years later

The beating of a massive wooden drum attached to a high pole, signals a warning alarm to the villagers of Furuichi. Its deep, vibrating, thuds echo through the streets striking fear into the hearts of the war-weary citizens. This alarm, however, is not warning of approaching war planes; rather it has been sounded because a river bank has broken. Floodwater is heading Furuichi's way.

The Kano home is more susceptible to floods than others in their neighborhood. Although the house sits on high ground, the main entrance is a few feet lower than street level. The mansion and grounds will be flooded.

When the drum sounds everyone in the household stops what they are doing. Shizue takes baby Tosh into her arms and Yorie by the hand and rushes upstairs. The maid and Shunichi help Aunt Kome to a higher level, safe from the rising water. Aunt Kome stays with Yorie as Shizue and the maid hurry up and down the stairs carrying essential household items. Moments later, floodwater rushes through the gate.

Shunichi, Aunt Kome, and the new maid, Hana, watch the inundation from an upstairs window. Shizue stands at the top of the stairs, holding little Tosh in her arms, as murky water, laced with yellowish froth, climbs the steps. Shizue silently calls to Obaasan to protect her babies.

261

The floodwater rises, step by step. Halfway up the staircase the water hesitates. A swell or two attempts to top the next step; then, with a lapping sigh of defeat, stops rising.

The family huddles together thankful for their lives. Now, they wait for the floodwater to retreat.

At the time of the flood, Toshiyuki is in Hiroshima City with his crew, repairing a bridge. By the time he hears the news and rushes home, the floodwaters have receded. The damage to the mansion is unbelievable. A foot of silt covers everything inside and outside their beautiful home.

"How did this happen? I have not sleep for three days. Now there is more destruction at home! Why did you let this happen, Shizue?"

"We are alive," says Shizue. Her baffled expression and pragmatic comment do not redirect Toshiyuki's irrationality.

With the pressure of demand upon demand wracking Toshiyuki's nerves, rational thinking has taken its leave. He goes into a rage.

"Everyone depends on me! Who can I depend on? No one! " He grabs his jacket and heads out the door. "I have no time for this! You clean up this mess. I'm going back to city."

Neighbors, who have come to help haul away mud and items damaged beyond repair, overhear Toshiyuki's outburst.

Shizue runs down the hallway crying. The neighbors retreat.

Toshiyuki, embarrassed by his dishonorable and unreasonable outburst, finds Shizue and begs her forgiveness. "I will go get more help. I'll be back as soon as I can."

He leaves Shizue crying.

Toshiyuki sends two of his men to help clean up the overwhelming mess.

Kind neighbors continue to assist the stricken family. Shizue prepares meals for everyone helping with the cleanup. The monumental task goes on for weeks. Everyone is completely exhausted.

All the downstairs tatamis, 6' x 8' about 2 inches thick, are dug out of the mud and piled up outside while the floors are mopped. Next, the hundreds of water soaked mats, weighing as much as one hundred pounds each, are stacked on carts to be hauled to the river to be washed.

At the river, everyone helping out has a specific job. Shizue rips off the cloth trim so the woven straw can drain. This chore keeps her waist deep in the river all day.

When the tatamis are as clean as can be reasonably expected, they are carried back to the mansion grounds, stood on end and leaned one against another in an A-shape to dry. When the tatamis are thoroughly dry, the trims are reattached.

Before the large mats can be returned to the house, Shizue pounds them with a bamboo swatter to release the fine, moldy dust that permeates the straw.

There are fewer neighbors helping now. Toshiyuki's men stayed only long enough to see the most strenuous work completed. Shizue, left with the finishing details, begins to show signs of extreme fatigue. Her back aches as if breaking, but she doesn't complain to anyone. She loses her appetite. Her already slight weight drops.

Toshiyuki comes for a visit after not seeing her for two weeks. He comments on her unhealthy appearance. She tells him she is tired, like everyone, and there is no need to worry.

Mr. Miyao, an uncle by marriage and the only relative still helping out, is concerned. He urges her to see a doctor. Shizue says there is no need for a doctor. Now that the emergency is behind her, she can rest and regain her strength. Time and rest, she insists convincingly, will be her cure.

In spite of Shizue's positive outlook, her strength does not return. Sharp pains in her stomach grow stronger. Pain soon becomes unbearable. Her agony can no longer be hidden. She sends a message to Toshiyuki in Hiroshima.

Toshiyuki immediately consults Dr. Yoshida, who suggests she travel to Hiroshima City the following day, or as soon as possible, for a check-up. Due to bridge repair commitments, Toshiyuki will be unable to accompany her.

The following afternoon, Shizue, although in considerable pain, walks to the train station and travels to the city alone.

An x-ray reveals that sections of her small intestines have fused together.

"How did this happen?" Dr. Yoshida's elfish manner is fatherly and protective. "Have you been in an accident? Fallen downstairs?"

"There has been no accident," replies Shizue.

"I see." Dr. Yoshida's eyes reveal other considerations. "Times are hard. No one is themselves." He pulls a stool up close to Shizue, sits and leans over, looking squarely into her eyes as he asks, "How are you and Toshiyuki getting along? Does he lose his temper?"

"No!" Shizue stiffens and draws back at his implication.

"I think you answer too strongly."

Shizue retreats with a rigid jaw and silence.

"Something caused this condition. It will help if I know." Yoshida's upside-down, v-shaped eyebrows rise above his spectacles. "What strenuous work have you done outside your ordinary daily chores?"

Shizue tells the doctor about the flood, the many weeks repairing tatamis in the river, and the effort it took to clean their home.

The doctor nods as she recounts the weeks of arduous labor.

"Yes," his nose twitches, "this certainly could have caused the problem."

The physician informs Shizue she must have surgery immediately to separate the small intestines. He instructs her to call her family and have them bring enough bedding, towels, cloths, pots and pans for a two week period of hospitalization.

Shizue agrees to follow his instructions.

Toshiyuki is unavailable. Shunichi will not know what to bring for her. Shizue leaves the doctor's office and although in excruciating pain, walks to the train station. From the last station in Furuichi, she trudges home to obtain the items necessary for her stay in the hospital.

Shunichi clicks off the radio when Shizue announces she will be away for two weeks.

"Two weeks! Who is going to take care of us?" Her father-in-law does not seem to have heard the words: doctor, hospital, and surgery.

"The maid," Shizue holds a sheet of paper in her hands. "I am making a list of things for her to do. She will do her best."

"The maid's best! Not good enough!"

Shizue leaves Shunichi to his grumbling, gathers the necessary items for her hospitalization, and packs them in a satchel.

Later that day, Toshiyuki, having spoken to Dr. Yoshida, and being certain that Shizue did not remain in Hiroshima as instructed, returns to Furuichi. The next morning, he accompanies her back to the city.

Dr. Yoshida explains the surgical procedure. He invites Toshiyuki into the operating room to observe what is causing his wife's pain.

Medical necessities are in short supply. General anesthesia is not available. Shizue is given several local anesthetics around her abdomen and back and a stick to bite on. The doctor waits for the anesthesia to take effect and then asks his nurse to hand him a knife. He makes the first incision below Shizue's navel. Blood spurts out. "Damn!" Yoshida is not averse to modest swearing. He tosses the knife aside.

"That knife is dull!" he snaps at the nurse. "Where is your head? Hand me another. Properly sharpened!"

Blood gushing from his wife's abdomen turns Toshiyuki gray and green. He covers his mouth and nearly faints.

"Nurse! Get him out. Quickly! I do not need two patients in the room."

Toshiyuki hurries out wondering about the doctor's skills as a surgeon.

Near the end of the procedure, the local anesthesia begins to wear off. Although the pain is extreme, Shizue bites on the stick and makes fists to tolerate it. The doctor notices her discomfort, but Shizue insists he go ahead with the surgery.

The operation is a success. A nurse wheels Shizue to a private room and instructs her to lie flat and still for 10 days.

Two days later, Yorie and little Tosh visit. For what to them feels like forever, they have been without the one person of whom they can emotionally depend. The children beg their mother to please come home. When Shizue gently explains that Mommy cannot come home yet, Yorie and Tosh do not understand. Toshiyuki takes them from the room crying inconsolably.

A week later, Dr. Yoshida removes Shizue's stitches. The incision has healed perfectly. In a few weeks there will remain only a slight visible horizontal scar under her navel.

Shizue returns home to Furuichi, thin and pale.

Only two days later, neighbors see her walking down the road toward the village holding Tosh in her arms and Yorie by the hand.

Two neighbor women approach and ask how she is doing.

"Thank you. Thank you," she replies. "I am feeling much better. The children and I are going to the studio for a portrait."

The neighbors whisper as Shizue, Yorie, and Tosh continue on their way. One covers her mouth and leans in to the other, "She looks terrible. I think she is dying."

"Yes. Look how unsteady she walks. She should be in bed. Why do you think she is going to have a portrait taken?"

"Maybe she knows she is dying," suggests the other.

At the studio, posing for the photograph, Shizue remembers an old saying she has forgotten until just now. "Three is not a good number," she tells the photographer. "Someone in this photograph will die unless we make it four. We need another person. I will come back another time."

"No wait," says the photographer. He hurries to a backroom and returns carrying a teddy bear for little Tosh to hold. Shizue is satisfied with the solution. Now there are four.

Concerned neighbors and friends check on the family every day. They offer to help out any way they can to aid in her recovery. But, with each knock on Shizue's door, they expect to find her dead.

To everyone's surprise, Shizue's health improves. In less than a month, she has regained her strength.

Life at the mansion in Furuichi returns to difficult and demanding post war "normal".

To ease their financial burden, Shizue resumes selling and bartering items sent from relatives in Hawaii for food.

One morning, as she dresses for a trip into town with Toshiyuki to visit the temple containing Toshio's ashes, she cannot find her favorite sweater.

"Toshiyuki, have you seen my sweater?"

"Which sweater?"

"My favorite ... the expensive cashmere ... the one my father gave me."

"I don't remember. What color is it?"

"Dear, of course you remember. It's white. You tell me every time I wear it how much you like it."

"Oh ... the white one ... yeah. I had to sell it. I needed money for construction business."

"You sold it? Toshiyuki, that sweater was not for sale. How could you..." Shizue's outburst drops cold as a distressing possibility presents itself. She wonders if her husband has given it to a woman. "Did you sell it?" she asks.

"Did I sell it? What else would I do with it?"

Shizue knows expressing her doubts about Toshiyuki's fidelity will only be confronted with denial. She mumbles a defeated reply, "Nothing. I ... I am just sad and disappointed to lose my beautiful sweater."

"You have other sweaters."

"Not like that one. It was special."

"Ask your father to send another ... or make another."

Shizue cannot replace the special sweater from her father meant only for her. She writes a letter to Waichi, explaining what happened and expressing how sorry she is to have "lost" it. She is also sorry she did not wear it more often.

In a return letter, Waichi promises to send another, if she promises to hide it from Toshiyuki. He also informs his daughter that her Uncle Sumida has moved back to Japan.

When the family learns of their uncle's situation, Shunichi locates Sumida and offers him a room at the mansion. Uncle Sumida politely declines Shunichi's offer to live in their home.

Shunichi makes another offer. The family's 20 acres of land is in desperate need of restoration. If Sumida will agree to live there and work as grounds keeper, he will take a huge burden from Toshiyuki and Shizue's shoulders as they work to improve their family's desperate postwar circumstances. There is a factory building located on the property used by the previous owner to breed silk worms. Living quarters are on the second level.

Sumida accepts the offer of room and board in return for work as the groundkeeper and moves in.

Toshiyuki works long, hard hours to make a success of his construction business. It ultimately proves unprofitable. He moves back to Furuichi and begins searching for another business venture.

While he is out searching for a new opportunity, he comes across a field of yellow mustard flowers. Seeing possibilities for profit, he locates the owner and offers to purchase the rights to the blossoms. The owner has no use for the blooms and tells Toshiyuki he is welcome to harvest them without charge.

Toshiyuki returns home excited. He will go into the mustard seed oil business. All he needs is equipment to extract oil from the seeds.

Shunichi and Shizue are modest in their enthusiasm. There is a rather huge obstacle. They don't have capital to start a business that requires a large investment of cash.

Toshiyuki is way ahead of them. After the attack on Pearl Harbor, his gambler uncle Waichi had won a fortune in a card game. Waichi had bought a large house and purchased a bait and tackle shop. Toshiyuki will ask him for assistance.

Toshiyuki sends his proposal by letter.

Waichi is hesitant. He phones Toshiyuki and listens to his nephew's eager proposal. Enthusiasm eventually convinces him that the project will be profitable. Waichi loans a large sum of money to start the business.

Toshiyuki begins his plan cautiously, purchasing one oil-extracting machine to test its productivity. He is fully satisfied with the outcome. With additional equipment, the new venture can go into full production. His family's financial struggles will come to an end and, in addition, as business owners, their prestige and community respect will be regained.

Toshiyuki speaks with local business owners about his plan, seeking suggestions from these respected men as to the best way to go about obtaining equipment. One directs him to a merchant who buys machinery at a discount.

Toshiyuki makes contact and invites the man to his home later that evening to discuss his objective.

Shizue wants to be included in the meeting. Toshiyuki curtly refuses. Wives do not get involved in husbands' business and financial affairs.

Shizue expounds her request. It could do no harm to have a second opinion. Shunichi does not care to be present at the meeting, preferring the excitement of a special wrestling broadcast. She suggests that her instincts as a woman could be beneficial in assessing the stranger's motives and ethics.

Toshiyuki's answer is, again, a firm "No". He is the head of this family and is capable of evaluating the man's character and his business proposal without the assistance of a woman.

When their guest arrives, Shizue graciously serves the business man, Mr. Saitou, a cup of tea. She lingers for a moment, to subtly look him over. He is a boney man, meticulously over-dressed for the occasion. Shizue has seen her father leave home many nights dressed in this same manner. Dressed to impress and bluff another gambler. She is suspicious.

Toshiyuki clears his throat with a glance at Shizue. She bows and excuses herself. She is not allowed to even exercise her discerning eye in "man's business".

Shizue doesn't go far. She positions herself around a corner just out of sight where she will not miss a word of the conversation.

Toshiyuki and his professional contact work out an innovative "get the most for your money" business deal in order to obtain oil-extracting equipment from a manufacturer in Osaka. There are two conditions to obtain the best price on the equipment. One, the contract is only verbal. Two, the businessman needs the money in cash, up front.

With his reason clouded by the exhilarating possibilities of his new venture, plus a vision of restored wealth and respectability, Toshiyuki hands over, in cash, all the money he borrowed from his uncle Waichi.

The stranger promises Toshiyuki the machines will be delivered within the next two months.

Toshiyuki shows Mr. Saitou out.

"It is done." he says to Shizue as she gathers and carries the tea utensils to the kitchen.

"Yes. I know." Shizue admits to overhearing some of their conversation and expresses concerns to her husband. She sensed deceit in the stranger's voice. She asks Toshiyuki to be very careful in his dealings with this man. *"If it isn't already too late,"* she thinks to herself.

Toshiyuki reminds her that this is not her affair. Mr. Saitou is a well-known, successful business man. Yes, he is new to Furuichi, but it is not uncommon to move in difficult times. He noticed nothing in his demeanor to warrant suspicion or caution. Toshiyuki stomps out Shizue's concerns like the butt of one of his cigarettes. He labels her sense of deception as nothing but the worry of a simple woman who knows nothing of big business.

In the weeks that follow, Toshiyuki eagerly awaits the dawning of a new and brighter future. He is happier than Shizue has seen him in years. He is light hearted, even playful.

Shizue cannot genuinely share his enthusiasm. She fears her instincts are right about the stranger's lack of integrity. She tries to be excited for Toshiyuki's sake. Every night she prays her husband's dreams will materialize into a successful business venture; one that will restore his pride and the family's prestige.

With each passing week bringing delivery of the oil extracting equipment closer, Toshiyuki's exhilaration for his new business heightens. His family's financial worries will soon be over.

Toshiyuki and Shizue's relationship takes a welcome leap forward during this time of hope.

"Toshiyuki," Shizue says as they lie together one night, "I've changed my mind."

"Changed your mind about what?" he draws the last bit out of a cigarette.

"About us. We didn't marry for love."

"Yeah, that is so," Toshiyuki crushes the butt and turns onto his side, propping up with one elbow.

"I once told you that I do not ever want to love a man," continues Shizue.

"Yes. I remember. I understand that you do not love me."

"But, I want to love you."

Toshiyuki springs up. "You ... what?"

"Yes. I have changed my mind about love. Obaasan said we would be happy one day. Sometimes, I think ... when you smile..." Shizue smiles, "I think we can find love."

"You think we can be in love?"

"Yes. What do you think?"

"You told me I am not the husband you want."

"Yes, but, Toshiyuki, I am no longer the same woman you married. The things I want have changed."

"And now, Shizue ... what do you want now?"

Shizue sits up to look squarely into her husband's eyes. "I want..." lamplight sparkles in her eyes. "I want someone I can talk to. I want someone who understands my nightmares ... someone who has walked with me through war and poverty ... someone who knows me."

"This is all?" says Toshiyuki with a hint of amusement.

"That is all," Shizue says in all seriousness. "Enough, I think, for now. The rest will come, if we want it."

Toshiyuki takes her hands into his, "A new start then ... if that is what you want."

Shizue whispers, "Yes." She fears that if she speaks her wish too loudly it will shatter at the stroke of midnight.

"Okay, then. Yeah..." Toshiyuki nods. "We do that."

Toshiyuki turns onto his back. Within seconds he is snoring softly.

"Yes. Yes, we will do that." Shizue drifts off to sleep.

Two good months pass. Months filled with new hope for the family and the future.

One morning, Shizue finds Toshiyuki standing in front of a calendar counting days. He has not heard from Mr. Saitou, the businessman who took his borrowed money with the promise of delivering oil extracting equipment. The delivery deadline has passed. Shizue suggests he go to the man's home immediately.

Toshiyuki has been entertaining suspicions about the good faith transaction for days, but he is too proud to admit his concern to Shizue.

"It's okay. Big business deals take time." Toshiyuki does not want to be embarrassed by appearing anxious.

Another month passes. No oil extracting equipment has been delivered. He asks around the village about Mr. Saitou. No one has seen him for ... well ... they are not quite sure how long it has been since they saw him.

Toshiyuki hurries home and asks his father to go into the village, to Mr. Saitou's home and talk with the man into whose hands he placed a small fortune.

Shunichi, a seasoned go-getter, has no qualms about confronting Mr. Saitou. He goes to the street and house as directed by Toshiyuki.

The gate is open. He knocks on the door.

"Mr. Saitou!" he calls out. "Mr. Saitou!"

He knocks again. There is no answer and no sound from within.

He knocks at the house next door. The neighbor informs Shunichi the family he is seeking moved out weeks ago.

Shunichi returns home with the devastating news.

"Gone?" Toshiyuki cannot believe his ears. "No one is there? You went to right house? You are sure?"

Yes. Shunichi is certain.

Toshiyuki grabs his jacket and bolts out the door. Shizue follows and stops him outside.

"Dear, where are you going?"

"There is mistake. There must be a mistake. Father went to wrong house. I will go. I will find Mr. Saitou."

"Yes. Yes, you should. Your father does show signs of confusion at times."

Toshiyuki returns home with the same crushing news. He knocked on every door on the street. All Mr. Saitou's neighbors repeated the same story. The family left during the night, taking very little with them. Thieves took the possessions they left behind. No one knows where they went.

Toshiyuki has been swindled. The business capital Uncle Waichi loaned him is gone. He cannot start a vegetable oil business with only one oil extraction machine.

Shunichi pats his son on the back. "It's okay, Son. You will find another business opportunity. I will help you."

His father's support adds humiliation to Toshiyuki's disillusionment. Only now does Shunichi hear from his son that not only is Mr. Saitou gone, all the money borrowed from Waichi was handed over in cash. There is no money for another investment.

Shunichi is furious. He storms away to his room. At mealtime, he does not look upon or speak to Toshiyuki.

Shizue remains supportive. Although Toshiyuki did not listen to her concerns about the stranger, her husband is guilty only of trusting someone. She knows that feeling.

"We have one machine, dear. There must be something we can..."

Toshiyuki, sitting slumped over, holding his head in his hands, interrupts Shizue's optimism. "One machine? Worthless! There is nothing I can do with one machine."

The next morning at breakfast, Toshiyuki's mood has changed. During the night, he came up with an idea. One machine isn't much, but making use of the oil it produces would allow them to open a Tempura shop in Hiroshima City.

"A tempura shop? In Hiroshima?" contemplates Shizue.

"Yeah. Like you say ... one machine is good for something. One is all we need for cooking oil."

"Yes, but ... Hiroshima?"

"Yes. Yes, Shizue. You are right. We can do this."

Toshiyuki wastes no time locating a small shop in Hiroshima City; a very small shop, with sitting room for six customers. Although Shunichi is skeptical that any profit can be realized and suggests he not waste his time, Toshiyuki's mind is made up. A slim chance at success is better than nothing. Shizue stands with her husband.

The Tempura shop opens and the possibility of a brighter future for the Kano family takes shape again. Accustomed to the daily chores such a shop demands, Shizue sees, long before her husband does, that their brighter future will not be born without many hours and hard labor.

Every night before bed, she prepares vegetables to be fried the next day; cleaning, peeling, chopping, and sorting. Early the next morning, Toshiyuki transports his wife, Yorie, and little Tosh on a motorized three wheel truck to the rented shop. They bundle the children in blankets for the sixteen-mile drive from Furuichi to the city, where Mother and Father serve lunch to factory workers.

A homeless man stops by to scrounge through the garbage behind the shop. He removes the rotten parts of oranges and other edible refuse and voraciously devours the remainder. His clothes are tattered and filthy. His hair matted with black greasy dirt as though he just climbed out of a chimney. He is one of many veterans, an ex-soldier who lost everything including his family and his health, in the bombing of Hiroshima.

His plight wrenches Shizue's heart. Every day thereafter, she prepares a plate of vegetables and fish for him as if he is a regular paying customer.

277

Now, instead of rummaging through the garbage, he waits behind the shop for Shizue to find a moment to take food out to him.

On little Tosh's better days, when sickness does not keep him inside the shop, he goes outside to play tag with Yorie. Today, he runs around a corner of the shop headlong into the homeless veteran. Tosh scrambles to his feet and races to his mother screaming.

"Mama! Kaiju, Kaiju! (Monster) He's going to eat me! Monster is going to eat me!"

The unfortunate man only smiled and reached a hand out to help the boy off the ground. But, with every other tooth missing, his jack o'lantern smile struck terror into Tosh's little heart. Having witnessed the ragged, sooty man eating anything he could get his hands on, Tosh is certain his own flesh will be the man's next meal.

The following morning, at home in Furuichi, Tosh won't stop crying when Shizue puts him into the truck as they prepare to leave for Hiroshima. He begs not to go.

"The kid is a sissy," sneers Toshiyuki.

"He's only a baby, dear."

"Yeah. Worse than girl. Yorie doesn't cry over every nothing-thing."

"She is older. Tosh will grow and be brave too. He fought for his life with the heart of a warrior. One day, he will be the son you want."

"One day is not today. How can we work long hours with crybaby? Leave him home."

Shizue agrees, reluctantly. Both children are left at home in Shunichi's care.

278

The grandchildren's noisy play makes it difficult for Shunichi to listen to his beloved radio broadcasts. Tiring of their disruptions, he directs them to amuse themselves in the yard of their cousin, Taichi, who lives across the street. Shunichi disregards Shizue's instructions to keep the children inside, within sight. He does, however, give them stern instructions to stay in their cousin's yard. They must go no farther, especially to the river.

"The river is flooding again," Grandfather Shunichi warns them. "The current is strong and dangerous. Chickens and pigs get washed away every day. Stay away from the river."

"Yes Grandpa."

Taichi listens to their grandpa's warning with adventure brewing his thoughts. As soon as Grandpa is out of sight, he starts running toward the river. "Come on! Let's see! Let's go see the chickens and the pigs in the water!"

Yorie follows her cousin. Little Tosh trots behind Yorie.

At the river, it is just as Grandpa described.

"Look!" Taichi shouts over the sound of rushing water.

There is, indeed, an old pig in the water trying desperately to stay afloat among the branches and fragments of wood being carried downstream in the turbulent water.

"Over here!" Taichi shouts. "Look!"

Yorie moves closer to the river's edge, then stops … frightened by the grumbling roar of the floodwater. She backs away. Tosh does not.

"Stop, Tosh! Stop! Grandpa said…"

Before Tosh can obey his older sister, a quick push from his mean-spirited cousin, sends Tosh tumbling into the roiling current.

The water swallows her brother. In seconds, Tosh is out of sight ... bobbing and then disappearing. Yorie screams for help. There is no one other than Taichi near enough to hear her over the water's turbulence.

"Grandpa! Tosh! Grandpa!" Yorie scrambles frantically toward the house, falling twice.

Alarmed at the trouble he might now be in, Taichi runs along the river bank yelling at Tosh, until he can't see his cousin any longer.

Downstream, a woman is bent over the bank washing clothes. She stands up to stretch her aching back muscles and notices what appears to be a child being swept toward her, but out of reach. Without hesitation, she dives into the river. An incredibly strong swimmer, she moves with the current cutting diagonally across the path where she thought she saw the child. She reaches Tosh, seizes him by the back of his shirt and pulls him to the shore, where she administers mouth to mouth resuscitation until he revives.

The woman washing clothes on the riverbank happened to be an athlete, a contender in the 1936 Summer Olympic Games. Another miracle saved little Tosh.

Shizue is furious when she hears what happened. Toshiyuki only stares at his father, as Shunichi relates the circumstances.

"Yorie and Tosh are too spirited to keep inside all day," Shunichi declares with the authoritative manner of a judge passing sentence. "They disobeyed me. I told them to stay away from the river. They have learned a hard lesson. Next time, they will listen to me!"

"There will be no next time!" Shizue gathers her children and exits the room.

"Toshiyuki! Are you going to allow her to use that tone with me? Straighten her out."

"No, Father. Leave her alone."

Shizue will never leave the children with Shunichi again. Yorie and Tosh are now forbidden to play with their cousin, Taichi.

Toshiyuki and Shizue continue to work hard to make the tempura business successful. All their energy and all their money go into it ... still the shop barely breaks even. They are forced to reconsider their decision. The long hours and exhausting work is taking its toll on them, physically and emotionally. That, along with the travel being so hard on the children, brings Shizue to the point of surrender. Toshiyuki does not want to give up. He decides they must continue on, hoping they can at the very least, recover some portion of their investment.

Two years later, the tempura shop fails.

The family is more financially desperate than ever.

Weeks pass. There is no income. There are no prospects for employment. Worry increases along with tension in the family.

Within the week, another threat to the family's survival surfaces.

The police chief stops by the home with a warning for Toshiyuki. There's a rumor going around town that the family receives packages from Hawaii containing great sums of money. He is concerned for their safety.

Toshiyuki and Shizue are, of course, shocked by the ridiculous gossip. While it is true they receive packages from Hawaii, the boxes certainly don't contain money, but rather common household supplies, clothing, and treats.

Nevertheless, the police chief cautions, the rumor is out. People believe the boxes contain money. It will be wise to be more careful than usual.

Burglars are also targeting large houses and Kura (storage houses). Thieves robbed the police chief's best friend's house and took everything of value.

The Kano family wastes no time moving what few valuables they have in their Kura inside the mansion to a secret room hidden behind a fake wall.

Toshiyuki then contacts an electrician who sells and installs security alarms. The alarm system is a simple one. Long strings of wire attached to stakes at about knee height, surround the property. If disturbed, the strings trigger a loud bell.

The alarm can also be triggered manually by a switch. Toshiyuki installs the switch mechanism in the bedroom near his futon.

The alarm wires must be taken down every morning and restrung at night. Shunichi volunteers to perform this task.

Within days, a burglar enters the property. Somehow he does not trip the alarm wires. He breaks into their Kura and finds it empty of anything of real value. Having already scaled the wall surrounding the property, and unwilling to discontinue his quest for ill-gotten gains, he sneaks toward the main house. As he attempts to open a window, a squeaky porch floor plank announces his presence.

The sound awakens Toshiyuki. He nudges Shizue, who listens and verifies the sound of an intruder.

Toshiyuki waits for the right moment to pull the string as he does not know how many intruders there may be on the grounds or how dangerous they could be if they might feel cornered.

Little Tosh wakes up as his father is poised to sound the alarm. Toshiyuki puts his hand over his mouth and touches a finger to his own lips signaling him to keep quiet. Yorie stays sound asleep. Toshiyuki, Shizue, and Tosh listen to the burglar rummaging through the house and dropping items into a sack.

"Switch the alarm," whispers Shizue.

"Not yet," Toshiyuki whispers back. "They are too close."

They hear the sound of a window opening, then a rattling thump as the burglar drops the bag of stolen items from the second floor to ground level.

Toshiyuki flips the alarm switch. The ding-dang of the warning bell startles the burglar. Thinking he can still get away with the stolen goods, he jumps from the window.

Shunichi, sleeping soundly, unaware of the intruder's entrance, yells, "Help! Help! Thief! Robber! Wake up! Help!"

Everyone in the home has been instructed to yell FIRE when a burglar is discovered on the property. Neighbors will come to help, if only to protect their own homes from the flames. They are too frightened to assist when someone screams "burglar" or "intruder" or even "help".

Startled out of his sleep, Shunichi didn't remember the procedure. His cries for help are in vain.

Toshiyuki and Shunichi search the grounds and find shoe imprints in the soil beneath the window where the burglar jumped. He barely missed a pointed stake supporting a cucumber vine. Another inch over and he would have been impaled. The intruder ran off so quickly he left the bag of stolen items behind.

The rumor about the family receiving boxes of money and valuables from the mainland spreads.

While the family is away attending a summer festival, burglars enter the property and attempt to haul their massive safe away. Unable to move it more than a few feet, they break into it. The safe contains only letters, birth certificates, etc., no money, jewelry, or other valuable items. The thieves are so angry they leave human excrement inside the vault with a note saying, "Nani no tame ni kansha." In effect, "Thanks for nothing!"

Shunichi checks the property for missing items and discovers a basket covered with a towel on the ground outside the kitchen window. He removes the towel and finds another mound of human excrement. This is not an insult personally directed at his family. It is a custom. Burglars believe they will not be detected as long as such leavings remain warm.

Toshiyuki goes into town the next day and returns with a new safeguard against burglars ... a five-month-old black and white puppy.

"She is our guard dog," announces Toshiyuki.

Yorie and Tosh squeal with delight as the puppy licks their faces.

"Does she have a name?" Yorie asks.

"Her name is Mary."

"Mary. Mary. Mary," the children chant. "Let's go play!"

"She is a guard dog," Toshiyuki calls after them.

"Okay, Daddy," Yorie shouts back. "We'll give her lots of exercise so she will grow up big and strong."

"Yorie is too smart," grumbles Toshiyuki.

"Mary. A scary name for guard dog," Shizue notes with a giggle.

Tosh runs in circles shrieking with delight at the antics of their new pet. Shizue smiles to a secret thought, "Perhaps lots of exercise will help my little Tosh grow big and strong too."

The small Border collie mix turns out to have a big bark. After Mary joins the family, there are no more burglaries.

Mr. Kubota recovers from radiation burns to his face, chest, abdomen, and arms, with no disfiguration. His skin is as fresh and pink as a baby. He obtains a teaching position in the village of Furuichi at a Junior High School. The family moves out of the teahouse.

Life at the mansion in Furuichi returns to normal ... for a while.

CHAPTER TWENTY-THREE

Desperate Spirits

If you believe the stories whispered in the dark, Japan is one of the most haunted places on Earth. The Japanese believe in supernatural powers, magical energy, and ghosts. They fear ghosts. They also honor them.

Little Tosh's encounter with the homeless veteran at the tempura shop in Hiroshima City is the first of many experiences with scary monsters. His next frightening encounter is at the end of a train ride with his grandfather.

Grandfather Shunichi takes Tosh to visit the Hiroshima Dome. At the time of the bombing, the building was the Hiroshima Prefectural Promotion Hall for arts and educational exhibitions. Located in the large business district next to the Aioi Bridge, it is the only structure left standing near the bomb's hypocenter. Inside is a huge desk with a model of Hiroshima City as it was before the bomb. The building itself has been left as it was after the bomb. Huge steel girders stand like a giant twisted skeleton. Rain falls through the metal bones creating craters in the dust. Tosh clings to his grandfather Shunichi. The giant, gaunt, distorted image of this place will visit him in nightmares.

Tosh often wakes up crying, whether from nightmares or the pain of seemingly endless illnesses. He is uncommonly susceptible to infections of every kind ... likely because of his exposure to radiation while still in the womb. He remains a crybaby and a sissy in his father's eyes.

On his good days, Tosh plays with his big sister, Yorie, in the beautiful mansion grounds that has now been lovingly restored by their Uncle Sumida.

Shizue scolds the children repeatedly for disrespecting the beauty of their sanctuary; particularly for trampling the thick, forest green lichen as they run and play hide-and-seek.

Today, Yorie and Tosh find the soft, carpet-like growth too delightful to resist. Like children in Eden, they revel in walking barefoot through the luxurious living carpet.

Evidence of their disobedience is obvious. The penalty for their transgression is to be cast from the garden by their angry mother. They are banished to the house. For three days, they must stay inside, contemplate the error of their mischief, and learn to respect the beautiful family garden, and especially, their mother's wishes.

Yorie takes the sentence lightly. Tosh, who has spent the greater part of his young life indoors, and whose playtime outside is already limited, cries for hours.

He begs his mother to let him go out and play.

Shizue will not reconsider her decision.

Toshiyuki comes home, once again, to the whimpering of his "crybaby sissy son". He decides then and there that it's time to take action. He devises a plan to toughen up Tosh.

At bedtime, he sits between Tosh and Yorie's futons.

"Would you like Daddy to tell you a story?"

Yorie and Tosh only look at each other. Daddy never tells them bedtime stories.

Shizue speaks first. "Daddy asked you a question? Do you want to hear a story?"

The children nod.

Toshiyuki begins by telling Tosh and Yorie about the Kano family's illustrious past, their noble Samurai heritage and of the honor they owe their ancestors.

"You must be brave. You must be strong or..." Toshiyuki pauses, baiting the children.

"Or what?" asks Yorie.

"...or," continues Toshiyuki, "or I will not be able to protect you. Can you be brave and strong?"

"Yes. Yes," they answer.

"Okay, then. A long time ago, there was this Samurai who behaved dishonorably. He left his wife alone and sorrowful while he go away for adventure. Many years pass. He misses his wife and is sorry he left her. He goes home. The house is the same as when left. A light is on. He goes inside and finds his wife very glad to see him. She welcomes her husband. They talk for a long time and then go to sleep like happy family. Next morning, Samurai wake up with dead wife in his arms. Long time dead! Her flesh smells bad. It is rotten and shriveled. She has no eyes ... only hollow sockets. Her long black hair sticks to bone. Yellow teeth grin from dead face. In morning light, the house is rotted and falling down. Suddenly, Samurai see wife's long hair moving like a snake. It crawls toward him, wraps around his neck and chokes him to death."

Yorie stares wide-eyed at her father. Little Tosh pulls the cover over his head.

"Do you want to know why this happened to Samurai?"

Yorie shakes her head. Tosh doesn't answer.

"I think they've heard enough," says Shizue. "It's getting late. They need to sleep."

"No. I will tell them. When Samurai husband go away, sorrow broke wife's heart and took her life. She died alone with no one to give her funeral. Her body stay where she die. Her spirit linger and wait, watching for bad, selfish husband to return."

Little Tosh pulls his covers tighter.

"Are you crying under there? You better not cry. Be brave boy. You must! Ancestors watch always."

Tosh whimpers.

Toshiyuki jerks the cover off his head. "Aha! Is that a tear? Do I see tear? Oh no!" Toshiyuki's eyes widen as if in fright. He peers around the room as though searching for the ghostly shape of a rotting apparition. "Better don't cry!" his warning scrapes against pretended fear, "Are you crying?"

"No. No."

"Okay. Go to sleep, But, don't forget what happen to bad Samurai."

Toshiyuki feels certain this strategy will strengthen his son. Shunichi likes the idea and joins in with his own ghost tales. Shizue remains overly protective.

Since the day Tosh almost drowned in the river, he has not been allowed outside the mansion gate. This began the onset of Tosh's "why" questions.

"Why can't I go outside the gate? Yorie goes. I want to go. Please let me go, Mama."

"No."

"Why? Why not? Why can't I go?"

"Because..." Shizue thinks better of reminding him of that awful day when he almost drowned in the river ... the day she almost lost him. "Just obey mother."

His mother's silence only makes Tosh more curious.

Yorie spends less time playing in the mansion yard now that Uncle Sumida is the grounds keeper and gardener. She and her rambunctious friends have been chased out of the vegetable garden and strawberry patch with arms waving and shouting, repeatedly... repeatedly, because now, they do it for fun.

It isn't just her uncle's loud commands that scare them away. Skinny Uncle Sumida is a seriously scary man. His intense scrutinizing gaze and grating voice has been the force behind neighbors doors clicking locked. Suits Sumida. Distance keeps good neighbors good and children where they belong, instead of destroying gardens and berry patches.

The rumor among neighbors is that Sumida fell in love only once in his life, met with rejection and his broken heart never healed.

With Yorie and her friends chased away to play in neighborhood yards, he is left with one child to deal with ... little Tosh. He follows his Uncle Sumida around as he cares for the grounds. Tosh takes particular care to stay out of the strawberry patch. Shizue has warned him that if he eats another green berry his nose will turn green and bumpy.

Today Sumida is going into the village. As he is leaving, Tosh, fueled by curiosity about the world beyond the 12 foot high wall, looks around, sees no one watching and slips out the gate behind him.

Sumida is not aware he is being followed by Tosh, who is being followed by his dog, Mary. Tosh and Mary trot behind Uncle Sumida, but a little boy's short legs cannot keep up. Tosh loses sight of his uncle.

He turns around, but doesn't know which road will take him back home. Mary doesn't help. She enjoys the outing, sniffing about, chasing chickens, barking at cats and other dogs. When Tosh calls her name and tries to catch her, she thinks it's a game of tag.

It isn't long before Tosh's distress attracts attention. Strange people surround him. Dead samurai wives, maybe. He begins to cry.

"Who are you, little boy?"

"Where do you live?"

Terrified by the unfamiliar faces and the bombardment of questions, he refuses to speak. One woman reaches out to comfort him. Tosh backs away.

The women look at each other puzzled. They have never seen the child before.

"What is your name? Tell us your name. We can help you."

"Uncle!" Tosh runs to his Uncle Sumida, who has returned by the same path and finds his nephew in distress.

Tosh escapes the frightening circle of strangers, but does not escape a severe scolding from Shizue.

"You must never do that again! Do you understand mother? I told you. Stay inside the walls where it is safe."

Tosh nods and sniffs tears away.

Toshiyuki walks into the room as the scolding ends. "Tosh ... are you crying again? What is it now?"

Tosh's sobbing begins anew as Shizue tells his father what happened.

Toshiyuki motions to his son. "Come with me."

"Where are you going?" asks Shizue.

"My son and I are going for a walk."

Tosh backs away. Toshiyuki motions for him, again.

"A walk? But it's almost dark."

"Yeah. Me and dark night are going to cure crybaby of your pampering."

Tosh clings to his mother's slacks.

His father takes hold of one hand and pulls him. Tosh holds onto Shizue with the other.

"Let go. You are coming with me."

Toshiyuki tells another story as he walks his son to the river.

"In old village called Ozaka, there was a rickety wooden bridge stretching across a mountain ravine to a neighboring village.

Very late one night, a man who lives near ravine hears whispering voices and creaking sounds, like someone, or something, crossing bridge. Crossing bridge is dangerous in the dark. So, this man rushes out to warn the traveler. He hurries to bridge. He looks around. No one is there.

Next night, he hears the same creaking and rattling, ghostly whispering and mournful weeping."

When Toshiyuki and little Tosh reach the bridge, Toshiyuki squats beside his son and continues his story.

"Man scared. Hide behind bush. He see bad thing ... scary thing! He see parade of dead people marching into Hell."

Toshiyuki draws a long breath and looks around. "It's getting dark. We must hurry across the bridge. You go first. You are Samurai ... son of Samurai. You must not cry."

Toshiyuki nudges his son toward the bridge. Together, they step onto it and tread forward. Tosh's eyes widen. He wants to cry, but brave Samurai do not cry.

At the middle of the bridge, Toshiyuki stops as if listening for something. The sounds of the night; voices of things hidden in darkness; the choked gurgling of the water below; strike fear into little Tosh. But, father and son move forward glancing over their shoulders as they go.

Toshiyuki sighs with pretended relief as they reach the other side.

Nothing happened! No rattling bones. No whisperings. No weeping. No parade of dead people. They made it across alive!

"You see? You were brave little Samurai. You did not cry. That made us safe."

Tosh doesn't feel safe until he reaches home and runs to his mother's side.

The little Samurai's curiosity about the world beyond the gate lessens after his walk in the dark. Soon though, it becomes clear, very clear, that he is not safe anywhere. Not within the walls of the grounds or even inside the mansion.

The massive mansion grows even larger in the dark. The high beamed ceilings groan. The old wooden floors creak and pop under the boney feet of unknown nocturnal wanderers. The ancient ancestral home whispers and sighs throughout the night. Clearly they are sounds made by ghosts and dead things, monsters that haunt the night.

Shunichi brings the children's' night fears to life when he tells them his favorite monster story. *Tenjo-name*, a towering, bony creature with a long tongue floats in the upper reaches of bedrooms waiting eagerly for naughty children to open their eyes when they are supposed to be sleeping.

Grandfather tells Yorie and Tosh to listen carefully and they will hear the monster licking the ceiling.

"When you hear this sound…" Shunichi imitates the moist, smacking sounds of licking, "you must keep your eyes closed and stay very, very, very quiet or *Tenjo-name* will grab you and whisk you away. You will wake up cold and hungry in a dark place far away from home."

Now, when little Tosh wakes up from a nightmare and feels like crying, he holds back his tears for fear of being captured by *Tenjo-name*. No matter the provocation, he keeps his eyes tightly shut. He does not want to wake up cold and hungry far away from home.

Tosh is satisfied staying inside the walls of the estate, until Yorie's tales about what fun she has playing with friends in the neighborhood increase. Tosh's curiosity restarts his "why" questions. Every attempt to give him a reason for denying his pleas is met with another "why." Tosh wears his mother down. She decides it is time to allow Tosh to explore beyond the gated walls as long as he is with Yorie. The children are even allowed to go to the river when it is low and placid. They play happily underneath Kandabachi Bridge wading and splashing in the shallow water.

Tosh tries to catch tadpoles with his little hands, like Yorie, but the slimy, black wigglers slip between his stubby fingers every time. Little Tosh has a big imagination. He comes up with a brilliant idea. He will use his underpants as a net!

A neighbor lady crossing the bridge spots Tosh running about bare bottomed. She tromps directly to Shizue, feigning shock.

Yorie and Tosh return home with a bucket full of tadpoles. Shizue breaks into laughter at the sight of her son. Tosh's once white underwear, now soaked, muddy, and stretched by their use as a fishing net, hang down to his knees.

With new freedom comes new adventures and unexpected encounters. Now well-versed in stories of monsters, spirits, and ghosts, Tosh is about to experience the dangers of another spirit power ... electricity.

One of Tosh's responsibilities is helping his grandfather clean the glass chimneys of oil lamps and fill them with fuel. The Kano house has electricity only in the kitchen and the guest room. Tosh is fascinated by the magical appearance of light at the touch of a switch.

Shizue buys light bulbs from a neighbor across the street that operates a small front room electrical supply shop. Today, she must go over to purchase a replacement for a burned out bulb. Not knowing what mischief Tosh might get into while she is gone, she takes him with her.

Considering their limited funds, this is an important purchase. The shopkeeper screws the bulb into a socket at the base of the wall to make sure it works.

He removes the operational lightbulb and hands it to Shizue. While she pays for the bulb, curious Tosh sticks his finger into the socket to see what's in there that causes light. The jolt knocks him back. He cries, more from surprise than pain.

Shizue tries to comfort him, but her wide-eyed attention only increases his wailing.

"Tosh. Look at mother. You are okay. Stop crying. If you stop now, I won't tell your father."

Tosh stops crying, but he doesn't understand why something in the socket wanted to hurt him. Monsters are everywhere. He adds one more goblin to his list of fears.

Yorie and Tosh hear at least one new ghost story each week. One, the most frightening, *Tenjo-name*, they ask to hear again and again. Toshiyuki, aided by Shunichi, is determined to toughen Tosh up, make him strong and brave; worthy of his Samurai heritage.

Shizue believes in spirits and the supernatural as much as anyone, maybe more; however, she doesn't like Toshiyuki and Shunichi filling the children with fear. She loosens her protective grip on Tosh hoping to prove that he is growing stronger and braver and thus end the litany of ghost stories.

Shizue assigns Tosh a new responsibility worthy, according to his father and grandfather, of a Samurai. His duty is to protect the family by closing the massive gate to the property before dark.

The huge gate is large enough for a truck to pass through, but counterbalanced so that a woman or child can close it. A push from Tosh's small hand swings it shut and a latch drops into place and locks it. Tosh loves this job. It makes him feel powerful. There is one drawback. Ghosts and monsters hide in the dark.

Now, every night he must traverse 100 feet from the house to the gate, close it, and get back to the house before anything can snatch him away or gobble him up. Walk he does not. Run he does. As soon as the gate latch clicks into place, he pivots and scrambles to the house as fast as his short little legs will propel him.

The long path from the gate to the relative safety of the old mansion creeps and crawls with eerie sounds and unknown dangers; the haunting hoot of owls, hidden in pine branches; screeches from shadowy forms; staring round yellow eyes. Tosh is determined not to cry! He is Samurai ... son of Samurai!

Yorie, knowing her little brother's fear of the dark and being the loving sister that everyone would want to have, hides along the path so she can jump out screaming like a banshee, happy to show how much she cares!

Even in the daylight, there are sources of fear. Toshiyuki's older sister, Nishiyo, who now lives in Hiroshima, visits the family mansion on occasion ... one occasion too often for Shizue. Her very presence strikes fear in the hearts of the children. She is harsh to everyone and strict and mean, especially to Yorie.

It is Japanese custom that shoes are not allowed in the house. But, children are children, and they forget. To Nishiyo, wearing shoes in the house is a cardinal sin; as most childlike antics and innocent mistakes are, according to her.

Energetic Yorie is able to run into the house and flip off her sandals as she goes. Today she runs in too fast and her shoes stay on. Nishiyo grabs Yorie by the arm and drags her to an old storage building, a Kura. She does this whenever she feels Yorie needs discipline, which is often. The Kura is dark inside with musty smells. Yorie begs not to be left there. She tells her aunt she is sorry and that she will be good. Her tears and pleas are only fodder for Nishiyo's anger. Auntie pushes the child inside and locks the door behind her.

She allows no one to let the frightened child out, not even Shizue. Yorie is left alone in the dark Kura for an hour at a time weeping, staring into the shadows for signs of monsters that live there.

After spreading her special rendition of joy, Nishiyo leaves with promises to visit again soon.

Shizue releases Yorie and comforts her. Yorie doesn't understand why her aunt punished her for something that was an accident.

"My shoes didn't slip off," she tells her mother. "I didn't mean to."

"You were running a little too fast," says Shizue. "I am not angry with you. And I don't want you to be angry with Auntie Nishiyo. One day she will have children. Maybe she will have a daughter much like you, only not as good as you. Do you know what I think is going to happen to your Auntie?"

"No. What?"

"I think..." Shizue kneels down, face to face with Yorie, "I think her little girl will run inside the house with her shoes on and will not obey Nishiyo when she tells her to stop."

"Will Auntie put her in the Kura," asks Yorie.

"She will ... once or twice, but because her little girl is so much like her mother, your Auntie, she will not obey. Auntie Nishiyo's daughter will run all around the house with her shoes on, tracking mud, twigs, and leaves all over the tatamis."

Yorie beams.

"Then," Shizue continues, "Auntie Nishiyo will be sorry she punished you."

"Will she tell me she's sorry?"

"Probably not ... but you and I will know and be happy many times."

Yorie is satisfied.

A few years later, Auntie Nishiyo does have a daughter. Her daughter will be allowed to run around the tatami rooms with her shoes on. Nishiyo will just laugh and say "No. No. Reiko, do not run".

Both children are assigned additional responsibilities as they are able to handle them. Tosh now helps Yorie feed the horses, pigs, cows, and a pair of pet rabbits. Unfortunately, Yorie, the experienced animal attender, is a child and gives Tosh no safety pointers.

As Tosh feeds a carrot to the horse, he keeps a firm hold on one end, expecting the animal to take a polite bite and wait for permission for another nibble. Horses are, however, horses, and thereby, not well-mannered dinner guests. The always hungry horse gobbles up the carrot and Tosh's hand. There is no serious injury; however horses are now on Tosh's growing list of scary monsters.

Tosh's learning experiences are far from over.

One morning, Uncle Sumida is late for breakfast. Shizue asks Tosh to fetch him. Full of bounce and eagerness to please his mother, he hurries to his uncle's room on the second floor of the factory.

He finds his Uncle Sumida out of bed, washing his face and performing daily manly rituals. Something is amiss. An eye stares at Tosh from beside the basin. He shrieks in terror! Uncle Sumida's head turns and with one good eye stares at his reactive little nephew. Sumida grins, picks up the eye, rinses it and places it back into his empty eye socket. He turns once more to grin at Tosh. Tosh dives for the door and dashes to the main house, yelling for his mother.

He runs headlong into her in the kitchen. Between gasps, he tells his mother the awful thing he has seen.

Shizue explains to Tosh that his uncle lost his eye driving a railroad spike. The eye he saw is not real. It is glass. This makes no sense to Tosh, but because it sparks his curiosity, Uncle Sumida does not land on his list of monsters. Instead, the glass eye begins Tosh's new list: curiosities. Tosh hangs around Uncle Sumida every chance he gets, now, hoping to get another look at his strange eye.

One sunny summer day, outside his uncle's room, he sees a bright yellow thing hanging on a low branch out of reach. It looks like a balloon his father once brought home to him. Of course, he wants to play with it. He finds a long bamboo stick and pokes at the balloon trying to get it down. He misses. Mary jumps and barks. Before he can swing again, Mary grabs the stick and starts a tug of war. Tosh scolds her, wrestles the stick away and tries again to knock the balloon down. His second try is successful.

The yellow curiosity falls, but doesn't act like a balloon. It lands on the ground and breaks into pieces releasing a horde of angry wasps.

Shocked by the unexpected ambush and stunned by the searing pain of multiple stings, Tosh doesn't even try to run. Mary leaps onto his chest and knocks him to the ground. Snarling and snapping, she takes the brunt of the attack from the angry insects by standing her ground over her little master.

Tosh's agonized screams bring Uncle Sumida running outside to see what is happening. He rushes back into his room for a blanket, quickly covers Tosh and scoops him away to safety, suffering stings for his efforts. Her master saved, Mary runs yelping for the bamboo forest.

Yellow balloons and bees are added to Tosh's list of monsters.

Toshiyuki doesn't scold Tosh or punish him for crying.

Tosh will soon make his father proud.

Yorie and Tosh are still forbidden to play in Taichi's yard, because he pushed Tosh into the river. Taichi has responded to the rejection by being angry at his cousins. Now, every time he sees them playing in their yard, he taunts them and teases them, calling them names while throwing rocks at them. Sometimes the missiles hit their target, sending the children crying to their mother.

Shizue does nothing about it. This is children's business. She has much too much to do. "Stay away from him," she says. This is her only advice.

Stay away? Not enough for Yorie. Sometimes, mothers just don't understand. She comes up with a plan. The next time Taichi crosses the road headed their way, she and Tosh will teach their little bully cousin a lesson.

They hide in the bushes near the main gate, lying in wait to deal with their common enemy.

Taichi pokes his head through the gate slates to see where his cousins are. Yorie jumps on him and wraps her arms around his neck, holding him while Tosh punches him in the nose.

Taichi wrestles out of Yorie's grip and hightails it home, crying.

Yorie and Tosh peek out to see what is going to happen when he reaches home.

Taichi's dad and grandfather, bearing down on long, heavy steps, head toward the Kano house for a double-barreled confrontation.

Uh-oh!

Yorie and Tosh disappear behind bushes and then follow at a safe distance while Taichi's father and grandmother march the 100 yards up to the house and pound on the front door. When Shizue opens it, they demand the children be punished for beating their poor innocent Taichi without cause.

Shizue, who did not witness the incident, but who has been informed of every single one of Taichi's assaults on her children, informs her neighbor relatives the thrashing was a justified act of vengeance in retaliation for Taichi's insufferable habit of throwing rocks at her innocent children.

Taichi's father and grandmother do not believe Shizue. They escalate their voices and insistence that her children be punished in their presence. They demand to witness justice.

Shizue slams the door in their faces.

After dinner, she describes the incident to Toshiyuki. He is elated that the children defended themselves against their bully cousin. He is especially delighted that Tosh drew "first blood".

"Yeah!" he chuckles. "My son is going to be okay after all."

Little Tosh has made it alive through his rite of passage. But will his family make it through theirs? The Kano's financial situation has worsened. They can no longer pay property tax on the home. Tensions rise.

CHAPTER TWENTY-FOUR

Leaving Home

Toshiyuki arrives home late after another day of searching for work in Furuichi. Shizue is ironing clothes in a corner of the kitchen. He sits down near the children who are playing pick-up sticks.

"No work." There is a worn-down edge in his voice.

"Will you look again tomorrow?" Shizue asks.

"Yeah," he sees Yorie reaching for the wrong stick. "No Yorie. Not that one ... that one." He points, then lies back on the tatami.

"That's not fair," complains little Tosh.

Yorie makes a ya-ya face at her brother when she successfully removes another stick.

"If there is no work..." Shizue presses hard on a stubborn wrinkle, "why go every day? Stay home with us."

"No, I keep looking." Toshiyuki yawns.

Shizue puts the iron aside and hands her husband a small, folded paper.

"What is this?"

"A note ... it was in your pocket. I found it when I washed your jacket."

Toshiyuki opens the notepaper. "Oh this? It's nothing."

"It's a note from a woman."

"I say it's nothing, Shizue!"

"You are lying."

Toshiyuki springs to his feet.

The children look up.

303

With quick steps, Toshiyuki is in Shizue's face.

"What did you say?"

"You are a liar!"

Toshiyuki smacks Shizue across the face and bolts out the door.

Shizue covers her mouth with a trembling hand. The children watch their mother open a cabinet door, grab a plate and slam it to the floor. Yorie and Tosh have never seen their mother like this. Shizue grabs another plate and another, smashing each on the floor. Years of pain from subservience, abuse, and betrayal rises to the surface. She glares at the shattered pieces of heirloom porcelain. She is always cleaning up this family's messes.

Shizue reaches for another plate. Yorie and Tosh take off out of the room.

Shizue is as angry over Toshiyuki's attempt to deceive her about the note as she is about another obvious betrayal. How stupid he must think she is.

"I glow when you cast your light," the note reads. *"Dawn will not return until you return."*

Shizue slams another plate to the floor, remembering the night she and Toshiyuki sat together on the hill, watching Hiroshima burn.

Shizue paces the kitchen speaking out loud. "You betray me with Mieko. You say you are sorry. Now, there is another woman ... a woman in our small village. That is why neighbors whisper when I pass by. You are sorry? No, Toshiyuki and neither am I. I will never be sorry again. I will never cry again." She smashes another plate.

Shizue moves her belongings and the children's to a bedroom far away from her husband.

At the dinner table that night, Shunichi notices her bruised cheek and swollen lip. Shizue tells him she stumbled and struck a wall. Toshiyuki joins in the ruse. He laughs and calls Shizue clumsy.

Along with the chill in the house, winter approaches.

Tosh and Yorie go out to feed their pet rabbits and discover the cage door standing ajar. The rabbits are missing. They look everywhere, under, around and behind, before going to their mother with the bad news.

Shizue finds herself in the unfortunate position of delivering worse news. Their rabbits did not escape. Their father killed the rabbits for food. He has taken their skins to a man who is making warm gloves for them.

"I don't want gloves. I want my rabbits!" says little Tosh.

"The rabbits are dead, Tosh." Yorie puts her arm around her brother. She has already learned the practicalities of impoverished living. "Mother will make a good stew for us."

Tosh shrugs her arm off. "I won't eat it. You can't make me."

"Tosh," says Shizue gently, "you remember how cold it is in the winter. How I rub your hands to get them warm. Gloves will keep you warm."

"I don't care. I won't wear them."

"I will, Mama," says Yorie.

"Thank you, Yorie. And please thank your father when he gives the gloves to you. He didn't want to kill your pets. If you thank him, he will feel better."

"Yes Mama. Tosh…" Yorie waggles a finger in her brother's face, "You must thank father too."

"No. I will not."

Tosh is as good as his word. No matter how much his parents insist, no matter how cold gets, Tosh never wears the rabbit fur-lined gloves.

Toshiyuki has no luck finding employment in the village of Furuichi. The family could have made-do a little longer, if not for repaying the money Uncle Waichi loaned for the mustard seed oil extraction machines. Toshiyuki promised to repay the debt.

All options for the family's survival have been exhausted except for the ultimate sacrifice. They must sell the beautiful estate that has been their family's home for hundreds of years. They must move to a larger city for employment opportunities.

Shunichi is heartbroken. However, faced with the irreversible facts, he agrees that the estate must be sold.

Desperate circumstances do not allow the family time to wait for the highest bidder. They sell their home to the first buyer, for pennies on the dollar.

They sell most of their household items and personal belongings, as they most certainly will be moving into a much, much smaller house.

Relatives, using trucks and carts, haul away everything the family is unable to sell or take with them. Toshiyuki's and Shizue's aunts, uncles, and cousins look like soldier ants swarming through the mansion. They squabble over items, picking over precious family heirlooms like vultures.

Toshiyuki immediately goes to Tokyo where he hopes to find work. He finds a small house for rent. It does not begin to compare with their beloved Furuichi home. Their new house is no bigger than the kitchen in the mansion. There are two rooms, plus a tiny kitchen and a toilet. There is no tub for bathing. The family must use a public bath.

Shunichi will stay behind in Furuichi to hand over the house to the new owner. When the purchase details are settled, he will join the family in Tokyo.

This is a sad day ... the end of an era of prosperity and influence.

CHAPTER TWENTY-FIVE

Rites of Passage

Tosh has come into his own as a brave little man. Shunichi begins to pay special attention to him. He is, after all the heir apparent to the family name. Before the family leaves for Tokyo, Grandfather decides to honor his little protégé by cooking him a special chicken dish.

Every morning Tosh collects eggs for breakfast. He has become attached to the chickens and given them names.

Shunichi scoops up a hen by its legs. It is Kuroba (Clover). The bird squawks and flutters in protest. Tosh watches in horror as Shunichi lays Kuroba's neck on a chopping block and hacks the head off with one swift blow from a hand ax. The headless chicken darts about, slams into a wall and collapses.

Grandfather Shunichi hangs the headless Kuroba by her legs for the blood to drain. He then scalds it in the boiling water to make the feathers easier to strip off the carcass.

Tosh watches; tears welling in his eyes. He begins to feel nauseous, runs outside, and throws up. Poor Kuroba.

Shunichi prepares dinner. His grandson has witnessed the slaughter of a pet with a name and personality.

At the dinner table, Shunichi places chicken stew before Tosh alone. Tosh does not appreciate this special coming of age gift from his grandfather. He does not want to eat the chicken stew. But, he knows better than to simply refuse. He makes excuses. None are accepted. After more enthusiastic prodding from his grandfather, he puts a bit into his mouth. His mind floods with visions of the murder scene. He just can't chew his pet.

Tosh swallows the piece and others whole. It is a miserable last supper.

Grandfather Shunichi is happy. That is all that matters.

The next morning, everyone except Grandfather Shunichi and the dog, Mary, who they must leave behind, takes their belongings to the gate and waits for the bus to Hiroshima station.

Friends and neighbors gather to say farewell.

A neighbor, who owns a knitting shop, gives each family member a ball of yarn. When the bus arrives, they board and dangle one end of the yarn out a window. Neighbors and friends take hold of it. The ball of yarn gets smaller and smaller as the bus leaves, disappearing along with friends, neighbors, Grandpa, Mary, and the family home which will never be theirs again.

At Hiroshima station, they catch a steam locomotive to Tokyo. The huffing chunka-chunka of the engine and the hiss of steam as it settles down to wait for passengers, the exciting, deafening blast of the engine whistle, the sound of steel wheels click-clacking on tracks, the hollow dark passage through tunnels, is alternately, exciting, frightening and fascinating to Tosh.

The train puffs to a stop at every city along the way. Men and women swarm underneath the open windows selling souvenirs: bento boxes, treats, and small toys. More passengers embark than disembark. Soon there is standing room only.

Outside Nagoya, a team of Sumo wrestlers board the train. About this time Tosh's stomach begins to rumble and cramp. He must get to the bathroom quickly. Yorie shows him the way. The train is so packed the children can barely squeeze between the voluminous Sumo wrestlers blocking the aisle. They finally make it ... and none too soon!

Yorie closes the door behind her little brother. The toilet is a hole in the floor. Tosh looks down. Railroad ties swish past underneath. Tosh hesitates; afraid he will fall through. He barely manages to take care of his business in time. This is a greater adventure than any small child would ever want.

Tosh is the only one affected by diarrhea. He is still a sickly child, but Toshiyuki suspects that Shunichi, who is not exactly at home in the kitchen, did not cook the chicken well enough.

At Osaka station, Toshiyuki buys boxed lunches and ice cream for everyone. Tosh has never seen such a thing. It's like a party. Everything looks wonderful, but he can't eat a thing. Yorie eats ice cream from a wooden box and then eats his.

Early the next morning, the train huffs into Tokyo station. They take a taxi to their new rented home on the outskirts of the city. The owners of the house, Mr. and Mrs. Moriya, a friendly older couple, who live across the street, escort the family inside.

The front room contains only four tatamis (their former home had hundreds). The tiny kitchen consists of a sink, a counter beside the stove, and an icebox. The living room has one window. Outside, there is a small shed for storage. A narrow yard about four feet wide surrounds the house. The east side is adjacent to a construction yard where lumber, bamboo, and handcarts are stored.

The family's few items, furniture and clothes were shipped ahead and are waiting in the storage shed, ready to be unpacked and placed inside the house. Toshiyuki orders Yorie and Tosh to stay put and quiet in a corner of the front room out of the way. Brother and sister huddle together.

Mrs. Moriya compliments Shizue and Toshiyuki on their well-behaved children. Most youngsters, she says, run around getting in everyone's way.

Shizue's sewing machine is placed near the children. Tosh amuses himself by playing with the wide foot pedal until his mother tells him to stop.

The local ice man stops by with a huge block of ice on a handcart. He cuts a chunk, about a cubit foot, for the family's icebox.

Once they squeeze their possessions into the tiny house, life settles down. Shizue enrolls Yorie in an elementary school half a block away. Tosh is enrolled in a newly established kindergarten, four blocks from the house.

On his first day of school, Shizue walks Tosh the few blocks there. The school building sits on a hill overlooking the town, Yutakacho. Shizue meets Tosh's teacher then turns to leave. Tosh didn't know he had to stay at this strange new place. He begs to go back home with his mother. The teacher holds his hand. Tosh tries to wriggle free. He reaches out for his mother, crying as if he will never see her again.

Tosh's classmates gather around him, curious about the new kid at school. His clothing is different, not like theirs. He wears wooden Geta sandals. The city children can barely understand his country dialect. Some classmates are fascinated. Others laugh and point fingers at him. Tosh simply does not know what to do with staring eyes and pointing fingers.

On the first rainy day, Tosh walks to school under his bamboo and oil paper umbrella. The other children carry western style metal and cloth umbrellas.

After class, on his way home, several bigger boys follow Tosh and surround him. They make fun of his old fashioned umbrella and try to snatch it from him. Tosh holds on tight. The boys poke holes in it with the pointed metal end of their umbrellas. Tosh's oil paper covering is soon shredded. He stands in the street soaking wet, crying. His tears invite more harassment. The bullies dance in a circle around him chanting, "Inakamono! Inakamono!" (Country bumpkin) "Tosh is a *country bumpkin*."

A neighbor sees what is happening. She hurries to Tosh's home and informs Shizue. Shizue rushes to his rescue, shoos away the bullies, and takes her wet and shaken son under her wing.

It may be a while longer before her little Tosh becomes a man.

Toshiyuki obtains a job in Tokyo, working in the import/export business. His responsibilities include involvement in the manufacture and distribution of women's cosmetics. There is an increased demand for beauty aids because of the injuries suffered during the war. Japan is being westernized. New products are being tested.

He brings one of the products home for Shizue to try. It is a cold cream to be used overnight. She spreads it on her face and goes to bed. The next morning, she wakes up to horror. The product burned her skin, leaving dark patches. It takes weeks to heal.

Shizue is certain her husband used her to test the product. Toshiyuki denies the accusation. Shizue does not believe him. They speak little in the following weeks. Avoidance has become their normal way of existing since Shizue discovered the love note in her husband's jacket pocket.

Toshiyuki has minimal positive interaction with Tosh. Tosh is still weak and sickly and has not consistently demonstrated the bravery he showed in the altercation with his cousin, Taichi.

So, it comes as a happy surprise when Toshiyuki tells Tosh they are going on a train ride to the country ... just the two of them. Tosh is excited to ride the train again. He is also excited that his father, who gives him no positive attention, is going to take him on a trip.

From Tokyo station, the train stops at two towns. Father and son get off at the third station and trudge on forever, or so it seems to little Tosh. At the end of a road winding through silk worm farms is a weather worn house, a barn barely standing, and a chicken coop.

Toshiyuki knocks on the front door. No one answers. He has just turned to leave when a young woman shouts his name and comes running from the barn.

"Toshiyuki!" The sight of Toshiyuki is so exhilarating she almost gallops toward him. Her excitement wanes and her pace slows when she notices the boy.

"Oh. Is this little Tosh?"

"Yeah," answers Toshiyuki.

"He's so cute," she pats the top of Tosh's head. Her smile fades. "Why is he here? Are you..." her smile returns, "are you leaving Shizue?"

"Tosh, stay here." Toshiyuki takes the young woman by the arm and escorts her away.

Tosh's father and the young woman talk. Short sentences pass back and forth, until she says, loud enough Tosh can hear, "No!

Please! No! You can't! What will I do?" The girl collapses to her knees, sobbing. "You promised! You promised me."

A grey haired man and a woman with her head wrapped in a scarf, peer out a window of the farm house. They watch as Toshiyuki leaves the young woman crying.

Toshiyuki strides away. "Come on, Son. Hurry."

Tosh trots after him. It is a long walk back to the train station, but another fun train ride back to Tokyo.

Shizue helps Tosh remove his jacket, "Did you have fun?"

"My feet hurt." Tosh removes his cap and scratches his head.

"Your feet hurt? From a train ride?"

"The woman cried."

"What woman … a woman on the train?" questions Shizue.

"Yeah. A woman on the train," says Toshiyuki.

Tosh sees Yorie in the adjoining room and limps over to see what she is reading.

"Tosh, wait. Who was crying?" asks Shizue.

"Leave him alone," snaps Toshiyuki. "What you want from sissy?"

Soon after, Toshiyuki obtains employment with the U.S. Navy, rebuilding bases in Okinawa. The job requires that he move 955 miles away from home. It will be a long time before he can afford to return to Tokyo for a visit. He promises to send money as soon as possible.

Months pass and no money arrives from Toshiyuki.

Shizue stretches the resources on hand, as she waits for help.

Winter arrives. Tosh has outgrown his warm jacket. There is no money for a new one and no money to buy material to make him one. Before sending him off to school one particularly cold morning, Shizue stuffs newspaper under his sweater.

"This will keep you warm. When your father sends money, I will buy you a wonderful new coat."

Tosh marches to school like a small-scale robot, his clothing stuffed with newspaper. Classmates laugh and point at him until the teacher scolds them for making fun.

After school, he attempts a quick getaway. He isn't fast enough. Several of the more aggressive boys catch up with him and run alongside, poking at the newspaper under his clothing.

Shizue, who watches the street every day now for her son's safe return, sees what is happening and shouts, "Hey! Stop that!" The bullies take off running.

That evening, Shizue rummages through scraps of fabric. There is little heavy material, only leftover odds and ends. She stays up all night making a coat for Tosh.

The next morning, she presents him with a coat that looks like a checkerboard. He is delighted. It's better than being stuffed with newspaper. He proudly wears his colorful new coat to school. But, once again, becomes the butt of cruel laughter and ridicule.

Tosh adds a new monster to his list. The Bully.

Meanwhile, Shunichi ties up the loose ends of selling the family's grand house in Furuichi and moves to Tokyo. He brings with him sad news. Their dog, Mary, who waited by the gate every day after they left, watching for their return, was run over by a passing truck. She died instantly.

Shizue and the children cry. They will never see their faithful pet again.

Shunichi has more bad news. Because they were forced by their dire circumstances to sell the house quickly and did not get a good price, he has paid the family debts in Furuichi and there is not enough money left to repay Waichi the money he loaned Toshiyuki to start the mustard seed oil extracting business. He gives Shizue all their profit. She stares at the bills in her hand ... barely two months' rent.

Shizue is devastated. Toshiyuki has sent no money. Now, there is no substantial surplus from the sale of the house.

Shunichi notices tears streaming down Shizue's face.

"What's wrong?" he asks.

"Nothing. It's just ... I really miss that big, old mansion."

Her reason for crying is a lie. Shunichi does not know Toshiyuki has sent no money to support his family. Shizue does not tell her father-in-law otherwise. She does not want Shunichi to think poorly of his son when money could arrive any day.

Shunichi settles into the Tokyo home and resumes his daily routine. He sets up his radio in a corner of the front room and sits day after day, listening to baseball broadcasts and professional Sumo wrestling. As in the past, this is his only pastime. Hour after hour, day after day he does nothing but listen to the radio, bent over, one ear tuned to the speaker, shuffling his feet when his legs become cramped or fall asleep. Soon, he wears a hole in the tatami.

His stats books grow in volume. He records every detail; who lost, who won; the contestants names, the teams, the wrestling matches, the baseball games, the hits, the strikes, the tags-outs, everything. The radio becomes his mistress, his profession, his life, his reason for being.

In the close quarters of the Tokyo home, Shunichi gets to know Shizue better. They spend some quiet times together when the children are away at school or sleeping. They talk about the good old days.

Shunichi never apologizes for past behavior, but Shizue can see his heart has changed. He no longer believes his daughters' critical accusations or the gossip Mrs. Kubota spread about her.

Soon, Shunichi begins to spend more time with Tosh and less time listening to the radio. He favors his grandson. Tosh hears stories of his grandfather's past success, the money, the power, and the prestige he enjoyed in Hawaii before the war. He assures his grandson that one day he will regain the family's lost land taken by the United States government.

"Don't worry." Shunichi holds Tosh by the shoulders, believing every word he speaks. "Everything will get better. When my property is returned, the family will be rich and you will never have to work for a living."

Shunichi often walks Tosh to kindergarten class. Returning home one day, his left leg gives out. He tries to stop the fall with his cane. The cane snaps in half. Shunichi falls and scrapes his face when he hits the ground. His health continues to decline. It appears paralysis is starting to set in.

Another month passes; still no money arrives from Toshiyuki. Shizue pinches resources to make ends meet. Necessities are scarce. The burden of caring for the family is, again, squarely on her shoulders.

There's a happy interlude when Shizue's father, Waichi, comes to visit bringing gifts and treats for the children. Tosh and Yorie stare wide-eyed at the treasure trove of Mars bars, Baby Ruth's, Wrigley's chewing gum, and a candy lei. He brings a special gift for Shizue, a beautiful diamond watch.

Waichi stays in Tokyo for a week and then returns to Hawaii.

In December Tosh and Yorie learn from children at school about a holiday called Christmas and an old man named Santa Claus. They have never been told about Santa Claus and are very excited to hear about Christmas trees, elves, reindeer, a flying sleigh, and the unusual way Santa Claus enters houses to leave presents. Tosh pouts when he realizes their house has no chimney for Santa to enter.

"We don't have a chimney. How will I get a present from Santa Claus?"

Shizue knows of this American custom from living in Hawaii. Although her family never observed the holiday, Yorie and Tosh are so excited, she plays along. "You are not the only little boy and girl whose house does not have a chimney. Are any of the children at school that have no chimney worried about getting a present?"

"I don't know."

"Then, I will tell you. They are not worried. Do you know why?"

"No," answers Tosh.

"Because ... Santa Claus is magic!"

"Magic? Really, Mama?"

"Yes. Really."

Magic is a very acceptable answer to Tosh. Thoughts of Santa Claus spark little Tosh's imagination.

A few days before Christmas, Tosh comes home from school and finds his mother alone and crying. He asks what's wrong. She tells him there is no money left to buy food.

"I can get money," says Tosh. "You can turn your diamond watch into money. I know how. I'll show you."

"No, son." Shizue shakes her head, thinking Tosh's thoughts are filled with too much Christmas magic.

"Why not?" he asks.

"Tosh ... dear ... there isn't any real magic in the world. Santa Claus is pretend magic."

"But, this isn't magic, Mamma."

"Tosh..." Shizue glances at the kitchen cabinets and the icebox, both empty of food.

"Come on. Let's go. We can go now."

Persuaded by her son's insistence, Shizue allows Tosh to lead her through the streets of Tokyo.

She wonders what she is doing. "Where are we going?"

"It's not far," says Tosh.

"But, it's so cold. We should go back."

"No, Mama. Come on." Tosh pulls his mother by the hand, pressing forward as though he knows exactly where he is going.

In an exclusive Japanese neighborhood, Shizue follows Tosh to a house with a moat separating the road and the wall. They cross the footbridge and knock at the entrance. A gray haired gentleman opens the gate.

"Hello."

Tosh looks up at him. "We want money."

"Tosh! No! I ... I'm so sorry," Shizue stammers. "My son said I could turn my watch into money. We are here ... I thought he..." She stops, flustered and embarrassed. "We are sorry to disturb you." She takes Tosh's hand and turns to leave.

"No. Wait," says the gentleman. "You are cold. Come inside."

The gentleman escorts Shizue and Tosh to a sitting room off the main entrance. A servant brings a tray with steaming green tea for Shizue and warm broth for Tosh.

The stately gentleman asks to see the watch. He examines it with a jeweler's loupe and asks Shizue how much she wants for it.

Shizue doesn't know how much to ask. She explains that her husband went to Okinawa to work and has not yet sent money to the family. She has no money to buy food.

"Tosh told me I could turn my watch into money." Shizue laughs nervously. "He led me here."

The man turns to Tosh and asks how he knew about him.

Tosh shrugs.

The gentleman, who introduced himself as, Mr. Watanabe, asks Shizue, again, how much she wants for the watch.

Shizue has no idea and will not commit. She explains that she hadn't intended to sell the watch as it is a gift from father.

"Well..." He inspects the watch again. "How about ten thousand yen? Is that fair?"

"I ... I don't know..."

"Take the money. I will hold the watch. When your husband sends money, you can pay me back a little at a time."

"Pay you back?"

"Yes ... as little or as much as you can spare. And then I will return the watch to you."

Shizue accepts.

On the way home, she questions Tosh. "How did you know about that man? Who told you?"

"I saw a sign on an electric pole on our street. It says "Takara" (Treasure). An arrow points to a house. It says a man there gives money."

These were the signs for the "Shichiya" pawnshop in their neighborhood. It was a miracle that little Tosh understood what it meant. Shizue didn't even know that kind business existed.

For Shizue, the incident is nothing less than divine intervention. God helped her family survive.

Yes. She thinks to herself as she tucks Tosh and Yorie into bed with a full stomach. *Yes. There is magic in the world.*

Shizue's next purchase is a loom. She weaves Tosh a gray jacket with a hood. He is no longer the laughing stock of his classmates.

Money borrowed on the value of the diamond watch supports the family for months. Finally, money arrives from Toshiyuki.

Every month, Shizue pays the gentleman back a portion of the ten thousand yen. Eventually the debt is paid and the diamond watch is returned. Shizue visits the pawnshop several times after that when she needs funds to survive.

Shizue had managed to keep the financial worries from Shunichi. There was nothing he could do to help.

As time passes, Shunichi spends less and less time in front of the radio listening to sports broadcasts; instead he goes out for long walks. Shizue thinks he is as aware as she, that unless he takes better care of himself, he may not live long enough to see his lost fortune returned.

One evening, Tosh sees his grandfather come out of the public bath, holding a towel and a metal bowl used for rinsing. Shunichi stumbles forward. "Tosh! Help! Help me. I can't stop."

Tosh tries to stop his grandfather's fall, but is knocked down. Shunichi staggers into a pole. A finger gets caught between the metal dish and the pole, resulting in a serious gash. Tosh helps his grandfather home.

Shizue is worried. Shunichi's paralysis is definitely worsening.

She takes him for a checkup. At the hospital, a doctor speaks with Shunichi about his symptoms. This doctor calls in several other doctors. The physicians examine him thoroughly and then gather in a corner of the room and whisper to each other.

Shizue and Shunichi cannot hear their conversation. A few minutes later, one of the doctors brings a medication for Shunichi. It is quinine.

Shunichi tells Shizue he has taken the medication before, when he was young.

Shizue remembers conversations with her grandmother about Shunichi and the paralysis and sufferings of his late wife, Tonoyo. Thinking like an engineer's wife, she puts two and two together. She suspects her father-in-law has syphilis. After many years, the disease has come out of remission.

It is a frightening prospect. Shizue boils all Shunichi's clothes. From then on, she washes his separately from the rest of the family's clothing. She thinks this will protect her and the children from the horrible disease.

And then ... good news! Shunichi receives a letter from his youngest daughter, Shigemi, in Honolulu. Shunichi has a chance to get his land back. He must return to Honolulu immediately and appeal to the United States government for the return of his property. The letter stresses that the appeal must be made in person.

Shunichi wastes no time preparing to return to Hawaii to regain his stolen land. December 28, 1952 he purchases his plane ticket to Hawaii. The flight is scheduled to leave from Haneda Airport in Tokyo the following day. He is packing a bag when he stops to go to the bathroom.

Shizue hears a yelp and a dull thump. She calls out to Shunichi, but he doesn't answer. She tries to open the bathroom door. Something is blocking it. She pushes harder and sees Shunichi slumped forward against the door.

"Yorie! Tosh! Come here! Quickly! Mother needs your help!" Tosh and Yorie are outside gathering charcoal for the stove. The children run inside to help, but it is too late. Grandfather Shunichi has passed away. He suffered a massive stroke as he attempted to rise from a squatting position.

Shizue notifies Dr. Kibe, their landlord's daughter. Toshiyuki rented a room from her and her husband while attending Tokyo University. Mr. and Mrs. Kibe treated him as if he was their own son and became good friends when his family moved to Tokyo.

Dr. Kibe examines Shunichi and signs the death certificate.

Shizue notifies Toshiyuki of his father's death and contacts a mortician, who prepares Shunichi's body at their home.

Yorie and Tosh watch as the undertaker puts cotton into their grandfather's nose and mouth, dresses him in a formal kimono, puts a triangle shaped headdress on him and places him into a coffin, set up in the living room.

As Shizue and the landlady, Mrs. Moriya, prepare for the funeral, Shizue starts showing signs of the influenza spreading throughout Japan that year. Then, both Yorie and Toshiharu start showing the same symptoms. The three become so sick they can only lie on their futons, which are laid out on tatamis. The living room has only six tatamis. There is barely enough room to walk around the coffin. Mrs. Moriya takes care of all the funeral arrangements for Shizue.

While they are preparing Shunichi's wake, two gentlemen show up at the front door demanding to see Shunichi's remains. They are from the Tokyo Health Department. They claim Dr. Kibe did not go through the proper channels to issue the Death Certificate. They insist on examining his body. They open the coffin and examine Shunichi for any suspicious markings. They are satisfied with their findings, sign the Death Certificate and leave.

It was hard enough to deal with the death of Shunichi. Now, they had to endure the horror of strangers cutting his clothing off and poking his body to see if there were any signs of foul play involved in his death.

Toshiyuki arrives from Okinawa.

The family, neighbors, and acquaintances say farewell to Shunichi. They spend the night and early morning talking and drinking sake to celebrate his life.

Shunichi is gone.

The family estate in Furuichi is lost forever.

Shizue's unfaithful husband will never be the man she dreamed of marrying.

Yorie and Tosh are the future of the family.

Another phase in the family's journey begins.

The next school year, Shizue decides she doesn't want Tosh to go to the school Yorie attended. The quality of teaching there is not good enough. She gets permission from Dr. Kibe to use her address in an upscale part of town, to get Tosh and Yorie into a better educational facility, eight miles away from their home. Shizue's secondary expectation is that in a school located in a better part of the city, little Tosh will not be the target of bullies and Yorie can take care of her little brother. Yorie enrolls in the Fourth grade and Tosh into the First grade.

The first day of class she dresses Tosh in the required military style uniform; a black coat fastened with brass buttons down the right side. Over the left breast is a badge with his name, grade, and classroom. Knee length black shorts, knee-high black socks, black shoes, and a black hat complete the uniform. He wears a white shirt, with the collar exposed over the coat. He carries a pigskin backpack and a rubber bag containing slippers for the classroom. Yorie is dressed in the girl's uniform.

Shizue walks Tosh and Yorie to the bus stop, intending only to show them which bus to take to get to school. But, as she turns to walk away, she can't. Tosh is trying to be brave, but she is certain it's only for her sake. Shizue rides with them to school so she can show them where to catch the bus home.

She walks with them to the gate of the school yard, then turns and begins the long walk home. Shizue doesn't look back. She can't bear to see little Tosh growing smaller and smaller as the distance between them grows.

Tosh watches his mother turn a corner and then runs behind a broad leafed bush to hide.

Yorie encourages him to come out, but he won't. The little Samurai cannot summon the strength to go any farther.

"Tosh, come on. We'll be late," says Yorie. "Come out of there."

Other students march through the gate and go inside. One little girl sees Tosh peeking from behind the bush.

"Hey. What's wrong?"

Tosh tells her he is afraid to go inside. The girl is Chiyoda, also a first grade student. She looks at Tosh's badge. "You're in my class. Come with me."

Yorie persuades Tosh to follow her and Chiyoda to his classroom. Tosh and his new friend, Chiyoda, go inside together.

As days and months pass, Shizue deals with the usual incidents of children's growth and learning.

Yorie is nine years of age now and, to all appearances, healthy.

Tosh, six years of age, is often sick and unable to attend school. A twelve-week fetus when the bomb was dropped on Hiroshima, his body was most affected by the radiation exposure. He struggles to keep up with his class work. He also struggles to declare independence from his mother. Because of her son's health issues, Shizue won't allow him to do anything she considers dangerous. No tree climbing, no bicycle riding. No eating cotton candy or popsicles.

More than anything in the world, Tosh wants to ride a bicycle. To a young boy dealing with health issues and an overprotective mother, these wonderful vehicles represent speed and freedom. He comes up with a clever idea worthy of an industrial entrepreneur. He removes two large magnets from Grandpa Shunichi's old radio speakers. Ties them to strings and drags them up and down streets in the neighborhood. The powerful magnets attract nails, screws and other metal odds and ends left over from the reconstruction of the neighborhood. He gathers the metal objects every day for a month. The neighbors applaud his community service, clearing the road of nails that flatten tires. His intent, however, is purely commercial. He sells his precious pile of scrap metal for enough money to rent a bicycle for one hour.

Tosh picks out a bright red bike for his maiden voyage and wobbles down the street. He does pretty well, considering he has no one to instruct him. Forty-five minutes into his hour, a swerve of the bicycle gets him sideswiped by a truck. The truck's mirror scrapes skin from his shoulder down to his wrist and sends him tumbling into a ditch. Tosh does not cry. He has experienced his first manly adventure worthy of a Samurai. His financial investment is secure as well because there is no damage to the bicycle.

Tosh returns home holding the injured arm behind his back.

"What's wrong with your arm?" Shizue asks.

"I fell."

"You fell?"

"Yes." Tosh thinks his escapade is best hidden in simple answers.

"Yes … you fell! Off a bicycle! Mrs. Moriya saw you get hit by a truck." Shizue, angry her son took such a risk and concerned about his injuries, begins to realize her little boy may not be the crybaby coward her husband makes him out to be.

Shizue says no more about the incident.

The next morning at the breakfast table she says, "Okay. I will buy you a bicycle. It will have to be a used one. And you must ride it only in the school yard nearby. Not on the streets."

"I can have a bicycle?" Tosh thinks he's dreaming.

"Yes. I'll ask around the neighborhood for one."

Shizue locates a gray bike for sale; in good shape, outgrown by a neighbor's cousin's boy.

Tosh polishes his bicycle and its shiny silver bell every day.

A year passes. Toshiyuki supports his family, but remains an absent parent. Tosh enjoys newfound freedom. Yorie is a popular girl, fast becoming a young lady. Old challenges join new ones.

Tosh is seven years old and in the second grade. He continues to miss class often due to recurrent illnesses caused by his weakened immune system. Every time he catches cold, it turns into bronchitis or tonsillitis or a nagging sinus infection.

And then, adding madness to injury, one school day, without Shizue's knowledge, Tosh and his classmates are required to remove their clothes. Naked, boys and girls alike are herded together into the schoolyard. They stand exposed, as a plane dives down and dumps DDT on them to eliminate lice. The children return to class with the acrid smell and taste of poison in their noses and mouths.

Shizue makes an appointment with school authorities and with no uncertain words, sees to it that Tosh will receive no further exposure to poison.

Because, Hibakushas, people exposed to radiation from the bombs dropped on Hiroshima and Nagasaki, keep their status secret for fear of social rejection, a rumor spreads rapidly among the teachers. Little Tosh's mother is a tiny bit toppyoushimonai (crazy).

With more and more homework heaped on him while suffering from illnesses that never seem to end, Tosh is unable to keep up with this schoolwork. He loses the will to study.

Constant battles with mysterious illnesses leave him in a chronic weakened condition. His poor health grows worse until he is kept at home most of the time. To ease his breathing, Shizue wraps a hot cloth around her son's chest and changes it every two hours. Tosh's condition does not improve. He loses his appetite. To keep up his strength, Shizue prepares okayu, rice cooked to a gooey paste. She serves the pasty rice with pickled plum. This is the only food he can keep down.

One morning at breakfast, Tosh's breathing is so heavy his shoulders move up and down with the effort. Shizue takes him to the doctor immediately. Tosh has tuberculosis.

Treatment for tuberculosis requires injections, three times a week for three weeks. Tosh is prohibited physical exercise and not allowed to go to school. Shizue picks up his classwork assignments and tries to help him at home.

After the course of injections he is allowed back in the classroom, but must avoid physical exertion for six months. Tosh sits in his classroom alone, while the other students go out at recess and on their lunch break. It will be a year before he recovers from the tuberculosis. The disease destroys twenty percent of his left lung.

Shizue dreads facing his teachers. They tell her she must push her son to study harder. There is little Shizue or Tosh can do.

After several occurrences of tonsillitis, Tosh's infected and ineffectual tonsils are finally scheduled to be removed. In the surgeon's office, are three reclining chairs that serve as operating tables.

A boy Tosh's age is undergoing tonsil removal in the same room, visible to all. The child fights and screams in pain and fear. Tosh watches in horror. The doctor, a tough old ex-army surgeon, gruffly commands the boy to be still and take it like a man. "Stop fighting me! Do not move. If you move you will die!"

Too disoriented to listen, much less comply, the frightened young patient continues to choke and struggle. The doctor roughly inserts a frame into the boy's mouth to hold it open. He puts his knee on the boy's chest to keep him from moving while he cuts away at the infected tonsils. Finally, the boy passes out.

Tosh is quite certain he is dead.

"You're next." The physician motions to Tosh. "Get in the chair."

Tosh complies.

"Here! Hold this dish under your chin and open your mouth."

Tosh opens his mouth.

The physician inserts the frame, and then picks up a huge needle. Terror paralyzes Tosh. He cannot utter a sound. The injection stings like a hot poker. Tosh doesn't move, fearing the doctor's warning, "Don't move or you'll die!"

Without waiting long enough for the medication to take effect, the impatient doctor makes the first incision. Tosh feels a stab of pain and fights to breathe through the thick, salty taste of blood.

After the tonsils are removed, Tosh's head is tilted forward as his adenoids are snipped. Blood gushes out into the dish he holds beneath his chin. Masses of flesh tumble into the receptacle, looking like bloody, raw meatballs.

"The boy can't eat anything for three days," the surgeon tells Shizue. "He can sip liquid through a straw. That's all. Put ice on his throat."

Tosh is sent home. His throat burns. Drinking cold water is unbearable.

After the tonsillectomy, adenoidectomy, and recovery from tuberculosis, Tosh's health improves somewhat.

Toshiyuki now spends time with his family once a year, staying for two weeks, from the middle of December until New Year's Day.

On his first yearly visit he brings boxes of chocolates, a doll for Yorie, and a solid steel yellow grader for Tosh. The grader is large enough for Tosh to sit on and play with in his sandbox.

Tosh enjoys the gifts his father brought, but he resents his father's visits. Toshiyuki scolds him for his poor grades and criticizes him for being weak. Worse, he and Yorie cannot sleep in the same room with their mother during their father's visit. They must sleep alone in a tiny room by the front door.

During this visit, a neighbor informs Toshiyuki that Shizue frequently entertains a male visitor in his home. The frequent visitor is her landlady's son, who is ten years older than Yorie. He enjoys visiting Yorie and Tosh. Later, he confesses to his mother that he wants to marry Yorie.

Toshiyuki confronts Shizue if the rumor is true.

"Yes," answers Shizue.

"Why does he come here?"

"He is a friend."

"A friend … only a friend?"

"He enjoys being with Yorie and Tosh," she replies, "not me. Why? What are you asking? Do you accuse me of sleeping with him? Are you going to kill me? You are a hypocrite! It is okay for you to have affairs but I cannot? I am sorry to disappoint you! I am not like you; I am not sleeping with him. I have pride and I am raising two children all by myself. Your jealousy is blinding you. Think what you like. You don't think when you hurt me, cavorting with other women … embarrassing me. Now you know how it feels."

Toshiyuki grabs his jacket and stomps out of the house.

331

He returns an hour later. Nothing more is said about Shizue's frequent male visitor. The unresolved tension thickens the air in the home.

Toshiyuki's two week visit passes slowly. Finally, it is time for him to return to Okinawa. Shizue and the children see him off at Haneda Airport.

They wave goodbye and smile with all sincerity. Toshiyuki is glad to leave. Shizue and Tosh, not so much Yorie, are glad to see him go. Absence will not make their hearts grow fonder. For Shizue, with her husband hundreds of miles away ... well, what she doesn't know...

CHAPTER TWENTY-SIX

Summers to Remember

The next year, Shizue transfers Tosh to a private school in the city of Iwai 80 miles northeast of Tokyo in the Chiba prefecture. Shizue chooses the school for its oceanfront location. There Tosh can breathe clean air, eat fresh fish, and drink fresh milk. This environment, she believes, will improve her son's health.

For the second time, Shizue lied to get Tosh into a better school.

Tosh's new experiences begin with his first breakfast there. The breakfast consists of Miso soup, a bowl of hot rice, pickled radish, and an egg, raw in the shell. Tosh doesn't know what to do with the raw egg.

The kid next to him cracks the egg into the bowl of hot rice; mixes it together and adds soy sauce. Sight of the slimy, raw egg soaking into the rice and soy sauce turns Tosh's stomach. He eats everything except the egg.

The second day, Tosh gives the raw egg and rice a try. It turns out to be delicious.

The students drink raw milk with their meals, fresh, sometimes warm from the cow. Although Tosh has been drinking fresh milk all his life, somehow he never learned where it comes from. Today, Tosh takes a swallow and asks the boy next to him why the milk is warm. The farm boy explains in great detail, the process of extracting milk from a cow's teats; cleaning the teats, drying them, and trying not to get any udder hair into the milk. Tosh eyes the creamy, warm substance, gags and will not drink another drop. He cleans his plate of food, but leaves the noxious liquid. A teacher notices the glassful of milk. Tosh tells her he doesn't like it. She tells him the milk is good for him and she won't allow him to waste it. In fact, he will sit there until he consumes it. Tosh considers his options and drinks the milk while holding his breath.

Tosh settles in and loves his new life at the oceanfront boarding school. Science becomes his favorite subject. He raises his grade from D to C.

When not in class, the children, both boys and girls, play games on the beach. Tosh especially likes baseball and ping pong. The beach strand turns into a classroom at night for studying heaven's constellations. Students eat, sleep, and bathe together. Tosh makes friends with a boy, Fumio, who is fascinated with poisonous plants. He also has his first crush on a girl, although he never even speaks to her.

Tosh is an excellent ping pong player. He and Fumio are the top two competitors. A championship match is set up. Fumio wins. Tosh cries. His life-long struggle to meet his father's and teacher's expectations; to be "Number 1" at something, finds its release.

But, there's still baseball. After playing the game on the beach one day and hitting three home runs; one grand slam, Tosh wakes up the next morning to find both legs swollen so badly, he cannot walk. A school official phones his mother to come right away.

The following morning, about 5 a.m., a nurse stops at his bedside to check on him. Tosh is awake. He tells the nurse he had a dream that his mother will walk through the school gate at 10 a.m. In the dream he saw her doing Shiatsu on his legs. The swelling went down and he could walk again.

"Okay, the nurse says. We will watch the clock and see if your dream comes true."

The dream does come true. Shizue walks through the gate at exactly 10:00 a.m. Everything happens just as Tosh saw it.

Once a month, a day is set aside for parent visitation. Toshiyuki, still working in Okinawa, hundreds of miles away, cannot visit. Shizue is able to visit only three times, twice during the summer and once when Tosh's legs were swollen.

Eighteen months later, Tosh returns home from the boarding school. After a year and a half of breathing fresh ocean air and eating wholesome foods, Tosh's health issues have improved, but he continues to have bouts with bronchitis.

Tosh treasures his memories of the ocean front boarding school, especially the summers. Fortunately, in most every child's life there is more than one summer to remember. For Tosh, there comes another, in 1957. Two airline tickets arrive in the mail for a trip to Naha, Okinawa; a ticket for Shizue and one for Tosh. Toshiyuki could only afford two tickets, so Yorie, now fourteen years old, will stay behind, being looked after by their landlady, Mrs. Moriya, who lives across the street.

At Haneda International Airport, Shizue and Tosh board a Lockheed Constellation tripletail aircraft. This is Tosh's first flight. He has watched his father leave many times by plane and is excited to experience it for himself.

The two inner propellers rumble as the plane prepares for takeoff. Suddenly, their speed increases. Gray smoke billows out from behind them. Then, the two outer propellers start up. Smoke billows out from the other two as their speed escalates. The plane begins to turn. A screeching sound accompanies the plane's movement. It taxies into take off position. On the runway, the aircraft picks up speed, grumbling with a low pitched hum, as it lifts into the air.

Tosh is flying. He presses his face to the window. City lights sparkle like diamonds on the ground as the plane climbs higher through wispy clouds.

Too soon for Tosh, there is only darkness outside his window. Lulled by the humming of the plane, his eyes grow heavy. He is almost asleep when the pilot's voice blasts out over the intercom. The aircraft is approaching a typhoon so massive it will be safer to fly through it rather than around.

"Brace yourself," warns the pilot. "It's going to be a rough ride until we get to the eye."

The pilot fails to inform the less traveled and knowledgeable passengers that after passing through the eye, they will experience more turbulence as they exit the typhoon.

One hundred mile an hour force wind and rain pounds the wings. The metal and bolt aircraft jerks, dips, and vibrates violently. The wings will surely be ripped off.

An air pocket drops the plane without warning. Tosh twists against the restraint of the seat belt and buries his face against his mother. Shizue holds his hand with assurance that everything is going to be okay.

Both Shizue and Tosh expect the plane to crash. How can the aircraft possibly withstand the relentless force?

The powerful turbulence lasts over an hour. Then, as suddenly as it began … calm. The plane enters the eye of the storm. The sky is clear again, filled with stars.

Exhausted from fear and his consequential imaginings, Tosh relaxes and falls asleep. It's a short night's sleep. The plane begins to vibrate again. They have exited the eye and reentered the tempest. The already rattled wings will surely be ripped away now.

Tosh's knuckles are white by the time the plane lands safely at Naha Airport in Okinawa. A massive sigh escapes the passengers, followed by anxious chatter. A smile aches on every face as they exit the plane. There are no strangers in survival. They are joined by comradery.

Toshiyuki waits at the airport to pick up Shizue and Tosh. He heard about the storm. Concern etches his face.

It surprises Shizue how happy she is to see her husband. Perhaps it is only relief that she and Tosh are alive. Or maybe their near death experience sparked another flame of hope for their relationship.

Toshiyuki walks them to his jeep.

He points to his boarding house as they drive into Naha, noting that his room is on the second floor at the far end of the hallway. But that isn't where they get out.

"My room is too small for you. Noisy too. You and Tosh will stay at the home of a friend who is out of town. He is grateful to me for getting him a government construction contract that made him rich. He has a   never- married daughter who lives nearby on the beachfront. She is excited to show you and Tosh the city."

Toshiyuki drives to a magnificent mansion on a hill, overlooking the entire town.

"It's beautiful," comments Shizue. "But Toshiyuki, I'd rather you show us around than a stranger's daughter."

"This is your vacation, not mine. I have to work."

"I see."

Toshiyuki's brow furrows, "I will show you my room before you leave."

The home where Shizue and Tosh stay in Okinawa is an aesthetic paradise. Giant white columns grace the entrance, evoking an image of strength and protection. The grounds are impeccable. Shizue sighs … for her love of beauty itself … for the loss of their mansion in Furuichi … and for the persistent, tortuous hope that is never far from the thorns of her reality. Are she and Tosh here at this wonderful home because Toshiyuki experienced a rare moment of thoughtfulness or does her husband have a secret motive?

Servants live in small homes on the property. They take care of all Shizue's and Tosh's needs.

Bunko, the unmarried daughter, arrives every morning to plan their day. Her name is completely at odds with the young woman's appearance. The name Bunko means "literary child". The real Bunko drives a jeep, wears an Australian type bush hat, shorts, and military boots.

Toshiyuki joins his wife and son in the evenings for dinner, but is away the rest of the three days that follow.

Shizue grows more suspicious. The next morning, she asks Bunko to entertain Tosh for the remainder of the day. Shizue wishes to go out on her own.

Tosh is excited. Today he can go where he wants to go, have some fun on the beach instead of visiting temples and gravesites.

Bunko drops Shizue off on the town's main street.

"Thank you, Bunko. I'm going to enjoy a little shopping and then walk back to the house. So, please, you and Tosh have fun without any concern for me."

"Yes, we will," assures Bunko.

Shizue waves as they pull away and then heads straight for Toshiyuki's boarding house.

She remembers the way and Toshiyuki's directions to his room. She climbs the stairs. Her mind flashes back to the day Colonel Kubota asked to speak with her in private; the day she learned of Toshiyuki's betrayal with Mieko. Why is she remembering that now? She will knock on her husband's door. He will not answer and she will leave feeling guilty over her suspicions, as she returns to Main Street and browses through the shops.

At the door to his room, she draws a quiet breath and knocks.

A young woman, younger than Shizue, opens the door, smiling. Her teeth are yaeba (snaggletooth), crooked and protruding.

"Who are you?" the young woman asks.

"Who are *you*?" asks Shizue.

"You should know. You knocked on Mr. Kano's door. I am Mrs. Kano."

"Hmmm…" Shizue looks over the woman serving up attitude and rudeness to a stranger. "Then, Mr. Kano has two wives."

"You are Toshiyuki's wife?" She laughs. "No, you are not."

"Hey!" Toshiyuki appears at the top of the stairs and rushes toward Shizue and Atsuko.

"Atsuko … I…" Toshiyuki pants, out of breath, "I told you I am married."

"And I told you I don't believe you," says Atsuko. "You do not have a wife. You have a new girlfriend. You cannot get rid of me by trickery."

"Shizue, please … tell her."

339

"You need to leave, Atsuko. Our son, Tosh, is waiting downstairs. I do not want him to see you."

"Show him to me! I want to meet your son."

"Toshiyuki?" Shizue's jaw juts forward. "What is happening here?"

"She ... Atsuko moved things in when I was away at work." His eyes cast downward all the while he speaks. "Atsuko refused to leave when I tell her to go. She does not believe I am married. She does not go when I ask her to go."

"I see. She does not leave when you *ask* her to go. So, this is why ... *she* is why you said you would show me your room before our vacation ends?"

"Yeah," Toshiyuki confesses.

"I am not going to ask Atsuko to leave," says Shizue.

"But, I..." Toshiyuki stammers. "I..."

"I will *tell* her to leave. Gather your belongings, Atsuko."

Atsuko laughs, again. "I will not be tricked so you can move in. I love Toshiyuki. I will be with him. Not you!"

"Toshiyuki, where are this woman's belongings?"

He points here and there in the room.

Shizue gathers clothing hanging from hooks on the wall. "This? And this?"

Toshiyuki nods.

Shizue presses the clothing against Atsuko. "If you want anything else, get it now. You are leaving."

Atsuko bundles the items and a few others into a scarf.

On her way out the door she faces Shizue, "He will get tired of you, too." Turning to Toshiyuki she says, "Then what will you do?"

Atsuko patters down the stairs.

Shizue walks past Toshiyuki and out the door.

"Shizue... Where are you going?"

"I'm going to get my son. We came here to have fun and that is what we are going to do."

"But you ... what about ... about Atsuko."

"I know all I need to know about Atsuko. But you ... my dear husband... You brought me here to get rid of a girlfriend you no longer wanted. How could you?"

In the days that follow, Shizue and Tosh explore the town and the seashore. They also, to Tosh's dismay, visit more burial sites and temples.

During a walk on the beach, Tosh gets thirsty and asks for something to drink. That day, eleven year old Tosh, tastes an American Pepsi for the first time. It is love! From then on, the fizzy, sweet soda is all he wants to drink. Shizue doesn't mind. The water available has an odd taste. She thinks it is too dirty to drink.

Toshiyuki takes a case of Pepsi to the house on the hill for Tosh. Tosh can't get enough. He drinks five bottles every day.

In late afternoons, tired out from whatever adventure the day has brought, Tosh climbs a narrow stairway opening onto the flat roof of the house. From there, he can see the whole city and watch for a cloud of dust as his father comes bumping up the road, driving his jeep. Tosh has lugged a discarded cardboard box up to the roof. He sits inside it for shade, as he waits for his father, drinks Pepsi, and eats tuna from a can.

Today it's too hot on the roof. He goes down to the courtyard and lies beneath a shade tree. He watches a breeze rustling through the branches and falls asleep. He awakens when something thuds on his shirt. Staring into his eyes is an also startled lizard; dark green with bright neon green bumps and a tail circled in black stripes. There are hundreds of them in the branches of the tree.

The treasure trove of lizards attracts ducks and chickens, who roam the yard looking for a tasty treat. The smell of duck and chicken dung is strong. Locals tolerate the odor because the dung keeps Habu away, one of the world's most poisonous snakes. The Habu, a pit viper greenish yellow in color, closely related to the adder, bites with two inch fangs causing death from convulsions, before the victim can take ten steps.

Into the second week of their visit, a typhoon, one of the most powerful ever, approaches Okinawa. House servants board the windows of the main house and retreat to their homes. Toshiyuki, Shizue, and Tosh take shelter in the basement of the mansion.

The typhoon hits the island from the south, goes north, turns around and hits them again. Gusts break the wind gage at 185 miles per hour.

At the first sign of a decrease in wind velocity, Toshiyuki sends Tosh upstairs for water and food. By the time Tosh reaches the kitchen, the wind has returned with a vengeance. Windowpanes pop and shatter from the pressure. Rain drives through breaks in the boards in a horizontal spray. Tosh runs back toward the basement without food or water. Reaching the stairs leading to the basement he is soaking wet and not a little scared.

He tries to close the heavy steel door at the top of the stairs when a tree crashes through the upper part of the house, through the floor, and down to the staircase.

Toshiyuki and Shizue rush out to the stairway.

Tosh barely escaped injury. A massive tree trunk lies only feet away.

Toshiyuki, Shizue, and Tosh huddle together, expecting the house to collapse upon them. Eventually, the wind dies. The rain fades to a light sprinkle and then stops. There is silence; an eerie suffocating hush.

The battery operated radio crackles as the local station comes back on the air.

The eye of the typhoon is over them. Food and water is running low. The steel door will not open fully as it is blocked by the fallen tree. Toshiyuki, Tosh, and Shizue duck under the tree and squeeze through the doorway.

Outside are blue skies.

The yard previously crowded with squawking chickens, quacking ducks, and lizards is silent. The powerful wind blew them all away.

Shizue and Tosh hurry to the local market where they buy as much Pepsi and snacks as they carry back to the house.

Toshiyuki cuts the fallen tree into sections before another round of killer wind attacks.

The storm stays with them four more days. Finally, it leaves Okinawa, headed for the mainland of Japan.

Super Typhoon Faye hit on September 18 and finally dwindled out on September 27th. Fifty people die. Seventy are missing.

Servants remove boards from windows as Shizue cleans up water and debris blown inside. Toshiyuki and Tosh hop into the inexplicably undamaged jeep and drive around surveying the storm's damage.

All the western style houses are severely damaged or simply blown away leaving only their foundations. Older, native homes are still standing, most with very little disturbance.

Tosh is baffled. Why do some houses remain and others are gone? Toshiyuki explains that the old style houses, standing on stilts and having no walls, allow the wind to pass through. Western style houses cannot release the tremendous wind pressure and collapse.

The last day of Shizue and Tosh's visit arrives. The servants prepare a customary farewell meal. The main course is roasted pig. The head servant cuts off one of the pig's ears and places it in front of Tosh, who is the guest of honor. Serving the ear of a pig is a sign of respect and farewell.

Tosh stares at the ear, as everyone stares at him. What's he supposed to do with it? Surely, they don't expect him to eat it.

The servants wait for little Tosh to accept the honor.

"Don't embarrass me," Toshiyuki mumbles under his breath. "Eat it."

Tosh picks the pig ear up with two fingers, breaks off a piece and shoves it into his mouth. As it was with the pet chicken stew his grandfather made, Tosh cannot chew it. He holds his breath and swallows the bite whole. The servants clap their hands and the family begins eating.

The servants have another surprise for Tosh ... a poisonous Habu, preserved in a jar. This gift is for Tosh to take back to school and show his classmates and teachers.

Tosh can hardly sleep the first night back in Tokyo. It's like Christmas Eve, waiting to carry his treasure to school and present the Habu to the principal. Tosh is not disappointed. The principal and teachers alike are excited over Tosh's generosity. Their recognition of him for bringing back a rare and dangerous specimen from his travels is overwhelming. It is Tosh's first moment of glory. The Habu will be kept in the school lab as a display and labeled as a gift from the Kano family.

Boarding school on the beachfront, the summer of 1957 in Okinawa and a dead Habu in a jar top the list of Tosh's happiest memories.

His one moment of glory is short-lived. Still suffering the effects of radiation, still sickly, missing school and unable to keep up with his studies, he continues to be alternately teased and shunned by classmates and ignored by teachers. When the children choose sides for games on the playground, Tosh is chosen last or simply left out. On class field trips, the students are required to hold someone's hand so they will not get separated from the group. No one will hold his. Tosh's hands are covered in warts, a result of his weakened immune system.

So his life continues: overprotected by a doting mother, and unaccepted by his prideful father. No friends. No hope for the things other children take for granted. Even Yorie grows more distant as her attention turns to "grownup" interests.

Tosh is never a child, in the beautiful sense being a child implies. To Japan, he is the defective offspring of nuclear war. His exposure to radiation drastically narrows, possibly eliminates, his chances of employment and marriage. People fear bomb survivors may spawn an epidemic of malformed children.

Toshiyuki works in Okinawa for ten years. His visits with the family do not increase. They remain once a year for a two week period in the winter.

Shizue, who sacrificed her own dreams on the bank of the Ota River when she learned of her husband's infidelity, focuses her attention on Yorie and Tosh.

345

Tosh spends his youth struggling to improve his grades in order to meet Japan's high standards of achievement. Acquiring this, he is certain, will also acquire his father's acceptance. Although his health gradually improves, his grades never meet expectations. Gaining his father's acceptance is also a goal he does not attain.

By his teenage years, Tosh has, according to his father and teachers, failed on every level. He sees no worth or value to his family or himself. There is a way out. Suicide. Tosh begins to contemplate ending his existence. In Samurai tradition, suicide is an honorable choice; a way to die without disgrace. Suicide restores family honor.

Tosh considers seppuku (hari-kari to the western world), plus other ways to end his life. He stands beside a railroad track imagining throwing himself in front of a train. He considers slitting his wrists and hanging.

Tosh does not carry through.

He spends most of his time alone, reading and living in the world of his imagination. Otherwise, every day is more of the same. Until, news arrives about their beautiful and beloved mansion in Furuichi.

It happened that the new owner's son broke up with his girlfriend. She retaliated by setting the house on fire. The huge mansion burned for hours, visible from miles away; the largest fire to occur ever in the village of Furuichi.

It had been heartbreaking to leave their ancestral home and now they have lost it for all time. They will never return to the magnificent old house their family once proudly called home.

Toshiyuki finishes his project in Okinawa and returns home.

Shizue has been saving money from the allowances Toshiyuki sent her from Okinawa. She has saved a large sum of money. She presents the savings book to Toshiyuki and suggests they buy a house. Toshiyuki is shocked! He was receiving 100,000 yen per month and kept 60% of it. Shizue had to feed and care for three people with 40%. She was not a tightwad; she just spent her money wisely and made most of their clothes. She did not hesitate to purchase nutritious food for the family and was very generous to neighbors and acquaintances.

Toshiyuki and Shizue buy a house on a hilltop overlooking the town of Oasaki. It is much larger than the house they have lived in for the last ten years. Their dream of living in a beautiful home again is granted. Yorie is now 16. Toshiharu is 12.

Their happiness does not last. Toshiyuki is not able to find a job.

A Chinese friend in Taiwan suggests Toshiyuki be his partner in his construction business. He invites him to Taiwan, where he is in the process of acquiring a contract to build a large housing complex. Toshiyuki accepts the offer and moves to Taiwan.

Six months pass, a year and then two years. Toshiyuki spends all his money waiting for his friend's business to take off. All the while, Shizue urges him to return home to Oasaki. Stubborn Toshiyuki insists he needs more time. He has not learned to trust Shizue's instincts.

Toshiyuki's friend does not get the contract.

While in Taiwan, Toshiyuki manages to get another mistress. He cannot be left alone! He betrays Shizue again.

He finally returns home to Oasaki having drained the precious family funds Shizue built over the years.

Now what?

Fortunately a friend of Toshiyuki's, Mr. Fukunaga, offers him a job with his small Import/Export business in Tokyo. There are only two employees, his buddy and a "Girl Friday". Toshiyuki works there for only a year. Mr. Fukunaga cannot pay him enough to support his family.

In January 1961, Toshiyuki and Shizue get their American citizenship reinstated with the help of Senator Fong of Hawaii and the United States Congress.

Within the week, a decision is made. For years, both Toshiyuki and Shizue have dreamed of returning to the place of their birth, Honolulu. The family will leave for Hawaii as soon as possible.

Tosh informs his teacher that he will soon be leaving the country. To Tosh's surprise the teacher replies, "A great day for the United States. A sad day for Japan."

Toshiyuki's and Shizue's beloved Hawaii is nothing like they remember. The nature of the island has changed drastically. It presents extreme temptations, especially for a teenage boy. They decide to look for another place to live.

Salt Lake City, they are told by relatives, is a great place to make a home and raise children. Good schools, reasonable home prices, low utilities cost, museums, art, and music.

In May, they make the move to Salt Lake City, where Tosh attends Granite High School.

After moving to Salt Lake City, Shizue sees the fireball a third time. She is talking to Toshiyuki's sister, Nishiyo, who has also moved to the city and is seated on the couch. Shizue is standing nearby. Both face a window. The fireball appears, coming and going in the same manner as the first and second appearances. The sister stands up and yells, "What happened? Did you see it? What was it?"

Misao's spirit has followed the family to Salt Lake City. Later, Shizue goes to the spot outside where the fireball appeared. There is scorched vegetation where it shot up. She tells Toshiyuki about the physical evidence of the fireball. Finally, she has proof for him that she was not dreaming and is not making it up. Toshiyuki dismisses the incident. He did not see it.

Toshiyuki, Shizue, Yorie, and Tosh begin their lives anew.

In December of 1967, Toshiyuki obtains a job with the United States Navy in Thailand. Toshiyuki, Shizue, and Yorie move to Thailand. Tosh is left behind in Utah to complete his college education at the University of Utah, majoring in Engineering.

In the summer of 1968, Tosh travels to Thailand for a visit.

Toshiyuki rents a room at a beach resort hotel for him and his son. The last day there, they sit together on the strand facing the setting sun as it pours liquid rose gold over water. Toshiyuki speaks with Tosh about his future. He has his son's life all planned out, in great detail. He has a job interview lined up for Tosh upon graduation from college. Tosh is to go to a certain company, ask for a certain man, etc. Once settled into a job, Tosh can start thinking about marriage and children.

Then Toshiyuki speaks candidly about his infidelities.

"Son, you know your mother and I did not marry for love, but for family."

Tosh, age 22, nods. It is true. He has never seen any form of affection pass between his parents.

"Promise me something," says Toshiyuki.

"What is it, Dad?"

"Son … over many years, I had other women. I hurt your mother deeply. Because of our class in Japanese culture, wealth and

349

power, all men in our family had mistresses. There were no exceptions." Toshiyuki smashes a cigarette in a souvenir ashtray brought from Honolulu.

Tosh waits to hear the promise Toshiyuki wants a son to give his father.

"Since moving to United States, your mother and I have found love. Yeah ... just as Grandmother said. We are happy. Tosh, I want you to be happy. Don't make the mistakes I made. Break the chain. Promise God and me you will be faithful to your wife when you marry. Don't hurt your wife. Can you promise this?"

"Yes. I promise. I will never have a mistress or an affair with another woman. I swear to God and to you."

"Thank you, Son." Toshiyuki rises from his chair.

"Dad ... wait. I think it will be good if you tell mother you are sorry for hurting her so much."

"You are right. Yeah, I will do that."

Living conditions in Bangkok are not pleasant. It is very humid (100% humidity) all year around.

Toshiyuki has a minor heat stroke. After a short recovery time, he decides to return to the United States. He obtains a job in California at El Toro Marine Air Station. Toshiyuki, Shizue, Yorie and their cat Tonko come back to the United States. Their cat Tonko has been with them since 1964 and traveled with them wherever they went.

Toshiyuki works at the El Toro until 1976. Then, he finds a position in Iwakuni, Japan as a Civil Engineer. Again, Toshiyuki, Shizue, Yorie and Tonko move; this time to Iwakuni, Japan in May

1975. In August, Yorie decides to move back to California, as she is not able to find a job in Japan.

Toshiyuki fares better. He is able to get his dream job in Yokosuka, Japan as a liaison between the United States and Japan.

He is diagnosed with cancer just as he is ready to move to Yokosuka. His Commander in Charge and doctors suggest he returns to the United States for treatment.

He and Shizue fly back to California. He is admitted to St. Joseph Hospital in Orange, California. The cancer spreads throughout his body and doctors are not able to treat him.

After 10 days of hospitalization, Toshiyuki passes away. It is August, 1976. The day after the funeral service, Tosh approaches his mother as she sits quietly looking through a box of photographs. He reveals the conversation with his father in the summer of 1968 in Thailand; Toshiyuki's request that Tosh break the chain of infidelity in the family and stay faithful to his future wife.

Tosh learns that his father did not express his sorrow and regret to Shizue, as he said he would.

Shizue's eyes fill with tears. "Yes. We did find the love Obaasan promised us. I wish your father had told me he was sorry..." Shizue hesitates, "but ... he did ... in a way. Because he told you this ... because he asked you to promise you will not hurt a woman as he hurt me, he has told me that he is truly sorry."

CHAPTER TWENTY-SEVEN

A Celebration for World Peace

August 25, 1990

Tosh left Salt Lake City, Utah at 8 a.m. this Saturday morning, driving 120 miles across the barren Bonneville Salt Flats to a small desert town on the border of Utah and Nevada. He is scheduled to speak about his first brush with death on that fateful day in Hiroshima, August of 1945. This isn't his first visit here. He has been to Wendover, a casino town, many times to play the slot machines.

Today, however, he travels by invitation as a guest speaker at the dedication of the Composite Group Monument erected in the parking lot of West Wendover's Visitor Center. This monument honors members of the 509th Composite Group, United States Air Force, who trained at the Wendover base in 1944 and 1945 for the vital, secret mission of delivering the first atomic bombs on Japanese targets. It was in this arid location the crew of the World War II B-29 bomber, the Enola Gay, trained before being deployed to Tinian Island for the mission which bombed Hiroshima, Japan, the city where Tosh's family lived. For this reason, and the fact that he is the youngest known survivor of the devastation and fallout of "Little Boy", he has been invited to speak at the gathering in Wendover. Its theme is to promote and celebrate World Peace.

As the miles pass, Tosh's anticipation mounts. There is much time on the lonely road to think about the event that brought him to this day, 45 years after the bombing. Outside distractions are few. Other than the comings and goings of visitors to the casinos, nothing ever changes on the strip of I-80 between Salt Lake City and Wendover. There are no houses along the way, no people, except in passing cars, rarely a sign of living creatures except the occasional lizard or wandering seagull en route to or from the Great Salt Lake. Side roads veer off with signs naming places that can't be seen, with the admonition, "No food. No services."

Stark sand etched in white salt stretches for miles, ending far in the distance at the bottom of hazy purple mountains. Here and there along the roadside, plastic flowers lay beneath a wooden cross staked into the ground where someone died in an auto accident; most often a one car accident caused by alcohol, speed, ice, or the hypnotic boredom of driving through this flat, featureless desert. Outside Wendover is a road sign tallying the deaths along the strip for the previous year.

When the Utah tree, an odd, concrete structure with branches bearing big, odd colored balls, comes into view, travelers know that Wendover is only 25 miles away.

Through a gap in the mountains, Tosh sees a patch of nondescript buildings. He's almost there. It will feel good to get out of the car and stretch. The drive today seemed much longer than usual. Tosh chalks up the anomaly to anticipation and apprehension surrounding the ceremony celebrating world peace.

When it comes to world peace, the paths people take in its name are, too often not peaceful at all … standing like a coin on edge, with opposing sides facing opposite directions. As a United States citizen and a Japanese man who was in Hiroshima when the A-bomb exploded, Tosh has a special understanding of opposing views.

Off the freeway, at the overpass approaching the Montego Bay Casino, a banner stretched across the road flaps wildly as gusts of hot, dry August air whip the desert terrain. The bold print on the banner announces Tosh's destination by location as well as purpose: *A Celebration for World Peace*

Tosh has always believed in "signs". The coincidence of that sudden atmospheric disturbance rattling the sign announcing the celebration of peace is significant. This day of celebration will not end as planned or anticipated.

He turns his car into a packed parking area. There are no spaces available. Pulling into a dusty field, he steps out of his air conditioned car, weaves around cars and over hot asphalt, to the area where the celebration is to take place. Some of the vehicles are overheated and hissing like exhausted locomotives.

Approaching the area where the stage has been set up, Tosh sees a familiar face in the distance. An acquaintance, Richard "Dick" Sherwood is walking away from the platform.

Dick, a former military pilot, was in a plane accompanying the Enola Gay over Hiroshima the day of the bombing. He witnessed the devastation of the city from the tail-gun section of a plane taking   low-level photographs to record the effectiveness of the new atomic bomb. The magnitude of destruction he saw, shocked him to his core. Dick's life changed forever. After leaving the military, he became an avid peace activist.

Tosh first heard about Dick from a colleague who knew his connection to Hiroshima. A few weeks later, Mr. Sherwood and Tosh met. Tosh reached out to shake his hand. Dick got down on his knees and with tears in his eyes, expressed his happiness that Tosh survived the bomb.

"Dick!" Tosh calls out. His friend continues walking away with a steadfast and noticeably annoyed gait.

Tosh approaches the gathering of around 500 people wondering why an eye witness to that day in Hiroshima would be leaving the ceremony.

Dick disappears from view as the national anthem of the United States begins to play. Tosh grabs a program and claims an empty chair in the back row.

The program shows the national anthem of Japan scheduled next, right after the United States anthem. However, the anthem of Japan does not play. No explanation is given. The ceremony moves forward without honoring Tosh's homeland.

Retired Brigadier General Paul Tibbets, commander of the 509th Composite Group and pilot of the B-29, the Enola Gay, on August 6, 1945, leads the dedication and uncovers the monument, a 16-foot granite obelisk supporting a bronze replica of the famous World War II bomber.

After the unveiling and applause, the former General thanks everyone for dedicating the memorial to his crew. The official ceremony soon approaches its end. The chaplain of the 509th closes with a prayer: "We thank thee, God, for the atom bomb, through which peace came to our world."

The microphone screeches, a squadron of jet fighters thunders overhead and the band jumpstarts a rousing tune.

The words of the chaplain's prayer whirl in Tosh's head. *We thank thee, God, for the atom bomb?*

"Tosh!"

Tosh looks around. Approaching him is Miss Underwood, the hostess who asked him to speak at the occasion.

She squeezes through the crowd. They exchange the usual pleasantries.

"Why was there no Japanese anthem?" The tone of Tosh's voice is not as delicate as he intended. "Do you know?"

She motions for Tosh to follow her away from the chattering crowd.

"Tosh … last night there was a press dinner and questions presented by journalists to the Enola Gay crew. One of the Japanese press members condemned the crew for killing the people in Hiroshima. He called the men aboard the bomber murderers. It was a very tense and unpleasant scene, as you can imagine. For safety reasons, security escorted the Japanese press from the room. General Tibbets and his crew did not want the Japanese anthem played at the dedication. They also asked me to cancel your speech at the dinner later. I am so sorry."

It saddens Tosh and Miss Underwood that an opportunity to advance peace in the world, began in such a way. The hostess apologizes repeatedly. Tosh has come a long way, both literally and figuratively to attend this celebration and promotion of the hope of peace. She knows how important his participation in this historical event is to him.

She invites him to join the other invitees at the dinner at which she had originally scheduled him to speak.

"Are you certain that will be okay? I'm not sure I should after what happened."

"It'll be fine." She appears to reflect on her words as she glances around the crowd. Then, looking back at Tosh, she smiles weakly and draws a breath. "Yes, I'm sure it's okay. I'll see you at 6:30 p.m. in the hanger that once housed the Enola Gay. Do you know the way?"

"I'm sure I can find it. Okay. I'll be there at 6:30."

Miss Underwood nods and walks away, glancing back once, before quickening her pace.

Tosh returns to the hotel, happy to get out of the heat. After showering, he lies down and falls asleep. The unexpected nap causes him to be half an hour late for the dinner.

Driving to the hanger, he passes the decades old buildings formerly used for barracks. They are an eerie sight now. Peeling paint hangs from weathered wood. Windows are dusty, dull, and empty. Thirsty ground and shriveled weeds surround the structures. They remind Tosh of the aftermath of the bomb dropped on Hiroshima. Photographic images too graphic to forget, witnesses of mutilation, pain and suffering pass through his mind like ghosts as he opens the door of the hanger.

At least 100 people are seated on folding chairs at long white clothed tables. The room that once housed the Enola Gay is filled with festive chatter and the inviting aromas of a feast of celebration.

Tosh enters. The door closes behind him. Everyone stops talking. The festive atmosphere goes from chatter to dead silence in five seconds.

Tosh is being digested in the belly of a giant, metal beast.

Alerted by the sudden change and directed by the turn of heads, Miss Underwood rushes to his side.

"Tosh! So glad you made it."

"Maybe I shouldn't be here."

"Of course you should. Please come on in."

Tosh is not reassured. Everyone stares critically at him, the late arrival, a middle-aged Japanese man in a conservative business suit, wearing coke bottle glasses held up by a heavy mustache.

The hostess takes his arm and escorts him to a table in the corner. She babbles praise for the caterers, describes the food and drinks available, and successfully pulls his focus from the awkward moment.

When Tosh ceases to be the center of attention, she points out General Tibbets.

"General Tibbets," Tosh repeats his name, feeling as if he is awakening from a forgotten dream. "I've wanted to meet him for such a long time. Do you think it's okay if I go over and say hello to him and his crew?"

"No!" The hostess is emphatic. "No, Tosh, I don't think so. Please... enjoy your dinner and know how much I appreciate your effort to be a part of the event. I'll speak with you again before you leave."

Tosh nods, thoughtfully.

The meal is delicious, especially the barbeque chicken. By the time Tosh finishes eating, he has decided to ignore the hostess's caution. He has waited for this moment far too long to turn and walk away. He will talk to the General and his crew.

Tosh maneuvers around tables and between chairs towards General Tibbets. The General, engaged in casual conversation, is unaware of his approach.

Toshiharu Kano, survivor of the A-bomb dropped on Hiroshima, taps General Tibbets, pilot of the Enola Gay, on his left shoulder.

The General turns. His eyes flash with surprise and then fix on the Japanese man.

One by one, heads turn. Conversations stumble to a stop. One by one, words fall like dominoes. Silence filters through the hanger once again.

"May I shake your hand?" Tosh asks the General.

The General glances at a man sitting across the table, who immediately resumes his dropped conversation. The other guests follow suit.

Once the rising banter affords a degree of privacy, the General replies, "Shake my hand ... what for?"

"I've seen you on TV in World War II documentaries, General Tibbets. My name is Toshiharu Kano. I was in Hiroshima when you dropped the bomb."

Tosh reaches out his hand again.

The former general withholds his.

"General, I know what happened last night. I understand your reluctance considering the unexpected turn of events. I assure you, there's no need for apprehension with me. You were given an order by the President of the United States to drop a bomb on Hiroshima. As I see it, you were fulfilling a mission. Dropping the bomb wasn't your decision. You only followed orders. If I were given such a mission, knowing only what you knew then, I would have done exactly what you did. I would defend my country. You and your crew did not know what the bomb would do. You and your crew were soldiers doing your duty."

The General stares at Tosh with a tilt of his head.

"Mr. Kano, my crew and I were condemned by people in Japan and the United States. For you, a survivor of the A-bomb, to say to us that we were assigned a mission and were only doing our duty, means a lot to me and it will mean a lot to my men."

General Tibbets reaches out his hand. "I'm glad to shake your hand. Let me introduce you to the rest of the crew."

As the two men walk toward the others aboard the B-29 bomber on August 6, 1945, the General asks, "How close were you to detonation?"

"My family was one-half mile from the center of the blast," Tosh informs him.

The former pilot of the Enola Gay stops and shakes his head.

"Mr. Kano, I was there. I saw what happened with my own eyes. The Enola Gay barely escaped the concussion force of the bomb." He shakes his head again. "You couldn't have survived at that distance. You couldn't have survived even at much greater distances. You must be mistaken."

General Tibbets waits for a retraction of the information Tosh has given him.

"My family and I were there … less than half a mile away from the hypocenter. It is documented."

"You were that close?" he questions again.

"Yes. We were .8 kilometers from the hypocenter."

Within an expanse of silence, the General appears to reflect on what he saw that day in the sky over Hiroshima. He shakes his head three times; the last more firm than the first.

"Mr. Kano. I saw what that bomb did to Hiroshima. No one could have survived at that distance. It's impossible."

CHAPTER TWENTY-EIGHT

Potted Plants and Nesting Birds

Twenty-three Years Later

"Hello?" Tosh's sister, Yorie, answers the phone.

"How was your trip?" Tosh asks.

"It was good. I had fun."

Today, Tosh notices the accent they both carry with them through the years.

"Any luck?"

Yorie has been at the Indian casinos an hour drive from her home in Costa Mesa, California. She enjoys making the rounds from one to another, Pechanga, Harrah's, and Valley View.

"Not really. I came out about even this time."

Things are better between Yorie and Tosh now. They were estranged for seven years. She did not speak to her brother as a consequence of him refusing to honor his parents' wishes.

In college, Tosh met and fell in love with, Annette, a tall, German and Swede blonde, born in North Dakota. Tosh proposed. Annette accepted. They planned to marry on December 24.

Soon after, a close friend of Shizue's invited Tosh to have dinner with her and her daughter. Tosh arrived at the home with his fiancée, Annette. Tosh had no idea this woman had hoped to make a love connection between Tosh and her daughter.

Tosh informed her that he and Annette were engaged to be married, but to please not tell anyone, as he had not yet told his father the news.

At her first opportunity, the woman phoned Thailand and told Shizue that Tosh was engaged to be married. Shizue informed Toshiyuki.

Toshiyuki, felt humiliated and betrayed by Tosh. Not only had Tosh not asked his permission to marry, he had heard the news second hand.

He called Tosh from Thailand.

"What's this about you getting married on December 24?" He doesn't give Tosh time to speak. "Wait until I return to Utah. We will talk about this. Do not get married. I order you. You will obey me."

Toshiyuki then asks to speak with Annette. The conversation goes on for 40 minutes. He orders Annette not to marry Tosh. Annette tells him that she is not his subordinate and will do as she pleases. It was the same reply she had given her own father when he told her he would not allow her to marry a "Jap".

Tosh and Annette were married on December 24.

Toshiyuki disowned his only son. "You are no longer my son!"

Tosh's mother, Shizue, felt compelled to honor her husband's decision, although she spoke to Tosh by phone.

Father and son reconciled in 1973 when Tosh and Annette's son, Cliff, was born.

All that is behind the brother and sister now.

Yorie is retired from her career as a Computer Technical Analyst and lives a quiet life. She goes about her day caring for a patio garden, watering potted flowers, and checking on the birds nesting outside her front door. This afternoon she will visit the Buddhist temple where Toshiyuki and Shizue's ashes rest. Although Yorie survived the devastation of Hiroshima, at an "impossible" one-half mile distance, nothing about her draws any special attention.

Tosh, too, attracts no special attention. He is a good citizen, a quiet friendly neighbor, an engineer. He looks like any other American business man.

Today, he drives his silver Subaru Impreza to his office at Holladay City Hall, only five minutes from his home in Olympus Cove, in the foothills of the Wasatch Mountains of Utah.

He is usually thinking of some upcoming meeting and considering his point of view in a particular issue and how he can best present his thoughts as the resident consulting engineer.

This spring morning, however, his thoughts are on a different path. The spot of blood he noticed while brushing his teeth carried his thoughts to a past neither he nor his sister can completely escape.

Deep in their flesh remain the wounds of radiation from the atomic bomb dropped on Hiroshima in 1945 … a long time ago …for some. For Tosh in Utah, and his sister a thousand miles away in California, the reality of the bomb is ever present.

Still, it is just another day.

Yorie stands for a moment, appreciating the sparkle of the sun on dew drops gracing her patio flowers. She walks through her condo to the front door where she whispers a greeting to the baby birds in a nest built in a flower arrangement. She then climbs the stairs to her mother's room, stands in the doorway and gazes at the bed where her mother Shizue died peacefully after slipping into a coma, at the age of ninety three.

Yorie keeps everything exactly as her mother left it. She spent many sweet years with her mother, after her father died. A breeze entering through the open window directs her gaze past the empty bed, out her mother's bedroom window, through the branches of a Jacaranda tree laden with flowers dripping purple petals on the ground beneath. As if in a trance, her mind drifts back through her own memories and her mother's tales of her family's past.

Flashing yellow lights pull Tosh's thoughts back to the present.

He slows his car at the intersection near Howard Driggs Elementary School. A crossing guard steps off the sidewalk, holding a red and white stop sign. Tosh eases his Subaru to a standstill.

Children cross the street on the way to their classes, some walking, others pushing bikes, chatting, teasing, pushing, pulling, laughing on the way to their future. Some are accompanied by a parent or watched from a distance, as did his own mother, to ensure their safe arrival at school.

It is an idyllic scene; a peaceful day in the city, as all days should be; a bright spring day radiating the intense beauty of new life. Splashed everywhere is Tosh's wife's favorite color combination; pink, white, and green, with a touch of yellow. Daffodils, lilacs, and pansies push up through flowerbeds. Delicate, defiant wild violets poke up through new grass. Songbirds electrify the morning with hope and promise.

Tosh is soberly aware, however, that bright futures are always delicately balanced on the secret thoughts and secret intentions of powerful, but not always beneficent minds.

The miles between brother and sister are thin today. Both Tosh and Yorie reflect on another day, like this one. One day … that's all it takes to change the world forever.

Tosh waits at the school intersection, drawing a deep breath to relax as glimpses of that day and its consequences disappear and reappear like blinking fireflies in a jar.

The school crossing guard escorts the last of the children to the other side of the street and waves him forward. He resumes his drive to work, but his thoughts stay in 1945.

He remembers the stories his parents told him and Yorie, as he approaches the next intersection where a boy dashes across the street, barely avoiding a speeding car. The boy's near miss brings back memories of the birth of his son, Cliff, and the fear he felt throughout his wife's pregnancy, that due to his own exposure to extreme radiation, his son might not be healthy or normal. Tosh relives their relief at his birth.

The boy crossing the street stumbles onto the sidewalk and then runs wildly in the direction of the elementary school. It is unlikely he will make his class before the tardy bell rings at 8:35 a.m.

The young boy is certainly unaware his carelessness and apparent lack of discipline could be shaping a destiny he may one day regret with all his heart. It was this sort of seemingly innocent childhood behavior that began Tosh's family's journey toward Hiroshima.

With a left turn at the corner gas station, Tosh arrives at Holladay City Hall, a renovated 1930's elementary school. He parks behind the building, the west side, and approaches the back door. Ascending the steps, he notices the scent of smoke in the air.

Unseen, but not far from the city, are fields bearing the remains of last season's crops. This time of the year, smoke rises into the air as farmers' burn off irrigation ditches.

The awareness of a distant fire is both bitter and sweet. It signifies death and yet out of the ashes new life will grow. As the door closes, Tosh remembers it was in this way his life began. He grew and still grows out of the deadly radioactive ashes of Hiroshima.

The Nekomoto/Kano family's survival of the A-bomb dropped on Hiroshima was a miracle by natural and scientific laws. But as amazing as the miracle was, it is only the axis of a much larger and more important story. Before the Nekomoto family became survivors of a nuclear powered weapon, they were victimized by crimes of the heart; pride, stubbornness, lies, and betrayal. By the grace of God they were given the chance to see the vicious outgrowth of these human frailties and from there find peace in their lives, become instruments of forgiveness, and promote peace for the world.

As Tosh told General Tibbets years earlier, his family survived the atomic bomb, at a distance that should have incinerated them, but did not. This miracle must have meaning. Perhaps it was intended by a power greater than mankind's that the emissary of world peace be born in the cauldron of international violence.

The lives of those affected cannot be bound within the moment of the explosion of the first nuclear weapon or the day the physical wounds finally healed. War has no sharp edges. It does not begin on this day nor end on another. It is especially so with nuclear war. The world is altered forever by the presence of a monster ironically named, as though to feign innocence, "Little Boy."

Having been once unleashed, this dragon lives forever. Though chained by law within the deep abyss of international treaties, agreements, and intents and guarded by the angel of peace, the beast still lives. We must never allow it to break free of its restraints.

Better ... that the dragons cease to exist. Let us endeavor to make ultimate peace possible.

POSTSCRIPT 1

Written by Tosh and Yorie's father, Toshiyuki Nekomoto/Kano:

"As you have read my experiences, you have felt the true feelings of the Japanese people. It is better to hear, see or read about both sides. For this reason I have written my memoirs, 'The Other Side of the Fence'.

Near the end of the war, Japan and the Japanese people were in deep distress. They were tired, fatigued and close to starvation. Even a slight breeze could have blown them down. The people were dragged along by the heavy pressure of the Military. They were moving mechanically with their empty stomachs, and obeying their superiors who still believed in victory.

Japan could have been easily invaded any way on the island because of the weak defense lines and the lack of war supplies. There were only a few places that were fortified by rapid constructions, where it was believed the Americans would land.

Was Hiroshima and Nagasaki necessary? Why two cities? Wasn't one enough? (Look Magazine, September 22, 1970 issue) Was it an act of revenge to the Japanese bombing of Pearl Harbor? Wasn't it un-Christian and un-American? Was it a mistake to drop the A-bomb?

My family and I had gone through the hard life and experienced many difficulties in the war time Japan. We were lucky to survive the first A-bomb dropped on Hiroshima; even though we were only 800 yards away from the center of the blast.

I met many people asking if the people in Hiroshima still hate the United States. I will honestly say, no. They don't hate United States, but the war.

I was lucky to survive the war, the first atomic bomb, although I have lost my mother in the beginning of the war and my son at the end of the war. This was my fate. What will happen to all of us, we don't know. All we can do is leave it to the fate.

I have not written my memoirs for mercy or pity. I wrote as I felt and really saw. It is not deliberately exaggerated. I want you to build up the image of the bomb's destructive power and realize the facts of dead from the fire, infection and even the radiation sickness. Also in such a situation people panic with no help. I want you to remember the endless primitive treatment of Mrs. Kubota for her husband. Someday this experience of mine may be some kind of help to you as I believe that the next war will be more destructive than this. I hope you will recall my experiences, if alive. And that next war never occur.

LET BYGONES BE BYGONES. LET US NOT HAVE HATRED AGAINST EACH OTHER BUT BETTER UNDERSTANDING AND LIVE TOGETHER IN PROSPERITY, PEACEFUL AND UNITED."

POSTSCRIPT 2

Toshiharu and Rita, we finally did it. Rita, we could not have done this without your support. We love you for spending numerous hours to complete our father's dream book.

It has been over 50 years since our father started to write this book. In the early 1960s, he started with an old Smith Corona manual typewriter with old-fashioned transcript paper (pre-printed with squares and lines). He was not a proficient typist. He would type one letter at a time with his stubby two index fingers. It must have taken several times longer than an average typist, but he was determined to put his thoughts on paper. As he was completing his manuscript, he tried to acquire a publisher but no one came forward to show any interest in the manuscript. He submitted it to Readers Digest, but was told it was too long for their publication. He even submitted it to Playboy, but received a formal rejection from them. However, he did not give up his dream of publishing his book. He decided to wait for the right time to do so.

In the early 1970s, our father consulted Toshiharu's late wife, Annette, for help editing his manuscript. She assisted him on basic grammar and had him modify his manuscript.

In 1975, he had an opportunity to go to Iwakuni, Japan as Director of Engineering Branch for the U.S. Navy Public Works Department. There, he was reunited with Geoffrey Adams. Col. Adams was one of the British prisoners of war when our father was in charge of the Japanese Army regiment in Malaysia. He showed Mr. Adams the manuscript hoping Mr. Adams could find a publisher who would be interested in publishing his book in England. Mr. Adams took his manuscript with him when he returned to England. Before he could get any answer from Mr. Adams, my father was diagnosed with cancer and had to come back to the United State for possible treatments. However, he passed away in August 1976. A few years later, Mr. Adams contacted us and returned the manuscript along with Mr. Adams' published memoir.

Like my father, I did not give up pursuing his dream to publish his book. In 2003, I decided to transfer his typewritten manuscript into my computer (Microsoft Word). I did not want to re-enter the entire manuscript by hand. I purchased a scanner to copy the manuscript into my Word. The scanner did not work most of the time and I ended up re-entering the entire manuscript by hand. There were too many corrections and written in notes on the manuscript and the scanner did not come across clean. It took me a while to do this but I was able to transfer the manuscript and edit it, as there were many misspelled (bad grammar as well) words to pass the SPELL CHECK.

After his first wife's death, my brother met Rita and he re-married in 2011. What a coincidence, she is a professional writer. Rita suggested updating the manuscript with additional information to make it more salable. I inserted some information that I heard from my mother and others and Toshiharu did the same. Finally, the manuscript is complete! It has been a very long journey.

Rita, we are very grateful for your encouragement to pursue our father's dream. We thank you for your dedication and compassion.

My father's dream never materialized in the manner he intended. My brother, Toshiharu and I believe that what we have done with our family's story will give him peace.

Yorie Kano

A letter of testament from British Colonel Geoffrey Adams:

"Toshiyuki Nekomoto was born in Hawaii a Nisei (i.e. of Japanese immigrant parents) on January 15, 1914. During much of the period of narrative, whilst in the Imperial Japanese Army, he had the name, Nekomoto, and was known by this to brother officers of the 5TH Engineering Regiment, IJA and to those British and Australian POWs who met him in the period of May to October of 1942.

To those of you who have read my own book 'No Time For Geishas' published in 1973 you will already know that the 5th Engineering Regiment was also called TAMURA BUTAI (i.e. Tamura's Regiment or Group) after their Colonel Yasuji Tamura. Further, you will know that they treated the POWs in their charge so much better than any other Japanese personnel did in three and a half years. Had we stayed with them for our entire captivity we would have been much happier prisoners!

Tosh was a good and truthful interpreter for POWs and IJA alike. Many came to know him in the Bukit Timah camps of 1942 and I found none who had cause to complain of him. He actively assisted the POWs without being a traitor to his own, however temporary, and allegiance to the Imperial Japanese Army. His own words tell his story of his war.

He was known too in Changi for once a week he met our GOC, Lt-Gen Arthur Percival, and was the officer who obtained for our General the Spanish books, which he made his captivity hobby at that time. He also maintained good relations with the then Bishop of Singapore, Leonard Wilson.

There was in Tamura Butai a reasonable attitude engendered from the top, from Colonel Tamura himself. My own recollections include knowledge of Tosh, and others such as Nakano, Matsuzawa, Kageyama, Oda, Fukuda, Hashimoto, Tamahiro, Kamiyama and others whose names I forget.

The author was perhaps fortunate in his return to Japan from Rabaul, for his comrades of Tamura Butai went on to the Solomon and South West Pacific campaigns, suffering heavy casualties throughout those disease-laden islands, until they in their turn were isolated, starved and contained by firstly US forces then Australian forces, until the Emperor ordered their surrender in 1945. This enabled them to be repatriated in mid-1946, to their families and to their homes, if they still existed after the holocausts of Allied bombing of Japan, which hastened the end of the war.

Nevertheless, Tosh's story is not of those who went into the infernos of Japanese defeat in the SW Pacific as American and Australian military might slowly regained from Japan the fruits of their easy victories of 1942. Theirs is another saga of endurance, stoic courage and separation from their loved ones at home.

In 1976, I was going to tour Japan and the countries of the Orient where I had been a captive of war. Having maintained a long established correspondence with several ex-members of Tamura Butai, it was a very happy arrangement that brought me face to face with Tosh at Fukuoka International Airport in Kyushu one fine day in June of that year. He became a valuable interpreter for me in TV interviews, press confrontations and simply getting around.

He was of course a United States citizen and had worked for many years for the US Armed Forces, in particular the US Marine Corps, in the continental USA. In 1976, he was the Chief Civil

Engineer at the giant US Marine Corps Air Station at Iwakuni, Honshu, a base shared with the Japanese maritime Self-Defense Force (many Japanese, now so dedicated to peace, refuse to call it their Navy!) He entertained me, with his wife, Shizue, at his rented home at Iwakuni and at the airfield, where I met his USN and Japanese Navy counterparts. There too he played a leading role in the Japanese-American Cultural Society, welding together the Americans of the base with the citizens of Iwakuni-shi.

In his home one evening he showed me a few pages of a manuscript written to show the Japanese side of the war (the other side of the fence, as he called it) – I was fascinated and suggested he get it published though he said he had written it down really for his family. He was about to move to a more senior post near Tokyo, some 50 miles north, and said he'd finish the book, correct any faulty English, and then send it to me in England, or hand it to me in Tokyo.

Together we traveled to that famous Japanese shrine Itsukushima Miyajima, where there was a reunion of Tamura Butai fellows just for me. He interpreted for further TV and press interviews, before that night leaving me in the care of his old comrades who then became my guardians for my entire tour of Japan – and everywhere I was given full VIP treatment whether with Nakano, Matuzawa, Kageyame, Bendai, Tamahiro, Oda or Fukuda. Colonel Tamura had died in 1952, but his 90-year old widow sent her thoughts and best wishes to us all.

Tamahiro and others were my hosts in Hiroshima where I saw the sense Tosh describes so graphically in his book, and though the city is a new one after that day in August 1945, one can get the atmosphere in the museums.

The story has a sad ending, rather like the death of his son from radiation after the Atom Bomb, which finished a dreadful war.

Having written to Tosh and received no reply, Ko Matuzawa wrote to me in August 1976 to say he had visited Tosh in the US Naval Hospital at Yokosuka and had discovered he had cancer, diagnosed a few days after I left him in Miyajima; had been given a few days to live, and the US Navy was flying him home to California.

The final news came early September in a letter from his daughter, Yorie, who told how he had died peacefully. His papers and effects would arrive later from Japan.

In due course, they sent his narrative to me and said Tosh was thrilled that I'd said I'd seek an English publisher for him, and hoped his untimely death would not stop me from at least trying.

It truly is worth remembering those few who accorded fair treatment to us POWs.

I close by quoting from my own book: "...not all our Japanese captors were the devil incarnate."

It is of interest that during my long stay in Japan in 1976 (not 1955/45) it was to me a telling point that very, very few IJA units ever have reunions, but Tamura Butai have one every year, and in 1975, some 300 men of all ranks traveled great distances to be present. That is a spirit rather like the British Army comradeship."

Made in the USA
San Bernardino, CA
25 April 2018